THE LAST MRS. PARRISH

THE LAST MRS. PARRISH

[A NOVEL]

Liv Constantine

HARPER

An Imprint of HarperCollins*Publishers*

THE LAST MRS. PARRISH. Copyright © 2017 by Lynne Constantine and Valerie Constantine. All rights reserved. Printed in the United States of America. No part of this book may be used or reproduced in any manner whatsoever without written permission except in the case of brief quotations embodied in critical articles and reviews. For information, address HarperCollins Publishers, 195 Broadway, New York, NY 10007.

HarperCollins books may be purchased for educational, business, or sales promotional use. For information, please email the Special Markets Department at SPsales@harpercollins.com.

FIRST EDITION

Designed by Bonni Leon-Berman

Library of Congress Cataloging-in-Publication Data has been applied for.

ISBN 978-0-06-266757-1

17 18 19 20 21   LSC   10 9 8 7 6 5 4 3 2 1

LYNNE'S DEDICATION:
*For Lynn, the other bookend, for reasons
too numerous to mention*

VALERIE'S DEDICATION:
For Colin, you make it all possible

[PART I]

AMBER

ONE

Amber Patterson was tired of being invisible. She'd been coming to this gym every day for three months—three long months of watching these women of leisure working at the only thing they cared about. They were so self-absorbed; she would have bet her last dollar that not one of them would recognize her on the street even though she was five feet away from them every single day. She was a fixture to them—unimportant, not worthy of being noticed. But she didn't care—not about any of them. There was one reason and one reason alone that she dragged herself here every day, to this machine, at the precise stroke of eight.

She was sick to death of the routine—day after day, working her ass off, waiting for the moment to make her move. From the corner of her eye, she saw the signature gold Nikes step onto the machine next to her. Amber straightened her shoulders and pretended to be immersed in the magazine strategically placed on the rack of her own machine. She turned and gave the exquisite blond woman a shy smile, which garnered a polite nod in her direction. Amber reached for her water bottle, deliberately moving her foot to the edge of the machine, and slipped, knocking the magazine to the floor, where it landed beneath the pedal of her neighbor's equipment.

"Oh my gosh, I'm so sorry," she said, reddening.

Before she could step off, the woman stopped her pedaling and retrieved it for her. Amber watched the woman's brow knit together.

"You're reading *is* magazine?" the woman said, handing it back to her.

"Yes, it's the Cystic Fibrosis Trust's magazine. Comes out twice a year. Do you know it?"

"I do, yes. Are you in the medical field?" the woman asked.

Amber cast her eyes to the floor, then back at the woman. "No, I'm not. My younger sister had CF." She let the words sit in the space between them.

"I'm sorry. That was rude of me. It's none of my business," the woman said, and stepped back onto the elliptical.

Amber shook her head. "No, it's okay. Do you know someone with cystic fibrosis?"

There was pain in the woman's eyes as she stared back at Amber. "My sister. I lost her twenty years ago."

"I'm so sorry. How old was she?"

"Only sixteen. We were two years apart."

"Charlene was just fourteen." Slowing her pace, Amber wiped her eyes with the back of her hand. It took a lot of acting skills to cry about a sister who never existed. The three sisters she did have were alive and well, although she hadn't spoken to them for two years.

The woman's machine ground to a halt. "Are you okay?" she asked.

Amber sniffed and shrugged. "It's still so hard, even after all these years."

The woman gave her a long look, as if trying to make a decision, then extended her hand.

"I'm Daphne Parrish. What do you say we get out of here and have a nice chat over a cup of coffee?"

"Are you sure? I don't want to interrupt your workout."

Daphne nodded. "Yes, I'd really like to talk with you."

Amber gave her what she hoped looked like a grateful smile and stepped down. "That sounds great." Taking her hand, she said, "I'm Amber Patterson. Pleasure to meet you."

Later that evening Amber lay in a bubble bath, sipping a glass of merlot and staring at the photo in *Entrepreneur* magazine. Smiling, she put it down, closed her eyes, and rested her head on the edge of the tub. She was feeling very satisfied about how well things had gone that day. She'd been prepared for it to drag out even longer, but Daphne made it easy for her. After they dispensed with the small talk over coffee, they'd gotten down to the real reason she'd elicited Daphne's interest.

"It's impossible for someone who hasn't experienced CF to understand," Daphne said, her blue eyes alive with passion. "Julie was never a burden to me, but in high school my friends were always pushing me to leave her behind, not let her tag along. They didn't understand that I never knew when she'd be hospitalized or if she'd even make it out again. Every moment was precious."

Amber leaned forward and did her best to look interested while she calculated the total worth of the diamonds on Daphne's ears, the tennis bracelet on her wrist, and the huge diamond on her tanned and perfectly manicured finger. She must have had at least a hundred grand walking around on her size-four body, and all she could do was whine about her sad childhood. Amber suppressed a yawn and gave Daphne a tight smile.

"I know. I used to stay home from school to be with my sister so that my mom could go to work. She almost lost her job from taking so much time off, and the last thing we could afford was for her to lose our health insurance." She was pleased with how easily the lie came to her lips.

"Oh, that's terrible," Daphne clucked. "That's another reason my foundation is so important to me. We provide financial assistance to families who aren't able to afford the care they need. It's been a big part of the mission of Julie's Smile for as long as I can remember."

Amber feigned shock. "Julie's Smile is *your* foundation? It's the same Julie? I know all about Julie's Smile, been reading about all you do for years. I'm so in awe."

Daphne nodded. "I started it right after grad school. In fact, my husband was my first benefactor." Here she'd smiled, perhaps a bit embarrassed. "That's how we met."

"Aren't you preparing for a big fund-raiser right now?"

"As a matter of fact we are. It's a few months away, but still lots to do. Say . . . oh, never mind."

"No, what?" Amber pressed.

"Well, I was just going to see if maybe you'd like to help. It would be nice to have someone who understands—"

"I'd love to help in any way," Amber interrupted. "I don't make a lot of money, but I definitely have time to donate. What you're doing is so important. When I think of the difference it makes—" She bit her lip and blinked back tears.

Daphne smiled. "Wonderful." She pulled out a card engraved with her name and address. "Here you are. Committee is meeting at my house Thursday morning at ten. Can you make it?"

Amber had given her a wide smile, still trying to look as though the disease was first in her mind. "I wouldn't miss it."

TWO

The rocking rhythm of the Saturday train from Bishops Harbor to New York lulled Amber into a soothing reverie far removed from the rigid discipline of her workday week. She sat by the window, resting her head against the seat back, occasionally opening her eyes to glance at the passing scenery. She thought back to the first time she'd ridden on a train, when she was seven years old. It was July in Missouri—the hottest, muggiest month of the summer—and the train's air-conditioning had been on the blink. She could still picture her mother sitting across from her in a long-sleeved black dress, unsmiling, back erect, her knees squeezed together primly. Her light brown hair had been pulled back in its customary bun, but she had worn a pair of earrings—small pearl studs that she saved for special occasions. And Amber supposed the funeral of her mother's mother counted as a special occasion.

When they'd gotten off the train at the grubby station in Warrensburg, the air outside was even more suffocating than the inside of the train had been. Uncle Frank, her mother's brother, had been there to meet them, and they piled uncomfortably into his battered blue pickup truck. The smell is what she remembered most—a mixture of sweat and dirt and damp—and the cracked leather of the seat digging into her skin. They rode past endless fields of corn and small farmsteads with tired-looking wooden houses and yards filled with rusted machinery, old cars on cinder blocks, tires with no rims, and broken metal crates. It was even

more depressing than where they lived, and Amber wished she'd
been left at home, like her sisters. Her mother said they were too
young for a funeral, but Amber was old enough to pay her respects.
She'd blocked out most of that horrendous weekend, but the one
thing she would never forget was the appalling shabbiness surrounding her—the drab living room of her grandparents' home,
all browns and rusty yellows; her grandfather's stubby growth
of beard as he sat in his overstuffed recliner, stern and dour in a
worn undershirt and stained khaki pants. She saw the origin of
her mother's cheerless demeanor and poverty of imagination. It
was then, at that tender age, that the dream of something different and better was born in Amber.

Opening her eyes now as the man opposite her rose, jostling
her with his briefcase, she realized they'd arrived at Grand Central Terminal. She quickly gathered her handbag and jacket and
stepped into the streaming mass of disembarking passengers. She
never tired of the walk from the tracks into the magnificent main
concourse—what a contrast to the dingy train depot of all those
years ago. She took her time strolling past the shiny storefronts
of the station, a perfect precursor to the sights and sounds of the
city waiting outside, then exited the building and walked the
few short blocks along Forty-Second Street to Fifth Avenue. This
monthly pilgrimage had become so familiar that she could have
done it blindfolded.

Her first stop was always the main reading room of the New
York Public Library. She would sit at one of the long reading tables as the sun poured in through the tall windows and drink in
the beauty of the ceiling frescoes. Today she felt especially com-
forted by the books that climbed the walls. They were a reminder
that any knowledge she desired was hers for the asking. Here, she
would sit and read and discover all the things that would give

shape to her plans. She sat, still and silent, for twenty minutes, until she was ready to return to the street and begin the walk up Fifth Avenue.

She walked slowly but with purpose past the luxury stores that lined the street. Past Versace, Fendi, Armani, Louis Vuitton, Harry Winston, Tiffany & Co., Gucci, Prada, and Cartier—they went on and on, one after another of the world's most prestigious and expensive boutiques. She had been in each of them, inhaled the aroma of supple leather and the scent of exotic perfumes, rubbed into her skin the velvety balms and costly ointments that sat tantalizingly in ornate testers.

She continued past Dior and Chanel and stopped to admire a slender gown of silver and black that clung to the mannequin in the window. She stared at the dress, picturing herself in it, her hair piled high on her head, her makeup perfect, entering a ballroom on her husband's arm, the envy of every woman she passed. She continued north until she came to Bergdorf Good-man and the timeless Plaza Hotel. She was tempted to climb the red-carpeted steps to the grand lobby, but it was well past one o'clock, and she was feeling hungry. She'd carried a small lunch from home, since there was no way she could afford to spend her hard-earned money on both the museum and lunch in Manhattan. She crossed Fifty-Eighth Street to Central Park, sat on a bench facing the busy street, and unpacked a small ap-ple and a baggie filled with raisins and nuts from her sack. She ate slowly as she watched people hurrying about and thought for the hundredth time how grateful she was to have escaped the dreary existence of her parents, the mundane conversa-tions, the predictability of it all. Her mother had never under-stood Amber's ambitions. She said she was trying to get too far above herself, that her kind of thinking would only land her in trouble. And then Amber had shown her and finally left it all—though maybe not the way she'd planned.

She finished her lunch and walked through the park to the Metropolitan Museum of Art, where she would spend the afternoon before catching an early-evening train back to Connecticut. Over the past two years she had walked every inch of the Met, studying the art and sitting in on lectures and films about the works and their creators. At first her vast lack of knowledge had been daunting, but in her methodical way, she took it step-by-step, reading from borrowed books all she could about art, its history, and its masters. Armed with new information each month, she would visit the museum again and see in person what she had read about. She knew now that she could engage in a respectably intelligent conversation with all but the most informed art critic. Since the day she'd left that crowded house in Missouri, she'd been creating a new and improved Amber, one who would move at ease among the very wealthy. And so far, her plan was right on schedule.

After some time, she strolled to the gallery that was usually her last stop. There, she stood for a long time in front of a small study by Tintoretto. She wasn't sure how many times she had stared at this sketch, but the credit line was engraved on her brain—"A gift from the collection of Jackson and Daphne Parrish." She reluctantly turned away and headed to the new Aelbert Cuyp exhibition. She'd read through the only book about Cuyp that the Bishops Harbor library had on its shelves. Cuyp was an artist she'd never heard of and she'd been surprised to learn how prolific and famous he was. She strolled through the exhibit and came upon the painting she'd so admired in the book and had hoped would be a part of the exhibit, *The Maas at Dordrecht in a Storm*. It was even more magnificent than she'd thought it would be.

An older couple stood near her, mesmerized by it as well.

"It's amazing, isn't it?" the woman said to Amber.

"More than I'd even imagined," she answered.

"This one is very different from his landscapes," the man offered.

Amber continued to stare at the painting as she said, "It is, but he painted many majestic views of Dutch harbors. Did you know that he also painted biblical scenes and portraits?"

"Really? I had no idea."

Perhaps you should read before you come to see an exhibit, Amber thought, but simply smiled at them and moved on. She loved it when she could display her superior knowledge. And she believed that a man like Jackson Parrish, a man who prided himself on his cultural aesthetic, would love it too.

THREE

A bilious envy stuck in Amber's throat as the graceful house
on Long Island Sound came into view. The open white
gates at the entrance to the multimillion-dollar estate gave way
to lush greenery and rosebushes that spilled extravagantly over
discreet fencing, while the mansion itself was a rambling two-
story structure of white and gray. It reminded her of pictures
she'd seen of the wealthy summer homes in Nantucket and Mar-
tha's Vineyard. The house meandered majestically along the
shoreline, superbly at home on the water's edge.

This was the kind of home that was safely hidden from the eyes
of those who could not afford to live this way. That's what wealth
does for you, she thought. It gives you the means and the power
to remain concealed from the world if you choose to—or if you
need to.

Amber parked her ten-year-old blue Toyota Corolla, which
would look ridiculously out of place among the late-model Mercedes and BMWs that she was sure would soon dot the court-
yard. She closed her eyes and sat for a moment, taking slow,
deep breaths and going over in her head the information she'd
memorized over the last few weeks. She'd dressed carefully
this morning, her straight brown hair held back from her face
with a tortoiseshell headband and her makeup minimal—just
the tiniest hint of blush on her cheeks and slightly tinted balm
on her lips. She wore a neatly pressed beige twill skirt with a
long-sleeved white cotton T-shirt, both of which she'd ordered

from an L.L.Bean catalog. Her sandals were sturdy and plain, good no-nonsense walking shoes without any touch of femininity. The ugly large-framed glasses she'd found at the last minute completed the look she was after. When she took one last glimpse in the mirror before leaving her apartment, she'd been pleased. She looked plain, even mousy. Someone who would never in a million years be a threat to anyone—especially not someone like Daphne Parrish.

Though she knew she ran a slight risk of appearing rude, Amber had shown up just a little early. She'd be able to have some time alone with Daphne and would also be there before any of the other women arrived, always an edge when introductions were made. They would see her as young and nondescript, simply a worker bee Daphne had deigned to reach down and anoint as a helper in her charity efforts.

She opened the car door and stepped onto the crushed stone driveway. It looked as if each piece of gravel cushioning her steps had been measured for uniformity and purity, and perfectly raked and polished. As she neared the house, she took her time studying the grounds and dwelling. She realized she would be entering through the back—the front would, of course, face the water— but it was, nevertheless, a most gracious facade. To her left stood a white arbor bedecked with the summer's last wisteria, and two long benches sat just beyond it. Amber had read about this kind of wealth, had seen countless pictures in magazines and online tours of the homes of movie stars and the superrich. But this was the first time she'd actually seen it up close.

She climbed the wide stone steps to the landing and rang the bell. The door was oversize, with large panes of beveled glass, allowing Amber a view down the long corridor that ran to the front of the house. She could see the dazzling blue of the water from where she stood, and then, suddenly, Daphne was there, holding the door open and smiling at her.

"How lovely to see you. I'm so glad you could come," she said, taking Amber's hand in hers and leading her inside.

Amber gave her the timid smile she'd practiced in front of her bathroom mirror. "Thank you for inviting me, Daphne. I'm really excited to help."

"Well, I'm thrilled you'll be working with us. Come this way. We'll be meeting in the conservatory," Daphne said as they came into a large octagonal room with floor-to-ceiling windows and summery chintzes that exploded with vibrant color. The French doors stood open, and Amber breathed in the intoxicating smell of salty sea air.

"Please, have a seat. We have a few minutes before the others arrive," Daphne said.

Amber sank into the plush sofa, and Daphne sat down across from her in one of the yellow armchairs that perfectly complemented the other furnishings in this room of nonchalant elegance. It irked her, this ease with wealth and privilege that Daphne exuded, as though it were her birthright. She could have stepped out of *Town & Country* in her perfectly tailored gray slacks and silk blouse, her only jewelry the large pearl studs she wore in her ears. Her lustrous blond hair fell in loose waves that framed her aristocratic face. Amber guessed the clothes and earrings alone were worth over three grand, forget the rock on her finger or the Cartier Tank. She probably had a dozen more in a jewelry box upstairs. Amber checked the time on her own watch—an inexpensive department-store model—and saw that they still had about ten minutes alone.

"Thanks again for letting me help, Daphne."

"I'm the one who's grateful. There are never too many hands.

I mean, all of the women are terrific and they work hard, but you understand because you've been there." Daphne shifted in her chair. "We talked a lot about our sisters the other morning, but not much about ourselves. I know you're not from around here, but do I remember you telling me you were born in Nebraska?"

Amber had rehearsed her story carefully. "Yes, that's right. I'm originally from Nebraska, but I left after my sister died. My good high school friend went to college here. When she came home for my sister's funeral, she said maybe it would be good for me to have a change, make a fresh start, and we'd have each other, of course. She was right. It's helped me so much. I've been in Bishops Harbor for almost a year, but I think about Charlene every day."

Daphne was looking at her intently. "I'm sorry for your loss. No one who hasn't experienced it can know how painful it is to lose a sibling. I think about Julie every day. Sometimes it's overwhelming. That's why my work with cystic fibrosis is so important to me. I'm blessed to have two healthy daughters, but there are still so many families afflicted by this terrible disease."

Amber picked up a silver frame with a photograph of two little girls. Both blond and tanned, they wore matching bathing suits and sat cross-legged on a pier, their arms around each other. "Are these your daughters?"

Daphne glanced at the picture and smiled with delight, pointing. "Yes, that's Tallulah and this is Bella. That was taken last summer, at the lake."

"They're adorable. How old are they?"

"Tallulah's ten, and Bella's seven. I'm glad they have each other," Daphne said, her eyes growing misty. "I pray they always will."

Amber remembered reading that actors think of the saddest thing they can to help them cry on cue. She was trying to summon a memory to make her cry, but the saddest thing she could come up with was that she wasn't the one sitting in Daphne's chair, the mistress of this incredible house. Still, she did her best to look downcast as she put the photograph back on the table.

Just then, the doorbell rang, and Daphne rose to answer it. As she left the room, she said, "Help yourself to coffee or tea. And there are some goodies too. Everything's on the sideboard."

Amber got up but put her handbag on the chair next to Daphne's, marking it as hers. As she was pouring a cup of coffee, the others began filing in amid excited hellos and hugs. She hated the clucking sounds groups of women made, like a bunch of cackling hens.

"Hey, everyone." Daphne's voice rose above the chatter, and they quieted down. She went to Amber and put her arm around her. "I want to introduce a new committee member, Amber Patterson. Amber will be a wonderful addition to our group. Sadly, she's a bit of an expert—her sister died of cystic fibrosis."

Amber cast her eyes to the floor, and there was a collective murmur of sympathy from the women.

"Why don't we all have a seat, and we'll go around the room so that you can introduce yourselves to Amber," Daphne said. Cup and saucer in hand, she sat down, looked at the photo of her daughters, and, Amber noticed, moved it just slightly. Amber looked around the circle as, one after another, each woman smiled and said her name—Lois, Bunny, Faith, Meredith, Irene, and Neve. All of them were shined and polished, but two in particular caught Amber's attention. No more than a size two, Bunny had long, straight blond hair and large green eyes made up to show their maximum gorgeousness. She was perfect in every way, and she knew it. Amber had seen her at the gym in her tiny shorts and sports bra, working out like mad, but Bunny looked at her blankly, as if she'd never laid eyes on her before. Amber wanted to remind her, *Oh, yes. I know you. You're the one who brags about screwing around on your husband to your girl posse.*

And then there was Meredith, who didn't at all fit in with the rest of them. Her clothing was expensive but subdued, not like the flashy garb of the other women. She wore small gold earrings and a single strand of yellowed pearls against her brown sweater. The length of her tweed skirt was awkward, neither long nor short enough to be fashionable. As the meeting progressed, it became apparent that she was different in more ways than appearance. She sat erect in her chair, shoulders back and head held high, with an imposing bearing of wealth and breeding. And when she spoke, there was just the hint of a boarding-school accent, enough to make her words sound so much more insightful than the others' as they discussed the silent auction and the prizes secured so far. Exotic vacations, diamond jewelry, vintage wines—the list went on and on, each item more expensive than the last.

As the meeting came to a close, Meredith walked over and sat beside Amber. "Welcome to Julie's Smile, Amber. I'm very sorry about your sister."

"Thank you," Amber said simply.

"Have you and Daphne known each other a long time?"

"Oh, no. We just met, actually. At the gym."

"How serendipitous," Meredith said, her tone hard to read. She was staring at Amber, and it felt as if she could see right through her.

"It was a lucky day for both of us."

"Yes, I should say." Meredith paused and looked Amber up and down. Her lips spread into a thin smile, and she rose from the chair. "It was lovely to meet you. I look forward to getting to know you better."

Amber sensed danger, not in the words Meredith had spoken but from something in her manner. Maybe she was just imagining it. She put her empty coffee cup back on the sideboard and walked through the French doors that seemed to invite her onto the deck. Outside she stood looking at the vast expanse of Long Island Sound. In the distance she spotted a sailboat, its sails billowing in the wind, a magnificent spectacle. She walked to the other end of the deck, where she had a better view of the sandy beach below. When she turned to go back inside, she heard Meredith's unmistakable voice coming from the conservatory.

"Honestly, Daphne, how well do you know this girl? You met her at the gym? Do you know anything about her background?"

Amber stood silently at the edge of the door.

"Meredith, really. All I needed to know was that her sister died of CF. What more do you want? She has a vested interest in raising money for the foundation."

"Have you checked her out?" Meredith asked, her tone still skeptical. "You know, her family, education, all those things?"

"This is volunteer work, not a Supreme Court nomination. I want her on the committee. You'll see. She'll be a wonderful asset."

Amber could hear the irritation in Daphne's voice.

"All right, it's your committee. I won't bring it up again."

Amber could hear footsteps on the tile floor as they left the room, and she stepped in and quickly pushed her portfolio under a pillow on the sofa, so it would look like she'd forgotten it. In it were her notes from the meeting and a photograph, tucked into one of the pockets. The lack of any other identifying information would ensure that Daphne would have to root around to find the photo. Amber was thirteen in the picture. That had been a good day, one of the few her mother had been able to leave the cleaner's and take them to the park. She was pushing her little sister on the swings. On the back, Amber had written "Amber and Charlene," even though it was a picture of her with her sister Trudy.

Meredith was going to be tricky. She'd said she was looking forward to getting to know Amber better. Well, Amber was going to make sure she knew as little as possible. She wasn't going to let some society snob screw with her. She'd made sure that the last person who tried that got what was coming to her.

FOUR

Amber opened the bottle of Josh she'd been saving. It was pathetic that she had to ration a twelve-dollar cabernet, but her measly salary at the real estate office barely covered the rent here. Before moving to Connecticut, she'd done her research and chosen her target, Jackson Parrish, and that's how she ended up in Bishops Harbor. Sure, she could have rented in a neighboring town for much less, but living here meant she had many opportunities to accidentally run into Daphne Parrish, plus access to all the fabulous town amenities. And she loved being so close to New York.

A smile spread across Amber's face. She thought back to the time she'd researched Jackson Parrish, googling his name for hours after she read an article on the international development company he'd founded. Her breath had caught when his picture filled the screen. With thick black hair, full lips, and cobalt-blue eyes, he could have easily been on the big screen. She'd clicked on an interview in *Forbes* magazine that featured him and how he built his Fortune 500 company. The next link—an article in *Vanity Fair*—wrote about his marriage to the beautiful Daphne, ten years younger than he. Amber had gazed at the picture of their two adorable children, taken on the beach in front of a gray-and-white clapboard mansion. She'd looked up everything she could about the Parrishes, and when she read about Julie's Smile, the foundation founded by Daphne and dedicated to raising money for cystic fibrosis, the idea came to her.

The first step in the plan that developed in her mind was to move to Bishops Harbor.

When she thought back to the small-time marriage she'd tried to engineer back in Missouri, it made her want to laugh. That had ended very badly, but she wouldn't make the same mistakes this time.

Now she picked up her wineglass and lifted it in salute to her reflection in the microwave oven. "To Amber." Taking a long sip, she rested the glass on the counter.

Opening her laptop, she typed "Meredith Stanton Connecticut" into the search bar and the page filled up with link after link about Meredith's personal and philanthropic efforts. Meredith Bell Stanton was a daughter of the Bell family, who raised Thoroughbred racehorses. According to the articles, riding was her passion. She rode horses, showed horses, hunted, jumped, and did anything else you could do with horses. Amber wasn't surprised. Meredith had "horsewoman" written all over her.

Amber stared at a photograph of Meredith and her husband, Randolph H. Stanton III, at a charity event in New York. She decided old Randolph looked like he had a yardstick up his ass. But she guessed banking was a pretty dry business. The only good thing about it was the money, and it looked like the Stantons had piles of it.

Next, she searched for Bunny Nichols, but didn't find as much. The fourth wife of March Nichols, a prominent New York attorney with a reputation for ruthlessness, Bunny looked eerily similar to the second and third wives. Amber guessed that blond party girls were interchangeable to him. One article described Bunny as a "former model." That was a laugh. She looked more like a former stripper.

She took a last sip from her glass, corked the bottle, and logged onto Facebook under one of her fake profiles. She pulled up the one profile that she checked every night, scanning for new photos and any status updates. Her eyes narrowed at a picture of a little boy holding a lunch box in one hand and that rich bitch's hand in the other—"First day at St. Andrew's Academy" and the insipid comment "Mommy's not ready," with a sad-face emoji. St. Andrew's, the school back home she had yearned to attend. She wanted to type her own comment: *Mommy and Daddy are lying skanks*. But instead she slammed the laptop shut.

FIVE

Amber looked at the ringing phone and smiled. Seeing "private" on the caller ID, she figured it was Daphne. She let it go to voice mail. Daphne left a message. The next day, Daphne called again, and again Amber ignored it. Obviously, Daphne had found the portfolio. When the phone rang again that night, Amber finally answered.

"Hello?" she whispered.

"Amber?"

A sigh, and then a quiet "Yes?"

"It's Daphne. Are you okay? I've been trying to reach you."

She made a choking sound, then spoke, louder this time. "Hi, Daphne. Yeah, sorry. It's been a rough day."

"What is it? Has something happened?" Amber could hear the concern in Daphne's voice.

"It's the anniversary."

"Oh, sweetie. I'm sorry. Would you like to come over? Jackson's out of town. We could open a bottle of wine."

"Really?"

"Absolutely. The children are sleeping, and I've got one of the nannies if they should need anything."

Of course one of the nannies is there. God forbid she should have to do anything for herself. "Oh, Daphne, that would be so great. Can I bring anything?"

"No, just yourself. See you soon."

When Amber pulled up to the house, she got out her phone

and texted Daphne: **I'm here. Didn't want to ring and wake the girls.**

The door opened, and Daphne motioned her in. "How thoughtful of you to text first."

"Thanks for having me over." Amber handed her a bottle of red wine.

Daphne hugged her. "Thank you, but you shouldn't have."

Amber shrugged. It was a cheap merlot, eight bucks at the liquor store. She knew Daphne would never drink it.

"Come on." Daphne led her into the sunroom, where there was already a bottle of wine open and two half-filled glasses on the coffee table.

"Have you had dinner?"

Amber shook her head. "No, but I'm not really hungry." She sat, picked up a wineglass, and took a small sip. "This is very nice."

Daphne sat down, picked up her own glass, and held it up.

"Here's to our sisters who live on in our hearts."

Amber touched her glass to Daphne's and took another swallow. She brushed a nonexistent tear from her eye.

"I'm so sorry. You must think I'm a basket case."

Daphne shook her head. "Of course not. It's okay. You can talk about it to me. Tell me about her."

Amber paused. "Charlene was my best friend. We shared a room, and we'd talk late into the night about what we were going to do when we grew up and got out of that house." She frowned and took another long sip of her wine. "Our mother used to throw a shoe at the door if she thought we were up too late. We'd whisper so she wouldn't hear us. We'd tell each other everything. All our dreams, our hopes . . ."

Daphne kept quiet while Amber continued, but her beautiful blue eyes filled with compassion.

"She was golden. Everybody loved her, but it didn't go to her head, you know? Some kids, they would have become bratty, but not Char. She was beautiful, on the inside and out. People would just stare at her when we were out, that's how gorgeous she was." Amber hesitated and cocked her head. "Sort of like you."

A nervous laugh escaped from Daphne's lips. "I would hardly say that about myself."

Yeah, right, Amber thought. "Beautiful women take it for granted. They can't see what everyone else does. My parents used to joke that she got the beauty, and I got the brains."

"How cruel. That's terrible, Amber. You are a beautiful person—inside and out."

It was almost too easy, Amber thought—get a bad haircut, leave off the makeup, don a pair of eyeglasses, slouch your shoulders, and voilà! Poor homely girl was born. Daphne needed to save someone, and Amber was happy to oblige. She smiled at Daphne.

"You're just saying that. It's okay. Not everyone has to be beautiful." She picked up a photo of Tallulah and Bella, this one in a cloth frame. "Your daughters are gorgeous too."

Daphne's face lit up. "They're great kids. I'm extremely blessed."

Amber continued to study the photograph. Tallulah looked like a little adult with her serious expression and hideous glasses, while Bella, with her blond curls and blue eyes, looked like a little princess. There was going to be a lot of rivalry in their future, Amber thought. She wondered how many boyfriends Bella would steal from her plain older sister when they were teenagers.

"Do you have a picture of Julie?"

"Of course." Daphne got up and retrieved a photograph from the console table. "Here she is," she said, handing the frame to Amber.

Amber stared at the young woman, who must have been around

fifteen when the picture was taken. She was beautiful in an almost otherworldly way, her big brown eyes bright and shining.

"She's lovely," Amber said, looking up at Daphne. "It doesn't get any easier, does it?"

"No, not really. Some days it's even harder."

They finished the bottle of wine and opened another while Amber listened to more stories of Daphne's tragic fairy-tale relationship with her perfect dead sister. Amber threw a full glass down the sink when she went to the bathroom. As she returned to the living room, she added a little wobble to her walk, and said to Daphne, "I should get going."

Daphne shook her head. "You shouldn't drive. You should stay here tonight."

"No, no. I don't want to put you out."

"No arguments. Come on. I'll take you to a guest room."

Daphne put an arm around Amber's waist and led her through the obscenely large house and up the long staircase to the second floor.

"I think I'm going to need the bathroom." Amber made the words sound urgent.

"Of course." Daphne helped her in, and Amber shut the door and sat down on the toilet. The bathroom was enormous and elaborate, with a Jacuzzi tub and shower big enough to accommodate the entire royal family. Her studio apartment would have practically fit inside it. When she opened the door, Daphne was waiting.

"Are you feeling any better?" Daphne's voice was filled with concern.

"Still a bit dizzy. Would it be all right if I did lie down for a minute?"

"Of course," Daphne said, guiding her down the long hallway to a guest room.

Amber's keen eye took it all in—the fresh white tulips that looked beautiful against the mint-green walls. Who had fresh flowers in a guest room when they weren't even expecting guests? The shiny wood floor was partially covered with a thick white flokati rug that added another touch of elegance and luxury. Billowy gauze curtains seemed to float down from the tall windows.

Daphne helped her to the bed, where Amber sat and ran her hand over the embroidered duvet cover. She could get used to this. Her eyes fluttered shut, and she didn't need to pretend that she felt the dizzying sensation of impending slumber. She saw movement and opened her eyes to see Daphne standing over her.

"You're going to sleep here. I insist," Daphne said, and, walking to the closet, opened the door and took out a nightgown and robe. "Here, take your things off and put on this nightgown. I'll wait out in the hallway while you change."

Amber peeled off her sweater and threw it on the bed, and stepped out of her jeans. She slipped into the silky white nightgown and crawled under the covers. "All set," she called out.

Daphne came back in and put a hand on her forehead. "You poor dear. Rest."

Amber felt a cover being tucked around her.

"I'll be in my room, just down the hall."

Amber opened her eyes and reached out to grab Daphne's arm. "Please don't go. Can you stay with me like my sister used to?"

She saw the briefest hesitation in Daphne's eyes before she went over to the other side of the bed and lay next to Amber.

"Sure, sweetie. I'll stay until you fall asleep. Just rest. I'm right here if you need anything."

Amber smiled. All she needed from Daphne was everything.

SIX

Amber flipped through the pages of *Vogue* as she sat listening to the whiny client on the other end of the phone continuing to bitch about the $5 million house that had been sold out from under her. She hated Mondays, the day she was asked to sit in for the receptionist at lunchtime. Her boss had promised her she'd be free of it as soon as the new hire began in another month.

She'd started as a secretary in the residential division of Rollins Realty when she first moved to Bishops Harbor, and she'd hated every minute of it. Almost all of the clients were spoiled women and arrogant men, all with a hugely elevated sense of entitlement. The kind of people who never slowed their expensive cars at a four-way stop because they believed they always had the right-of-way. She'd set appointments, call them with updates, set up appraisal and inspection appointments, and still they barely acknowledged her. She did notice that they were only a little more courteous to the agents, but their lack of manners still infuriated her.

She used that first year to take evening classes in commercial real estate. She checked books out of the library on the subject and read voraciously on weekends, sometimes forgetting to eat lunch or dinner. When she felt ready, she went to the head of the commercial side of Rollins, Mark Jansen, to discuss her thoughts on a potential opportunity regarding a zoning change vote she'd read about in the paper and what a successful vote could mean for one of their clients. He was blown away by her knowledge and understanding of the market, and started stopping by her desk occasionally to chat about his side of the business. Within a few months she was sitting right outside his office, working closely with him. Between her reading and his tutelage, her knowledge and expertise increased. And to Amber's good fortune, Mark was a great boss, a devoted family man who treated her with respect and kindness. She was right where she had planned to be from the start. It had just taken time and determination, but determination was one thing Amber had in spades.

She looked up as Jenna, the receptionist, walked in with a crumpled McDonald's bag and a soda in her hands. No wonder she was so fat, Amber thought in disgust. How could people have so little self-control?

"Hey, girlie, thanks so much for covering. Did everything go okay?" Jenna's smile made her face even more moonlike than normal.

Amber bristled. *Girlie?* "Just some moron who's upset because someone else bought her house."

"Oh, that was probably Mrs. Worth. She's so disappointed. I feel bad for her."

"Don't waste your tears. Now she can cry on her husband's shoulder and get the eight-million-dollar house instead."

"Oh, Amber. You're so funny."

Amber shook her head in puzzlement at Jenna and walked away.

Later that night, as she sat soaking in the tub, she thought about the last two years. She'd been ready to leave it all far behind—the dry-cleaning chemicals that burned her eyes and nose, the filth from soiled clothing that clung to her hands, and the big plan that had gone awry. Just when she thought she'd finally grabbed the brass ring, everything had come crashing down. There was no question of her hanging around. When she left Missouri, she'd made sure that anyone looking for her wouldn't find even a trace to follow.

The water was turning cooler now. Amber rose and wrapped herself in a thin terry-cloth robe as she stepped out of the bath. There'd been no old school friend to invite her to Connecticut. She'd rented the tiny furnished apartment just days after she arrived in Bishops Harbor. The dingy white walls were bare, and the floor was covered with an old-fashioned pea-green shag that had probably been there since the 1980s. The only seating was an upholstered love seat with worn arms and sagging pillows. A plastic table sat at the end of the small sofa. There was nothing on the table, not even a lamp, the single lightbulb with its fringed shade hanging from the low ceiling being the only illumination in the room. It was hardly more than a place to sleep and hang her hat, but it was only a placeholder until her plan was complete. In the end, it would all be worth it.

She quickly dried off, threw on pajama bottoms and a sweatshirt, and then sat at the small desk in front of the only window in the apartment. She pulled out her file on Nebraska and read over it once again. Daphne hadn't asked her any more questions about her childhood, but still, it never hurt to refresh. Nebraska had been her first stop after leaving her hometown in Missouri, and it was where her luck had begun to change. She bet she knew more about Eustis, Nebraska, and its Wurst Tag sausage festival than even the oldest living resident. She scanned the pages, then put the folder back and picked up the book on international real estate she'd gotten from the library on her way home that night. It was heavy enough to make a good doorstop, and she knew it was going to take some very long nights and lots of concentration to get through it.

She smiled. Even if her place was small and cramped, she had spent so many nights longing for a room of her own when she and her three sisters were packed in the attic her father had turned into a bunkhouse of sorts. No matter how hard she'd tried, the room was always a mess, with her sisters' clothes, shoes, and books strewn all over. It made her crazy. Amber needed order— disciplined, structured order. And now, finally, she was the master of her world. And of her fate.

SEVEN

Amber dressed carefully that Monday morning. She had quite accidentally run into Daphne and her daughters at the town library late yesterday afternoon. They'd stopped to chat, and Daphne had introduced her to Tallulah and Bella. She had been struck by their differences. Tallulah, tall and thin with glasses and a plain face, appeared quiet and withdrawn. Bella, on the other hand, was an adorable little sprite, her golden curls bouncing as she cavorted around the shelves. Both girls had been polite but uninterested, and had leafed through their books as the two women spoke. Amber had noticed that Daphne didn't seem her usual cheery self. "Is everything all right?" she said, putting her hand gently on Daphne's arm. Daphne's eyes had filled. "Just some memories I can't shake today. That's all."

Amber had gone on full alert. "Memories?"

"Tomorrow is Julie's birthday. I can't stop thinking about her." She ran her fingers through Bella's curly hair, and the child looked up at her and smiled.

"Tomorrow? The twenty-first?" Amber said.

"Yes, tomorrow."

"I can't believe it. It's Charlene's birthday, too!" Amber silently berated herself, hoping she hadn't overplayed her hand, but as soon as she saw the look on Daphne's face, she knew she'd struck just the right chord.

"Oh my gosh, Amber. That's unbelievable. I'm beginning to feel like the heavens have brought us together."

"It *does* seem like it's meant to be," Amber had said, then paused for a few seconds. "We should do something tomorrow to celebrate our sisters, to remember the good things and not dwell on the sadness. How about if I pack us some sandwiches, and we can have lunch at my office? There's a small picnic bench on the side of the building near the stream."

"What a good idea," Daphne had said, more animated then. "But why should you go to the trouble of packing a lunch? I'll pick you up at your office, and we'll go to the country club. Would you like that?"

That was precisely what Amber had been hoping Daphne would suggest, but she hadn't wanted to seem too eager. "Are you sure? It really isn't any trouble. I pack lunch every day."

"Of course I'm sure. What time shall I pick you up?"

"I can usually duck out around twelve thirty."

"Perfect. I'll see you then," Daphne had said, and shifted the pile of books in her arms. "We'll make it a happy celebration."

Now Amber studied herself in the mirror one last time—white boat-neck T-shirt and her one nice pair of navy slacks. She'd tried on the sturdy sandals but exchanged them for white ones. She wore faux pearl studs in her ears and, on her right hand, a ring with a small sapphire set in gold. Her hair was pulled back with the usual headband, and her only makeup was a very light pink lip balm. Satisfied that she looked subdued but not too frumpy, she grabbed her keys and left for work.

By ten, Amber had checked the clock at least fifty times. The minutes dragged unbearably as she tried to concentrate on the new shopping center contract in front of her. She reread the final four pages, making notes as she went along. Ever since she'd found an error that could have cost the company a bundle, her boss, Mark, didn't sign anything until Amber had reviewed it.

Today was Amber's day to cover the phones for Jenna, but Jenna had agreed to stay so that Amber could go out for lunch.

"Who are you having lunch with?" Jenna asked.

"You don't know her. Daphne Parrish," she answered, feeling important.

"Oh, Mrs. Parrish. I've met her. A couple years ago, with her mother. They came in together 'cause her mom was going to move here to be closer to the family. She looked at tons of places, but she ended up staying in New Hampshire. She was a real nice lady."

Amber's ears perked up. "Really? What was her name? Do you remember?"

Jenna looked up at the ceiling. "Lemme see." She was quiet a moment and then nodded her head and looked back at Amber. "I remember. Her name was Ruth Bennett. She's a widow."

"She lives alone?" Amber said.

"Well, sort of, I guess. She owns a B&B in New Hampshire, so she's not really alone. Right? But on the other hand, they're all pretty much strangers, so she kind of does live alone. Maybe you could say she lives semi-alone, or only alone at night when she goes to bed," Jenna prattled on. "Before she left, she brought a real nice basket of goodies to the office to thank me for being so nice. It was really sweet. But kinda sad too. It seemed like she really wanted to move here."

"Why didn't she?"

"I don't know. Maybe Mrs. Parrish didn't want her that close."

"Did she say that?" Amber probed.

"Not really. It just seemed like she wasn't too excited about her mom being so close by. I guess she didn't really need her around. You know, she had her nannies and stuff. One of my friends was her nanny when her first daughter was a baby."

Amber felt like she'd struck gold. "Really? How long did she work there?"

"A couple years, I think."

"Is she a good friend of yours?"

"Sally? Yeah, me and her go way back."

"I bet she has some stories to tell," Amber said.

"What do you mean?"

Is this girl for real? "You know, things about the family, what they're like, what they do at home—that kind of thing."

"Yeah, I guess. But I wasn't really interested. We had other stuff to talk about."

"Maybe the three of us could have dinner next week."

"Hey, that would be great."

"Why don't you call her tomorrow and set it up? What's her name again?" Amber asked.

"Sally. Sally MacAteer."

"And she lives here in Bishops Harbor?"

"She lives right next door to me, so I see her all the time. We grew up together. I'll ask her about dinner. This'll be really fun. Like the three musketeers." Jenna skipped back to her desk, and Amber went back to work.

She picked up the contract and put it on the desk in Mark's empty office so they could discuss it that afternoon when he got back from his appointment in Norwalk. She looked at her watch and saw that she had twenty minutes to finish and freshen up before Daphne's arrival. She returned two phone calls, filed a few loose papers, and then went to the bathroom to check her hair. Satisfied, she went to the front lobby to watch for Daphne's Range Rover.

It pulled up at exactly twelve thirty, Amber noticed, appreciating Daphne's promptness. As Amber pushed open the glass door of the building, Daphne rolled the car window down and called out a cheerful hello. Amber walked to the passenger side, opened the door, and hoisted herself into the cool interior.

"It's great to see you," Amber said with what she hoped sounded like enthusiasm.

Daphne looked over at her and smiled before putting the car into gear. "I've been looking forward to this all morning. I couldn't wait for my garden club meeting to be over. I know it's going to make the day so much easier to get through."

"I hope so," Amber said, her voice subdued.

They were both quiet for the next few blocks, and Amber leaned back against the soft leather seat. She turned her head slightly in Daphne's direction and took in her white linen pants and sleeveless white linen top, which had a wide navy stripe at the bottom. She wore small gold hoops and a simple gold bangle bracelet next to her watch. And her ring, of course, the rock that could have sunk the *Titanic*. Her slender arms were nicely tanned. She looked fit, healthy, and rich.

As they pulled into the driveway of the Tidewater Country Club, Amber drank it all in—the gently winding road with precision-cut grass on either side, not a weed in sight; tennis courts with players in sparkling whites; the swimming pools in the distance; and the impressive building looming before them. It was even grander than she had imagined. They drove around the circle to the main entrance, and were met by a young guy in a casual uniform of dark khakis and a green polo shirt. On his head was a white visor with the Tidewater logo embroidered in green.

"Good afternoon, Mrs. Parrish," he said as he opened her door.

"Hello, Danny," Daphne said and handed him the keys. "We're just here for lunch."

He walked around to open Amber's door, but she had already stepped out.

"Well, enjoy," he said, and got into the car.

"He's such a nice young man," Daphne said as she and Amber walked up the wide stairs into the building. "His mother used to work for Jackson, but she's been very ill the last few years. Danny takes care of her and is also working to put himself through college."

Amber wondered what he thought about all the money he saw thrown around at this club while he nursed a sick mother and worked to make ends meet, but she bit her tongue.

Daphne suggested they eat on the deck, and so the maître d' led them outside, where Amber breathed in the bracing sea air she loved so much. They were seated at a table overlooking the marina, its three long piers filled with boats of all shapes and sizes bobbing up and down in the choppy waters.

"Wow, this is just beautiful," Amber said.

"Yes, it is. A nice setting to remember all the wonderful things about Charlene and Julie."

"My sister would have loved it here," Amber said, and meant it. None of her perfectly healthy sisters would have even been able to imagine a place like this. She tore her gaze away from the water and turned to Daphne. "You must come here a lot with your family."

"We do. Jackson, of course, heads right for the golf course whenever he can. Tallulah and Bella take all kinds of lessons—sailing, swimming, tennis. They're quite the little athletes."

Amber wondered what it would be like to grow up in this kind of world, where you were groomed from infancy to have and enjoy all the good things in life. Where you made friends almost from birth with the right people and were educated in the best schools, and the blinds were tightly drawn against outsiders. She was suddenly overwhelmed with sadness and envy.

The waiter brought two tall glasses of iced tea and took their lunch order—a small salad for Daphne and ahi tuna for Amber.

"Now," Daphne said, as they waited. "Tell me a good memory about your sister."

"Hmm. Well, I remember when she was just a few months old, my mom and I took her for a walk. I would have been six. It was a beautiful, sunny day and Mom let me push the carriage. Of course she was right next to me, just in case." Amber warmed to her subject, embellishing the story as she continued. "But I remember feeling so grown-up and so happy to have this new little sister. She was so pretty, with her blue eyes and yellow curls. Just like a picture. And I think from that day on, I sort of felt like she was my little girl too."

"That's really lovely, Amber."

"What about you? What do you remember?"

"Julie and I were only two years apart, so I don't remember much about when she was a baby. But later, she was so brave. She always had a smile on her beautiful face. Never complained. She always said if someone had to have cystic fibrosis, she was glad it was her because she wouldn't have wanted another child to suffer." Daphne stopped and looked out at the water. "There was not one ounce of unkindness in her. She was the best person I've ever known."

Amber shifted in her chair and felt a discomfort she didn't quite understand.

Daphne went on. "The part that's hard to think about is all she went through. Every day. All the medications she had to take." She shook her head. "We used to get up early together, and I would talk to her while she had her vest on."

"Yes, the vibrating contraption." Amber remembered reading about the vest that helped dislodge mucus from the lungs.

"It became routine—the vest, the nebulizer, the inhaler. She spent more than two hours a day trying to stave off the effects of the disease. She truly believed she would go to college, marry, have children. She said she worked so hard at all her therapies and exercised because that's what would give her a future. She believed to the very end," Daphne said, as a single tear ran down her cheek. "I would give anything to have her back."

"I know," Amber whispered. "Maybe our sisters' spirits have somehow brought us together. It sort of makes it like they're here with us."

Daphne blinked back more tears. "I like that idea."

Daphne's memories and Amber's stories continued through the lunch, and as the waiter took their plates away, Amber felt a flash of brilliance and turned to him. "We're celebrating two birthdays today. Would you bring us a piece of chocolate cake to share?"

The smile that Daphne bestowed on Amber was filled with warmth and gratitude.

He brought them the cake with two lighted candles, and with a flourish said, "A very happy birthday to you."

Their lunch lasted a little over an hour, but Amber didn't have to hurry back since Mark wasn't due back in the office until at least three o'clock, and she had told Jenna she might be a little late.

"Well," Daphne said when they'd finished their coffee. "I suppose I should get you back to the office. Don't want to get you in trouble with your boss."

Amber looked around for their waiter. "Shouldn't we wait for the check?"

"Oh, don't worry," Daphne said, waving her hand. "They'll just put it on our account."

But of course, Amber thought. It seemed the more money you had, the less you had to actually come into contact with the filthy stuff.

When they pulled up to the realty office, Daphne put the car in park and looked at Amber. "I really enjoyed today. I've forgotten how good it is to talk to someone who really understands."

"I enjoyed it too, Daphne. It helped a lot."

"I was wondering if you might be free on Friday night to have dinner with us. What do you say?"

"Gosh, I'd love to." She was thrilled at how quickly Daphne was opening up to her.

"Good," Daphne said. "See you on Friday. Around six o'clock?"

"Perfect. See you then. And thank you." As Amber watched her drive away, she felt like she had just won the lottery.

EIGHT

The day after her lunch with Daphne, Amber stood behind Bunny in the Zumba class at the gym. She laughed to herself, watching Bunny trip over her feet trying to keep up with the instructor. What a klutz, she thought. After class, Amber took her time dressing behind the row of lockers next to Bunny's in the locker room, listening to the trophy wife and her sycophants discuss her plans.

"When are you meeting him?" one asked.

"Happy hour at the Blue Pheasant. But remember, I'm with you girls tonight, if your husbands ask."

"The Blue Pheasant? Everyone goes there. What if someone sees you?"

"I'll say he's a client. I do have my real estate license, after all."

Amber heard snickering.

"What, Lydia?" Bunny snapped.

"Well, it's not exactly like you've been doing much with it since you married March."

March Nichols's net worth of $100 million stuck in Amber's head—that and the fact that he resembled Methuselah. Amber could understand why Bunny looked elsewhere for sex.

"We won't be there long, anyway. I reserved a room at the Piedmont across the street."

"Naughty, naughty. Did you book it under Mrs. Robinson?"

They were all laughing now.

Old husband, young lover—there was a certain poetry to it.

Amber had what she needed, so she jumped into the shower, then rushed back to the office, excuse at the ready to explain her long absence.

Later that day, she got to the bar early and sat with her book and a glass of wine at a table near the back. As it began to fill up, she tried to guess which one he was. She'd settled on the cute blond in jeans when McDreamy walked in. With jet-black hair and bright blue eyes, he was a dead ringer for Patrick Dempsey. His camel-colored cashmere jacket and black silk scarf were meticulously sloppy. He ordered a beer and took a swig from the bottle. Bunny came in, eyes laser-focused on him, and, rushing to the bar, she flung her arms around him. Standing so close a matchbook wouldn't have fit between them, they were obviously besotted with each other. They finished their drinks and ordered another round. McDreamy put his arm around Bunny's waist, pulling her even closer. Bunny turned up that adorable little face to him and locked her lips against his. At that precise moment, Amber turned her iPhone to silent, raised it, and snapped several photos of their enraptured display. They finally pulled apart long enough to gulp down the second drink they'd ordered and then leave the bar arm in arm. No doubt they were not going to waste any more time at the bar when the hotel across the street beckoned.

Amber finished her drink and scrolled through the pictures. She was still laughing as she walked to her car. Poor old March would be getting some very enlightening photographs tomorrow. And Bunny—well, Bunny would be too distraught to continue with her duties as Daphne's cochair.

NINE

Amber had been counting the days until Friday. She would finally get to meet Jackson at dinner, and she was giddy with anticipation. By the time she rang the doorbell, she felt ready to burst.

Daphne greeted her with a dazzling smile, taking her by the hand. "Welcome, Amber. So good to see you. Please, come in."

"Thanks, Daphne. I've been looking forward to this all week," Amber said as she entered the large hallway.

"I thought we might have a drink in the conservatory before dinner," Daphne said, and Amber followed her into the room. "What will you have?"

"Um, I think I'd like a glass of red wine," Amber said. She looked around the room, but Jackson was nowhere in sight.

"Pinot noir okay?"

"Perfect," Amber said, wondering where the hell Jackson was.

Daphne handed her the glass and, as if reading her mind, said, "Jackson had to work late, so it'll just be us girls tonight—you, me, Tallulah, and Bella."

Amber's exhilaration evaporated. Now she'd have to sit and listen to the mind-numbing chatter of those kids all evening.

Just then Bella came tearing into the room.

"Mommy, Mommy," she wailed, thrusting herself forward onto Daphne's lap. "Tallulah won't read to me from my *Angelina Ballerina* book."

Tallulah was right behind her. "Mom, I'm trying to help her read it by herself, but she won't listen," she said, sounding like a miniature adult. "I was reading way harder books at her age."

"Girls. No quarreling tonight," Daphne said, ruffling Bella's curls. "Tallulah was just trying to help you, Bella."

"But she knows I can't do it," Bella said, her face still in Daphne's lap and her voice muffled.

Daphne stroked her daughter's head. "It's all right, darling. Don't worry, you will soon."

"Come on, ladies," Daphne addressed them all. "Let's go out to the deck and have a nice dinner. Margarita made some delicious guacamole we can start with."

Summer would be coming to an end soon, and there was a slight breeze that held just a hint of cooler days to come. Even a casual dinner on Daphne's deck took on an air of style and sophistication, Amber thought. Triangular dishes of bright red sat on navy blue place mats, and napkin rings decorated with silver sailboats held blue-and-white-checked napkins. Amber noticed that each place setting was identically placed. It reminded her of the British films about aristocracy, where the waitstaff actually measured every item placed on the dining table. Couldn't this woman ever relax?

"Amber, why don't you sit there," Daphne said, pointing to a chair directly facing the water.

The view, of course, was stunning, with a velvety lawn gently sloping to a sandy beach and the water beyond. She counted five Adirondack chairs clustered on the sand, a few yards back from the water's edge. How picturesque and inviting it looked.

Bella was eyeing Amber from across the table. "Are you married?"

Amber shook her head. "No, I'm not."

"How come?" Bella asked.

"Darling, that's a rather personal question." Daphne looked at Amber and laughed. "Sorry about that."

"No, it's okay." Amber turned her attention to Bella. "I suppose I haven't met Mr. Right."

Bella narrowed her eyes. "Who's Mr. Right?"

"It's just an expression, silly. She means she hasn't met the right one for her," Tallulah explained.

"Hmph. Maybe it's 'cause she's kind of ugly."

"Bella! You apologize this minute." Daphne's face had turned bright pink.

"Why? It's true, isn't it?" Bella insisted.

"Even if it's true, it's still rude," Tallulah offered.

Amber cast her eyes downward, trying to appear hurt, and said nothing.

Daphne stood up. "That's it. The two of you can eat by yourselves in the kitchen. Sit there and think about the proper way to speak to others." She rang for Margarita and sent the girls off, amid protests. She came over to Amber and put an arm around her shoulder. "I am so, so sorry. I'm beyond embarrassed and appalled by their behavior."

Amber gave her a small smile. "You don't need to apologize. They're kids. They don't mean anything by it." She smiled again, buoyed by the thought that now they could spend the rest of the evening unfettered by the little brats.

"Thank you for being so gracious."

They chatted about this and that and enjoyed a delicious dinner of shrimp scampi over quinoa and a spinach salad. Amber noticed, though, that Daphne had barely taken two bites of the scampi and not much more of her salad. Amber finished every bit of hers, not about to waste this expensive food.

It was beginning to get cool, and she was relieved when Daphne suggested they go back in the sunroom for coffee.

She followed Daphne until they reached a cheerful room decorated in yellows and blues. White bookcases lined the walls, and Amber lingered in front of one set, curious to see what Daphne liked to read. The shelves were lined with all the classics, in alphabetical order by author. Starting with Albee all the way to Woolf. She would bet there was no way Daphne had read them all.

"Do you like to read, Amber?"

"Very much. I'm afraid I haven't read most of these, though. I'm more into contemporary authors. Have you read all of these?"

"Yes, many of them. Jackson likes to discuss great books. We're only to the *H*'s. We're tackling Homer's *The Odyssey*. Not quite light reading." She laughed.

A lovely porcelain turtle, as blue as the Caribbean, caught Amber's attention and she reached out to touch it. She'd seen a few others throughout the house, each one unique and more exquisite than the last. She could tell they were all expensive, and she wanted to smash them to the floor. Here she was, struggling to make rent every month, and Daphne could throw money away collecting stupid turtles. It was so unfair. She turned away and took a seat on the silk love seat next to Daphne.

"This has been so much fun. Thanks again for having me."

"It's been wonderful. I enjoyed having another adult to talk to."

"Does your husband work late a lot?" Amber asked.

Daphne shrugged. "It depends. He's usually home for dinner. He likes the family to eat together. But he's working on a new land deal in California, and with the time difference sometimes it can't be helped."

Amber went to pick up the coffee cup from the table in front of her, and her grip slipped. The cup went crashing to the floor.

"I'm so sorry—" The horrified look on Daphne's face stopped Amber midsentence.

Daphne flew from her chair and out of the room, returning a few minutes later with a white towel and a bowl with some sort of mixture in it. She started blotting the stain with the towel, and then rubbing it with whatever concoction she had mixed up.

"Can I help?" Amber asked.

Daphne didn't look up. "No, no. I have it. Just wanted to make sure I got to it before the stain set."

Amber felt helpless, watching Daphne attack the stain as if her life depended on it. Wasn't that what the help was for? She sat there, feeling like an idiot, while Daphne scrubbed furiously. Amber began to feel less bad and more annoyed. So she'd spilled something. Big deal. At least she hadn't called anyone ugly.

Daphne stood, took a last look at the now-clean rug, and gave Amber a sheepish shrug. "Goodness. Well, can I get you a new cup?"

Was she for real? "No, that's okay. I really should be going anyway. It's getting late."

"Are you sure? You don't have to go so soon."

Normally Amber would have stayed, played things out a little longer, but she didn't trust herself not to give her annoyance away. Besides, she could see that Daphne was still on edge. What a clean freak she was. She'd probably examine the rug with a magnifying glass once Amber left.

"Absolutely. This has been such a great evening. I've really enjoyed hanging out with you. I'll see you next week at the committee meeting."

"Drive safely," Daphne said as she closed the door.

Amber glanced at the time on her phone. If she hurried, she could get to the library before it closed and check out a copy of *The Odyssey*.

TEN

By the third committee meeting, Amber was ready to execute the final stage of Operation Bye-Bye Bunny. Today she was wearing a thin wraparound sweater from the Loft over her best pair of black slacks. She dreaded seeing the other women and enduring their condescending glances and too-polite conversation. She knew she wasn't one of them, and it infuriated her that she let it get to her. Taking a cleansing breath, she reminded herself that the only one she needed to worry about was Daphne.

Forcing a smile, she rang the bell and waited to be escorted inside.

The housekeeper opened the door in uniform.

"Missus will be down shortly. She left a paper in the conservatory for you to look at while you wait."

Amber smiled at her. "Thanks, Margarita. By the way, I've been meaning to ask you. The guacamole you made the other evening was divine—never had any as good. What's your secret ingredient?"

Margarita looked pleased. "Thank you, Miss Amber. You promise not to tell?"

Amber nodded.

She leaned in and whispered, "Cumin."

Amber hadn't actually tasted the green goo—she hated avocados—but every woman thinks her own recipes are so special, and it was an easy way to get on someone's good side.

The room was set up with a breakfast buffet: muffins, fruit, coffee, and tea. Grabbing a mug, Amber filled it to the brim with coffee. She had already reviewed the agenda when Daphne walked into the room, perfectly turned out as usual. Amber rose and gave her a hug. Holding up the piece of paper, she frowned and pointed at the first item. "New cochair needed? What happened to Bunny?"

Daphne sighed and shook her head. "She called me a few days ago and said she had a family emergency to deal with. Something about having to leave town to care for a sick uncle."

Amber affected a perplexed expression. "That's a shame. Wasn't she supposed to have finished organizing the silent auction by today?" It was a huge job, requiring good organizational skills and attention to detail. All of the items had been secured, but Amber was quite sure that Bunny had left plenty of work that still needed to be completed, given that her world had collapsed a week ago.

"Yes, she was. Unfortunately, she just let me know yesterday that she hadn't finished organizing all of it. Now we're really behind the eight ball. I feel so bad asking someone to step in and take over. They'll have to work nonstop to have everything ready in time."

"I know I'm the newbie here, but I've done this sort of thing before. I would love to do it." Amber looked down at her fingernails, then back up at Daphne. "But the other women probably wouldn't like it."

Daphne's eyebrows shot up. "It doesn't matter that you're new. I know you're here because your heart's truly in it. But it's an awful lot of work," she said. "All the item write-ups still need to be done, the bid forms have to be matched, and the bid numbers need to be set up."

Amber tried to keep her voice casual. "I managed one for my

old boss. The best thing is to have the bid form in triplicate, three different colors, and to leave the bottom copy with the item after the auction closes and take the other two to the cashier. It eliminates confusion."

She'd hit her mark from her Google research from the night before. Daphne looked duly impressed.

"It would make me feel like I was doing something for Charlene," Amber continued. "I mean, I don't have the money to make big donations, but I can offer my time." She gave Daphne what she hoped was a pitiful look.

"Of course. Absolutely. I would be honored to have you as my cochair."

"What about the other women? Will they be okay with it? I wouldn't want to ruffle any feathers."

"You let me worry about them," Daphne said and lifted her coffee mug in salute to Amber. "Partners. For Julie and Charlene."

Amber picked up her mug and touched it to Daphne's.

A half hour later, after eating Daphne's food and catching each other up on their scintillating lives, the women all finally got down to the business of the meeting. It must be nice to have all morning to fritter away like this. Once again, Amber'd had to take a vacation day to be there.

Amber held her breath as Daphne cleared her throat and addressed the room. "Unfortunately, Bunny had to resign from the committee. She's been called out of town to care for an ailing uncle."

"Oh, what a shame. I hope it's not too serious," Meredith said.

"I don't have any other details," Daphne said, then paused. "I was going to ask one of you to step in as cochair, but Amber has graciously offered to do it."

Meredith looked at her, then at Daphne. "Um, that's very generous, but do you think that's really wise? No offense intended, but Amber just joined us. It's a lot to get up to speed on. I'd be happy to do it."

"The main thing left is to handle the silent auction, and Amber has experience with it," Daphne replied in a nonchalant tone. "Plus, Amber has a very personal stake; she wants to honor her sister as well. I'm sure she would welcome your help and that of everyone on the committee."

Amber turned her gaze from Daphne to Meredith. "I would be so appreciative of any advice you're willing to give. Once I've assessed where we are, I can divvy up some assignments." The thought of having that rich bitch reporting to her made her flush with pleasure. She didn't miss the look of irritation on Meredith's face and struggled to hide a smirk.

Meredith cocked an eyebrow. "Of course. We're all happy to do our part. Bunny had planned on laying out all the items in her house and having a few of us come and help with the bid sheets and descriptions. Should we plan on coming to your house, Amber?"

Before Amber could respond, Daphne dove in to rescue her. "The items are already here. I sent for them yesterday afternoon. No sense in moving them again."

Amber fixed her eyes on Meredith as she spoke. "I'm planning on automating the forms anyhow. It will be much more efficient for me to e-mail them to each of you with a picture of the item, and you can fill out the descriptions and send them back. Then I can have them printed and set with the items. I'll send everyone an e-mail tonight with the groupings, and you can let me know which you'll write up. No need to waste time all sitting around together."

"That's a great idea, Amber. See, ladies? Nice to have some new blood."

Amber leaned back into her armchair and smiled. She felt Meredith's appraising eyes on her, and noticed once again how everything about her screamed old money, from her double strand of pearls to the slightly worn camel jacket. Minimal makeup, no particular style to her hair, quiet wristwatch and earrings. Her wedding ring, a band of sapphires and diamonds, looked like a family heirloom. Nothing ostentatious about this woman except the distinct aura of *Mayflower* lineage and trust funds. Her arrogance reminded Amber of Mrs. Lockwood, the richest woman in the town where she grew up, who would bring her cashmere sweaters, wool suits, and formal gowns into the dry cleaner's every Monday morning, putting them gingerly on the counter as if she couldn't bear for her sacred garments to touch the clothes of the underclass. She never greeted Amber and never responded to a hello with anything but a forced, sour smile that looked as if she'd smelled something rotten.

The Lockwood family lived in a huge home at the top of a hill overlooking the town. Amber had met Frances, their only daughter, at a county fair, and the two had become fast friends. The first time Frances took Amber to her home, Amber had been awestruck at its size and magnificent furnishings. Frances's bedroom was a young girl's dream, all pink and white and frilly. Her dolls—so many!—were lined up neatly on built-in shelves, and on one long wall stood a case filled with books and trophies. Amber remembered feeling like she never wanted to leave that bedroom. But the friendship had been short-lived. After all, Amber was not the sort Mrs. Lockwood wanted as a friend for her precious daughter. As quickly as the two girls had connected, the cord was severed by Frances's imperious mother. It had stuck in Amber's craw ever since, but she'd found a way to get even when she met Matthew, Frances's handsome older brother. Mrs. Lockwood hadn't known what hit her.

And now, here she was, confronting the same condescension from Meredith Stanton. So far, though, it was Amber one, Meredith nothing.

"Amber." Daphne's voice startled her from her reverie. "I'd like to get a picture for a little advance publicity. Let's have you and the rest of the auction committee with some of the items. I'm sure the *Harbor Times* will publish it with a blurb about the fundraiser."

Amber couldn't move. *A picture? For the newspaper?* She couldn't let that happen. She had to think quickly. "Um." She paused a moment. "Gee, Daphne, I'm so new to the group. I don't think it's fair for me to be in the photo. It should include members who have worked on this longer than I have."

"That's very gracious of you, but you are the cochair now," Daphne said.

"I'd really feel more comfortable if other people's accomplishments were highlighted." Looking around, Amber realized she'd scored points for humility. It was a win-win. She could maintain the rank of poor but sweet and unassuming little waif to these privileged snobs. And most importantly, no ghosts from the past would come sniffing around. She just needed to keep a low profile for now.

ELEVEN

The next morning Jenna came dancing into Amber's office, her smile so wide that her cheeks practically obscured her squinty little eyes. "Guess what?" she demanded breathlessly.

"No clue," Amber said flatly, not even bothering to look up from the commission reports she was working on.

"I talked to Sally last night."

Amber's head shot up, and she put her pen down.

"She said she'd like to come to dinner with us. Tonight."

"That's great, Jenna." For the first time, Amber was thankful for Jenna's doggedness. She had pestered Amber from her first day on the job, and every time Amber refused her invitations, she had bounced back up like a Punchinello toy and asked her again, until finally Amber relented. Jenna had gotten what she wanted, and now it was all about to pay off for Amber too.

"What time, and do we have a place in mind?"

"Well, we could do Friendly's. Or Red Lobster. Tonight they're having all the shrimp you can eat."

Amber pictured Jenna sitting across from her, cocktail sauce dripping down her chin as she devoured all those little pink shrimp. She didn't think she could stomach that. "Let's go to the Main Street Grille," she said. "I'm free right after work."

"Okay. I'll tell Sally to meet us around five thirty. This is going to be so much fun," Jenna squealed, clapping her hands together and prancing out of the office.

When Amber and Jenna arrived at the Grille, they were

seated in a booth near the back of the restaurant, with Jenna facing the door so she would see Sally when she arrived. Jenna began yammering away about a new client who had come in today looking for properties in the $5 million range and how nice and friendly she was, then suddenly stopped and waved her hand. "Here's Sally," she said and stood up.

As Sally approached the table, Amber knew her surprise registered on her face. This woman was not at all what she'd expected.

"Hi, Jenna." The newcomer gave Jenna a hug and then turned to Amber. "You must be Amber, the one Jenna is always talking about." She smiled, reached a slender arm across the table, and shook Amber's hand. Sally wore fitted jeans and a long-sleeved white T-shirt that showed off her trim figure, tanned skin, and luxuriant brown hair. As she took the seat next to Jenna, Amber was struck by her eyes, so dark they were almost black, with thick, long eyelashes.

"It's nice to meet you, Sally," Amber said. "I'm glad you could make it tonight."

"Jenna and I have been promising to get together for ages, but we've been so busy with work that we haven't had time. I'm glad we finally made it happen." Amber wondered what these two could possibly have in common besides living on the same street.

"I'm starving. Do you two know what you want?" Jenna said.

Sally picked up her menu and quickly scanned it.

"The grilled salmon with spinach sounds good," Amber said, and Jenna wrinkled her nose.

"Yes, I think I'll have the same." Sally put down the menu.

"Yuck. How can you choose salmon instead of a hot turkey sandwich with mashed potatoes and gravy? That's what I'm getting. And no spinach."

The waitress took their orders, and Amber ordered a bottle of the house red. She wanted everyone relaxed and loose-tongued tonight.

"Here," she said, and poured the wine into their glasses. "Let's sit back and enjoy. So tell me, Sally, where do you work?"

"I'm a special education teacher at a private school, St. Gregory's in Greenwich."

"That's great. Jenna told me that you had been a nanny. You must love kids."

"Oh, I do."

"How many years did you nanny?"

"Six years. I only worked for two families. The last one was here in town."

"Who was that?" Amber asked.

"Geez, Amber, did you forget? The day you had lunch with Mrs. Parrish, I told you Sally used to work for her," Jenna said.

Amber gave her a hate-filled look. "Yes, I did forget." She turned back to Sally. "What was it like—working there, I mean?"

"I loved it. And Mr. and Mrs. Parrish were great to work for."

Amber wasn't interested in a fairy tale of how perfect the Parrish family was. She decided to take another tack. "Nannying must be a tough job at times. What were the hardest parts, do you think?"

"Hmm. When Tallulah was born, it was sort of tiring. She was small—only weighed five pounds at birth—so she had to eat every two hours. Of course the nurse took the night feedings, but I would get there at seven in the morning and stay till she came back at night."

"So the nurse fed her through the night? Mrs. Parrish didn't nurse the baby?"

"No, it was sad, really. Mr. Parrish told me she tried at first, but her milk wouldn't come in. He asked me not to say anything because it made her cry, so we never talked about it." Sally took a forkful of salmon. "I sometimes wondered about it."

"What do you mean?"

Amber detected discomfort in Sally, who seemed to be trying for nonchalance. "Oh, nothing, really."

"It doesn't sound like nothing," Amber pressed.

"Well, I guess I'm not telling you something everybody doesn't already know."

Amber leaned in closer and waited.

"A while after Tallulah was born, Mrs. Parrish went away. To a sort of hospital where you rest and get help."

"You mean a sanitarium?"

"Something like that."

"Did she have postpartum depression?"

"I'm really not sure. There was a lot of gossip at the time, but I tried not to listen to it. I don't know. There were police involved somehow. I remember that. There were rumors that she was a danger to the baby, that she shouldn't be alone with her."

Amber tried to hide her fascination. "Was she? A danger?"

Sally shook her head. "I had a hard time believing that. But I never really saw her again. Mr. Parrish let me go right before she came home. He said they wanted someone to speak French to Tallulah, and I had been thinking about going back to school full-time anyhow. Later, they did end up hiring my friend Surrey for the weekends. She never mentioned anything strange."

Amber was wondering what had happened to make Daphne require hospitalization. Her mind was miles away when she realized Sally was still talking.

"I'm sorry. What were you saying?" Amber asked her.

"It was Mrs. Parrish who encouraged me to continue and get

my master's degree. She said the most important thing was for a woman to be independent and know what she wanted. Especially before she considers marriage." Sally took a sip of her wine. "Good advice, I think."

"I suppose. But she was pretty young when she married Mr. Parrish, wasn't she?"

Sally smiled. "In her twenties. It seems like they have a perfect marriage, so I guess it was a good decision."

What a load of crap, Amber thought as she divided the last of the wine between their glasses. "Jenna told me that Mrs. Parrish's mother was thinking about moving here at one time. Did you ever meet her?"

"I met her a few times. She didn't visit that often. She mentioned that she ran a B&B up north, but it still seemed odd that she wasn't there more, you know, to see the baby and all."

"Do you know why she decided not to move to Bishops Harbor?"

"I'm not sure exactly, but she seemed put off by all the help the Parrishes had. Maybe she thought she'd be in the way," Sally said, then sipped her wine. "You know, Mrs. Parrish has an extremely well ordered and tightly scheduled life. Precision is a hallmark in her house—nothing out of place, every room spotless, and every item perfectly placed. Maybe it was a little too regimented for Mrs. Bennett."

"Wow, it sure sounds like it." Amber had not failed to notice the very same thing every time she visited Daphne, which was more and more often lately. The house looked as if no one lived in it. The moment you finished drinking from a glass or emptied your plate, it was whisked away and disappeared. There was never a misplaced thing, which was hard to achieve with two young kids around. Even the girls' bedrooms were immaculate. Amber had looked into the rooms the morning after she'd spent the night and was astounded at the meticulous placement of books and toys. Nothing was out of order.

As she drank more wine, Sally seemed to be warming to her subject. "I heard from Surrey that Tallulah and Bella never get to watch cartoons or kid shows. They have to watch documentaries or educational DVDs." She waved her hand. "I mean, not that that's bad, but it is sad that they can't watch anything just for fun or entertainment."

"I guess Mrs. Parrish values education," Amber said.

Sally looked at her watch. "Speaking of which, I really should get going. School in the morning." She turned to Jenna. "If you're ready to go, I can give you a ride home."

"That'd be good." Jenna clapped her hands together. "What a fun night it's been. We should do this again."

They settled the check, and Jenna and Sally left. Amber finished her wine and sat back in her seat, reviewing the nuggets of information she'd gathered.

When she got home, the first thing she did was look up Daphne's mother. After a bit of searching, she found that Ruth Bennett owned and ran a B&B in New Hampshire. It was a quaint inn with lovely grounds. Nothing extravagant, but very nice nonetheless. The picture of her on the website showed her to be an older, not quite as beautiful version of her daughter. Amber wondered what it was between them, why Daphne'd been reluctant to have her mother move near her.

She bookmarked the page and then logged onto Facebook. There he was, looking older and fatter. Guess the last few years hadn't been so good for him. She laughed and shut the lid of her laptop.

TWELVE

Waiting on the platform, Amber sipped the hot coffee in her gloved hand, trying to stay warm. White vapor escaped from her mouth every time she opened it, and she marched in place to generate some heat. She was meeting Daphne, Tallulah, and Bella for a day of shopping and sightseeing in New York, the primary attraction being the Christmas tree at Rockefeller Center. She had purposely dressed like a tourist: sensible shoes, warm down jacket, and a tote bag to hold her treasures. Just what a gal from Nebraska would wear. The only makeup she had on was a cheap frosted lipstick she'd picked up at Walgreens.

"Amber, hi," Daphne called as she came running toward her, a little girl attached to each hand. "Sorry we're late. This one couldn't decide what to wear." She tilted her head toward Bella with a smile.

Amber smiled. "Hi, girls. Nice to see you again."

Bella eyed her suspiciously. "That's an ugly coat."

"Bella!" Daphne and Tallulah exclaimed in unison. Daphne looked mortified. "That's a terrible thing to say."

"Well, it's true."

"I'm so sorry, Amber," Daphne said.

"It's okay." Amber squatted down until she was eye level with Bella. "You're right. It *is* an ugly coat. I've had it forever. Maybe you can help me pick a new one out today." She wanted to smack the little brat. She was all of six or seven, and she was wearing a pair of silver sneakers that Amber recognized from a package that had been sitting open on the kitchen table when she'd dropped off gift certificates for the auction at the house the other day. She'd gone home and looked up the shoes to discover that they cost almost $300. The spoiled kid was already a fashion snob.

Bella turned to her mother and whined, "When is the train coming? I'm cold."

Daphne wrapped her arms around her and kissed the top of her head. "Soon, darling."

After another five minutes of Bella's complaints, the train pulled in and they scrambled aboard, luckily finding a vacant spot in the front of the car—two rows facing each other. Amber sat down, and Bella stood in front of her, little arms crossed over her chest.

"You took my seat. I can't sit backward."

"No problem." Amber moved to the other side and Tallulah took the seat next to Bella.

"I want Mommy to sit next to me."

Were they really going to let this little monster bark orders all day?

Daphne gave her a stern look. "Bella, I'm right across from you. Stop this nonsense now. I'm going to sit next to Amber."

Bella gave her a dark look and kicked her little foot against the seat across from her. "Why'd *she* have to come, anyway? This is supposed to be a family trip."

Daphne stood up. "Excuse us for a moment." She grabbed Bella by the hand and walked her to the end of the aisle. Amber could see her gesturing with her hands as she talked. After a few minutes, Bella nodded and the two returned.

Bella took her seat and looked up at Amber. "I'm sorry, Amber."

She didn't look one bit sorry, but Amber gave her what she hoped was a kind look.

"Thank you, Bella. I accept your apology." She turned her attention to Tallulah. "Your mom tells me that you're a Nancy Drew fan."

Tallulah's eyes lit up, and she unzipped the small backpack she carried and brought out *The Secret of the Wooden Lady*. "I have all my mom's old books. I love them."

"So do I. I wanted to be just like Nancy Drew," Amber said.

Tallulah started to soften. "She's so brave and smart and always on an adventure."

"Boooooring," the little furby next to her called out.

"How would you know? You can't even read," Tallulah responded.

"Mom! She's not supposed to say that to me," Bella said, her voice rising.

"All right, girls, that's enough," Daphne said mildly.

Now Amber felt like slapping Daphne. Couldn't she see that kid needed to be put in her place? A good spank across the rump would probably do wonders.

They finally pulled into Grand Central and poured out of the train into the crowded station. Amber stayed behind Daphne as she and the girls walked up the steps and into the main terminal. Her spirits lifted as she looked around at the magnificent architecture and thought again how much she loved New York.

Daphne stopped and gathered them together. "Okay, here's what's on our agenda. We're going to start by looking at all the holiday window displays, then lunch at Alice's Teacup, then American Girl Store, and finally ice-skating at Rockefeller Center."

Kill me now, Amber thought.

※

Amber had to admit that the window displays were fabulous, each one more elaborate than the next. Even the little princess was bewitched and stopped her whining. When they arrived at Alice's Teacup, Amber groaned inwardly at the long line, but apparently Daphne was well known there, and they were whisked right in. Lunch was fine, no major incidents, and Amber and Daphne actually got to have a conversation longer than five minutes.

While the girls took their time eating their French toast, Amber finished her ham and cheese croissant and sipped her tea.

"Thanks again for including me, Daphne. It's so nice to be a part of a family day this time of year."

"Thank *you*. You're making the day so much more fun for me. When Jackson bailed out, I almost canceled." She leaned in and whispered, "As you've seen, Bella can be a little bit of a handful. It's great to have some help."

Amber felt her back go up. Was that what she was? Help?

"Wasn't the nanny available today?" she couldn't resist asking.

Daphne didn't seem to notice the jab. She shook her head absently. "I'd already given her the day off since we had planned this." She smiled brightly at Amber and squeezed her hand. "I'm so glad you came with us. This is the kind of thing I'd be doing with my sister if she were alive. Now I have a special friend to enjoy it with."

"That's funny. When we were looking at the beautiful animations in the store windows, I imagined how much Charlene would have loved it. Christmas was her favorite time of year." In fact, Amber's childhood Christmases had been mean and disappointing. But if Charlene *had* existed, she might have liked Christmas.

"Julie loved Christmas too. I've never told this to anyone, but very late on Christmas Eve each year, I write a letter to Julie."

"What do you tell her?" Amber asked.

"All that's happened in the last year, you know, like those Christmas letters that people send out. But these letters are different. I tell her what's in my heart and all about her nieces—how much she would have loved them and they her. It keeps me connected to her in a way I can't explain."

Amber felt a brief stab of sympathy that quickly turned to envy. She had never felt that kind of love and affection for anyone in her family. She wondered what that would be like. She didn't know quite what to say.

"Can we go to American Girl now?" Bella was standing, pulling on her coat, and Amber was grateful for the intrusion.

They left the restaurant and grabbed a cab. Amber sat in front with the driver. The inside of the car smelled of old cheese, and she wanted to gag, but as soon as she rolled the window down, Queen Bella piped up from the backseat.

"I'm cold."

Amber gritted her teeth and put it back up.

When they arrived at Forty-Ninth and Fifth, the line going into the store went all the way around the block.

"The line is so long," Tallulah said. "Do we really have to wait?"

Bella stomped her foot. "I need a new dress for my Bella doll. Can't you get us in ahead of them, Mommy? Like you did at the restaurant?"

Daphne shook her head. "Afraid not, sweetie." She gave Tallulah a beseeching look. "I *did* promise her."

Tallulah looked like she wanted to cry.

Amber had an inspiration. "Say, I noticed we passed a Barnes & Noble just a few blocks back. Why don't I take Tallulah there, and you and Bella can meet us when you finish?"

Tallulah's eyes lit up. "Can we, Mom? Please?"

"Are you sure, Amber?" Daphne asked.

Was she ever. "Of course. This way, they're both happy."

"Super. Thanks, Amber."

As she and Tallulah began to walk away, Daphne called out. "Amber, please stay with her in the store."

She bit back a sarcastic retort. Like she'd really let the kid wander in Manhattan on her own. "I won't take my eyes off her."

As they headed south on Fifth Avenue, Amber seized the opportunity to get to know Tallulah better.

"You're not into American Girl dolls?"

"Not enough to stand in line for hours. I'd much rather look at books."

"What kinds of things *do* you like?"

She shrugged. "Well, books. And I like to take pictures, but with old cameras and film."

"Really? Why not digital?"

"The resolution is better, and I've found that . . ."

Amber tuned out the rest of her explanation. She didn't care. All she needed to know was what she liked, not the three paragraphs of science behind it. Tallulah was like a little professor masquerading as a kid. Amber wondered if she had any friends at all.

"Here we are."

She followed Tallulah around the enormous store until they reached the mystery section, and she pulled out an armful of books. They found a cozy place to sit, and Amber grabbed a few books off the shelves as well. She noticed Tallulah holding a collection of Edgar Allan Poe stories.

"Did you know Edgar Allan Poe was an orphan?" Amber asked.

Tallulah looked up. "What?"

Amber nodded. "Yes, his parents died when he was four. He was raised by a wealthy merchant."

Tallulah's eyes widened.

"Sadly, his new parents cut him out of their will, and he ended up very poor. Maybe he wasn't as nice to them as he was to his real parents." Amber smiled inwardly at Tallulah's shocked expression. It was a good lesson for the kid to keep in mind.

They spent the next two hours reading, Tallulah lost in her Poe book, ignoring Amber, Amber looking through a book on Formula One racing. She'd read that Jackson was an avid fan. When she'd had enough of that, she opened the Facebook app on her phone. Rage overcame her when she read the update. So, the bitch was pregnant. How could that have happened? The three of them smiling like idiots. Who was stupid enough to announce a pregnancy at only eight weeks? Amber consoled herself with the thought that maybe she'd miscarry. She heard someone approach and looked up to see Daphne, laden with shopping bags, rushing toward them.

"There you are!" Daphne was out of breath, and Bella's hand was in hers as she ran to keep up with her mother. "Jackson just called. He's going to meet us after all. We'll grab a cab and meet him at SixtyFive. We'll have dinner and then see the tree." She smiled.

"Wait," Amber said, grabbing the arm of Daphne's coat. "I don't want to intrude on your family time." In truth, she was surprised at how nervous she was at the prospect of meeting Jackson. The suddenness threw her off balance. She wanted advance warning, time to ready herself to meet the man she knew so much about.

"Don't be silly," Daphne gushed. "You won't be intruding. Now come on. He's waiting for us."

Tallulah got up immediately, putting all the books into a pile and picking them up.

Daphne waved her hand. "Leave them, sweetie. We need to get going."

THIRTEEN

He was waiting at the best table in the place. Its view was even more stunning than Amber had imagined. So was he, for that matter. The sex appeal practically oozed out of him. Drop-dead gorgeous. There was no other way to say it. And the impeccably tailored custom suit made him look like he'd just stepped off the set of a Bond movie. He stood as they approached, and when his dazzling blue eyes rested on Daphne, his smile widened, and he greeted her with a warm kiss on the lips. He was crazy about her, Amber realized with frustration. He crouched down, opening his arms, and the girls ran into them.

"Daddy!" Bella grinned, looking happy for the first time all day.

"My girls. Did you have a great day with Mommy?"

They both started chattering at once, and Daphne ushered them into their seats while she took the one next to Jackson. Amber sat in the remaining seat, across from him, next to Bella.

"Jackson, this is Amber. I told you about her; she's come to my rescue on the gala committee."

"Very nice to meet you, Amber. I understand you've been a great help."

Her eyes were drawn to the delectable dimple that appeared when he smiled. If he wondered what she was doing having dinner with them, he at least had the good grace not to show it.

They ordered cocktails for themselves and appetizers for the kids, and after a little while Amber blended into the background and sat observing them.

"So tell me about your day," Jackson said. "What was the high-light?"

"Well, I got two new dresses for my Bella doll, a stable set, and a tutu to match mine, so she can come to ballet with me."

"How about you, Lu?"

"I liked Alice's Teacup. It was cool. Then Amber took me to Barnes & Noble."

He shook his head. "My little bibliophile. You come to the city, and that's where you go? We have one right around the corner," he said, not unkindly.

"Yeah, but's it not huge, like here. Besides, we come here all the time. No big deal."

Amber swallowed her anger at Tallulah's sense of entitle-ment. No big deal, indeed. She'd like to ship her off to some rural location for a few years and let her see how the rest of America lived.

Jackson turned to Daphne, resting his hand briefly on her cheek. "And you, my darling? What was your highlight?"

"Getting the call from you."

Amber wanted to vomit. Were they for real? She took a long swallow from her wineglass. No need to pace herself; he could afford to keep it coming.

When he finally tore his eyes off his gorgeous wife, Jackson glanced at Amber. "Are you from Connecticut, Amber?"

"No, Nebraska."

He looked surprised. "What brought you east?"

"I wanted to expand my horizons. A friend of mine moved to Connecticut and invited me to room with her," she said, then took another sip of wine. "I fell in love with the coastline right away— and being so close to New York."

"How long have you been here?"

Was he really interested or just being polite? She couldn't tell.

Daphne answered before she could. "About a year, right?" She smiled at her. "She's in real estate too, works in the commercial division of Rollins Realty."

"How did you meet again?"

"I told you, it was quite by accident," Daphne said.

He was still looking at Amber, and she suddenly felt as though she was being interrogated.

"Helloooooo? This is boring," Bella sang out. Amber was grateful to the little wretch for distracting him.

Jackson turned his attention to her. "Bella, we don't interrupt adults when they're talking." His voice was firm. Thank God one of them has a backbone, Amber thought.

Bella stuck her tongue out at him.

Tallulah gasped and looked at Jackson, as did Daphne. It felt like time had stopped as everyone waited to see his reaction.

He burst out laughing. "I think someone's had too long a day."

Everyone at the table seemed to exhale.

Bella pushed her chair back and ran over to him, burying her head in his chest. "I'm sorry."

He stroked her blond curls. "Thank you. Now you're going to behave like a lady, right?"

She nodded and skipped back to her seat.

Score another point for the little hooligan, Amber thought. Who knew that the biggest thorn in her side was going to be this little pint-sized gremlin?

"How about another surprise?" he said.

"What?" the girls asked in unison.

"How about we go see the Christmas show at Radio City and then spend the night here?"

The girls' voices rose in excitement, but Daphne put her arm on Jackson's and said, "Sweetheart, I hadn't planned to stay the night. And I'm sure Amber wants to get home."

In fact, Amber was thrilled to stay. Her curiosity about the Parrishes' apartment outweighed any desire to get back home.

Jackson glanced at Amber as if she were a pesky problem to be solved. "Tomorrow's Sunday. What's the big deal? She can borrow a change of clothes." He looked right at Amber. "Is that a problem for you?"

Amber was dancing on the inside, but she gave him a sober and appreciative look. "That would be fine with me. I'd hate to disappoint Bella and Tallulah. They seem really excited to stay."

He smiled and squeezed Daphne's arm. "See? It's fine. We'll have a great time."

Daphne shrugged, resigned to the change in plans. They went into the theater and watched Santa and the Rockettes for the next hour and a half. Amber thought the show was moronic, but the girls loved every minute.

When they came out, it was snowing, and the city looked like a winter wonderland, with white lights twinkling on the bare tree branches now covered in the magic powder. Amber looked around in awe. She'd never seen New York this late at night. It was a sight to behold, the lights making everything shimmer and glow.

Jackson took the phone from his pocket, pulled off his leather glove, and, hitting a key, brought it to his ear and said, "Send the driver to the front entrance of Radio City."

When the black limousine with dark windows pulled up, Amber craned her neck to see what celebrity might step out, but as a tall, uniformed chauffeur got out and opened the back door, she realized that the limo was empty and that it was there for them. Now *she* felt like the celebrity. She'd never been in a limousine. She noticed that Daphne and the girls didn't look the least bit fazed. Jackson took Daphne's hand and guided her in first. Then he gave Bella and Tallulah a playful shove, and they followed after their mother. He gestured to indicate that Amber should enter next, but he barely looked at her. The car was large enough for the two women and two children to sit four across. Jackson spread out on the seat opposite them, his arm draped across the back of the seat and his legs spread wide. Amber tried with difficulty to keep her eyes off him. He was positively brimming with power and masculinity.

Bella was leaning against her mother, almost asleep, when Tallulah said, "Are we going right to the apartment, Daddy?"

"Yes, I—"

But before he got another word out, Bella shot up, now wide awake. "No, no, no. Not the apartment. I want to go where Eloise is. I want to sleep at the Plaza."

"We can't do that, sweetheart," Daphne had said. "We don't have a reservation. We'll do that another time."

Bella wasn't having it. "Daddy, please. I'll be the first one in my class to stay where Eloise lives. Everyone will be so jealous. Please, please, please?"

At first Amber had wanted to grab the little whiner and wring her selfish little neck, but there was something in her that Amber recognized, something that made her see how she could turn her into an ally instead of an enemy. And anyway, who cared whether they stayed at the apartment or the Plaza? Either one was a treat for Amber.

The next morning Amber rolled over, pulling the duvet closer around her until it touched her chin. She sighed and wriggled her body against the silky sheet, feeling its softness caress her. She'd never slept in such a sumptuously comfortable bed. In the one next to hers, Tallulah stirred. The suite had only two bedrooms—Bella had bunked with her parents, and though Tallulah hadn't looked too happy about sharing a room with Amber, she'd obliged. Amber threw off the covers, rose, and went to the window. The Grand Penthouse Suite looked out over Central Park, and New York lay before her as if for the taking. She scanned the beautiful room, with its tall ceilings and elegant furnishings. The suite was fit for royalty, larger than the average house. Jackson had succumbed to Bella's request, of course, had even sent his chauffeur to get clothes for everyone from the apartment. Unbelievable, how easy it was for the rich—how unfairly easy.

She slipped off the pajamas Daphne had lent her, then showered and dressed in the clothes she'd also been given last night: a pair of blue wool slacks and a white cashmere sweater. The material felt divine against her clean skin. She looked in the mirror, admiring the perfect cut and clean lines. When she glanced at the bed, she saw that Tallulah still slept, so she tiptoed quietly out of the room. Bella was already up, sitting on the green tufted sofa with a book in her hands. She looked up briefly as Amber entered, said nothing, and gave her attention back to the book. Amber sat on a chair opposite the sofa and picked up a magazine from the coffee table, not saying a word and pretending to read. They stayed that way for the next ten minutes, silent, uncommunicative.

Finally, Bella closed her book and stared at Amber. "Why didn't you go home last night? This was supposed to be a family night."

Amber thought for a moment. "Well, Bella, to tell you the truth, I knew everyone at my office would be envious if they knew I got to stay at the Plaza and have breakfast with Eloise."

She paused for effect. "I guess I wasn't thinking about the family thing. You're right about that. I should have gone home. I'm really sorry."

Bella tilted her head and gave Amber a suspicious look. "Your friends know about Eloise? But you're a grown-up. Why do you care about Eloise?"

"My mother read all the Eloise books to me when I was little." This was total bullshit. Her mother had never read anything to her. If Amber hadn't spent all her spare time in the library, she'd be illiterate now.

"Why didn't your mom take you to the Plaza when you were little?"

"We lived far away from New York. Have you ever heard of Nebraska?"

Bella rolled her eyes. "Of course I've heard of Nebraska. I know all fifty states."

This brat was going to take more than camaraderie and kid gloves.

"Well, that's where I grew up. And we didn't have enough money to come to New York. So, there you have it. But I do want to thank you for making one of my dreams come true. I'm going to let everyone at the office know that it was all because of you."

Bella's face was inscrutable, and before she answered, Jackson and Daphne came into the room.

"Good morning." Daphne's voice was cheery. "Where's Tallulah? It's time for breakfast. Is she up yet?"

"I'll go see," Amber said.

Tallulah was up and almost finished dressing when Amber knocked and went in. "Good morning," she said to her. "Your mom asked me to check on you. I think they're ready to go down to breakfast."

Tallulah turned to look at her. "Okay, I'm ready." And they walked together to the living room where the others waited.

"Did you girls sleep well?" Jackson's voice boomed as they headed to the elevator. They all spoke at once, and as the elevator descended, he looked at Bella and said, "We're going to have breakfast with Eloise in the Palm Court."

Bella smiled and looked at Amber. "We've been wanting to do that for a long time," she said.

Maybe she finally had this little hellion in her pocket, Amber thought. Now it was time to work on Jackson.

FOURTEEN

Amber and Daphne sat beside each other at the Parrish dining room table, which was covered in paper, including the list of attendees and a ballroom diagram of the table arrangements. Since almost all of these people were unknown to Amber, Daphne was dictating the seating for each table while Amber dutifully entered all the information into an Excel file. There was a lull as Daphne studied the names before her, and Amber took the opportunity to gaze around the room and out the long bank of floor-to-ceiling windows that looked out to the sea. The room could comfortably seat sixteen for dinner, but it still had a feeling of intimacy. The walls were a muted gold, a perfect backdrop for the magnificent oils of sailboats and seascapes in gilded frames. She could imagine the formal dinner parties they must have here, with elegant place settings of china, crystal, fine silver, and table linens of the highest quality. She was pretty certain that there was not a paper napkin to be found anywhere in the house.

"Sorry to take so long, Amber. I think I finally have table nine figured out," Daphne said.

"No problem. I've been admiring this beautiful room."

"It's lovely, isn't it? Jackson owned the house before we were married, so I haven't done very much to change things. Just the sunroom, really." She looked around and shrugged. "Everything was already perfect."

"Gosh, how wonderful."

Daphne gave her an odd look that passed quickly—too quickly for Amber to identify it.

"Well, I think we're finished with the seating. I'll send the list to the printer to make up the table cards," Daphne said, rising from her chair. "I can't thank you enough. This would have taken forever without your help."

"Oh, you're welcome. I'm happy to do it."

Daphne looked at her watch and then back at Amber. "I don't have to pick the girls up from tennis for another hour. How about a cup of tea and a bite to eat? Do you have time?"

"That would be great." She followed Daphne out of the dining room. "Could I use the restroom?"

"Of course." They walked a bit farther, and Daphne indicated a door on the left. "When you come out, turn right and keep walking to the kitchen. I'll put the tea on."

Amber entered the first-floor powder room and was stunned. Every room in the house offered a staggering reminder of Jackson Parrish's great wealth. With its polished black walls and silver picture-frame wainscoting, it was the epitome of quiet opulence. A waterfall slab of marble was the focus of the room, and on top of it sat a marble vessel sink. Amber looked around in wonder once again. Everything original, custom-made. What would it be like to have a custom-made life, she wondered?

She washed her hands and took one last look in the mirror, a tall, beveled piece of glass set in a frame that looked like rippled silver leaves. As she walked the length of the corridor to the kitchen, she slowed to look at the art on the walls. Some she recognized from her exhaustive reading and Met courses—a Sisley and a stunning Boudin. If these were the real thing, and they probably were, the paintings alone were worth a small fortune. And here they were, hanging in a little-trafficked hallway.

As she entered the kitchen, she saw that tea and a plate of fruit sat waiting on the island.

"Mug or cup?" Daphne asked, standing in front of an open cabinet door.

The shelves of the cabinet looked as if they could have been a display for a luxury kitchen showroom. Amber imagined someone using a ruler to measure an exact distance between each cup and glass. Everything lined up perfectly, and everything matched. It was disconcerting in some strange way, and she found herself mutely staring, mesmerized by the symmetry.

"Amber?" Daphne said.

"Oh. Mug, please." She sat on one of the cushioned stools.

"Do you take milk?"

"Yes, please," Amber said.

Daphne swung the refrigerator door open, and Amber stared again. The contents were lined up with military precision, the tallest at the rear and all labels facing front. The absolute precision of Daphne's home was off-putting. It felt to Amber like more than a desire for a neat home and more like an obsession, a compulsion. She remembered Sally's account of Daphne's time in a sanitarium after Tallulah's birth. Perhaps there had been more going on than just postpartum depression, she thought.

Daphne sat opposite Amber and poured their tea. "So, we have just two weeks before the big night. You've been amazing. I've felt such a wonderful synergy with you. We both have so much of our hearts invested in this."

"I've loved every minute of it. I can't wait until the fund-raiser. It's going to be a huge success."

Daphne took a sip of tea and placed the mug on the counter between her hands. Looking at Amber, she said, "I'd like to do something to show my appreciation for all your hard work."

Amber tilted her head and gave Daphne a questioning look.

"I hope you'll let me buy you a dress for the fund-raiser," Daphne said.

Amber had hoped this was going to happen, but she had to play it carefully. "Oh no," she said. "I couldn't let you do that."

"Please. I'd really love to. It's my way of saying thank you."

"I don't know. It feels like you're paying me, and I didn't work on this to get paid. I wanted to do it." Amber smiled inwardly at her brilliant show of humility.

"You mustn't think of it as payment. Think of it as gratitude for your immense help and support," Daphne said as she pushed back a blond wave, her diamond ring flashing brightly.

"I don't know. I feel sort of funny having you spend money on me."

"Well," Daphne said and paused. "How would you feel about borrowing something of mine, then?"

Amber could have kicked herself for protesting too much, but she guessed borrowing a dress was the next best thing. "Gee, I hadn't thought of that. I *would* feel better if you weren't spending your money." As if this woman didn't have millions to burn.

"Great." Daphne stood up from the stool. "Come upstairs with me, and we'll look through my closet."

They climbed the stairs together, and Amber admired the Dutch masters on the wall.

"You have magnificent artwork. I could spend hours looking at it."

"You're more than welcome to. Are you interested in art? Jackson is absolutely passionate about it," Daphne said as they reached the landing.

"Well, I'm no art expert, but I do love museums," Amber replied.

"Jackson too. He's a board member of the Bishops Harbor Art Center. Here we are," Daphne said, leading her into a large room—given its size, it could hardly be called a walk-in closet—filled with racks of clothing lined up in perfect, parallel rows. Every piece of clothing was in a transparent garment bag, and two walls were lined with shelves that held shoes of all styles, arranged by color. Built-in drawers on a third wall held sweaters, one each, with a small see-through panel to identify them. At one end of the room stood a three-way mirror and a pedestal. The lighting was bright but flattering, without the harshness of department-store fitting rooms.

"Wow," Amber couldn't help herself from remarking. "This is something."

Daphne waved her hand dismissively. "We attend a lot of functions. I used to go shopping for each one, and Jackson said I was wasting too much time. He started having things sent to the house for me to look at." She was leading Amber to a rack near the back when suddenly a young woman came walking into the room.

"Madame," she said. "*Les filles.* It is time to pick them up, *non?*"

"Oh my gosh, you're right, Sabine," she exclaimed, looking at her watch again. "I've got to go. I promised the girls I would get them today. Why don't you just look through these dresses till I get back? I won't be long." She patted Amber's arm. "Oh, and, Amber, this is Sabine, our nanny." She rushed out of the room.

"Nice to meet you, Sabine," Amber said.

Sabine, reserved, gave a small nod of her head and in thickly accented English responded, "My pleasure, miss."

"Mrs. Parrish told me you'd been hired to teach French to the girls. Do you enjoying working here?"

Sabine's eyes softened a moment before she regained her austere composure. "Very much. Now you will please excuse me?"

Amber watched as she walked away. So she was French—big deal. She was still just a nanny. But, Amber thought, Daphne's friends would all think it was so grand, not the usual Spanish-speaking nanny, but one who would teach her daughters French.

Amber looked around the room in wonder. Daphne's closet, indeed. This was more like having an exclusive department store at your disposal. She sauntered, slowly examining the rack upon rack of clothes, all meticulously sorted by color and type. The shoes were lined up with the same fastidiousness as the china in the kitchen cabinets. Even the spacing between garments was uniform. When she got to the three-way mirror, she noticed two comfortable club chairs on either side—apparently meant for Jackson or whoever was nodding approval as Daphne modeled her choices. On the rack Daphne had indicated, she began to look through the dresses. Dior, Chanel, Wu, McQueen—the names went on and on. This wasn't some chain department store sending clothes for Daphne to look at; these were couture houses making their designs available to a moneyed client. It boggled her mind.

And Daphne was so casual about all of it—the luxury, the fine art, the "closet" full of designer suits, dresses, and shoes. Amber unzipped one of the bags and brought out a turquoise Versace evening dress. She carried it to the three-way mirror and stepped onto the pedestal, holding the beautiful dress against her body and staring at her reflection. Even Mrs. Lockwood had never brought anything remotely like this to be dry-cleaned.

Amber hung the dress up and, when she turned away, suddenly noticed a door at the far end of the room. She moved toward it and paused with her hand on the knob only a moment before opening it. Before her was a sumptuous space that was a dazzling mix of luxury and comfort. She walked around slowly, her fingers brushing the yellow silk wallpaper. A white velvet chaise longue sat in a corner of the room, and the light from the Palladian window threw dazzling prisms of color on the walls as it pierced the crystals that hung from the large chandelier. She reclined onto the chaise, looking at the picture on the opposite wall, the only piece of art in the room, and felt herself drawn into the peaceful scene of trees and sky. Her shoulders relaxed, and she surrendered to the stillness and calm of this special place.

She closed her eyes and, imagining this was her room, stayed that way for a while. When she finally rose, she examined the space more closely, the delicate table with photographs of a young Daphne and her sister, Julie. She recognized the slight girl with long, dark hair and beautiful almond-shaped eyes from photographs she'd seen throughout the house. She moved to the front of an antique armoire with an abundance of small drawers. Reaching over, she opened one of them. Some lacy underwear. Another with exotic soaps. More of the same in the other drawers, all meticulously folded and placed. She opened the cabinet and found mounds of plush bath towels. She was about to close the door when she noticed a rosewood box toward the back. Amber took it in her hand, undid the catch, and opened it. Inside, nestled on rich green velvet, sat a small pearl-handled pistol. She gently lifted it from the box and saw etched on the barrel the initials YMB. What was this gun doing here? And who was YMB?

Amber wasn't sure how long she had been standing there when she heard the sound of voices and doors opening and closing. She quickly replaced the gun, took one more glance around the room to make sure she hadn't disturbed anything, and left. As she reentered the clothing room, the children came bounding in, Daphne close behind them.

"Hi, we're back. Sorry we were so long. Bella forgot her painting, so we went back to get it," Daphne said.

"It's fine," Amber said. "The dresses are all so beautiful, I can't decide."

Bella frowned and whispered to her mother, "What's she doing here?"

"Sorry," Daphne said to Amber and then took Bella's hand. "We're finding a dress for Amber to borrow for the fund-raiser. Why don't you and Tallulah help her? Wouldn't that be fun?"

"All right," Tallulah said with a smile, but Bella looked at Amber with undisguised hostility, turned on her heel, and stalked out of the room.

"Don't let her upset you. She just doesn't know you well enough yet. It takes Bella a while to warm up."

Amber nodded. She better get used to me, she thought. I'm going to be around a long, long time.

FIFTEEN

Amber was pissed. It was December 24, and Rollins was staying open until two o'clock. What kind of idiots looked at houses on Christmas Eve? Why weren't they at home, wrapping their big-ticket presents and decorating their twelve-foot trees? But they probably didn't do all those things themselves, she reflected. That's what people like Amber were for.

Around noon Jenna stood in the doorway of Amber's office. "Hey, Amber, can I come in?"

"What is it?" Just what I need now, she thought peevishly.

Jenna walked in with a large wrapped package in her hand and placed it on Amber's desk. "Merry Christmas."

Amber glanced at the gift and then at Jenna. She hadn't even thought to buy a present for Jenna, and was discomfited by her gesture.

"Open it!" Jenna said.

Amber picked it up and tore off the paper, then took the lid off the box. Inside was a glorious assortment of Christmas cookies, each one more delicate and delicious-looking than the last. "Did you make these?"

Jenna clapped her hands together. "Yes, me and my mom do it every year. She's a spectacular baker. Do you like them?"

"I do. Thank you so much, Jenna. It was really nice of you." Amber paused a moment. "I'm so sorry, but I didn't get you anything."

"It's okay, Amber. I didn't make them so you'd get me a gift. It's just something my mom and I love doing. I give them to everyone in the office. I hope you enjoy them. Merry Christmas."

"Merry Christmas to you too."

Amber slept late on Christmas morning. When she awoke, the sky was blue, the sun was shining, and only an inch of snow had fallen. She took a long, hot shower and, after wrapping her terry-cloth robe around her, made a strong pot of coffee. She took her mug back into the bathroom and began to blow-dry her wet hair into soft waves—plain but classic. She applied a little blush, a dab of very discreet eye shadow, and some mascara. She stepped back from the mirror to examine the finished product. She looked youthful and fresh but without a trace of sexiness.

Daphne had asked her to come over around two o'clock, so after she finished a cup of yogurt, she sat down to read *The Odyssey*, which she'd borrowed from the library last week. Before she knew it, it was time to dress and gather everything up. Hanging on the closet door was the outfit she'd chosen—gray wool slacks and a white-and-gray turtleneck sweater. Small pearl studs in her ears—not real, of course, but who cared—a simple gold-colored bangle on her left wrist, and only her sapphire ring on her finger. She wanted to look pure and virginal. She took one last look in the full-length mirror, nodded approval at her image, and swept the presents into a large shopping bag.

Fifteen minutes later, she pulled into the open gates and parked her car in the circular driveway. Grabbing the bag of presents, she strode to the door and rang the bell. She saw Daphne coming down the hall, Bella right behind her.

"Welcome! Merry Christmas. I'm so glad you could come," Daphne said, flinging open the door and embracing her.

"Merry Christmas to you. Thank you so much for letting me share this day with you and your family," Amber said.

"Oh, it's our pleasure," Daphne said as she shut the door.

Bella was dancing around next to Daphne like a jumping bean.

"Hi, Bella. Merry Christmas." Amber gave her a big fake smile.

"Do you have a present for me?" Bella asked.

"Oh, Bella, you didn't even say hello. That was very rude," Daphne scolded.

"Of course I brought you a present. How could I not give one of my favorite girls a present?"

"Goody. Can I have it now?"

"Bella! Amber hasn't even taken her coat off." She gave her daughter a little shove. "Let me have your coat, Amber, and let's all go into the living room."

Bella looked as if she was going to protest but did as she was told.

Jackson and Tallulah looked up from the dollhouse they were furnishing as Amber, Daphne, and Bella entered the room. "Merry Christmas, Amber. Welcome," Jackson said with a warmth that indeed made her feel welcome.

"Thank you for inviting me. My whole family is back in Nebraska, and I would have been alone today. You don't know how much I appreciate it."

"No one should be alone on Christmas. We're glad you're here."

Amber thanked him again and then turned to Tallulah. "Hi, Tallulah. Merry Christmas. What a cool dollhouse."

"Would you like to come see it?" she asked.

These kids were like night and day. She didn't like children, but at least Tallulah had manners, not like the little animal who thought the sun and the moon revolved around her. Amber went and sat down next to Tallulah in front of the dollhouse. She had never seen anything like it, even in photographs. What she and her sisters would have given for a toy like this, with all the fabulous furnishings and dolls to go with it! It was enormous, with three stories, real wood floors, tile bathrooms, electric chandeliers that actually worked, and beautiful paintings on the walls. As she looked closer, she realized it was a replica of the actual house they lived in. It had to have been custom-made. What must that have cost?

"How about a glass of eggnog, Amber?" Daphne asked.

"I'd love one, thank you." She continued to watch as Tallulah carefully placed sofas, tables, and chairs in the house. Bella was on the other side of the room, busy with her iPad.

As she sat there, Amber took in all of the presents sitting open under the tree. They were piled high upon one another, tissue and ribbon mingled in the mix and spilled far into the room. She thought back to the miserly Christmases of her youth and felt keenly sad. She and her sisters had always gotten presents that were utilitarian, like underwear or socks, never a gift that was a luxury or even just a fun toy to play with. Even their stockings had been filled with useful or edible things, like the huge orange at the bottom to take up room, pencils and erasers for school, and sometimes a little puzzle that would become tiresome after one day.

The display in the Parrishes' living room left her speechless. She saw what looked like silk lingerie peeking out from one of the boxes and several smaller boxes that must have contained more jewelry for Daphne. Tallulah's presents were stacked in a neat pile. Bella's, on the other hand, were haphazardly spread out over a large part of the room, and once she put down the iPad, she went from one to another in quick order.

The one thing missing from this scene, Amber thought to herself, was Daphne's mother. Why wouldn't the girls' grandmother, a widow living only a car ride away, not be invited to spend Christmas with her only daughter and granddaughters? It seemed to her that the value placed on lavish presents was way above that of family.

Daphne came back into the living room with three glasses of eggnog and put them on the mahogany butler's table between the two large sofas.

"Amber, come sit with me," she said, and patted the cushion next to her. "Will you have some time off before the new year?"

"I do, actually. That's the advantage of working on the commercial side of real estate." She took a sip of eggnog. "Are you and Jackson going away over the holiday?"

"As a matter of fact, we leave on the twenty-eighth for St. Bart's. We usually leave the day after Christmas, but Meredith is having a surprise fiftieth birthday party for Rand the day after tomorrow, so we pushed the date."

"How nice," Amber said, seething inside. She would be spending the rest of the holidays in her cheerless apartment trying to stay warm while they basked in the sun.

She rose from the sofa, hoping her expression hadn't betrayed her jealousy. "I've brought some presents. Let me get them," she said.

Bella jumped up from the floor and ran over. "Can I see my present? Can I, can I?"

Amber noticed Jackson smiling as he watched Bella jump around with anticipation.

"Here you go, Bella." Amber handed her the wrapped book set. Luckily, she had also gotten her a sparkly necklace and bracelet to match. Bella loved shiny things.

She ripped greedily into the paper, looked briefly at the books, and then opened the smaller box. "Ooh, pretty."

"How lovely. Let me help you put on the necklace," Daphne said.

"Here, Tallulah, this one is for you."

She slowly unwrapped the package. "Thank you, Amber. I love this book."

Bella, finished with the necklace and bracelet, began looking through the books Amber had given her and stomped her foot. "No fair. I already have this book in the series!"

Jackson swept her up in his arms and tried to console her. "It's okay, baby. We'll take it back to the store and get one you don't have, okay?"

"Okay," she whined and put her head on his shoulder.

Daphne retrieved a wrapped package from under the Christmas tree and handed it to Amber. "This is for you. I hope you like it."

Amber untied the red velvet ribbon and gently tore off the black-and-gold paper. The small box held an elegant gold chain with a single pearl. It was beautiful. For a moment Amber was overwhelmed. She'd never owned something so lovely. "Oh, Daphne, thank you. I love it. Thank you so much."

"You're so welcome."

"I have something for you too."

Daphne unwrapped the box and then held up the bracelet. When she read Julie's name on the charm, her eyes filled with tears. She slipped the bangle onto her wrist. "What a wonderful gift. I'll wear it always. Thank you!"

Amber held her arm out in front of her. "I have one too. We'll have our sisters with us all the time."

"Yes." Daphne choked up as she pulled Amber to her, hugging her tightly.

"Let me see, Mommy." Bella ran to the sofa and flopped onto her mother's lap.

"You see, a pretty bracelet with Aunt Julie's name engraved on it. Isn't it lovely?"

"Uh-huh. Can I wear it?"

"Maybe later, okay?"

"No, now."

"Well, just for a few minutes, and then Mommy wants it back." Daphne took the bracelet off and handed it to her. Bella pushed her fist through it, but the bracelet was too big to stay on her tiny wrist, and she passed it back to Daphne. "Here, Mommy. I don't like it. You have it."

Amber was furious that this unpleasant child had interrupted what should have been a serious bonding moment, but she picked up the other gift and held it out to Daphne, "One more that I thought you might like."

"Amber. Really, this is too much. You've gone overboard."

No, Amber thought, overboard is what is surrounding us in this room full of lavish presents amid discarded ribbons and wrappings. "It's nothing, Daph. Just a little thing."

Daphne opened the box and pulled out the turtle wrapped in tissue paper. As she unwound the paper and the crystal turtle came into view, she lost her grip and dropped it onto the floor.

Amber reached down to pick it up, glad to see that it hadn't broken. "Good"—she placed it on the coffee table—"still intact."

Jackson strode over to them, scooped up the turtle to examine it, and turned it over in his hands. "Look, Daphne. You don't have one like this. What a nice addition to your collection." Jackson set the turtle down. "Great gift, Amber. Now how about we go to the dining room for some Christmas dinner?"

"Oh, wait," Amber said. "I have a gift for you too, Jackson."

"You really needn't have done this," he said as he took the package she handed to him. She watched as he removed the decorative paper and stared at the book in his hands. He looked up at Amber in surprise, and for the first time she felt he was really looking at her. "This is amazing. Where did you find it?"

"I've always been interested in the cave paintings. It's apparent that you and Daphne are discerning art lovers, so when I came across it on an antiquarian book site, I thought you might be interested in them too." She'd searched the antiquarian bookstores online and had finally found one she thought he'd appreciate— *The Lascaux Cave Paintings* by F. Windels. She'd gulped when she'd seen the $75 price, but decided to go ahead and make this her one splurge. The paintings were over 17,000 years old, and the French caves had been named a UNESCO World Heritage Site. She had hoped he would be impressed.

Amber smiled to herself. She had definitely scored with this one.

Daphne rose from the sofa. "Okay, everyone, time for dinner."

"Just a second. One more thing." Amber handed her the box of cookies.

"Goodness, Amber. These look delicious. Look, girls, don't they look yummy?"

"I want one." Bella stood on tiptoe and looked in the box.

"After dinner, sweetheart. Amber, this is so sweet of you."

"Well, Rollins closed early yesterday, so I enjoyed baking them last evening."

"What? You made these?"

"It's not a big deal. It was fun, really."

They walked into the dining room together, and suddenly Bella was by Amber's side. She took hold of Amber's hand and smiled up at her. "You're a really good cookie maker. I'm glad you came today."

Amber looked down at the little brat and smiled back. "Me too, Bella."

She felt a swell of satisfaction rise inside her.

SIXTEEN

Amber had a New Year plan that she hoped would ramp things up. Her panicked phone call had done the trick, and now Daphne waited for her as she walked to the door.

A worried look crossed Daphne's face as she ushered Amber in. They went directly to the sunroom.

"What's happened?" Daphne asked with concern.

"I've been trying to work this out on my own, but I just can't take it anymore. I have to talk to someone about it."

"Come, sit." Daphne took Amber by the hand and led her to the sofa. "Now, what is it?" She leaned forward, her eyes focused on Amber's face.

Amber took a deep breath. "I was fired today. But it's not my fault, and I can't do anything about it." She began to cry.

"What do you mean? Back up and tell me everything."

"It started a few months ago. It seemed whenever I went into his office, Mark—my boss, Mark Jansen—would find some reason to touch me. Brushing something off my shoulder or putting his hand on mine. At first I thought it was nothing. But then, last week, he asked if I would go with him on a client dinner."

Daphne was staring at her intently, and Amber wondered if she thought she was too homely to be hit on.

"Is it usual for you to attend client dinners?" Daphne asked.

Amber shrugged. "Not really. But at the time I was flattered. I figured he valued my opinion and wanted my input. And maybe, you know, there might be a promotion in the future. I drove myself and met him at Gilly's. He was already there, but he was alone. He told me the client had called and was running late. We had a couple of beers, and I started to feel funny." She stopped again, taking a deep breath. "The next thing I knew, his hand was on my knee and then moving up my thigh."

"What?" Daphne's voice exploded in anger.

Amber wrapped her arms around herself and rocked back and forth. "It was horrible, Daph. He slid closer to me in the booth and stuck his tongue in my mouth and started fondling my breast. I pushed him away and ran."

"That pig! He won't get away with this." Her eyes were blazing. "You have to report him."

Amber shook her head. "I can't."

"What do you mean, you can't?"

"The next day, he claimed *I* had hit on *him*. Told me no one would believe me."

"That's ridiculous. We're going to march right over there and talk to Human Resources."

"I'm so ashamed to tell you this, but at the office holiday party a few weeks ago, I had too many drinks and ended up kissing one of the agents. Everyone saw. They're going to believe him, believe that I'm loose."

"Still, that's not the same thing as your boss taking advantage of you."

"I can't make trouble. He offered me two months' pay if I leave quietly. My mother is still paying off Charlene's medical bills, and I send her money every month. I can't afford not to take it. I'll find something else. I'm just so humiliated."

"He's paying you off to shut you up. I can help you with money until you find another job. I think you should fight it."

Now she was talking, but Amber had to up the ante and see the act through.

"And have every real estate firm in Connecticut afraid to hire me? No, I have to keep my mouth shut. Besides, maybe I *did* give him the wrong idea."

Daphne stood up, pacing. "Don't you dare blame yourself. Of course you didn't do anything wrong. That piece of garbage— he'll probably do it to someone else too."

"Believe me, I've thought about that too. But, Daphne, I have too many people depending on me. I can't report him and take the chance of not being able to get a job."

"Damn him. He knows he has you in a corner."

"He gave me a good reference. I just need to hit the pavement now." She smiled at Daphne. "And the upside is that my days are free, so I'm free to work full-time on the fund-raiser."

"You find the good in everything, don't you? I'll respect your wishes, even though I'd love to go over and let him have it. It's so noble of you, helping your mom." Amber watched Daphne's face as she grew quiet, seemingly contemplating something. Amber wondered if Daphne was thinking of her own mother and feeling guilty. "You know what? I'm going to talk to Jackson. There might be something for you at his company."

Amber made herself look surprised. "You really think so? That would be amazing. I'd be willing to do anything. Even starting as an administrative assistant or something like that would be great." This time her smile was genuine.

"Of course. They must have something for you. I'll speak to him tonight. In the meantime, let's do something to cheer you up. How about a little shopping?"

She must have noticed the look on Amber's face and realized

that shopping was the last thing she could afford now that she was out of work. Honestly, how long had it been since this woman had lived in the real world?

"Sorry, you must think me terribly insensitive. What I meant was, I'd love to take you shopping—my treat. And before you argue, remember, I didn't grow up with all this." She swept her arm across the room. "I'm from a little town in New Hampshire. Probably not that different from where you were raised. When I first met Jackson and saw this house, I thought it was ridiculous, all the excess. Over time, you get used to it—maybe too used to it. And spending time with the women here, I must admit, I've lost myself a little."

Amber kept silent, curious to see where Daphne's little confession was going.

"You've helped me remember what's really important, why I came here to begin with—to help other families and to ease the suffering of those with this terrible disease. Jackson's made a lot of money, but I don't want that to build a wall between you and me. For the first time since I lost my sister, I actually feel close to someone. Please, let me do this."

Amber liked the sound of that. The best part was that she could make Daphne feel like Amber was the one being generous. She wondered if she could get her to spring for a whole new work wardrobe.

She widened her eyes. "Are you sure?"

"Very."

"Well, I suppose I could use a few things for my job search. Can you help me pick out a new interview outfit?"

"I would love to."

Amber suppressed a laugh. Daphne was so nice, she almost felt guilty. She had figured it would take some subtle hinting and footwork to nudge Daphne into suggesting a job at Parrish International, but Daphne had bitten before she'd even tasted the bait. And poor, happily married Mark Jansen, whose reputation she had besmirched, had never made anything resembling an advance toward her. She would call Mark this afternoon and resign. The engine was humming. It was now just a matter of driving the car.

SEVENTEEN

The big evening had finally arrived and, despite herself, Amber was as nervous as an actress on opening night. The fundraiser began at eight, but Jackson and Daphne were picking her up at six so they could be there early and make sure everything was in order. Daphne had spared her the worry of how she would come up with the $250 for the ticket by purchasing the whole table and inviting her.

Amber poured herself a glass of chardonnay. The wine and music would relax her as she dressed. This was not her night to shine, but on the other hand, she didn't want to show up looking like some small-town hick. She went to the bed, where she'd laid out her clothes for the evening, picking up the black lace thong and slipping it over her slender hips. Nobody would see her underwear, but she would know how sexy she looked underneath that dress, and it would make a difference in the way she felt. Then the dress, the gorgeous Valentino she'd chosen from Daphne's closet. It was a simple, floor-length black number with a high neck, long sleeves, and draped back. Subtly sexy, but not in the least obvious. She pulled her hair back into a sleek chignon and applied minimal makeup. The only jewelry she wore was the pearl necklace Daphne had given her for Christmas and her small pearl earrings. She took one last look in the mirror and smiled at her reflection. Satisfied, she grabbed her handbag, a small silver clutch she'd picked up cheap at DSW. She caught a whiff of Daphne's perfume as she draped the silver silk shawl Daphne had lent her around her shoulders.

She stood at the door and, before turning out the light, looked back at the room she lived in. She tried to ignore her surroundings, but it was becoming more and more difficult as she was exposed to the way Daphne and her friends lived. She had graduated from the dreary home of her youth to this monklike existence. She sighed, banished the memories from her mind, and closed the door behind her.

At ten to six, she walked down the short path from the building to the street. At precisely six o'clock, the black Town Car pulled up. She wondered what her neighbors on her modest street were thinking as the chauffeur got out of the car and opened the door for her. She slid into the backseat across from Jackson and Daphne.

"Hello, Daphne, Jackson. Thanks so much for picking me up."

"Of course," Daphne said. "You look lovely. The dress looks like it was made for you. You should keep it."

Jackson looked at her a long moment and then turned away. He seemed slightly annoyed, Amber thought. Great, she'd been hoping to make a lasting impression on him, and she was, but for the completely wrong reason. She never should have agreed to borrow a dress from Daphne. What had she been thinking?

"I went to the hotel a little earlier to see the auction setup," Daphne said, smoothing over the awkwardness. "It looks beautiful. I think we'll do well."

"I think so too," Amber said. "The silent auction items are fabulous. Can't wait to see how much the villa in Santorini goes for."

The small talk continued as they drove to the hotel. She noticed that Jackson held his wife's hand for the entire drive, and when they arrived, he gently and lovingly helped her out of the car, leaving the chauffeur to lend Amber a hand. He was nuts about Daphne, Amber thought, and felt her determination wilt a bit.

They were not the first to arrive. The decorating committee was already there, putting the finishing touches on the auction table and placing the floral centerpieces on the fifty tables covered in pink tablecloths and black napkins. The band was setting up at the far end of the room, and the bartenders were arranging their stock; they'd be busy tonight.

"Wow, Daphne, it looks amazing," Amber said.

Jackson put his arm around Daphne's waist and, pulling her to him, nuzzled her ear. "Great job, my darling. You've outdone yourself."

Amber looked at them, Jackson resembling a movie star in his black dinner jacket, and Daphne absolutely gorgeous in a strapless chiffon gown of emerald green that hugged every curve of her body.

"Thank you, sweetheart. That means so much to me." She looked at Jackson and then pulled away. "I really need to check on my volunteers and see if anyone needs anything. You'll excuse me, yes?" Daphne turned to Amber. "Stay here and keep Jackson company while I see if Meredith has everything she needs."

"Sure," Amber said.

Jackson continued to watch Daphne as she walked across the ballroom, seemingly unaware that Amber was even there.

"You must be very proud of your wife tonight," Amber said.

"What?" He tore his eyes away from Daphne.

"I said, you must be very proud of your wife tonight."

"She's the most beautiful and accomplished woman in this room," he said with pride.

"Daphne's been wonderful to me. My best friend, really."

Jackson frowned. "Your best friend?"

Amber sensed immediately that she'd made a mistake. "Well, not best friend exactly. More like a mentor. She's taught me so much."

She saw him relax a little. This was proving to be an exercise in futility. Obviously, nothing in her plan was going to move forward tonight.

"I think I'll go see if I can be of any help," she said to Jackson.

He gestured absently. "Right-o, good idea."

The evening was a smashing success. The bidding was frenzied, and the crowd drank and danced until midnight. Amber walked around the room, taking it all in—the designer dresses and opulent jewels, the snippets of gossip and laughter from clustered groups of women, the men in black tie loudly discussing the latest S&P 500 losing streak. The world of the rich and mighty, mingling and toasting each other, smug and confident in their little one-percent corner of the world.

Despite being seated at Daphne's table, though, Amber felt as out of place here as she had at the dry cleaner's. She wanted to belong somewhere, to have people look up to her, fawn over her the way they did Daphne. She was tired of being the girl no one noticed or cared about.

But tonight was not turning out the way she'd hoped. Jackson never took his eyes off Daphne. He was always reaching for her hand or running his hand up and down her back. For the first time, Amber was discouraged, wondering if her plan was unworkable, if the prize was out of reach.

She watched the dancers from her seat, some of the May-December couples looking comically unsuited to one another. Something flashed in the corner of her eye, making Amber turn to see a photographer. She turned her head quickly as the flashing continued, praying her image had not been caught on camera.

Jackson and Daphne had been on the dance floor a good portion of the evening, and now they came walking back to the table. She saw Daphne give Jackson a discreet push, and he stood in front of Amber. "Would you care to dance?" he asked.

Amber looked at Daphne, who smiled and nodded at her. "I'd love to." She rose and took Jackson's hand as he led her to the dance floor.

She relaxed into Jackson's strong arms, inhaling the clean, masculine smell of him, enjoying the feel of his arms around her and his body against hers. She closed her eyes and pretended he belonged to her, that she was the envy of every woman in the room. The high lasted even though the dance ended. He didn't ask her again, but that one dance was enough to get her through the rest of the evening. At twelve thirty, Amber strode to the long table where volunteers sat waiting to help winning bidders check out. She sat down at the credit card machine next to Meredith.

"We did well tonight," Meredith said.

"Yes, it was a great success. Of course, you were a big part of that." Amber was laying it on thick, but Meredith wasn't biting.

"Oh please, it was a group effort. Everyone worked equally," she said stiffly.

Amber had nothing to say in response. This bitch would never accept her, so why should she even try? They continued to work side by side in silence as people checked out. As they were finishing up, Meredith turned to Amber. "Daphne tells me you're from Nebraska."

"I am."

"I've never been there. What's it like?" she said, with not one iota of curiosity in her voice.

Amber thought for a moment. "I come from a small town. They're pretty much all the same."

"Mm. I suppose they are. What town exactly?"

"Eustis. You've probably never heard of it."

Before Meredith could continue her interrogation, Daphne appeared in front of them.

"You're all amazing," she said to the volunteers at the table. "Thank you so much for this phenomenal night. Now go home and get some much-needed rest. I love all of you." She looked at Amber. "Are you ready to go?"

"Yes, we're all finished. I'll just get my things."

On the drive home, Jackson and Daphne looked like lovebirds, his hand firmly on her thigh.

"Your speech was good." Jackson squeezed her leg.

Daphne looked surprised. "Thank you."

"I wish you had let me look it over."

"You were so busy. I didn't want to bother you."

He stroked her leg. "I'm never too busy to help you, darling."

Daphne leaned her head against his shoulder and closed her eyes.

Amber grew disheartened as she watched their interaction. It was obvious to her that Jackson took a loving interest in every aspect of Daphne's life. Daphne had been easy pickings, but Jackson was going to be a different matter entirely. He was going to require all of Amber's cunning and ingenuity.

EIGHTEEN

I t had been a month since the fund-raiser, but Amber was still feeling off balance after seeing Jackson's devotion to Daphne that night. Her connection to Daphne was just getting stronger, though. She was on her way to Tallulah's eleventh birthday party, having become fully ensconced in Daphne's life and invited to almost all family events. Daphne was so trusting of her that it almost made her feel bad . . . almost. Amber had gotten Tallulah a book on the life of Edgar Allan Poe and had thought it wise to also pick up a little something for Bella. She was beginning to understand the workings of the little brat's mind and figured watching Tallulah open a ton of gifts would not be at the top of Bella's list of fun things to do.

When she entered the playroom, the children were seated in a big circle as two women unloaded cages with exotic birds and small zoo animals. Amber walked to where Daphne and an older woman stood watching the fun.

"Amber, welcome. Come meet my mother." Daphne clasped Amber's hand in hers. "Mom, this is my friend Amber."

The woman stretched her arm out for a handshake. "I'm pleased to meet you, Amber. I'm Ruth."

"Nice to meet you," Amber replied, juggling the presents she'd brought so that she could shake Ruth's hand.

"My goodness," Daphne said. "What have you got there?"

"Oh, just a few presents."

"Why don't you put them in with the others in the conservatory? The zoo show will start soon. You don't want to miss that," Daphne said.

When Amber entered the conservatory, she was startled once again by the excess. Not that she wouldn't have wanted the same kind of party as a kid, but she hadn't even known anything like this existed when she was little. The presents were piled high, and a large table had been moved into the room for the children's lunch. Each place was carefully set with colorful plates and napkins, and beautifully wrapped goodie bags were perched at each spot. It was completely kid-friendly and sublimely elegant at the same time. She put her gifts down and left the room. As she walked back to the party room, she saw Jackson coming down the hall. He gave her a charming smile.

"Hi there. So glad you could join us today," he said with enthusiasm.

"Um, thank you. I'm glad to be here," she stuttered.

He gave her another wide smile and held the playroom door for her.

They stood together and watched as the handlers brought out one animal after another and explained a little about them, Jackson with a drink in hand. Amber had difficulty keeping her eyes from straying to him. She wondered how long it would take to get him into bed. The thought that she could have this man of power and wealth under her spell exhilarated her. She knew how to please a man and suspected that after over a decade of marriage, the sex between him and Daphne had to be pretty boring and stale. Amber could picture the things she could do to make him want her if given half the chance. She resolved to take her time and carefully stick to her plan. No sense in rushing and messing things up like before.

When the show ended, the adults tried to calm the children as

they tromped into the conservatory for lunch. It was noisy and ri-
otous, with raucous laughter and high-pitched voices. Amber felt
like she was going to scream, and she noticed that Jackson wasn't
in the room where everyone was eating.

Finally, Margarita brought out the huge birthday cake covered
in chocolate icing and topped with eleven white candles in the
shape of ballerinas. Amber noticed a small chunk missing from
one side of the cake.

"Okay," Daphne said in a loud voice. "Time to sing 'Happy
Birthday,' and then Tallulah can open her presents."

Amber could see the storm clouds gathering behind Bella's eyes
as the children and adults sang to her sister. Her mouth was set in
a straight line, and her arms were crossed in front of her. She was
having none of it.

The minute the singing stopped and Tallulah had blown out
the candles, Daphne began handing her the presents. At the table,
the children were happy and occupied eating cake as Tallulah
unwrapped one after another and thanked the giver. After the
seventh one, Bella's voice rang out. "It's not fair. Tallulah's getting
all the presents. Where's mine?"

This was the moment Amber had been waiting for. "Hey, Bella.
I brought a present for Tallulah, but I brought one for you too. I'll
give Tallulah hers, and here's the one for you. I hope you like it."

Daphne smiled at her, and Ruth looked at her with an expression Amber couldn't quite read. Amber noticed that Jackson had
just come back into the room, and she hoped he had seen the exchange. Bella ripped off the wrapping paper and opened the box.
She held up the pink sweater with a white faux-fur collar and the
small pink handbag with its shiny handle and smiled. She ran to
Amber and flung her arms around her waist. "I love you, Amber.
You're my best friend ever."

Everyone laughed at this show of affection, but Amber noticed that Ruth didn't seem as amused as the rest of the guests. Tallulah was nearing the end of the presents, the last one a small box from Sabine. "Ooh, Sabine, *je suis très heureuse. Merci.*" Tallulah held up a gold chain with a slender cross.

"*De rien,*" Sabine said.

The local glitterati soon began arriving to pick up their little rich kids, who had once again been treated to splendiferous entertainment, yummy food, and expensive swag bags. No wonder they all grew up with a sense of entitlement. They knew nothing else.

After all the guests had gone, Surrey, the other nanny, gathered up the presents.

"Would you take the gifts upstairs with the girls? If you bathe them and get them into pajamas, we'll have a light dinner around six," Daphne instructed her.

Jackson poured himself another scotch. "Can I get anyone a drink?"

"I'll have a glass of wine, sweetheart," Daphne said. "Mom, would you like anything?"

"I'll have a club soda."

Jackson looked at Amber. "And you?"

"May I have a glass of wine too?"

Jackson laughed. "You may have anything you want."

That's what I'm hoping, Amber thought, but she simply smiled back at him.

"Daphne, have you showed Amber the photos from the fundraiser?" Ruth said, then looked at Amber. "There were some very good ones in the *Bishops Harbor Times.* You look very pretty in one of them."

Amber's heart stopped. Photos? In a newspaper? She'd been

so careful to avoid the photographer that night. When had he gotten a picture of her? Daphne brought the newspaper in and handed it to her. She picked it up with trembling hands and scanned the pictures. There she was, large as life, completely recognizable. Her name wasn't there, not that it would have mattered—her face was the problem. She just had to assume that this small-town newspaper with its limited range would not be seen farther afield.

"Would you excuse me?" She needed to get out of that room and calm her nerves. She closed the bathroom door, put the lid down on the toilet seat, and sat with her head in her hands. How could she have been so careless? After a while, her breathing settled and she promised herself she would be more vigilant in the future. She splashed some water on her face, stood up straight, and slowly opened the door. She could hear Ruth and Daphne as she walked back to the conservatory.

"Mom, you don't understand. I have my hands full here."

"You're right, Daphne, I don't understand. You used to love singing in the church choir. It seems to me you don't do any of the things you used to love. You've let all this money go to your head. If you know what's good for you, you'll remember your roots and come down off your high horse."

"That's completely unfair. You don't know what you're talking about."

"I know what I see—two nannies, for heaven's sake. And one that just speaks French. Really! A daughter who's spoiled rotten that you can't control. The club, all your lessons. For goodness sake, I practically have to make an appointment to see my granddaughters. What's happened to you?"

"That's enough, Mother."

For the first time, Amber heard real fury in Daphne's voice.

And then the sound of the nanny and the girls coming down the stairs. They all entered the conservatory at the same time, and the conversation between mother and daughter abruptly ended.

Bella ran to Daphne, putting her head on her mother's lap. Her cries were muted, and then she looked up and said, "Tallulah got so many presents, and I only got two. It's not fair."

Ruth leaned over and stroked Bella's face. "Bella, darling, it's Tallulah's birthday. When it's your birthday, you'll get all the presents. Right?"

Bella jerked away from her grandmother's hand. "No. You're ugly."

"Bella!" Daphne seemed horrified.

Jackson suddenly appeared, strode over to the sofa, and picked Bella up. She wiggled and squirmed, but he held her tightly and she finally was still. He put her down on the other side of the room and, kneeling so they were eye level, spoke quietly to her. After a few minutes, they came back together, and Bella stood before her grandmother.

"I'm very sorry, Grandmamma," she said, and bowed her head.

Ruth gave Daphne a triumphant look and took Bella's hand. "I forgive you, Bella. But you mustn't say things like that in the future."

Bella looked at her father and got only a stern look in return. "Yes, Grandmamma."

Margarita peered into the room and announced that dinner was ready. Jackson took Ruth's arm, and the two of them marched into the dining room together, Bella and Tallulah right behind them. As Daphne rose, Amber gave her a pat on the shoulder.

"It's been a long day. Bella's just overtired. Don't let them all get to you," she said to her.

"Sometimes that's really hard," Daphne said.

"You're a wonderful mom. Don't let anyone tell you that you're not."

"Thanks, Amber. You're such a good friend."

In a way, Daphne was a wonderful mother. She gave her kids everything, especially love and affection. She was certainly a better mother than Amber's, who'd made it clear every day of her life that her kids were a loathsome burden.

"Don't leave yet. Stay and have dinner with us," Daphne said.

Amber wasn't sure that dinner with an exhausted, exasperated Bella and a disapproving grandmother was going to further her plans in any way. "I'd love to, Daph, but I have tons of laundry and cleaning to do. Thanks for asking, though."

"Oh, all right," Daphne said, linking her arm in Amber's. "At least come to the dining room and say good night to everyone."

She obediently followed Daphne into the room where the family was all seated and being served by Margarita.

"Good night, all," Amber said, waving her hand. "It was a wonderful party."

A chorus of farewells came from the group, and then Jackson's smooth voice rang out. "Good night, Amber. See you tomorrow at the office."

NINETEEN

Amber dressed carefully for her first day at Parrish International. Her hair was pulled back into a ponytail, and she wore plain gold-colored hoop earrings and minimal makeup. Getting up at four o'clock to catch the 5:30 train was murder, but she had to make a good impression. How anyone could stand doing this on a long-term basis was beyond her. Hopefully, it would only be temporary.

The glass tower that housed Jackson's company was enormous, and she marveled that he owned it. It must have cost a fortune to own a building like this in Manhattan. The lobby was empty except for security, and she nodded as she scanned her identity badge and was green-lighted through the turnstile. When she reached the thirtieth floor, she was surprised to see a few people already in their offices. She'd have to get an even earlier train tomorrow. Her tiny cubicle was outside her boss's office. She would be reporting to his first assistant, Mrs. Battley, or Mrs. Battle-Ax as Amber thought of her after their meeting last week at orientation. The Battle-Ax was somewhere between sixty-five and seventy-five with steel-wool-gray hair, thick glasses, and thin lips. She was the very definition of no-nonsense, and Amber hated her on sight. She had made it clear that she wasn't pleased that Amber had been thrust upon her. It was going to be a challenge getting the old bird to like her.

"Good morning, Mrs. Battley. I'm going to get some coffee. Would you like some?"

She didn't look up from her laptop. "No. I've already had my one cup. I have some filing for you, so please see me when you've gotten yours." Amber cast a discreet glance in the direction of Jackson's corner office. His door was closed, but she could see movement through the slatted blinds covering one glass wall.

"Do you need something?" Battley's gravelly voice interrupted her thoughts.

"Sorry, no. My coffee can wait. I'll take the filing now."

"Here you are," she said, handing Amber a pile of papers. "And here's a list of new clients to add to the database. I've left instructions on your desk on how to do so. You'll also need to add their websites and all social media channels to their profiles."

Amber took the folder and returned to her tiny cube. She'd traded in her office with a window view for this claustrophobic cube, but at least now her plan was progressing. The hours passed as she immersed herself in her work, determined to be the most efficient assistant Old Battle-Ax had ever had. She'd brought a bag lunch and ate at her desk, working without a break. At six o'clock, Battley was standing at her cube with her coat on.

"I didn't realize you were still here, Amber. You can leave at five, you know."

She stood up and gathered her things. "I wanted to finish up. I like to come in to a clean desk in the morning."

This actually elicited a smile from the older woman. "Quite right. I've always felt the same way."

She turned to leave, but Amber called out, "I'll walk down with you."

They walked in silence to the elevator bank, and when they got on, Amber gave her a shy smile.

"I want to thank you for giving me this chance. You don't know how much it means to me."

Battley raised her eyebrows. "Don't thank me. I had nothing to do with it."

"Mrs. Parrish told me how valuable your opinion is to Mr. Parrish," Amber said. "She made it quite clear that I was here on a probationary basis. If you don't find me up to snuff, then I'll have to look elsewhere."

Amber could tell that the woman's pride made her believe this bullshit. Battley stood a little straighter. "We shall see, then."

Yes, we shall, Amber thought.

After a month, she'd still had no direct contact with Jackson, but Old Battle-Ax had begun to rely on her more and more. Amber would arrive at least fifteen minutes before her, so that she could bring Battley her morning coffee with a little something extra in it. Amber had a three-month supply of Elavil from her internist. She had told him that she was having panic attacks, and he'd recommended it. He did mention some possible side effects: short-term memory loss and confusion. She'd started dosing low, and hoped that Battley's predilection for flavored creamer obscured any trace of the pills in her coffee.

Battley arrived that morning, seemingly more confused than normal. Amber noticed that her pace had become slower and that she paused often, looking around her desk as if unsure of what to do next.

When Battley got up to go to the bathroom, Amber quickly went into her office and took the woman's keys from her purse and moved them. She then refiled a folder that was sitting on her desk. Battley came back to her office and searched for the missing file, panic in her eyes. At the end of the day, Battley opened her purse and looked inside. Amber watched as she moved the contents around and finally poured everything out on her desk. No keys. She looked stricken. "Amber," she called. "Have you seen my keys?"

Amber hurried into Battley's office. "No, I haven't. Aren't they in your handbag?"

"No," she said, almost in tears.

"Here," Amber said, taking the purse from the desk. "Let me look." She pretended to root around. "Hmm. You're right. Not here." She stood a moment as if thinking. "Have you looked in your drawers?"

"Of course not. I never take them from my pocketbook. I would never put them in my desk," she insisted.

"Why don't we look, just in case."

"Ridiculous," Battley huffed, but opened the drawer. "See, they're not there."

Amber leaned over to look and then glanced past them, at the wastebasket next to the file cabinet. She pulled it toward her.

"They're in the trash can." Amber reached in and pulled them out, handing them to Battley.

Battley stood still, staring at the ring of keys in her hand as she swallowed hard. It was apparent that the woman was distraught, but all she said was good night before turning and leaving without another word. Amber smiled as she watched her walk away.

A few days later Amber rearranged the cards in Battley's Rolodex—she must have been the last person on earth to still have one. As the weeks wore on, the stress was having the intended effect—a haunted look of constant worry was in the older woman's eyes. Amber felt a little bad about what she was doing, but the woman really needed to retire. Her time would have been much better spent with her grandkids. She'd told Amber she had five and complained that she didn't get to see them enough. Now she'd get to be with them more, and Jackson would probably give her a good retirement package—especially if he believed she had dementia. Amber was doing her a favor, really.

And didn't Jackson deserve someone more hip and this-century helping him out? He was probably keeping her on out of loyalty. Amber was doing them both a favor, when she thought about it. This morning, she'd printed off a paper with gibberish and slipped it in between the pages of a report Battley had just finished. She knew the woman would think she'd really lost it when she saw it, and of course, she'd never mention it to anyone. Amber figured it would only take another few weeks. Between her eroding self-confidence and the mistakes she was soon to make, arousing Jackson's suspicions, Amber would be sitting pretty in Battley's office in no time.

TWENTY

t took much longer than Amber anticipated, but after three months, it had all become too much for Battley, and she handed in her resignation. Amber was now filling in while Jackson began the search for a new head assistant. She was still in her tiny cubicle, while Battley's office remained vacant, and while it bothered Amber that he hadn't yet considered letting her step in permanently, she was confident he would soon find her indispensable. She had already spent the past seven nights learning everything she could about his newest clients from Tokyo—it was amazing what people put on their social media profiles. Even if they did have the smarts to set up their privacy settings properly, what they didn't realize was that every photo they were tagged in linked to someone else's page, and not everyone was as diligent. Between using her background-check software and trolling all the social sites, she had a comprehensive picture of each of them, including their disgusting predilections. She had also conducted a thorough search of their recent business deals to get an idea of their negotiating skills and any tricks they might have up their sleeves.

Jackson summoned her to his office, and she gathered the report on the client. He was leaning back in his black leather chair, reading something on his iPhone. His jacket was off and his shirtsleeves rolled up, showing off his tanned forearms. The Parrishes had just returned from Antibes. She figured they were able to practice the French language they seemed to worship. He didn't look up as she entered the office.

"I'm slammed today, but I forgot Bella's play at camp is this afternoon. I have to duck out after lunch. Move my appointments."

What must it be like to have a powerful father who cared
enough about you to take time from his busy schedule to come
to your play? And the little brat appreciated nothing. "Of course."

"Did you make reservations at Catch for Tanaka and his team
tomorrow?"

"Actually, no."

His head snapped up. She had his full attention. "What?"

"I made them at Del Posto. Tanaka loves Italian, and he's allergic to shellfish."

He looked at her with interest. "Really? How do you know
that?"

She handed him her report. "I took the liberty of doing some
research. On my own time, of course," she added quickly. "I
thought it would be helpful. With social media it's not that hard
to find things out."

He smiled widely, giving her a glimpse of his perfect teeth, and
reached out for the report. After thumbing through it, he looked
up again. "Amber, I'm very impressed. Great initiative. This is
fantastic."

She beamed. She bet Battley didn't even know how to use Facebook.

She stood up. "If there's nothing else, I'll go take care of sorting
your appointments."

"Thanks," he mumbled, immersed in the report again.

She was making progress with him, although she was a little disappointed that he didn't seem to notice how good her legs
looked in the short skirt and high heels she'd worn that day. He
was that rare commodity—a man who only had eyes for his wife.
Daphne, on the other hand, seemed complacent, like she took it

for granted that he worshipped her. It irritated Amber. It was obvious to her that Daphne wasn't as passionate about Jackson as he was about her, and that she really didn't deserve him.

She opened up Jackson's calendar on her computer and began contacting his afternoon appointments to reschedule. As she was about to make another call, he appeared.

"Amber, why don't you sit in Mrs. Battley's office until we find her replacement? It'll be more convenient to have you right outside. Give Facilities a call; they can move your things."

"Thank you, I will."

She watched him as he strode away, his Brioni suit looking as though it had been hand-crafted by the gods. She wondered what it would be like to wear a garment that cost more than some people made in a year.

She picked up her phone and texted Daphne.

Are you free tomorrow? Would love to meet for a drink.

Her text tone sounded. **Sure. I'll have Tommy pick you up and we can go to Sparta's. Seven thirty good?**

Great! See you tomorrow.

If Daphne was having Tommy drive them, it meant she was in the mood to drink, which was perfect because Amber was ready to get her to spill her guts. She had discovered that after one martini Daphne became much more relaxed, making it easy to pour a few more down her throat.

TWENTY-ONE

The Parrish Town Car was waiting outside her apartment right on time. She was about to call out a hello to Daphne when she realized the backseat was empty.

"Where's Mrs. Parrish?" she asked Tommy as he opened the door for her.

"Mr. Parrish came home unexpectedly. She asked me to collect you and drop you at Sparta's, then swing around for her."

She felt annoyance choke out her good mood. Why hadn't Daphne just called and asked if they could move the time back? She felt like an appointment being handled. And why should it matter that Jackson came home? Why didn't Daphne just tell him she already had plans? Where was her backbone?

When she got to the bar, she chose a cozy table in the corner and ordered the 2007 Sassicaia. It was $210, but Daphne would be picking up the bill, and it served her right for making Amber wait. She took a sip of the red delight and savored the opulent flavor. It was amazing.

She looked around as the lounge began to fill and wondered if any of Daphne's so-called friends would be coming in tonight. She hoped not—she wanted Daphne all to herself.

Daphne finally arrived, looking harried and, frankly, a little unkempt. Her hair was a bit frizzy and her makeup splotchy.

"I'm sorry, Amber. Just as I was leaving, Jackson came in, and . . ." She threw her hands up. "Not even worth getting into.

I need a drink." She glanced at the bottle, and a little frown furrowed her brow.

"I hope you don't mind that I ordered a bottle. I forgot my reading glasses and couldn't really see that well, so I asked the waiter for a recommendation."

Daphne started to say something and then seemed to think better of it. "It's fine."

A glass appeared, and she poured herself a generous serving. "Mmm. Delish." She took a deep breath. "So, how are things going at Parrish International? Jackson tells me you're proving to be quite valuable."

Amber studied her for any traces of suspicion or jealousy but saw none. Daphne looked genuinely happy for her, but there was also a touch of concern in her face.

"Is everyone treating you well? No problems, right?"

Amber was surprised by the question. "No, none at all. I'm loving it. Thank you so much for recommending me. It's so different from Rollins. And everyone is really nice. So, what was the big emergency?"

"What?"

"Jackson coming home—what did he need that disrupted your plans?"

"Nothing. He just wanted a few minutes with me before I went out."

Amber arched an eyebrow. "A few minutes for what?"

Daphne turned red.

"Oh, *that*. He can't seem to get enough of you. That's pretty amazing. You've been married, what, nine years?"

"Twelve."

Amber could tell she was making Daphne uncomfortable, so she switched tactics. She leaned in and lowered her voice. "Consider yourself lucky. One of the reasons I left home was because of my boyfriend, Marco."

"What do you mean?"

"I was crazy about him. We'd been dating since high school. He was the only one I'd ever been with, so I didn't know."

Now Daphne was bending closer. "Didn't know what?"

She squirmed and made herself look embarrassed. "That it wasn't normal. You know. That guys should sort of be . . . ready. I had to do things just to help him be able to make love to me. He told me I wasn't pretty enough to get him excited without some help." She was laying it on pretty thick, but it seemed like Daphne believed it.

"The last straw was when he asked me to bring another man into the bedroom."

"What?" Daphne's mouth fell open.

"Yeah. Turned out he was gay. Didn't want to admit it or something. You know how those small towns can be."

"Have you dated anyone since?"

"A few guys here and there, but no one serious. Truthfully, I'm a little nervous about sleeping with someone again. What if I find out that it really was me?"

Daphne shook her head. "That's crazy, Amber. His sexual orientation had nothing to do with you. And you're lovely. When you find the right man, you'll know it."

"Is that how you felt when you found Jackson?"

Daphne paused a moment, taking a sip of her wine. "Well . . . I guess Jackson swept me off my feet. My father became ill after we began dating, and Jackson was my rock. After that, things moved really quickly, and before I knew it, we were married. I never expected it. He dated sophisticated and accomplished women. I wasn't quite sure what he saw in me."

"Come on, Daph, you're gorgeous."

"That's sweet, but so were they. And they were wealthy and worldly. I was just a girl from a small town. I didn't know anything about his world."

"So what do you think it was that made you special?"

Daphne refilled her wineglass and took a long swallow. "I think he liked having a blank canvas. I was young, only twenty-six, and he was ten years older. I was so focused on building Julie's Smile, I wasn't taken in by him. He told me later that he never knew whether the women he went out with wanted him or his money."

Amber found that hard to believe. Even if he'd been dead broke, he was still gorgeous, brilliant, and charming. "How did he know you didn't care about his money?"

"I actually tried to cool things off. He didn't really turn my head. But then, he was so wonderful to my family, and they all encouraged me not to let him get away."

"See, you *are* lucky. Look how wonderful it turned out. You have such a great life."

Daphne smiled. "Nobody's life is perfect, Amber."

"It sure seems it. It looks as close to perfect as you can pretty well get."

"I'm very fortunate. I have two healthy children. That's something I never take for granted."

Amber wanted to keep things focused on marriage. "Yes, of course. But your relationship seems like a fairy tale from the outside. Jackson looks at you like he worships you."

"He's very attentive. I suppose sometimes I just need a little breathing room. It can feel confining, having to fit into the mold of the CEO's wife. He has high expectations. Sometimes I'd like to just sit around and watch *House of Cards* instead of going to another charity function or business event."

Oh, boohoo, Amber thought. It must be so hard to have to dress up in designer gowns and drink expensive wine and munch on caviar. She mustered a sympathetic look. "I can see that. I would feel so out of place having to do all that. But you make it look so easy. Did it take you long to fit in?"

"The first couple of years were rough. But Meredith came to my rescue. She helped me navigate the treacherous social circles here in Bishops Harbor." She laughed. "Once you have Meredith on your side, everyone falls into line. She's been the foundation's staunchest supporter—until you, that is."

"You must have felt very lucky. Sort of like I feel having you."

"Exactly."

The bottle was empty, and Amber was about to suggest they order another when Daphne's phone lit up with a text.

She scanned it, then looked at Amber apologetically.

"It's Bella. She's had a nightmare. I need to go home."

That little brat. Even when she wasn't present, she was messing up Amber's plans.

"Oh, poor darling. Does that happen often?"

Daphne shook her head. "Not too often. Sorry to have to cut our evening short. If you don't mind, I'll have Tommy take me right away, then drop you home."

"Of course. Give her a kiss from Aunt Amber," Amber said, throwing it out there. Why not elevate her status?

Daphne squeezed her hand as they walked out to the waiting car. "I like that. I will."

Although she was disappointed that she wouldn't get another glass of that divine wine, she'd gotten some of what she'd wanted: the beginning of a profile of Jackson's perfect woman. She would build it, tidbit by tidbit, until she was an exact replica of what he found irresistible.

Only she would be a newer, younger version.

TWENTY-TWO

Amber inhaled the intoxicating smell of the ocean. It was a perfectly gorgeous Sunday morning, and she and Daphne had already been out on the water for the last hour. Jackson was in Brussels on business, and Daphne had invited Amber to spend the weekend. She had been slightly dubious when Daphne suggested they go kayaking, as she'd never done it before and wasn't sure she wanted her first foray to be on the deep waters of Long Island Sound. But she'd had nothing to worry about. The water was still as glass when they started out, and within a half hour, Amber was feeling sure and confident. They stayed close to the shore at first, and Amber marveled at the peacefulness of the early-morning quiet, the only sounds birdsong and the lapping of water against their paddles. Everything was still, so wonderfully devoid of the bustle and noise of everyday life. They glided along beside each other, both silent and content.

"Shall we go out a little farther?" Daphne broke the silence.

"I guess so. Is it safe?"

"Perfectly."

Amber worked to keep up with Daphne's sure strokes, breathing hard as she exerted herself. She was impressed with Daphne's stamina. As they moved farther from shore, the water took on an entirely different aura. The first time a boat passed them, she thought she would be swamped by its wake, but the second time it happened, she got an adrenaline rush riding the small swells.

"I love this, Daph. I'm so glad you made me come."

"I knew you'd like it. I'm glad. Now I'll have a partner. Jackson doesn't really enjoy kayaking. He'd rather be on the boat."

Well, Amber thought, the boat would be good too. She hadn't been on his Hatteras yet, but she knew it wouldn't be long before she got an invitation.

"Don't you like the boat?" Amber asked.

"Oh sure, I like it, but it's a completely different experience. It needed some work before going back into the water. Should be sometime in late June. We'll all go out together. Then you can make your own judgment."

"What's the name of it?"

"*Bellatada*," Daphne answered, her smile holding a touch of embarrassment.

Amber thought for a minute. "Oh, I get it. The beginning of each of your names. Jackson's three girls."

"A little silly, I guess."

"Not at all. I think it's sweet." Inwardly she was choking on her words.

"Shall we head back? It's almost ten." Daphne looked at her watch and adjusted her visor.

It didn't take long to reach the beach in front of the house and deposit the kayaks. As they walked up the path to the house, the sounds of laughter and girlish squeals reached them. Bella and Tallulah were splashing around in the swimming pool with their father.

Amber turned to Daphne. "I thought Jackson was coming back tonight."

"Me too," Daphne said and picked up her pace.

He looked up and ran a hand through his wet hair. "Hello, you two. Been out kayaking?"

"We have. When did you get home? I'm sorry I wasn't here, but

I thought you were coming in tonight," Daphne said, sounding strained.

"We finished up last night, so I decided to fly home this morning." Bella was holding on to his back and splashing with her feet. He turned to grab her, and she squealed with delight as he tossed her back into the water. She pushed up through the water and swam to him. "More, Daddy."

But he began walking to the shallow end of the pool, wiping the water from his face. "That's all, sweetie. Time to take a break."

For once there was no obnoxious complaining from Bella. It had to have been a first.

Jackson handed towels to the girls and started drying himself with his own. It was impossible not to look at his body, wet and glistening, as he stepped closer to Daphne and kissed her. "It's good to be home," he said.

Daphne had asked Amber to spend the day, but now that Jackson was home, Amber knew she had to deliver the obligatory I-don't-want-to-be-in-the-way speech. "I had a great time kayaking, Daph. Thanks a bunch. I'm going to let you have your family time now."

"What do you mean? You can't leave yet."

"I really should. I'm sure Jackson would like to be alone with you and the girls."

"Nonsense. You know how he feels about you. You're like family. Come on. We'll have fun."

"Absolutely," Jackson said. "You're more than welcome to stay."

"Are you sure?"

"Of course," Daphne said. "Let's go inside and make lunch. Margarita is off this weekend, so we're the cooks."

They worked together in the kitchen, but when they finished

loading the tortillas with refried beans, veggies, and cheese, they didn't end up with neat and beautiful burritos like Margarita's.

"They look pretty sad, don't they?" Daphne said with a laugh.

"What the heck. They'll taste good, anyway." Amber washed her hands and tore off a section of paper toweling while Daphne reached into a cabinet and pulled out two trays. "Here we go. I think everything will fit. We'll eat outside by the pool."

"Oooh, yummy," Bella called as they carried the food out.

They sat, the five of them, under the large umbrella, the reflection of the sun on the turquoise pool water making shimmery diamonds and triangles. A slight breeze sliced through the warmth—a perfect late-spring day. Amber closed her eyes a moment, pretending this all belonged to her. If anything, the last few weeks had shown her that Daphne now considered Amber her closest friend and confidante. Last night, after the girls had gone to bed, she and Daphne had sat at the kitchen table and talked late into the night. Daphne had told her all about her childhood, how much her parents had tried to make their lives seem completely normal despite the illness that crouched in the background, ready to pounce without warning at any moment.

"Mom and Dad encouraged Julie to do everything healthy kids can. They gave her the freedom to live her life the way she wanted, to try all the things she wanted to," Daphne had said.

At first, when Daphne talked about all the hospital stays, the hacking coughs that brought up gloppy mucus, the runny bowels and trouble digesting food, Amber had begun to feel sympathy. But when she compared her own childhood to Daphne's, and even Julie's, her resentment returned. At least Julie had grown up in a nice house with money and parents who cared about her. Okay, she was sick and then she died. So what? A lot of people were sick. A lot of people died. Was that a reason to make them saints? How about Amber and what she'd gone through? Didn't she deserve a little sympathy too?

She looked around the table at all of them. Bella, lazing back in her chair and swinging her legs back and forth, taking distracted bites out of her burrito without a care in the world, the pampered and indulged child of wealth. Tallulah, sitting up straight and concentrating on the lunch before her. Daphne, sun-kissed and casually beautiful, making sure her brood had refills and napkins and anything else they needed. And Jackson, the master of it all, sitting like a knighted lord watching over his vast domain and faultless family. Suddenly the terrible emptiness inside Amber was a physical gnawing, as if the very life were being squeezed from her. This was no time to go soft. She would win this time.

TWENTY-THREE

Things were so busy at work that Amber hadn't seen Daphne in two weeks, since their kayaking day. But Jackson was out of town again, so she'd called Daphne to see if she'd like to see a movie, and Daphne had invited her to the house instead.

She had started fantasizing about the day the house would belong to her. She wanted to leave her mark on it everywhere. On one occasion, when Daphne left her at the house alone to go pick up the girls, she'd tried on every pair of Daphne's underwear. Sometimes she'd go upstairs and use Daphne's bathroom, brush her hair with Daphne's brush, apply a little of her lipstick. They almost looked the same, she would think as she looked in the mirror at herself.

She arrived right at seven. Bella opened the door a crack and peeked out.

"What are you doing here?"

"Hi, sweetie. Mommy invited me over."

Bella rolled her eyes. "We're watching *The Wizard of Oz* tonight. Don't try and change it to some boring adult movie." She opened the door, then turned her back on Amber.

Now Amber rolled *her* eyes. *The Wizard of Oz.* If she had to listen to Dorothy keep saying "There's no place like home," she might kill herself.

"There you are. Bella said you were here. Come on in the kitchen." Daphne appeared, looking perfect in a romper that looked very much like a Stella McCartney Amber had seen in a recent *Vogue*.

Amber sat down at the enormous marble island.

"Can I get you a drink?"

"Sure, whatever you're having."

Daphne poured her a glass of chardonnay from the open bottle.

"Cheers." Daphne raised her glass.

Amber took a small sip. "I understand we've got *The Wizard of Oz* on tap for tonight."

Daphne gave her an apologetic look. "Yes, sorry. I forgot I'd promised the girls." She lowered her voice so Bella wouldn't hear. "Once we're half an hour in, we can sneak into the other room and chat. They won't notice."

Whatever, Amber thought.

The doorbell rang. "Is someone else coming?" Amber asked.

Daphne shook her head. "I'm not expecting anyone. Be right back."

A minute later, Amber heard voices, and then Meredith was there, following Daphne back into the kitchen. She looked determined.

"Hi, Meredith," Amber greeted her, feeling uneasy

Daphne had a look of concern on her face and put a hand on Amber's arm. "Meredith says she needs to talk to us in private."

Amber's thoughts raced. Could she have discovered the truth? Maybe the photo from the fund-raiser had been her undoing after all. She took a deep breath to stop the hammering in her chest. No need to get upset until she heard what Meredith had to say. She rose from her stool.

"Margarita, could you please feed the girls now? We'll be back in a little while." Daphne turned to Amber and Meredith. "Let's go into the study."

Amber's heart was still pounding as she followed them down the hallway and into the wood-paneled study. She stared straight ahead at the wall of books, willing herself to be calm.

"Let's all have a seat." Daphne pulled out a chair and sat at the mahogany card table in the corner of the room. Amber and Meredith followed suit.

Meredith looked at Amber as she spoke. "As you know, I run all our committee applications through a background check."

"Didn't you do that months ago?" Daphne interrupted.

Meredith put a hand up. "Yes, I thought I had. Apparently the agency misfiled Amber's. They ran it last week and called me today."

"And?" Daphne prodded.

"And when they ran the social, they discovered that Amber Patterson has been missing for four years." She held up a copy of a missing person flyer, with a photo of a young woman with dark hair and a round face, who looked nothing like Amber.

"What? That must be some sort of mistake," Daphne said.

Amber kept quiet, but her heartbeat slowed. So that was all. She could work with this.

Meredith sat up straighter. "No mistake. I called the Eustis, Nebraska, records department. Same social security number." She pulled out a photocopy of an article from the *Clipper-Herald* with the headline "Amber Patterson Still Missing" and handed it to Daphne. "Want to tell us about it, Amber, or whatever your name is?"

Amber put her hands up to her face and cried real tears of panic. "It's not what you think." She choked back a sob.

"What is it, then?" Meredith's tone was steely.

Amber sniffled and wiped her nose. "I can explain. But not to *her*." She spat out the last word.

"Give it up, girl." Meredith's voice rose. "Who are you, and what do you want?"

"Meredith, please. This isn't helping," Daphne said. "Amber, calm down. I'm sure there's a good explanation. Tell me what this is all about."

Amber sank back into the chair, hoping she looked as distraught as she felt. "I know it looks bad. I didn't want to have to tell anyone. But I had to get away."

"Away from what?" Meredith insisted, and Amber shrank back more.

"Meredith, please let me ask the questions," Daphne said and put her hand gently on Amber's knee. "What were you running away from, sweetie?"

Amber closed her eyes and sighed. "My father."

Daphne looked like she'd been struck. "Your father? Did he hurt you?"

Amber hung her head as she spoke. "I'm so ashamed to tell you this. He . . . he raped me."

Daphne gasped.

"I've never told another soul."

"Oh my God," Daphne said. "I'm so sorry."

"It went on for years, from the time I was ten. He left Charlene alone as long as I was around and didn't tell. That's why I had to stay. I couldn't let him hurt her."

"That's horrible . . . couldn't you tell your mother?"

She sniffled. "I tried. But she didn't believe me, said I was just trying to get attention, and she'd whip my butt if I ever told anyone else such a 'vile lie.'" A quick glance out of the corner of her eye assured her that Daphne believed her, but Meredith looked unconvinced.

"So what happened exactly?" Meredith's voice sounded almost mocking, and Amber saw Daphne give her a look.

"I stayed until Charlene died. He told me if I left, he'd hunt me down and kill me. So I had to change my name. I hitchhiked to Nebraska and met a guy in a bar. He found me a roommate. I worked waitressing and saved my money until I had enough to come here and start over. He worked at the hall of records and got me the information on the missing girl, introduced me to someone who made me an ID in Amber's name."

Amber waited a beat for the women to respond.

To her great relief, Daphne rose and took her in her arms. "I'm so sorry," she said again.

Meredith wasn't letting it go, though. "What? Daphne, do you mean to tell me you're just going to take her word for it and not investigate? I can't believe this."

Daphne's eyes were cold. "Please go, Meredith. I'll call you later."

"You have a blind spot where she's concerned." Meredith walked to the door in a huff and turned around before she left. "Mark my words, Daphne—this will not end well."

Daphne took Amber's hand. "Don't you worry. No one will ever hurt you again."

"What about Meredith? What if she tells people?"

"You let me worry about Meredith. I'll make sure she doesn't breathe a word."

"Please don't tell anyone, Daphne. I have to keep pretending I'm Amber. You don't know how he is. He'll find me, wherever I am."

Daphne nodded. "I won't tell another soul, not even Jackson."

Amber felt a little guilty for painting her father in such a bad light. After all, he'd worked nonstop at the cleaner's to support her mother and her three sisters, and he would never have touched any of his daughters. Of course, he'd also made all of them work at that damn store for free, which she was pretty sure was child slave labor, close enough to child abuse. So what if he never touched her? He still took advantage of her.

Suddenly she didn't feel so guilty anymore. She raised her head from Daphne's shoulder and looked her in the eye. "I don't know what I did to deserve a friend like you. Thank you for always being there for me."

Daphne smiled and smoothed Amber's hair. "You'd do the same for me."

Amber gave her a forlorn smile and nodded.

Daphne started to walk from the room, then turned back. "I'll tell Bella that *The Wizard of Oz* will have to wait. I think you deserve to pick tonight."

Amber smiled a genuine smile—she couldn't wait to see the look of disappointment on the little princess's face. "That would really help me get my mind off things."

TWENTY-FOUR

Growing up, Amber had always hated the Fourth of July. The only good thing about that day was that her father closed the dry cleaner's. She and her three sisters would watch the parade—the high school marching band that was always screechingly off-key, at least one majorette who would drop her batons, and some plump-faced farm girl who would wave with glee from a hay-filled wagon. It was all so hokey and embarrassing, Amber cringed every time.

But this year was different. Quite different. Amber sat with Daphne on the back deck of the Parrishes' sixty-five-foot Hatteras as it sped across the Sound. They were spending the entire weekend on the boat, and Amber was over the moon. She'd gone shopping with Daphne and spent more than she had planned, but she wanted to look her absolute best every moment since she'd be near Jackson twenty-four/seven. She bought a new white bikini and then splurged on a one-piece black suit with a long, low V in the front and cutouts on the sides. It was one of the sexiest suits she'd ever seen, and Daphne had nodded her approval when Amber walked out from the dressing room. Her cover-up was sheer, so her body would never be hidden from him. For when they went ashore, she'd gotten white shorts that barely covered her buttocks and tank tops that clung just a bit. She'd brought skinny white pants for evening, a few T-shirts, and a casual navy sweater to throw over her shoulders. She'd even gotten a spray tan. This was her time to shine.

Jackson stood at the controls, his legs tanned and muscular, in a pair of khaki shorts and white golf shirt. He moved with utter confidence and mastery. He turned to where Daphne and Amber sat and called to them over the noise, "Hey, sweetheart, can you get me a beer?"

Daphne reached into the cooler and brought out a can of Gordon Ale, dripping with cold water. She had to admit, Daphne's black bikini showed off her perfect body to its best advantage. She had hoped Daphne would be wearing something more matronly, but no such luck. Daphne handed it to Amber. "Here, why don't you give it to him? You can get a lesson on how to handle a boat."

Amber took the can from Daphne and jumped up. "Sure. . . . Hey." She tapped Jackson on the shoulder. "Here's your beer."

"Thanks." He opened it, took a sip, and Amber noticed his long fingers and fine hands, immediately imagining them on her body.

"Daphne said you'd give me a boat-driving lesson," she said coyly.

"Boat driving. Is that what she called it?" He laughed.

"Well, maybe not. I can't remember."

"Here," he said, moving slightly to the right. "Take the wheel."

"What? No. What if we crash?"

"You're cute. What are we going to crash into? You really don't have to move it much. Just point the end of the bow in the direction you want to go and don't make any sudden jerking moves."

She put her hands on the wheel and concentrated on the water, her nerves subsiding a bit as she got the feel of it.

"Good," he said. "Steady as you go."

"This is fun," she said, throwing her head back and laughing. "I could do this all day."

Jackson patted her on the back. "Great. It's good to have a partner up here. Daphne isn't crazy about the boat. Prefers the kayak."

Amber widened her eyes. "Really? I can't imagine that. This is way better than kayaking."

"Maybe you can convince my wife of that." He took another sip of ale and looked back to where Daphne sat, quietly reading *The Portrait of a Lady.*

Amber followed his gaze and put a reassuring hand on his arm. "I'm sure she likes it more than you think. I know I would."

She stayed at the wheel for the next hour, asking questions and praising Jackson for his depth of navigation knowledge. She made him promise to show her the charts later, so she could study them and learn about the waters around Connecticut. And every now and then, she'd move close enough that her body would barely touch his. When she thought it might be too obvious, she turned the wheel back over to Jackson and went back to sit with Daphne. They were approaching Mystic, and the sun was beginning to set.

Daphne looked up from her book. "Well, you seemed to be enjoying yourself. Did you learn a lot?"

Amber searched Daphne's face for any sign of annoyance, but she seemed genuinely delighted that Amber was having a good time. "I liked it," she said. "Jackson knows so much."

"This boat is his favorite thing. He'd be on it every weekend if I let him."

"You don't love it, do you?"

"I like it. I just don't like spending all my time on it. We have a beautiful home, the beach, and a pool. I like being there. On the boat there's just endless water, and it takes so much time to get anywhere. I start to get bored. And the girls begin to get antsy too. It's a small space, and it's hard to keep everything in order."

Amber wondered again at Daphne's obsession with neatness. Did she ever lighten up and relax?

"Well, you have to admit it's pretty exciting. The wind rushing through your hair and ripping through the water," Amber said.

"I especially don't enjoy speeding. To tell you the truth, I prefer sailing. It's quiet. I feel much more connected to nature when I'm on a sailboat."

"Does Jackson like it?" Amber asked.

"Not much. Don't get me wrong—he's a good sailor. Knows his stuff. But he can fly at top speed on this, and he likes fishing too." She pushed her hair back from her face. "My boyfriend in college grew up sailing, so we spent a lot of time on his family's sailboat. That's where I learned."

"I guess I can understand why you'd like that better," Amber said.

"It's fine, really. I make sure to bring a good book, and the girls bring games. And of course it's always fun to have a friend like you aboard."

"Thanks for asking me, Daph. It's a real treat for me."

"You're welcome," Daphne said, yawning and rising from her chair. "I'm going below to check on the girls. You don't mind if I lie down for a few minutes before dinner, do you?"

"Of course not. Go ahead and rest." Amber watched her go down the stairs and immediately took up her position next to Jackson again. "Daphne's taking a nap. I think she was getting bored."

She watched his face for a reaction, but if he had any irritation, he certainly didn't show it.

"She's a good sport about it."

"She is. She was telling me about all the fun she had in college when she and her old boyfriend would go sailing together." Amber noticed a slight twitch in Jackson's cheek. "I don't know. That seems so tame compared to this."

"Why don't you have another go? I'll grab us a couple of drinks."

She gripped the wheel and felt like she might finally, slowly, be taking control of the helm.

Later that night, after a leisurely dinner in Mystic, the five of them walked back to the marina under a warm, star-studded sky.

"Daddy," Tallulah said as they ambled. "Are we going to anchor out and watch the fireworks tomorrow night?"

"Absolutely. Just like we always do."

"Goody," Bella said. "I want to sit way up on the fly bridge all by myself. I'm old enough now."

"Not so fast, little one." Jackson took one of her hands and Daphne grabbed the other, and they swung her between them. "You can't go alone yet."

"I want to lie down on the forward deck like I did last year and watch from there," Tallulah piped up.

"Daddy will sit on the bridge with you, Bella, and I'll be on deck with Tallulah." She turned to Amber. "And you should go up with Jackson and Bella. It's a great place to watch from, especially since this is your first time."

That's fine with me, Amber thought.

It was a little past ten when they got back to the boat, and once again, Amber found herself alone with Jackson as Daphne took the children below to get them ready for bed. He had gotten some wine from the galley and was back with three glasses in one hand and the bottle of muscat in the other.

"Too early to finish the night. What do you say we have a glass before turning in?"

"Sounds great," Amber said.

They sat in the warm night air, sipping wine and chatting

about Parrish International's latest acquisition and how the financing would work. When Daphne appeared, Jackson poured another glass and handed it to her. "Here, sweetheart."

"No, thank you, darling. I'm feeling rather sleepy. Probably shouldn't have had such a big meal. I think I'll hit the sack."

Actually, Amber thought, Daphne really did look tired. But big meal? She'd hardly touched her food.

"Well, good night, you two." She smiled at Jackson. "I'll keep the night-light on for you."

"I'll be down soon. You get some rest."

After she disappeared, Amber poured herself another glass of wine. "I remember how tired my mother used to get, and how she stopped staying up late. My father would joke and say things had really changed from their hot dating days."

Jackson looked into his glass as he twirled the stem. "Are your parents alive?"

"Yes. They're back in Nebraska. Daphne reminds me a lot of my mom."

A faint hint of surprise registered on his face and was quickly replaced by his usual inscrutability. Amber was beginning to realize that he was particularly skilled at keeping his thoughts and feelings hidden.

"How are they alike?"

"Well, they're both homebodies. My mom liked nothing better than watching a sentimental movie with us kids. A lot of times, when you're away, Daph invites me over for movie night with Tallulah and Bella. It's fun, reminds me of home. And I think she gets sort of tired of all these charity events and art openings and all those things. At least, that's what she tells me."

"That's interesting," Jackson said. "What else?"

"Well, she likes quiet things, my mom, like Daphne. My mom

would have hated how fast this boat goes and all the wind in her face. Not that we had boats, but my dad did have a motorcycle. She hated it—the noise and the speed. She preferred her bicycle, slow and quiet." More crap, but she was making her point.

He was quiet.

"I thought it was thrilling, being at the helm and speeding across the water. But maybe tomorrow we should take it a little slower, so that Daphne enjoys it too."

"Yes, good idea," he said idly and finished the wine in his glass.

Things were humming along now. And she hoped that tomorrow night, there would be more fireworks than the ones in the sky.

TWENTY-FIVE

Right after the Fourth of July, Amber finally secured the coveted position of Jackson's first assistant. The résumés had dwindled, and anything that looked too good, Amber had tossed. She had made herself indispensable to Jackson since Mrs. Battley's departure, so when he called her into his office, she felt sure it was to tell her she was officially his new assistant. She took a pad and pen with her and sat in a leather armchair across from his desk, careful to cross her black-stockinged legs to their best advantage. She looked at him through thick lashes she had gotten plumped at the aesthetician's and slightly parted glossy lips. She knew her teeth, recently whitened at the dentist's, looked perfect against her lips.

Jackson stared at her a moment and then began. "I think you know how helpful you've been these last months. I've decided to suspend the search for a new assistant and am offering the position to you if you're interested."

She wanted to jump up and shout but didn't betray her glee. "I'm overwhelmed. I'm definitely interested. Thank you."

"Good. I'll talk to Human Resources." He looked down at a document in front of him, clearly dismissing her, and Amber rose. "Oh," he said, and she stopped and turned around. "Of course, there will be a substantial raise."

To get close to him, she would have worked there for nothing, but in truth, she had been working damn hard and felt she deserved her now-six-figure salary. It didn't take long for her to anticipate his needs in her new role, and in a very short time, they were working together with the precision of a fine Swiss watch. Amber loved the importance the job gave her, her proximity to the big boss. The admins looked at her with envy, and the executives treated her with respect. No one wanted to be on the wrong side of the person who had the ear of Jackson Parrish. It was a heady experience. She thought of that Lockwood son of a bitch back home and how he'd treated her—as if she were some piece of trash he could throw away.

She jumped when her buzzer sounded late Friday and got up and went to his office. When she approached his desk, she saw what looked like a stack of bills and a large checkbook. "I'm sorry to burden you with this. Battley used to take care of it, and I just don't have time to look this all over."

"Did you really just use that word with me? You should know by now that nothing you give me to do is a burden."

Jackson smiled at her. "Touché. You do it all with pleasure. I should put PA after your name on your business cards. Perfect Assistant."

"Hmm. Perfect Boss. I guess we're a team made in heaven."

"Here's the test," he said, with a wry smile.

"What is it?" she asked.

"Bills. They're all on auto pay, but I want you to go over them, match them to the receipts, and be sure they're accurate. And of course there are some bills that need to be paid by check. I've indicated which those are, so you'll write a monthly check for those—Sabine and Surrey, school expenses, those kinds of things."

"Of course. No problem." She picked up the pile and the checkbook but hesitated before leaving his office. "You know, I'm feeling like Telemachos."

Jackson's eyebrows went up in surprise. "What?"

"You know, from *The Odyssey*."

"I know who Telamachos is. You've read *The Odyssey*?"

Amber nodded. "A few times. I love it. I love the way he takes on more and more responsibility. So . . . don't ever feel like you're giving me too much."

The way he looked at her felt to Amber as if he was appraising her, and it seemed to her that she had definitely scored a lot of points. She smiled sweetly and left him still studying her as she walked out the door.

She dropped everything onto her desk and began going through the folders. It turned out to be a very interesting exercise. Amber was astounded at the enormous sums of money Daphne spent each month. There were charges at Barney's, Bergdorf Goodman, Neiman Marcus, Henri Bendel, and independent boutiques, not to mention the couture houses and jewelers. In one month alone she'd bought over $200,000 worth of merchandise. Then came the nanny salaries, and the housekeeper and the driver. Daphne's gym membership and private yoga and Pilates classes. The girls' riding and tennis lessons. The country-club dues. The yacht-club fees. The shows and dinners. The trips. It went on and on, like a freaking fairy tale.

Amber's new salary was a pittance compared to the money Daphne could access. One bill in particular stopped her in her tracks—it was for a red crocodile Hermès Birkin. She did a double take when she saw the price: $69,000. For a purse! That was more than half her annual salary. And Daphne would probably use it a couple of times, then throw it in her closet. Amber's outrage was so palpable, she thought she would choke. It was obscene. If Daphne really wanted to help families living with CF, why didn't she donate more of her own money to them and be satisfied with the dozen designer purses she already had? What a little hypocrite. At least Amber was honest with herself about her motives. When she was married to Jackson, she wouldn't waste her time pretending to care about charity work.

Daphne didn't have to lift a finger at home, could buy anything she wanted, and had a husband who loved her, and she couldn't even pay her own bills? How spoiled could you get? Amber would never be lazy enough to give someone else an inside view into her lifestyle. Now that she had seen even more deeply into the pampered life Daphne led, she realized how limitless Jackson's wealth was and became even more determined to carry out her plan.

It took her over an hour and a half to wade through all the bills and receipts, and by the time she was finished, she was positively steaming. She got up from her desk and went to the coffee bar down the hall. On the way back, she stopped in the ladies' room and looked at herself in the mirror. She liked what she saw, but it was time to up the ante, make herself just a bit sexier, but in a subtle way—have him wonder what was different about her. When she got back to her desk, she saw that Jackson had already left for the day. She put the bills and checkbook in her drawer, locked it, and drank her coffee. When she finally closed her office door and walked out of the building, plans were forming in her mind. She had the whole weekend to perfect them.

TWENTY-SIX

On Saturday she met Daphne at Barnes & Noble, and then they went to lunch at the small café across the street. They sat at a small booth near the back of the restaurant, and Amber ordered a green salad with chicken. She was surprised when Daphne ordered a cheeseburger and fries, but said nothing.

"So, Jackson tells me you're doing an amazing job. Do you like it?"

"I do. It *is* a lot of work, but I really love it. I can't thank you enough for recommending me."

"I'm so glad. I knew you'd be great."

Amber looked at the package on the seat next to Daphne, which she'd been carrying all morning. "What's in the bag, Daph?"

"Oh, that. It's a bottle of perfume I have to return. It's the one I used to wear when Jackson and I met, and he loved it. I haven't worn it in a long time, so I decided to try it again, but I must be allergic now. Broke out in hives."

"That's terrible. What's it called?"

"Incomparable. Ha. That's how I felt when I wore it."

Their food arrived, and Daphne dug into the cheeseburger as if she hadn't eaten in days. "Mm. Delicious," she said.

"What was it like? You know, when you and Jackson were dating?"

"I was so young and inexperienced, but in some crazy way, I think that appealed to him. He'd been with so many glamour girls who knew their way around, I think he liked that he could take me to places I'd never been and show me things I'd never seen." She paused and had a faraway look in her eyes. "I hung on his every word." She looked back at Amber. "He likes to be adored, you know." She laughed. "And it's pretty easy to adore him. He's one of a kind."

"Yes, he is," Amber agreed.

"Anyway, I guess nothing stays the same. Of course, now things are different."

"What do you mean?"

"Oh, you know. Children come along. Things become routine. Lovemaking isn't as passionate. Sometimes you're just too tired, and sometimes you just don't feel like it."

"Must be especially hard when you have a new baby. It must be so exhausting. You read all the time about new moms having postpartum depression."

Daphne was quiet and looked down for a moment. With her eyes still fixed on the floor, she said, "I'm sure it's a terrible thing."

After a few awkward minutes, Amber tried again. "Well, anyway. Having children didn't seem to put the damper on your romance. Every time I'm with you guys, it's obvious that he's crazy about you."

Daphne smiled. "We've been through a lot together."

"I hope I have such a great marriage one day. Like you and Jackson. The perfect couple."

Daphne took a sip of her coffee and looked at Amber a long moment. "Marriage is hard work. If you love someone, you don't let anything destroy it."

This is getting interesting, Amber thought. "Like what?"

"There was a bump in the road. Right after Bella was born." She paused again, tilting her head. "There was an indiscretion."

"He cheated on you?"

Daphne nodded. "It was just once. I was exhausted. Busy with the baby. We hadn't made love in months." She shrugged. "Men have their needs. Plus, it took me a long time to get back in shape."

Was Daphne seriously justifying what he did? She was even more gullible than Amber thought.

"I'm not saying what he did was right. But he was sorry after and swore it would never happen again." She gave Amber what looked like a forced smile. "And he never has."

"Wow. That must have been so hard for you. But at least you bounced back. The two of you seem very happy," Amber said. She looked at her watch. "Well," she said. "I guess we should be going. I have a salon appointment to get to."

After their lunch, Amber went home and ordered a bottle of Incomparable online. She looked up from the computer and smiled to herself, relishing her new piece of intel. He'd cheated before! If he could do it once, he could surely do it again.

Monday brought with it drowning rain and cold winds, which soaked Amber as she waited for the train. The only thing Amber disliked about her job was the long commute into the city. It was fine to come in for a leisurely day of checking out museums, but rush-hour travel was its own special torture. As she sat, still windblown and wet, wedged between a large man who smelled of cigars and a young boy with a dirty backpack, she read the advertisements above the windows across from her. She could practically recite them by heart now. She wondered what it was like to see your picture on the walls of trains or the side of buses. Did the models get a kick out of it? She fantasized about being the object of desire for thousands of men. Her body was certainly good enough, and with the right hair and makeup, she bet she'd look every bit as good as those stuck-up models, even though she was just five-seven, a few inches shorter than Daphne. They probably thought they were so special, sticking their fingers down their throats just to stay skinny. She would never do that— but then again, she was lucky to be naturally thin.

By the time she arrived at Fifty-Seventh Street, the hems of her pants were almost dry. The rain had stopped, but the wind was still whipping furiously. She nodded at the doorman and said good morning to the guard at the front desk.

"Good morning, Miss Patterson. Filthy weather out there. You still manage to look perfect though. New hairstyle?"

She loved that they all knew who she was. "Yes, thanks." She swiped her ID badge and walked to the elevator. Her first stop when she got upstairs was the ladies' room. She pulled out her cordless flat iron and smoothed her hair, now shoulder length and a light-champagne blond. After she dabbed a drop of Incompa-rable on her wrists, the tennis shoes came off, and on went the nude Louboutins. She wore a black turtleneck sweater dress and a black lace push-up bra that beautifully enhanced her ample as-sets. On her wrist was a wide silver cuff bracelet. The only other jewelry were her earrings, hammered silver and stylishly simple. She smiled in the mirror, confident that she looked like she had just completed a Ralph Lauren photo shoot.

When she entered her office, she saw that Jackson's door was closed and the windows still dark. She made it her business to be there early every day, but Jackson still managed to beat her. To-day was a rare exception. She started answering e-mails, and the next time she looked up, it was eight thirty. Jackson sauntered in after ten.

"Good morning, Jackson. Everything okay?"

"Morning. Yeah, fine. Had a conference at Bella's school." He unlocked his office door and then stopped. "By the way, we have a show tonight. Would you make a six o'clock dinner reservation for two at Gabriel's?"

"Certainly."

He started to go inside but stopped again. "You look very nice today."

Amber felt the heat rise on her neck. "Thank you. That's very kind of you."

"Nothing kind about it. Just the truth." He walked into his office and closed the door.

The thought of Daphne and Jackson having a romantic dinner and then sitting side by side in a Broadway theater pissed her off. She wanted to be the one sitting next to him in those primo seats, everyone looking at her with envy. But she knew that she had to keep her head about her. It wouldn't serve her to lose her cool and do something stupid.

Later that afternoon, she and Jackson were going over his itinerary for next week's trip to China when Daphne called his cell. Amber heard only his side of the conversation, but it was apparent he wasn't pleased. He clicked off and threw the phone onto the desk. "Shit. Totally screws up the plans for tonight."

"Is Daphne all right?"

He closed his eyes and rubbed the bridge of his nose. "She's fine. So to speak. Says Bella's not well. Doesn't want to come in for the play."

"I'm sorry," Amber said. "Shall I cancel the reservation?"

Jackson thought about this a few seconds and then gave Amber an appraising look. "Any chance you'd be interested in dinner and a show?"

Amber felt her stomach drop. This was too easy, falling into her lap like a gift from the heavens. "I'd love to. I've never been to a Broadway show." She hadn't forgotten that he liked innocence and first-timers.

"Good. These tickets for *Hamlet* are a hot item, limited run, and I don't want to miss it. Let's finish up by five thirty or so and we'll grab a cab to the restaurant. Reservation's at six?"

"Yes."

"Good. Let's get back to work."

Amber went back to her desk and phoned Daphne, who answered after one ring.

"Daphne, it's Amber. Jackson told me Bella's not well. I hope it's nothing serious."

"No, I don't think so. Just some sniffles and a low-grade fever. You know, she just wants Mommy. I didn't want to leave her."

"Yes, I can understand why you wouldn't." She paused. "Jackson asked me to fill in for you tonight. I just wanted to let you know. You don't mind, do you?"

"Of course I don't mind. I think it's a great idea. Enjoy yourself."

"Okay. Thanks, Daphne. I hope Bella's feeling better soon."

For once, Amber was filled with gratitude for the little nuisance.

They left the office at five thirty on the dot. She felt a rush sitting next to him in the taxi. It was better than the best high she'd ever experienced. When they walked into the restaurant, she was pleased by the admiring glances of those around her. Amber knew she looked good, and the man with his hand on her back was one of the richest men in the room. They were seated at a table in a quiet corner of the posh restaurant, bathed in candlelight.

"Wow, I've never been in a restaurant like this."

"This was one of the first places I brought Daphne when we started dating."

Daphne was the last thing Amber wanted to talk about, but if he insisted, maybe she could spin it to her advantage. "Daphne's talked a lot about your dating days, how different it was then."

He sat back in his chair and smiled. "Different? Yes, it was different then. There's nothing like the rush that comes with falling in love. And I fell hard, that's for sure. I'd never met anyone like her." He took a sip of wine, and once again, Amber admired his fine hands.

"Sounds like you were made for each other." She practically had to choke the words out.

He put the glass down and nodded. "Daphne has grown into such an amazing woman over the years. I look at all she's accomplished and am so proud of her. I have the perfect wife."

Amber almost gagged on her salad. Just when she thought he might be noticing the changes in her, the new, stylish, and attractive Amber, he was going on about his golden wife.

They talked mostly about business after that, and he treated her as any colleague he might have been dining with. When they got to the theater and took their seats—in a box—she let herself imagine again what it would be like to be married to him. If only he were interested in her as a woman and not just an assistant, the night would have been perfect.

When the curtain fell at eleven, Amber was not ready to end the evening. There were still plenty of bustling crowds on the street, and it looked as if all the restaurants and cafés were filled with patrons.

As they strolled toward Times Square, Jackson looked at his watch. "It's getting late, and we have an early day tomorrow—the meeting with Whitcomb Properties."

"I'm wide awake. Not tired at all," she said.

"You might feel different when your alarm—" He stopped

midsentence. "You're going to be exhausted in the morning. Daphne and I were going to stay at the apartment tonight, and when she couldn't make it, I told her I was going to go ahead and stay by myself. You could stay in the guest room. It seems foolish for you to take a train at this late hour, and you've stayed with us in the city before. I suppose the only problem is clothing."

"I'm sure Daphne wouldn't mind if I borrow something. After all, she lent me a designer gown for the fund-raiser. I'm only one size smaller than she is." Amber hoped he didn't miss the comparison.

"Okay, then." Jackson hailed a cab, and Amber sank back into the seat, happy with this turn of events.

The taxi let them off in front of an uptown building, and they walked under the long canopy to the entrance. "Good evening, Mr. Parrish." The doorman's face showed no reaction to Amber, whether because of discretion or lack of interest, she didn't know.

The private elevator opened directly into the foyer of the large space. It was unlike their house, a more modern and minimalist design, all in shades of white and gray. The focal points were the paintings on the walls, abstract art with bursts of color that fused it all together. She took it all in, overwhelmed.

"I'm going to grab a nightcap," Jackson said. "The guest bedroom is the third door on the right. Fresh towels and toothbrushes, everything you might need. But before that, why don't you take a look in Daphne's closet and pick something out for the morning?" He went to the glass cart that held bottles and decanters and poured himself a scotch.

"Okay. I won't be long." She walked into the sumptuous bedroom, wanting nothing more than for Jackson to swoop in and throw her onto the king-size bed. Instead, she searched the bureau for Daphne's lingerie. She pondered again the evidence of an uptight Daphne whose drawers were in such order as to be almost laughable. Pulling out black lace panties, she held them up and nodded. They would do. Next, she went to the closet, where each garment was evenly spaced, just as it was at home. She took out a delicious red Armani suit and white camisole. *Perfect. Now the stockings.* She opened several drawers before finding them and chose a pair of sheer and silky thigh-highs in beige. She'd look like a million bucks tomorrow.

Amber grabbed her items and reluctantly left the bedroom.

Jackson looked up from his drink. "All set?"

"Yes. Thank you, Jackson. It's been a wonderful evening."

"Glad you enjoyed it. Good night," he said and gave a little nod as he headed toward his bedroom.

The guest room was supplied to fulfill every possible need, just as Jackson had said. Amber stripped out of the day's clothes, showered, brushed her teeth, and got into bed. She relaxed into the soft feather mattress that seemed to hug her and pulled the down comforter up to her chin. It felt like she was resting on a cloud, but she was having a difficult time falling asleep, knowing that Jackson was lying in bed just a few rooms away. She hoped he would feel how much she lusted for him, and find his way into her bed, where he'd forget all about his perfect wife. After what seemed like an eternity, she realized it wasn't going to happen and fell into a fitful sleep.

The next morning, after she'd showered and dressed, she phoned Daphne to let her know she'd spent the night. She didn't want to give Daphne any reason to distrust her. Everything aboveboard—as far as Daphne was concerned, anyway. And Daphne, in her usual sweet manner, assured Amber that it was perfectly fine.

TWENTY-SEVEN

Now that Amber had a front-row seat to the finances under-pinning Daphne's world, she understood why Daphne always looked fantastic—who wouldn't, with that kind of money? From the top of her head to the bottom of her loofahed feet, people ministered to her on a daily basis. Amber got a taste of it when Daphne invited her to a small dinner party at the Parrish home. That's where Amber met Gregg, the perfect antidote to her paltry wallet.

They were seated next to each other at the dinner for fourteen. Gregg was young, and although he was good-looking, Amber thought his chin weak and the reddish tint to his hair not to her liking. But the more she examined him, the more she saw that other women would probably find him very attractive. It was just next to Jackson that he didn't measure up.

With so many individual conversations going on around the table, it was easy for Gregg to monopolize her for almost the entire evening. Amber found the conversation banal and Gregg boring beyond belief. He talked on and on about his work at the family's hugely successful accounting firm.

"It's so fascinating to see how it all balances out, how per-fectly it comes out in the end." He was talking about the profit-and-loss statements, and Amber thought she'd rather have been having a root canal than listening to him talk about these stu-pid numbers.

"I'm sure it's incredible. But tell me, what do you do outside of work? You know, what kinds of hobbies do you have?" Amber had asked, hoping he might get the message.

"Ah, hobbies. Well, let's see. I golf, of course, and I home-brew my own beer. I play bridge. Really enjoy that."

Was he for real? Amber examined his face to see if he was putting her on, but no, he'd been perfectly serious.

"How about you?" Gregg asked.

"I love art, so I visit museums whenever I can. I love to swim, and I've come to enjoy kayaking. I read a lot."

"I don't read much. I feel like, why read about someone else's life when you should be out living your own?"

Amber kept herself from spitting out her food in astonishment and simply nodded. "That's an interesting take on books. Never heard that one before."

Gregg smiled as if she'd handed him a blue ribbon or something.

She'd decided he would be useful, if tough to endure. He'd serve her purposes for the time being. He'd be her temporary ticket to dinners out, plays, and posh events. She figured she could easily get him to buy her expensive presents. She'd keep him by her side and hope that Jackson would look at him as a rival. She'd already seen his watchful eye on them tonight at dinner. And she'd seen too that Daphne looked pleased at Amber's apparent attentiveness to Gregg. But Amber wasn't interested in someone with a rich daddy. She wanted the rich daddy himself.

In the meantime, she strung Gregg along, letting him take her out to nice restaurants and buy her presents. He'd already sent her flowers to the office twice since the dinner, and she was delighted that Jackson looked none too pleased when he picked up the card and read it. She supposed Gregg was nice enough and good-looking in his way, but he was such a dolt. Boring as an old shoe. He was a good cover, though, and as she moved her plan into overdrive, he would serve her well in making sure Daphne didn't get suspicious or suddenly jealous of her.

A month had gone by since she and Gregg met at Daphne's dinner party, and tonight they were all having dinner at the country club. She'd manipulated Daphne into it the other night on the phone.

"I really want the four of us to get together," she said on the phone. "But I don't think Jackson wants to socialize with me, since I work for him."

Daphne hadn't answered right away. "What do you mean?" she finally asked.

"Well, you and I are so close. Best friends. And I want Gregg to get to know you, since I always tell him how we're like sisters. He's tried to arrange it with Jackson, but he always makes an excuse. Can you get him to do it?"

Of course Daphne had. She would pretty much do anything Amber wanted; Amber'd play the little-sister card, and Daphne would fold.

She suspected that Jackson was a snob at heart and didn't consider her worthy of him socially. She didn't hold it against him; she'd feel the same in his position. But she also noticed the way his body stayed a little closer to her when they were reviewing a document, the way his eyes held hers just a moment longer than necessary. And when he saw her with Gregg, she hoped the seeds of jealousy would take root and hasten the seduction.

She took her time getting dressed and dabbed on the perfume that Daphne was now allergic to. Maybe it would make her eyes water, Amber thought spitefully. The dress was just low-cut enough to show off her cleavage, but not so low as to be slutty. She wore five-inch heels, wanting to be taller than Daphne for a change since Daphne had hurt her ankle playing tennis and was stuck in sensible shoes until it healed.

Gregg picked her up right on time, and she ran down the stairs to his waiting Mercedes convertible. She loved slipping into the luxurious car and being seen in it as they drove around. Sometimes he let Amber drive it, and she loved the feel of this singularly superior vehicle. Gregg loved pampering her, and she milked it for all it was worth.

She got in, admiring the saddle leather, and leaned in close to kiss him. He was a good kisser at least, and when she closed her eyes, she could pretend it was Jackson's tongue in her mouth.

"Mmm, you're delicious," she said, sliding back over. "But we'd better get going. Don't want to keep Daphne and Jackson waiting."

Gregg took a deep breath and nodded. "I'd much rather sit here kissing you."

Even his lines were dull. She feigned desire. "Me too, but you promised you'd take it slow. I told you how hurt I was in my last relationship. I'm not ready yet." She gave him a pretty pout.

He took off, and they made small talk on the way to the club. They pulled through the gates right behind Jackson's Porsche Spyder.

"Park next to them, and we can walk in together."

She wanted Jackson to see her walking next to Daphne.

Daphne and she got out of their cars at the same time, and Amber walked over to give her a kiss, noticing that Daphne was carrying the new Hermès purse.

"Good timing!" Daphne smiled and gave her arm a squeeze.

"Love your bag," Amber said, trying to make herself sound sincere.

"Oh, thanks." She shrugged. "Just a little gift from Jackson." She looked over at him and smiled. "He's so good to me."

"Lucky lady," Amber said, wanting to spit.

The four of them walked in together, and Amber had to struggle to keep her eyes off Jackson and on Gregg.

After they'd been seated and gotten their drinks, Gregg lifted his glass. "Cheers. So glad we were finally able to get together." He put his arm around Amber. "I can't thank you enough for introducing me to this gem."

Amber leaned over next to Gregg and kissed him. When she sat back up, she tried to gauge Jackson's reaction, but his expression was unchanged.

"We're glad it worked out. I had a feeling you two would be perfect for each other," Daphne answered.

Amber snuck a glance at Jackson. He was frowning. Good. Licking her lips, she raised her glass of wine and took a long swallow, then looked at Gregg.

"You were right; this is a better choice than the house cabernet. I wish I knew as much about wines as you."

"I'll teach you," he answered with a smile.

"Actually," Jackson said, "the 1987 vintage was better." He gave Gregg an apologetic look. "Sorry, old chap, but I'm something of a sommelier. I'll order a bottle, and you'll taste the difference."

"No worries. That's the year I was born, so it was a good year," Gregg answered, perfectly seriously.

Amber had to struggle to keep from laughing. Gregg had put Jackson in his place even though he was too thick to realize it. But of course Jackson picked up on it right away. No matter how much more money or smarts Jackson had, he couldn't make himself fifteen years younger.

"Obviously age is what makes a wine so much more desirable. The older the better," Amber said, slowly moving her tongue along her lips and looking at Jackson.

TWENTY-EIGHT

Amber was about to get a new glimpse into the Parrishes' life. When she did the bills, she had seen that they rented a house on Lake Winnipesaukee from Memorial Day to Labor Day, although they probably used it less than an accumulated four weeks. Amber was curious to see what kind of place warranted such an exorbitant rental fee, and today she would. She was waiting for Daphne to pick her up for a weekend at the lake house in New Hampshire. Jackson was on another of his many business trips abroad.

At 8:30 sharp, the white Range Rover pulled up. Daphne jumped out of the car and opened the back hatch for Amber's luggage.

"Good morning." Daphne hugged her and then took the bag from her. "So glad you're coming with us."

"Me too."

It was a four-and-a-half-hour drive to Wolfeboro, but it seemed to go quickly with the girls sleepy and quiet in the back as Amber and Daphne chatted up front.

"How are things at the office? Are you still liking it now with all the responsibilities?"

"I really love it. Jackson's a great boss." She looked at Daphne. "But you must know that."

"I'm glad. By the way, I never thanked you for pinch-hitting for me the time you went to see *Hamlet* with him. Did you enjoy it?"

"I did. It was so different to see it onstage. I'm sorry you had to miss it."

"I'm not a huge Shakespeare fan." Daphne chuckled. "I know that's an awful thing to admit, but I'm more suited to Broadway musicals. Jackson, on the other hand, adores Shakespeare." She took her eyes from the road and glanced briefly at Amber. "He has tickets to *The Tempest*. I think it's the week after next. Since you enjoyed *Hamlet*, if you don't mind, I'll ask him to take you instead."

"I'm sure he would want you to go." Amber didn't want to seem overly anxious.

"He'll love the idea of introducing you to more Shakespeare. And besides, you'd be doing me a big favor. I'd much rather be at home with the girls than listening to language I don't understand half of."

This was too delicious. Daphne was practically handing Jackson to her on the proverbial silver platter. "Well, when you put it that way, I guess it would be okay."

"Good. That's settled, then."

"Will your mom be coming to stay at all? I imagine she's not too far from here."

She noticed Daphne's hand tighten on the wheel. "New Hampshire's bigger than you think. She's actually a couple of hours away."

Amber waited for her to go on, but there was an awkward silence. She decided not to press it. A few minutes later, Daphne looked in the rearview mirror and spoke to the girls.

"We've got about an hour left. Everyone okay, or do we need a bathroom break?"

The girls said they were fine, and Amber and Daphne chatted about their plans for the rest of the day once they got to the house.

They arrived at the charming little town of Wolfeboro around lunchtime and continued to the lake house, passing mile after mile of sparkling water and verdant hillsides. The homes along the banks were an exciting combination of old and new, some imposingly important and others small and eclectic. Amber was enchanted by the clear call of summer pleasures that seemed to hover over everything. Daphne pulled into the driveway, and the moment they opened the doors, the smell of honeysuckle and pine filled the car. Amber stepped onto the gravel, which was covered in pine needles, and breathed in the fresh air. This was paradise.

"If everyone grabs something, we can do this in one trip," Daphne called from the back of the Rover.

Bags in hand, with even Bella helping out, they walked down the dirt path leading to the house. Amber stopped and stared, openmouthed, at the structure in front of her, an immense three-story cedar house abounding with porches, balconies, and white railings. Beyond it stood a large octagonal gazebo and a small boathouse that overlooked the pristine waters.

The inside of the house was homey and comfortable, with old pine floors and cushioned furniture that invited relaxation. The front porch spanned the entire front of the house and looked over the lake.

"Mom, Mom, Mom." Bella had already gone upstairs and changed into her bathing suit. "Can we go swimming now?"

"In a bit, sweetheart. Wait till we all get into our swimsuits."

Bella plopped herself onto one of the sofas to wait.

The lake water was cold and clean. It took a while for them all to get used to it, but soon they were squealing and splashing and laughing. Amber and Daphne took a break and sat on the edge of the pier, legs dangling in the water as they watched the girls swim. The afternoon sun warmed their shoulders as the cold lake water dripped from their hair.

Daphne kicked up a splash of water and turned to Amber. "You know," she said, "I feel closer to you than anyone I know. It's almost as if I have my sister back." She looked out over the lake. "This is exactly what Julie and I would be doing now if she were alive—sitting here watching the girls, just enjoying being together."

Amber tried to think of a sympathetic response and then said, "It's very sad. I understand."

"I know you do. It hurts me to think of all the things I would love to be sharing with her. But now, with you, I can do that. It's not the same, of course, and I know you understand what I mean. But it makes me a little happier that we can make it hurt less."

"Just think, when Bella and Tallulah are grown, they'll sit together like this. It's nice that they'll have each other."

"You're right. But I've always felt it was a shame we didn't have more."

"Did Jackson want to stop at two?"

Daphne leaned back and looked up at the sky. "Quite the opposite. He was desperate for a son." She squinted and put her hand up to shield her eyes from the light. Turning to Amber, she said, "It never happened though. We tried and tried, but I never got pregnant after Bella."

"I'm sorry," Amber said. "Did you think of trying fertility treatments?"

Daphne shook her head. "I didn't want to be greedy. I felt like we'd been blessed with two healthy children, and I should be grateful for that. It was really only because Jackson had always wanted a boy." She shrugged. "He talked about having a little Jackson Junior."

"It could still happen. Right?"

"I guess anything is possible. But I've given up hoping for it."

Amber nodded solemnly, though she was dancing inside. So he wanted a boy, and Daphne couldn't deliver. This was the best news yet.

They were both quiet, and then Daphne spoke again. "I've been thinking; you shouldn't have to do that commute every day while the apartment is just sitting there, empty. You're more than welcome to stay at the apartment the nights Jackson isn't there."

Amber was genuinely floored. "I don't know what to say."

Daphne put her hand on top of Amber's. "Say nothing. That's what friends are for."

TWENTY-NINE

A mber was looking forward to sleeping in Daphne's bed tonight. She was going to take Daphne up on her offer to use
the apartment for the weekend. Since it was the last week in Au-
gust, and Jackson had been telecommuting from the lake, the
apartment was available. Amber had no big plans for the weekend, so she'd spend Saturday roaming around Manhattan. She
texted Daphne to let her know and to thank her.

She hadn't been there in a while and was taken aback again at
the sheer elegance and luxury. She imagined that bastard back
home and his snotty mother—if they could see her in this palatial
apartment! She flung off her heels and stepped barefoot onto the
fluffy carpet. Then, sinking into the white, half-moon sofa, she
surveyed her surroundings with pleasure. It almost felt as if it
were hers. She put her head back and closed her eyes, feeling incredibly indulged. After a few minutes, she went into the master
bedroom to search for a robe.

Amber chose a gorgeous Fleur number in silk and lace. It felt
like a warm, sultry breeze gliding over her skin. Next, she opened
Daphne's drawers and picked a white pair of Fox & Rose lace panties that made her feel like a seductress—not that she had anyone to
seduce, but it felt good nonetheless. She went into the bathroom and
brushed out her long hair, now even blonder from her frequent trips
to the salon. It fell loosely around her shoulders, thick and shiny.
Maybe not as beautiful as Daphne, but certainly younger.

She looked over at the bed, which was covered in a downy

pale-green comforter. She would sleep here tonight and pretend it was all hers, see how it felt to be Daphne. She sat on the bed and bounced a few times, and then she lay down and spread out. It was like being hugged by a thousand clouds. How lovely it would be to wake up whatever time she chose in this heavenly room and then explore the city. What could be a more perfect Friday and Saturday?

Amber nestled a little longer. The rumbling in her stomach reminded her that she hadn't eaten since breakfast. She reluctantly rose and padded into the kitchen. She'd picked up a salad from the market, and she scraped it out of its container and onto one of Daphne's china plates. She'd opened a bottle of malbec earlier and now poured herself a glass. After her dinner, she put a few jazz CDs in the player and sat with her second glass of wine, thinking about what she would do tomorrow. Maybe the Guggenheim or the Whitney. The third disc was playing when Amber heard a noise outside the apartment. She bolted to a standing position and listened. Yes. Definitely. It was the elevator. Suddenly, the doors opened and Jackson walked in.

He looked surprised. "Amber. What are you doing here?"

She pulled the robe tighter around herself. "I, uh, I . . . Daphne gave me a key and said I could use it if I was too tired to get the train. She said she told you. I figured with all of you at the lake, it would be empty. I'm sorry. I had no idea you were coming." She blushed.

He dropped his briefcase and shook his head. "It's fine. I should have let you know."

"I thought you were staying at the lake until Sunday night."

"It's a long story. Let's just say I've had better weeks."

"Well, I'll go and get my things and get out of your way." She hated to go, but figured he'd expect her to offer.

He shook his head and moved past her toward the bedroom. "It's late, you should feel free to stay till morning. I'm going to go change."

She heard him on the phone, but couldn't make out what he was saying. He stayed in the bedroom for close to an hour, and Amber wondered if he was ever going to come out. She debated changing from the robe into some clothes, but decided against it. She had a good feeling about tonight. She sat back down with her glass of wine and a magazine, waiting for him.

He finally came out, got a drink, and sat down on the other end of the sofa. He seemed to register what she was wearing for the first time. "That robe looks nice on you. A little tight for Daphne lately."

"She's gained a little weight. It happens to the best of us," Amber said, choosing her words carefully.

"She's not been herself lately."

"I've noticed that too. Whenever we're together, she seems distracted, like something's on her mind."

"Has she said anything to you? About being unhappy or anything?"

"I really wouldn't want to repeat anything she's said to me, Jackson."

He sat up straight. "So she *has* said something to you."

"Please, if she's not happy, that's something you and Daphne need to discuss."

"She told you she's not happy?"

"Well, not in so many words. I don't know. I don't want to betray a confidence."

He took a long swallow from his glass. "Amber, if there's something I should know, something that can help, then tell me. Please."

"I don't think you want to hear what I have to say."

"Tell me."

She let out a sigh and allowed the robe to fall open just enough to show a teasing bit of cleavage. "Daphne told me the sex is boring and routine. And that she's thrilled every month when she gets her period and knows she's not pregnant." She pretended to look nervous. "But please don't tell her I told you. She told me how much you want a boy, and she might not want you to know she doesn't feel the same way."

He was speechless.

"I'm sorry, Jackson. I didn't want to tell you, but you're right: you have a right to know how she feels. Just . . . please . . . don't say anything to Daphne."

He remained silent, his face red and set with a grim expression that Amber saw only rarely. He was furious.

She rose from the sofa and walked toward him. She made sure her robe opened slightly against her leg as she approached him. She stood in front of him and put her hand on his cheek. "Whatever is going on, I'm sure it will pass. How could anyone be unhappy with you, Jackson?"

He took her hand from his face and held it. Amber ran her other hand through his hair and he moaned, but then slowly pushed her away. "Forgive me, Amber. I'm not myself."

She sat next to him. "I understand. It's hard when you discover someone you love doesn't want the same thing you do."

He gazed steadily at her. "Did she really say those things? That she was happy every time she knew she wasn't pregnant?"

"She did. I'm sorry."

"I can't believe it. We've talked about how wonderful it would be. I just can't believe it." He put his head in his hands, his elbows resting on his knees.

Amber caressed his back. "Please don't tell Daphne I told you. She made me promise to keep her secret." She thought for a moment and then decided to go all the way. "You know," she said sadly, "she was kind of laughing about it, about how she fooled you and you never even realized." She prayed the lie wouldn't blow up in her face, but she needed to move this game forward.

When Jackson looked up at her, his eyes were filled with confusion and pain. "She laughed about it? How could she?"

She put her arms around his neck and pulled him close to her. "I don't understand it either. Let me help you," she said, kissing his cheek.

He pushed her away again. "Amber, no. This is wrong."

"Wrong? And what she's done is right? Betraying you? Laughing at you?" Amber rose and stood before him once again. "Let me make you feel good. It doesn't have to change anything."

He shook his head. "I can't think right now."

"I'm here for you. That's all you have to think about." She slowly untied the sash of her robe and let it fall from her shoulders, standing before him in only the lace panties. He looked up at her, and she pulled his head toward her until it was buried against her belly. She pushed him back so she could straddle his lap, and once she had, she put her mouth against his ear and whispered how much she wanted him as she moved her hips and ground against him.

She found his lips and thrust her tongue deep inside his mouth. She felt his resistance weaken as he pulled her closer to him and returned her kiss.

Their lovemaking was fierce and powerful. They barely let go of each other when they moved into the bedroom in the middle of the night. Finally, at dawn, they fell into a deep and satisfying slumber.

Amber awoke first. She turned on her side and looked at Jackson, sleeping next to her. He had been an expert lover, an added bonus and one she hadn't expected. She was so used to planning every move that it now seemed impossible that their being alone together in the apartment had happened so serendipitously. She closed her eyes and lay back against the pillow. Jackson stirred beside her, and then she felt his hand gliding up her thigh.

They stayed in bed until after twelve, dozing off and on. Amber was still half asleep when Jackson got up to shower and dress. He was in the kitchen making coffee when she came out, now in a long white T-shirt of Daphne's.

"Good morning, Superman." She moved toward him, but he backed away.

"Listen, Amber. This can't happen again. I'm sorry. I love Daphne. I would never want to hurt her. You understand, don't you?"

Amber felt as if she'd been struck. She took a moment to think things through, to alter her game plan. There was no way she was going to let him cast her aside. "Of course I understand, Jackson. Daphne's my best friend, and the last thing I would ever want is for her to be hurt. But don't beat yourself up. You're a man, and you have needs. There's no reason for you to be ashamed of that. I'm here for you whenever you want. Just between us. Daphne doesn't need to know."

Jackson looked at her. "That's hardly fair to you."

"I would do anything for you, so hear me again: Whenever you want. No questions asked, no strings attached, and no spilling secrets." She put her arms around his neck and felt his close around her.

"You're making it impossible for me to resist you," he whispered, his lips against her ear.

She pulled slightly away and looked up into his eyes as her hand moved below his waist to caress him.

"Ah." He put his head back and closed his eyes in pleasure.

"Why would you try to resist me?" Her voice was silky. "I told you. I'm here for you. Come to me for whatever you need. Our little secret."

THIRTY

Amber clutched a silky pillow to her, closing her eyes to get a few more minutes of sleep. She and Jackson had been sleeping together for over two months now, and they had stayed up all night making love. She was drifting off again when she felt him shaking her arm.

"You've got to get up. I forgot! Matilda's here to clean."

Her eyes flew open. "What should I do?"

"Get dressed! Go in the guest room and make it look like you stayed there last night. We'll have to make something up for Daphne."

Annoyed, she threw on the robe at the foot of the bed and ran down the hallway to the guest room. Would it be so terrible if Daphne found out? Yes, it was too soon. She had to make sure he was firmly in her grasp before anything happened to jeopardize her position. Outside of his office she was the consummate professional, but inside, with the door shut, she used every trick at her disposal to make sure he couldn't get enough of her. It got a little tiresome—especially his affinity for blow jobs—but she could retire her services after she had a ring on her finger. And afterward, she demanded nothing and went about the day as if they had nothing more than a professional relationship. They usually stayed together at the apartment a few nights a week. She loved that the best. Waking up next to him, in that fabulous apartment, as if it was all hers. Now she made sure to schedule late appointments and dinners for him so he'd be more inclined to spend the night, and she always had an overnight bag at the ready.

It was becoming harder and harder to play the part of Daphne's best friend. She hated having to pretend that she was nothing more than Jackson's assistant; that she didn't know every inch of his body probably better than his own wife did. For now, though, she had to play it cool. But when Daphne phoned to send her on an errand, she was livid.

"Amber, dear. Can you do me a big favor?" Daphne had asked.

"What is it, Daphne?"

"Bella has a party to go to and needs an accessory for one of her American Girl dolls. I just can't get into the city in time. Would you mind picking it up for me and bringing it to the house?"

She damn well did mind. She wasn't Daphne's servant. Amber had planned to stay overnight at the apartment, but now she had to change her plans.

"Certainly, Daphne, what is it?" she said with a distinct lack of enthusiasm.

"She wants the Pretty City Carriage. They're going to pretend they're in Central Park. I've called and charged it already. They're holding it in your name."

Amber was still fuming when her train got in to Bishops Harbor just before six. She took a cab right to their house and wondered if Jackson had returned from his business trip yet.

When she arrived, Daphne was in the kitchen with the girls, and Jackson was nowhere in sight.

"Ah, you're a doll. Thank you!" Daphne gushed. Tilting her

head toward Bella, she went on, "I would have had a major melt-down on my hands if you hadn't come through."

Amber forced a smile. "Can't have that."

"Drink?" Daphne held up a bottle of red wine, half empty. It was a little early for her, Amber thought.

"Just one. I have a date with Gregg tonight," she lied. She didn't want to get stuck here all night. "I see you've gotten a head start."

Daphne shrugged and poured a glass for Amber. "TGIF."

Amber accepted the glass and took a sip. "Thanks. Where's Jackson?"

Daphne rolled her eyes. "In his office, where else?" She lowered her voice so the girls wouldn't hear and stood closer to Amber. "Honestly, he's been gone all week, and the first thing he does when he gets home is complain that Bella left her shoes in the hall." She shook her head. "Sometimes it's easier when he's away."

Don't worry, honey, Amber wanted to tell her. *You won't have to put up with it for long.* She put on her concerned face instead. "You're ruining my fantasy of marriage." She laughed.

"It's okay. After he cooled down, he and I had a little afternoon delight. It was the first time in a while." She put her hand up to her mouth. "I can't believe I just told you that! Enough about me, tell me more about what's going on with Gregg." She linked her arm in Amber's, and they went into the sunroom, Daphne calling over her shoulder, "Sabine, please give the girls their baths when they've finished eating."

"I need to use the restroom," Amber said as she hurried past her. She went in and slammed the door, her back against it. Was he getting tired of her already? Daphne's smug expression infuriated her. It began as a tingling in her fingers, and then she was digging her fingernails into her hands to stop from screaming.

She was a furnace, ready to explode, adrenaline pumping through her so fast that she couldn't catch her breath. She wanted to break something. Her eyes went to the delicate green glass turtle on the shelf in front of her. She picked it up and threw it on the floor and stomped on it with both feet, grinding the pieces into the carpet. She hoped Daphne cut her feet on them. She flung the door open and headed back to the sunroom. This is what happened when he got out of her sight for too long. She would have to do something about it, and fast.

Daphne patted the seat next to her when Amber walked in. "So, spill. How's it going with Gregg?"

As far as Gregg was concerned, she saw him just enough to keep Daphne's suspicions at bay. She'd go to dinner with him, usually on a Friday or Saturday night, or she'd play the occasional tennis game at the club with him. He believed her story that she needed more time to get over the abusive ex-boyfriend she'd invented—the one that no one else but he "knew" about.

"He's very sweet and attentive. I don't see him as much as I'd like because of work." She put her hand up. "Not that I'm complaining. I appreciate my job, believe me."

Daphne smiled. "I know that. Don't worry. The boss's wife won't say anything."

Amber was inwardly seething. "I don't think of you as the boss's wife."

Daphne raised an eyebrow.

Amber reached out and squeezed her hand. "What I mean is, I think of you as my best friend. If I do ever get married, I'd want you to be my matron of honor."

"Aw. You're sweet. I'm probably a little old for that, though?"

Amber shook her head. "Of course not. Forty isn't old."

"Excuse me! I'm thirty-eight. Don't push me over the hill yet."

She knew exactly how old Daphne was. But really, thirty-eight, forty—what did it matter? Amber was twenty-six. There was no competing with that. "Sorry, Daph. I'm awful with ages. You look young, anyway."

"Oh, before I forget, I've got some clothes I'm getting rid of but thought I'd see if you want any of them first," Daphne said.

Amber didn't need her castoffs. She had a whole new wardrobe of her own, thanks to Jackson. But she couldn't show her hand—not yet.

"That's so nice. I'd love to look at them. Why don't you want them anymore? Do they not fit?" She couldn't resist.

The color rose in Daphne's cheeks. "Excuse me?"

Amber looked at the floor. How was she going to get out of this one? Before she could say anything else, Daphne spoke again.

"I *have* gained weight. I can't seem to stop snacking. I eat when I'm stressed, and I'm worried about Jackson. He's acting strange, and I don't understand it." She sighed loudly.

"Oh, Daph. I wasn't sure if I should tell you, but he *has* been spending lots of time with one of his vice presidents. She's a new hire, and her name is Bree. I don't know if anything's going on, but they've been taking some awfully long lunches . . ." Bree was a knockout who had started there a few weeks ago. Amber had actually been wary of her and ready to do some sabotage until she found out Bree was a lesbian. But Daphne didn't know that. Bree and Jackson had been working a lot together, but it was perfectly innocent—and now Daphne would start nagging him about her and drive him right back into Amber's arms.

Daphne's hand flew to her mouth. "I know who you mean. She's gorgeous."

Amber bit her lip. "I know. She's a real snake too. I've seen the way she looks at him. She's always putting a hand on his arm or crossing her legs and wearing short skirts. She's rude to me too, suddenly going straight to Jackson to make an appointment like she has special access or something."

"What should I do?"

Amber raised her brows. "I know what I'd do if it were me."

"What?"

"I'd tell him to get rid of her."

Daphne shook her head. "I can't do that. It's his business. He'll think I'm crazy."

Amber pretended to think. "I know. Go talk to her."

"I can't do that!"

"Sure you can. You come to the office and very quietly tell her that you're on to her, and if she values her job she'd better leave your husband alone."

"You really think so?"

"Do you want to lose him?"

"Of course not."

"Then, yes, get your tail in there and show her who's really boss. I'll make sure to keep him occupied while you do, so he doesn't find out."

Daphne took a deep breath. "Maybe you're right."

Amber smiled. It was perfect—Daphne would embarrass him at his office, which would make him livid. "I'll be behind you all the way."

THIRTY-ONE

I t was becoming more difficult to keep Gregg out of her bed. Not that she would have minded taking him for a spin—he was a decent enough kisser, and she could tell he was more than willing to please her. But she couldn't risk it. When she got pregnant, it would be with Jackson's kid, not Gregg's. Besides, as soon as her position with Jackson was assured, she'd be kicking Gregg to the curb. All she had to do until then was what she'd learned best in high school. Pushing herself up off her knees, she brushed his stomach with her lips, then kissed him on the lips before going into the bathroom to wash her mouth out. He was still standing there, a dazed look on his face, pants around his ankles.

He gave her a sheepish look and pulled his trousers up. "Sorry. You're really out of this world, baby." He pulled her to him, and she had to resist the urge to squirm out of his arms. "When are you going to be ready to make love? I don't know how much longer I can take this."

"I know, me too. My doctor said I need to wait another six weeks. Then everything will be healed up. It's killing me too." He was getting impatient, and she'd had to make up a new excuse. She told a lame story about having some cysts removed that necessitated holding off on intercourse. When she'd started to get graphic, he'd put his hands up and told her to stop, that he didn't need to know the details.

"Better get dressed, we'll be late for the play if we don't start dinner soon," she said sweetly. *Snap out of it*, she wanted to say.

They had come into New York to see *Fiddler on the Roof* and were spending the night at his parents' apartment across from Central Park. Amber had wanted to see *Book of Mormon*, but when she'd mentioned it, Gregg had said he wasn't interested in seeing a religious play.

She'd stupidly agreed to prepare dinner for them before the show—packaged grilled chicken over minute rice and a green salad. Now she was rummaging through cabinets for pots, bowls, and utensils when she felt Gregg bump into her from behind. She turned around and stared at him.

"Oh, sorry," he said. "I was trying to help you find things."

"I've found everything I need," she answered curtly.

As Amber turned on the faucet to fill the pot, Gregg's arm reached out in front of her.

"What are you doing?" she asked.

"I'm trying to help you. I was going to take the pot from you and put it on the stove."

"I think I can handle that," she said, walking to the stove, but Gregg ran ahead of her to turn the burner on, and they collided. The pot bobbled in Amber's hand, and water flew everywhere, soaking the front of Amber's dress.

"Oh my gosh. Are you okay?" Gregg said, grabbing a tea towel and pressing it against Amber's dress.

Are you a flipping moron? she almost yelled, but instead smiled thinly and said, "I'm fine. How about you go sit down, and I'll finish in here?"

They arrived at the Broadway Theatre in plenty of time, and he went to the bar to get them each a drink. Amber looked around at the magnificent theater while she waited, admiring the grand chandelier in the opulent lobby of red and gold. Gregg returned with their drinks, two glasses of white wine, even though she'd repeatedly told him she preferred red. Did the moron ever listen?

"I think you'll be pleased with the seats. Front-row orchestra," he said, brandishing the tickets with a flourish.

"Great. A front-row seat to all that singing." Amber had seen the movie, and she didn't really get what all the fuss was about. *Fiddler* was old news as far as she was concerned. These were his parents' tickets, and apparently even they weren't interested in going.

"Have you seen it before?" she asked.

He nodded. "Seven times. It's my favorite play. I just love the music."

"Wow, seven times. That must be a record," Amber said, looking distractedly around the lobby.

Gregg stood up straighter and said with pride, "My family are quite the theater aficionados. Dad buys tickets to all the best shows."

"How nice for you."

"Yes, it is. He's a great man."

"And what about you?" Amber asked without much interest.

"What do you mean?"

"Are you a great man?" she said, playing with him.

Gregg chuckled. "I will be one day, Amber. I am being groomed right now to be a great man," he said, looking at her in earnest. "And I hope you will be by my side."

Amber controlled the urge to laugh in his face and instead said, "We'll see, Gregg, we'll see. Shall we go take our seats now?"

Amber found she was enjoying the play despite her earlier reservations. Just when she'd begun to think the evening wasn't such a waste after all, Gregg started tapping his foot in time to the music. Next he was humming along, and the people around them began to look over.

"Gregg!" she hissed under her breath.

"Huh?"

"You're humming."

"Sorry! It's just so catchy."

He quieted down, but then began to bob his head back and forth in time to the music. She wanted to slug him.

Three hours later, they left the theater. Amber came away with a headache.

"Feel like a drink?" Gregg asked.

"I guess." Anything was better than going straight back to his parents' apartment and being pawed.

"How about Cipriani's?"

"That sounds fine. Can we grab a cab, though? I don't want to walk in the rain."

"Of course."

"I still don't get what the big deal was when the young daughter married the Russian," Gregg said as they were seated in the taxi. "I mean, geez, weren't the Jews complaining about being judged because of their religion, and then Tevye goes and does the same thing."

Amber looked at him in astonishment. "You do realize that the Russians were the ones making them leave, right? Also she was marrying outside of her religion." *He had seen this seven times and was still confused?*

"Yeah, yeah. I know. But I'm just saying. It's not very politically correct. But, whatever, the music sure is great."

"Do you mind if we skip drinks? My head is pounding; I really need to just go to sleep." If she had to spend any more time talking to him tonight, she might have to choke him.

"Of course, babe." He gave her a concerned look. "So sorry you don't feel well."

She smiled tightly. "Thanks."

When they got back to the apartment, she crawled under the covers and curled into a tight ball. She felt the mattress shift as he lay next to her, pressing his body close.

"Want me to massage your temples?" he whispered.

I want you to get lost, she thought. "No. Just let me try and fall asleep."

He draped an arm around her waist. "I'm right here if you change your mind."

Not for long, Amber thought.

THIRTY-TWO

A bright beam of light peeked through the heavy bedroom
curtains of Amber's room at the Dorchester Hotel, rousing
her. She jumped out of bed and pushed back the green drapery to
let the full radiance of the sun warm her body. Despite the early
hour, there was lots of activity in Hyde Park; joggers, dog walk-
ers, people on their way to work. They'd been in London three
glorious days, and Amber was lapping up every minute of it. She
was here as Jackson's assistant, as he had brought along the whole
family, and she had her own room just down the hall from the
family suite. Jackson and Amber worked during the day while
Daphne and the girls went sightseeing.

On their second night, they all went to St Martin's Theatre to
see *The Mousetrap*, but last night Daphne had decided to take
Tallulah and Bella to the Royal Ballet to see *Sleeping Beauty*
while Jackson and Amber went to a business dinner. The truth
was, there was no business dinner. Amber and Jackson had spent
those four hours in her room. He was frenzied after not being
able to be alone with her for the last three days. He wasn't used
to such long dry spells; she'd made sure of that, and when she had
her period she pleased him in other ways. Jackson now stayed at
the New York apartment at least three nights a week, and Amber stayed with him. Daphne could reach either one of them by
cell phone, so there was no way for her to figure out they were
together. On the weekends, Amber was usually hanging at the
Parrish house with her good friend Daphne, and on at least two

occasions, she and Jackson had had sex in the downstairs bath-room while Daphne was putting the girls to bed. The danger of it had been absolutely thrilling. And they had snuck out of the house late one night after Daphne fell asleep on the couch and gone skinny-dipping in the heated pool, then did it in the gazebo. He couldn't get enough of her. She had him lassoed, and as soon as she was pregnant, she would tighten the rope.

Amber draped her leg over Jackson's body and nestled against his shoulder. "Mmm. I could stay like this forever," she mumbled sleepily.

Jackson pulled her closer and stroked her thigh. "They'll be back soon. We need to put on our dinner duds and wait for them in the suite." He rolled over on top of her. "But first . . ."

Amber was meeting Daphne and girls for breakfast in the hotel, and when she walked in, the striking mix of copper, marble, and butterscotch-colored leather filled her senses once again. Daphne and the children were seated with Sabine at a round table near the middle of the restaurant.

"Good morning," Amber said as she took a seat. "How was the ballet last night?"

Before Daphne could say anything, Bella piped up. "Oh, Auntie Amber, you would have loved it. Sleeping Beauty was so beautiful."

"I guess that's why they call her Sleeping Beauty," Amber said.

"No, no. They call her that because she fell asleep and no one could wake her up until the prince kissed her." Bella's face was flushed with excitement.

"Aunt Amber was kidding. That was a joke, stupid," Tallulah said.

Bella hit the cereal bowl with her spoon. "Mom!"

"Tallulah, apologize to your sister at once," Daphne said.

Tallulah gave her mother a look. "Sorry," she muttered to Bella.

"That's better," Daphne said. "Sabine, will you take Tallulah and Bella for a walk in the park? The barge down the Thames to Greenwich doesn't leave until eleven."

"*Oui.*" She pushed her chair out and looked at Bella and Tallulah. "*Allez les filles.*"

Daphne was on her second cup of coffee when Amber's full English breakfast arrived, and she dug into it with gusto.

"You have quite an appetite this morning," Daphne commented.

Amber looked up from her plate. She realized that she and Jackson had never eaten last night. It had been the last thing on their minds.

"I'm absolutely famished. I hate dinner business meetings. Your food gets cold while you talk, and then it's completely unappetizing."

"I'm sorry you had to work and miss the ballet. It was superb."

"Me too. I would much rather have done that."

Daphne absently stirred her coffee for a moment before speaking.

"Amber." Her voice was low and serious. "I need to talk to you about something that's been bothering me."

Amber put down her knife and fork. "What is it, Daph?"

"It's about Jackson."

Amber pushed down the panic threatening to rise. "What about Jackson?" she said, her face a mask.

"I really do think he's seeing someone."

"Did you talk to Bree?"

"I know it has nothing to do with Bree. She's gay—I met her

partner at a party we attended recently. I'm so glad I never went to the office and accused her. But he's been very distant lately. He's spending most of the week at the apartment in New York. He never used to do that. Maybe a night here and there, but it was the exception. Now it seems to be the rule. And even when he's home, he's not really there. His mind is always somewhere else." She put her hand on Amber's arm. "And we haven't made love in weeks and weeks."

Nothing could have pleased Amber more. So he wasn't sleeping with Daphne any longer. It didn't surprise her. She made sure she left him satisfied in every way possible.

"I'm sure you're wrong," she said, putting her hand on Daphne's. "He's closing on that huge project in Hong Kong, and it's been brutal. Plus, the time difference between here and there has him on calls at all hours. He's totally exhausted and consumed by it. You have nothing to worry about. As soon as this deal closes, he'll be back to normal. Trust me."

"You really think so?"

"I do." Amber smiled. "But if it makes you feel better, I'll keep my eyes and ears open and let you know if anything looks suspicious."

"I'd appreciate that. I knew I could count on you."

Amber joined them later on the boat ride down the Thames to Greenwich, and together they wended their way up the big hill to the Royal Observatory. They ate lunch in the town and strolled around most of the afternoon, also visiting the National Maritime Museum. By the time they got back to the hotel, Bella and Tallulah were fading and ready for naps. Amber was feeling like she could use a quick nap too, and they all went to their rooms to rest. Amber was out in seconds, and when she awoke, it was six o'clock. She called the suite to see what the plan was for dinner.

"Did you get some rest?" Daphne asked when she picked up.

"I did. How about you?"

"Yes, we all slept. I've been up for a while, but Tallulah and Bella just got up. The girls are eating in tonight." Daphne's voice got a little softer. "I think you must be right. Jackson wants a romantic dinner, just the two of us. He apologized for all the nights away and his preoccupation with work. I should have known you were right. Thank you for setting me straight."

"You're welcome." Amber's voice was strangled. What the hell was he playing at? A romantic dinner with Daphne? After he had made love to Amber that morning?

Daphne's voice startled her. "Thanks again. See you tomorrow."

Amber put the phone down and sat on the bed, stewing. She was furious. Did he think he could just use her and then run back to Daphne? She heard her mother's words, repeated so often that Amber remembered wanting to stuff a rag in her mouth. *Don't be someone's trash can.* What a vile admonition, Amber had always thought when she heard her mother say it. But that's precisely what she felt like now.

She was putting the finishing touches on her makeup when she heard knocking at her door.

She opened it, and Jackson slid in. He looked at her, a puzzled expression forming.

"Are you going out?"

She smiled, put one leg on the bed, pulled up a sheer stocking, and clipped it to her garter.

"Daphne told me that you had plans, so I called an old friend, and we're meeting for drinks."

"What old friend?"

She shrugged. "Just an old boyfriend. I called my mom earlier today, and she told me he'd moved here a few years ago with his wife," she lied.

Jackson sat on the bed, still looking at her.

"Poor thing, he just got divorced. I thought he could use some cheering up."

"I don't want you to go."

"Don't be silly. He's ancient history."

He grabbed both her hands in his and pushed her backward until she was against the wall. Kissing her hungrily, he moved his body against hers and lifted her skirt above her thighs. Standing up and half undressed, they made love with urgency, and when they were finished, Jackson pulled her to the bed to sit beside him.

"Cancel on him," he said.

"You can't expect me to sit alone in this hotel room while you're out with Daphne. Besides, don't you trust me?"

He stood from the bed, his face red, his hands balled into fists, and glared at her. "I don't want you going out with another man." He pulled a box from his pocket. "This is for you."

He handed it to her, and when she opened it, there sat a magnificent diamond bracelet.

"Wow," she breathed. "I've never seen anything more beautiful. Thank you! Will you put it on me?" She gave him a long kiss. "I suppose I could cancel if it bothers you that much. How long will your dinner take?"

"I'll make it quick. Meet you back here in two hours."

The bracelet was the most amazing piece of jewelry she'd ever seen. And it was hers. All hers. She turned slowly and, never taking her eyes from Jackson, began to undress. When she was finally wearing nothing but the bracelet, she walked over to him and purred, "Hurry back, and then I'll show you how very grateful your girl is."

After he left, she pulled out her phone and took a selfie—a very erotic selfie. She waited an hour, knowing he'd be in the middle of dinner, then texted it to him. That ought to have him calling for the check.

THIRTY-THREE

Amber delighted in soaking in Daphne's bathtub, more often than not with Jackson. She luxuriated in the soft-as-silk sheets as she lay next to Daphne's husband and drove him mad with lust. And how liberating it was to know that no matter how many towels she used, no matter how mussed the sheets became, no matter how many glasses of wine or dishes of food she consumed, she could walk out the door in the morning and know the maid would have everything spick-and-span when she and Jackson returned in the evening. The doorman nodded politely to her on arrival and departure, a model of discretion, just like the new maid. Matilda, the old one, had been fired. Apparently she'd stolen some of Daphne's jewelry. The same jewelry that Amber had hocked for a little extra cash.

The night before, they'd gone to an art opening at a small gallery on Twenty-Fifth Street. The artist, Eric Fury, was one Jackson had discovered a few years ago and had introduced to his collector friends. The moment they'd entered the gallery, they had been surrounded. It'd been clear not only that Jackson was well known but also that people wanted to be in the orbit of his power and charm. Amber had been careful not to put her arm in his or appear too intimate.

As soon as Eric Fury saw Jackson, he'd rushed over to shake his hand.

"Jackson. Wonderful to see you." He swept his arm around to indicate the crowded room. "Isn't it great?"

"It is, Eric, and you deserve every bit of it," Jackson said.

"It's all thanks to you. I can never tell you how grateful I am."

"Nonsense. I just made the introductions. Your art speaks for itself. You wouldn't be here if you didn't have the talent."

Fury turned to Amber. "You must be Daphne."

"Actually, this is my assistant, Amber Patterson. Unfortunately, my wife was unable to be here, but she loves your work as much as I do."

Amber extended her hand. "It's a pleasure to meet you, Mr. Fury. I read recently that you're moving away from canvas and instead painting on wood you collect from old buildings."

Jackson had looked at her in surprise, and Fury said, "You are absolutely right, Miss Patterson. It's a statement about what we lose when we let historical edifices be torn down."

Suddenly a man appeared with a camera. "Hey, Mr. Fury. How about a photo for tomorrow's edition?"

Eric smiled and stood next to Jackson as Amber quickly moved away from the twosome. The last thing she needed was another picture of her in the newspaper.

"Okay, kid. Get back to your fans and sell some art," Jackson said when the photographer finished. When the artist walked away, Jackson walked over to where Amber stood admiring one of the works.

"I didn't realize you knew anything about Eric Fury," he said.

"I don't really. But when you asked if I wanted to go to the exhibit, I read up on him. I always like to know something beforehand. It makes the experience much more rewarding."

He nodded his head in approval. "Impressive."

Amber smiled.

"That was discreet of you. Moving out of the picture. I hope you didn't feel uncomfortable," he said.

That was funny. He thought she was protecting him. "Not at all. You know I'll always have your back." She smiled and moved a little closer to him. "And your front too," she whispered.

"I think it's time to split," he said.

"You're the boss."

As they circled the room, bidding everyone good night, Amber experienced just what it would feel like to be Jackson's wife, to be at the center of the universe with him—and it felt sublime. She only needed to bide her time.

They grabbed a taxi back to the apartment and were practically tearing each other's clothes off as the private elevator ascended. They never got to the bedroom, but made furious love on the living room floor. That was one of the things Amber especially loved—she made sure that they'd had sex in every room, even both of the girls' bedrooms. That one had been a challenge, but she wanted her scent everywhere, like an alley cat.

She heard the shower going and turned lazily to look at the clock on the night stand. Seven thirty! Jackson came out of the bathroom with a towel around his waist, his chest still shiny with dampness. He sat on the edge of the bed and ruffled her hair. "Good morning, sleepyhead."

"I didn't even hear the alarm. I'll get up."

"You put on quite a show last night. No wonder you're exhausted." He leaned down and gave her a long, sensuous kiss.

"Ooh, come back to bed," she cooed.

He ran his hand down the front of her body. "Nothing I'd like more, but remember? I have a ten o'clock with Harding and Harding."

"Oh, that's right. Sorry I kept you up so late."

"Don't ever apologize for that." He rose, dropped the towel, and began dressing. Amber snuggled against the pillow and admired the toned and muscular body that she now knew so intimately. He finished dressing as she slowly got out of bed. "I'm off," he said as he pulled her naked body to him. "Give me a kiss and hustle. We need to prepare for that meeting."

Amber hurriedly poured a glass of juice and then got into the shower. She chose the red Oscar de la Renta suit Jackson had bought for her last week and was out the door close to eight. She made it to the office by eight forty-five and strolled into Jackson's office. She knew he was watching her as she strutted in the fitted jacket and short skirt that hugged her bottom.

At twelve o'clock, the meeting in Jackson's office was still going on when Amber looked up to see Daphne approaching her desk. She looked like she had gained more weight and was not her usual, impeccable self. Her lipstick was mussed, her blouse so tight that the buttons were straining. Amber noticed, too, that she wore no jewelry other than her ring.

Amber rose from her desk. "Daphne, what a surprise. Is everything all right?" What was *she* doing here?

"Yes, everything's fine. I was in town and just wondered if Jackson might be available for lunch."

"Was he expecting you?"

"Well, no. I just took a chance. I tried calling you to get his schedule, but they said you weren't in yet. Is he here?"

Amber stood up straighter. "He's in a meeting with a group of investors. I'm not sure when they'll be finished."

Daphne looked disappointed. "Oh. Did the meeting just start?"

Amber shuffled some papers on her desk. "I don't know. I had car trouble this morning, so I missed my train. That's why I was late." She stared at Daphne.

"Well, maybe I'll wait a little bit. Do you mind if I sit in here with you? I won't bother you if you have work to do."

"Of course not. Please have a seat."

"By the way, that's a beautiful suit you're wearing."

"Thank you. I got it at a consignment shop here in the city. Amazing what you can find for cheap." She wanted to add, *and guess whose red bra and panties I'm wearing.*

Daphne sat, and Amber went back to the pile of work on her desk while fielding phone calls.

"You've really taken to this job, haven't you? Jackson says he wouldn't know what to do without you. I knew you'd be perfect for him."

Amber bristled. She was sick and tired of Daphne patronizing her. She was so out of tune with her own husband's needs and desires it was laughable.

Just then, the door to Jackson's office opened and the four-member Harding and Harding team stood there shaking hands and saying their good-byes. Amber could tell from the look on Jackson's face that the meeting had gone well. She was glad. This would mean a financial leap into a whole new stratosphere. Jackson, now standing alone, looked surprised to see Daphne.

"Hi, darling," she said, rising from her chair and embracing him.

"Daphne, how nice. What are you doing in New York?"

"Can we go into your office?" she asked in a sweet voice.

Jackson followed her in and closed the door behind them. After twenty minutes, Amber was fuming. What could possibly be going on in there? Suddenly, Jackson was at the door and said,

"Amber, can you come in and bring my schedule with you? I seem to have erased it somehow."

Daphne looked up as Amber entered. "You see, Amber? What on earth would he do without you? Jackson's just been telling me what an innovator you are."

"How's my afternoon looking, Amber? My wife wants to take me to lunch."

Amber pulled up the calendar on her iPhone. "It looks like you have a lunch appointment at twelve forty-five with Margot Samuelson from Atkins Insurance." He didn't, but Amber wasn't about to let Jackson and Daphne have a meal together. She turned to Daphne. "I'm so sorry you came in for nothing."

Daphne got up from her seat. "Don't worry. I had to come in for a foundation meeting this morning. It's no problem." She walked behind the desk and gave Jackson a kiss. "I'll see you tonight?"

"Absolutely. I'll be home for dinner."

"Good. We've missed you."

Amber walked her out, and Daphne gave her a hug. "I'm glad he's coming home tonight. The girls miss him. He never used to stay overnight in the city this often. Are you sure you're not noticing anything suspicious? No one calling here for him or anything?"

"Believe me, Daphne—no one is calling or coming around. I even stayed at the apartment one night when you and Jackson were at the lake, and there's no sign that anyone but Jackson has been there. It's just a super-busy season here. I'm sure there've been times like this before."

"Yes, I suppose you're right. There have been. It feels different this time, though."

"I think you're imagining things."

"Thanks for keeping me on an even keel."

"Anytime."

Once Daphne was gone, Amber went straight to Jackson's office. "What did she want?"

"She wanted to have lunch, just like she said."

"You were alone a long time. What was that all about?"

"Whoa. She's my wife, remember?"

Amber did her best to backpedal. "I know. Sorry. It's just . . ." She choked back fake tears. "It's just that I care about you so much, I can't stand the thought of your being with anyone else."

Jackson got up from his desk chair and opened his arms. "Come here, you little worrier." He hugged her, and she held on to him tightly. "Stop fretting. It will all work out, I promise you."

Amber knew better than to challenge him by asking him *how* and *when* it was all going to work out. "You're going back to Connecticut tonight?"

He moved her back, his hands on her shoulders, and looked into her eyes. "I have to. Besides, I want to check things at home. Daphne looks like she's having problems."

"Yes, I noticed that too. She's gained more weight, hasn't she?" Amber said.

"She looked sloppy, and that's not like her. I want to check on the girls too, make sure everything's okay."

Amber wiggled back into his arms. "I'll miss you so much."

He dropped his arms and walked to the office door. Amber was already unzipping her skirt as she heard the lock click.

THIRTY-FOUR

Jackson told Amber he had a surprise for her. The chauffeur picked them up from the apartment and drove them to Teterboro Airport, where a private jet waited for them. When Amber saw the airfield, she turned to Jackson. "What are we doing?" she asked.

Jackson pulled her closer to him. "We're taking a little trip."

"A trip? Where? I don't have any clothes with me."

"Of course you don't. But you won't be in them much anyway," he said with a laugh.

"Jackson!" Amber feigned outrage. "But really. I didn't pack anything."

"Don't worry—there are stores in Paris."

"Paris?" she cried. "Oh, Jackson. We're going to Paris?"

"The most romantic city in the world."

Amber unbuckled her seat belt, slid onto Jackson's lap, and kissed him. They almost undressed right there in the car, but they had pulled to a stop near the jet stairs. Jackson was the first to pull away. "Here we are," he said, and opened his door.

They boarded the plane, and Amber looked around while Jackson talked to the pilot. The only planes she'd been on were commercial airliners crowded with rows and rows of seats, and naturally, Amber had never sat anywhere but in economy. Even that time she'd met Jackson and the family in London, she had flown commercially. She knew that private jets existed, but she'd never imagined they looked like this. Supple leather sofas in a beautiful cream color sat on both sides of the plane, facing each other. There was a large-screen TV, and a dining table for four had a round crystal vase filled with fresh flowers. A door opened onto a bedroom with a king-size bed, and the bathroom was almost as luxurious as the one in the New York apartment. In fact, Amber thought, it was like being in a smaller but just as sumptuous home.

Jackson came up behind her and put his arms around her waist. "You like?"

"What's not to like?"

"Follow me," he said.

He led her into the bedroom, where he opened the closet doors. Indicating a mass of clothing hanging there, he said, "Look through them and decide what you want to keep. Keep all of them if you like."

"When did you have time to do this?"

"I took care of it last week," he said.

Amber went to the closet and went through the hangers one by one, examining the dresses, tops, pants, jackets, and sweaters, every one still with a tag on it. Obviously, he'd bought them just for her. She excitedly began pulling them out to try on, kicking off her shoes and removing her dress. Jackson sat on the bed. "You don't mind if I watch this little show, do you?"

"Not one little bit."

She tried on every last piece, modeling them for Jackson, who approved of it all. Of course, he had chosen everything, so it stood to reason that he would.

"There are shoes in there too. Up top, on the shelf," he said.

"You think of everything, don't you?"

"I do."

Amber looked up and counted fifteen shoe boxes with names

she had only dreamed about. Each pair cost about the same as her monthly rent, some of them even more. When she got to the Jimmy Choos with white suede, crystals, and ostrich feathers, she put them on and took off everything else, then wiggled into the delicious red and black lace corset he'd bought for her. She felt like a movie star, with her stupendously expensive duds, a private jet to travel in, and a gorgeous man dying to make love to her. She walked over to Jackson, still seated on the bed, and, running her fingers through his hair, pulled his face against her chest. She pushed him down and began to work her magic. In a matter of seconds, she would do her best to take him to another world.

Later they had dinner by candlelight, Amber still in her high heels, but now with a silk robe over her naked body.

"I'm famished," she said as she cut into her filet mignon.

"No wonder. You must have burned up five thousand calories."

"If I could stay in bed with you and never have to come up for air or food, I would be the happiest girl alive." She made sure to stroke his ego every chance she got.

Jackson raised his wineglass. "That would be a perfect world, my hungry little sexaholic."

When they landed at Le Bourget Airport in Paris, they were whisked by chauffeur to the Hotel Plaza Athénée. Amber loved the hotel, with its red awnings and crimson bouquets every-where you looked. She toured its 35,000-bottle wine cellar and was pampered at the Dior Institut spa. It was the most glorious week of her life, strolling along the Champs-Élysées and dining in intimate cafés with soft lighting and delectable food. The Eiffel Tower thrilled her. She was overwhelmed by the vast-ness of the Louvre and its masterpieces, moved by the grand edifice of Notre-Dame, and charmed by the city's amber hue as lights glowed in the twilight. And in between this eye-opening journey, she never let Jackson forget how virile and exciting she found him.

The visit had seemed to fly by, Amber thought as they boarded the private plane for their return. She sat without speaking for the next hour, while Jackson gathered papers from his briefcase and began making notes. When he finished, she went over and sat next to him.

"This has been the most wonderful week of my life. You've really opened up my world."

Jackson smiled but said nothing.

"It's been heaven having you all to myself. I hate the thought of sharing you with Daphne."

Jackson frowned, and Amber knew immediately that she'd made a mistake. She never should have mentioned her. Now he was probably thinking about Daphne and the girls. Damn. She usually didn't make that kind of slipup. She'd have to try to recover.

"I've been thinking," he finally said. "How would you feel about having your own apartment in New York?"

She was nonplussed. "Why would I want that? I like living in Connecticut. Besides, when I want to stay in New York with you, we have your place."

"But it's getting complicated. If you had your own apartment, you could have all your own things there. You wouldn't have to hide your clothes or make sure they're out of my apartment in case Daphne comes into the city."

She didn't want her own place. She wanted Daphne's place.

When she didn't answer, Jackson went on. "I'd buy it for you, of course. We'd furnish it together, buy all the art and books you love. It would be our own hideaway. Just ours."

Their hideaway. She didn't want to be hidden. She wanted to be very much out in the open, to be Mrs. Jackson Parrish.

"I don't know, Jackson. It might be too soon for something like that. Besides, wouldn't Daphne wonder how I got the money for a New York apartment? And what about Gregg? I've been able to hold him off, but if he thinks I'm a New York sophisticate, I won't be able to play the innocent little girl. And we have to keep up that little charade for Daphne's sake—although I'm having more and more trouble keeping Gregg's hands off me. I've stopped him a couple of times before he could finish what I think was going to be a proposal."

Jackson's face grew red, just as Amber had hoped. "Have you slept with him?"

"Really? Are you serious?" She took the napkin from her lap and threw it on the table. "I'm finished." She rose from her chair and strode into the bedroom. She wasn't going to be cast aside again. It felt like her plans were all going awry. Oh, Jackson was under her spell at the moment, and he was buying her expensive things and taking her on fabulous trips, but she wanted more— much more. And she'd be damned if she was going to let anything stand in her way, especially now that she'd missed two periods.

THIRTY-FIVE

Tonight was the night. Amber was now ten weeks pregnant and couldn't hide it much longer. Jackson thought she was on the pill, and she'd even made sure to get a prescription and take a pill out of the dispenser each day so he wouldn't be suspicious. Then she'd flush it. The only medication she was taking was Clomid, for fertility. She probably didn't need it, but she wasn't taking any chances. She needed to get pregnant before he tired of her. She had been a little worried about twins, but then she figured, if one was good, two would be even better.

She'd hoped to find out the sex at the last appointment, but it was apparently still too soon. With the computer skills she'd honed in months of night classes, she'd been able to doctor the image from the ultrasound, so she'd tell him it was a boy. By the time they were married, if she ended up having a girl, it would be too late for him to do anything about it anyway.

She'd gone to Babesta earlier in the day and bought a bib—"Daddy's little boy"—that she planned to give him tonight after they made love. Then he'd finally leave Daphne, and she could drop the facade and stop pretending to be her friend. She couldn't wait to see the look on Daphne's face when she found out that Amber was pregnant. It would be almost as delicious as telling Bella she wouldn't be the youngest anymore. *Move over, baby, you're old news now.*

Once she was Mrs. Parrish, those two brats were on borrowed time. They could go to community college as far as she was concerned. But she was getting ahead of herself; first, she had to convince Jackson to leave them.

When Jackson arrived at the apartment, Amber was wearing a black leather corset and collar. Daphne had complained to her on a recent night out that Jackson's tastes were becoming more unconventional. When she'd pressed for more details, the prude had turned red and mentioned something about restraints. Amber had decided to test the waters, and what she'd found was that Jackson was craving more adventure in the sack. She'd gladly given it to him, and together they'd scoured a few online stores and ordered all sorts of interesting sex toys. She encouraged him to push the limits, was ready to do whatever she had to, to make him compare Daphne unfavorably to her. She kept all their toys in a drawer in the guest room, half hoping Daphne might snoop when she was there and Amber could have a nice laugh at her expense. But Daphne never mentioned anything to her.

"That was amazing." She nuzzled closer to him. "If I were Daphne, I'd never let you out of my bed." She bit his earlobe.

"I don't want to talk about Daphne," he whispered.

She giggled. "She likes to talk about you."

He sat up, his brow furrowed. "What do you mean?"

"Oh, nothing. Just little wifely complaints. No big deal."

"I want to know. What did she say?" There was a hard edge to his voice.

She slid back so she could see his face, her finger tracing a pattern on his chest as she spoke. "Just stuff about how she's at a point in her life when she wants to chill out, and you're always pushing her to socialize. Said she'd rather stay home and watch old *Law &*

Order reruns. I told her she was lucky to go places with you, but she just shook her head and said she was getting too old for all these dinners and galas keeping her out late." It was a total lie, but so what. He'd never know.

She watched his face to see how he reacted, pleased to see his jaw clench.

"I don't appreciate the two of you discussing me." He slid from the bed and threw on his silk robe.

Amber went to him, still naked, and pressed herself against him. "We don't talk about you, I promise. She just complains and I defend you, then change the subject. I adore you, you know that." She hoped he believed that.

His eyes narrowed. He didn't look convinced.

She changed her approach. "I think Daphne's out of her element. You're so brilliant and accomplished. You know all about art and culture, and she . . . well, she's just kind of a simple girl. It's hard to keep up the pretense."

"I suppose," he said.

"Come back to bed. I have a surprise."

He shook his head. "I'm not in the mood."

"Okay, then. Let's go to the living room. I have a present for you." She grabbed his hand.

He yanked it back from her. "Stop telling me what to do. You're starting to sound like a nagging wife."

She felt tears of rage spring to her eyes. How dare he talk to her like that? She swallowed her anger and made her voice sweet. It wouldn't do to let him see how pissed she was. "I'm sorry, sweetie. Would you like a drink?"

"I'll get it myself."

She didn't follow him, but sat down and forced herself to read a magazine, then another to give him some time to cool off. After about an hour, she retrieved the small gold bag with the bib from inside the closet and carried it into the living room. He was sitting in one of the dining room chairs, still brooding.

"Here you go."

"What is it?"

"Open it, silly."

He moved aside the tissue paper and pulled out the bib. He looked up at her, puzzled.

She took his hand and put it on her belly. "Your baby is in here."

His mouth dropped open. "You're pregnant? With a boy?"

She nodded. "Yes. I couldn't believe it myself. I didn't want to say anything until I was sure. There's something else in there."

He rooted around and found the sonogram picture.

"That's our son." Her smile was victorious.

"A boy? Are you sure?"

"One hundred percent."

He stood up, grinning from ear to ear, and picked her up. "This is wonderful news. I'd given up on ever having a son. Now you have to let me get you a place here."

Was he serious? "A place here?"

"Well, yes. You can't very well stay where you are now."

The blood was pounding in her ears. "You're right, Jackson. I can't. And I don't want my son to grow up wondering why his father has him hidden in some back alley. He needs to be with family. Once he's born, we'll go back to Nebraska."

She turned and stomped from the room.

"Amber, wait!"

She threw on a pair of jeans and a sweatshirt and began packing a bag. Did he really expect her to go on being his secret now that she was giving him an heir? He was crazy if he thought she'd let Daphne continue to reap the benefits of being Mrs. Parrish while she worked in his office like a slave and he snuck in visits to his son. The hell with that.

"What are you doing?"

"Leaving! I thought you loved me. What a fool I've been. I don't see Daphne giving you a son, although she looks more pregnant than I do."

He grabbed her hands. "Stop. I was insensitive. Let's talk."

"What's there to talk about? Either we're going to be a family, or we're not."

He sat down on the bed and ran his hand through his hair. "I need to think. We'll figure this out. Don't even think about moving away."

"She doesn't appreciate you, Jackson. She told me she cringes when you touch her. But I love you so much. All I want to do is take care of you, be the wife you deserve. I'll always put you first—even before this child. You're everything to me." She got down on her knees, the way he liked, and showed him just how much she adored him. When she finished, he pulled her to him.

"How was that, Daddy?"

He gave her an inscrutable smile and stood up, picking up the sonogram picture again. His fingers traced it.

"My son." He looked up at Amber. "Does anyone else know? Your mother, your friends?"

She shook her head. "Of course not. I wanted you to be the first."

"Good. Don't tell anyone yet. I have to figure out a way to get out of this marriage without Daphne taking me to the cleaners. If she finds out you're pregnant, it could cost me a lot of money."

Amber nodded. "I understand. I won't breathe a word to anyone."

He continued to sit, a look of such deep concentration on his face that she was afraid to speak.

Finally he stood and began to pace back and forth. "Okay. This is how we're going to play it. You'll get everything out of this apartment, and we'll move you into a rental for now. If Daphne gets suspicious, the last thing we need is for her to find your things here."

"But Jackson," she whined, "I don't want to move to some awful rental. I'll be all alone."

He stopped pacing and stared at her. "What do you mean, 'Some awful rental'? What kind of cheapskate do you think I am? If you don't want an apartment, we'll get a large suite at the Plaza. You'll have people to wait on your every need."

"But what about you? When will I see you?"

"We have to be careful, Amber. I'm going to have to spend a little more time at home. You know, to allay any suspicion. You'll have to stop working once you're showing. Stay out of the way, so no talk gets back to Daphne."

"And what am I supposed to tell Daphne? She'll get suspicious if I stop hanging out with her."

He chewed his lip and then nodded. "You'll say someone in your family is sick. You're taking some time off to go help."

This was beginning to sound like a bad plan to Amber. She'd be stuck away in some hotel, completely dependent on his being true to his word. It felt like she was being put out on a boat without a life jacket or a paddle and could be swept away at Jackson's whim.

"I don't want to be in some impersonal hotel. It won't be good for me to be in some strange place that doesn't feel like home. It won't be good for the baby either."

He sighed. "Fine. We'll rent an apartment. A nice one that will feel like home. You can buy whatever you'd like for it."

She thought about that a few minutes. It was probably the best offer she was going to get at this point. "How long?"

"I don't know. Maybe a few months? We should settle it all by then."

She was angry and scared now, which made it easy to cry. "I hate this, Jackson. I love you so much, and now we're going to have to be separated. I'll be alone in some apartment that isn't even ours. It makes me feel so afraid, the way I used to feel when I was little and we moved all the time because we couldn't pay the rent." She sniffled and wiped the tears from her cheeks, hoping this tale of woe might move him.

He gave her a long look. "Do you want me to lose everything? You're just going to have to trust me."

He wasn't biting. She'd have to go along with the plan and hope he meant what he said until she could come up with something else. But what if he proved to be untrustworthy? Then what? She'd be shit out of luck, just like she was when she fled from Missouri. She wasn't going to let him get away with throwing her and this kid she was carrying aside, even if she had to take more drastic action this time. No more screwing Amber. Those days were over.

DAPHNE

THIRTY-SIX

I didn't use to be afraid of my husband. I thought I loved him, back when he was kind—or pretended to be. Before I knew what a monster looks like up close.

I met Jackson when I was twenty-six. I'd finished my graduate studies in social work and was in the planning stages of the foundation I was starting in honor of Julie. I'd gotten a job in operations at Save the Children and had been there for six months. It was a great organization, where I could work at something I loved while learning everything I'd need to run my own foundation one day.

A coworker recommended I get in touch with Parrish International, an international real estate firm with a reputation for giving back. She had an in—her father was a business associate. I had expected to be pawned off on some junior executive. Instead, I was granted an audience with Mr. Parrish himself. Jackson was nothing like the captain of industry I had read about. With me, he was amiable and funny, and he put me at ease from the start. When I told him my plans for the foundation and why I was starting it, he shocked me by offering to fund Julie's Smile. Three months later I'd quit my job and was the head of my own foundation. Jackson had assembled a board, which he joined, provided the funding, and found me office space. Things had remained professional between us—I hadn't wanted to jeopardize his support of the foundation, and to be honest, I was also a little scared. But over time, when the lunches turned into dinners, it seemed natural—inevitable even—that our relationship would turn more personal. His wholehearted embrace of my charity turned my head, I'll admit. So I agreed to go to his house for a dinner to celebrate.

The first time I saw his thirty-room estate, the vastness of his wealth hit me. He lived in Bishops Harbor, a picturesque town on the coast of Long Island Sound with a population of about thirty thousand. The town's shopping area could rival Rodeo Drive, with stores far too expensive for my budget, and the only domestic cars on its pristine roads belonged to household staff. The houses dotting the shoreline in the area were magnificent, set far back from the road, shielded by gates, and on grass so lustrous and green it didn't look real. When Jackson's driver pulled the car into the long driveway, it took a minute for the house to come into view. My breath caught in my throat when we approached the tremendous gray estate.

When we walked into the grand foyer, with a chandelier that would have been at home in Buckingham Palace, I gave him a strained smile. Did people really live this way? I remember thinking that the excesses surrounding me could pay so many medical bills for the CF families struggling to keep their heads above water.

"It's very nice."

"Glad you approve." He'd looked at me with a puzzled expression, called for the housekeeper to take our coats, and whisked me off to the deck, where a roaring fire awaited in an outdoor fireplace and we could take in the spectacular view of Long Island Sound.

I was attracted to him—how could I not be? Jackson Parrish was undeniably handsome, his dark hair the perfect frame for eyes bluer than the Caribbean. He was the stuff fantasies were made of—thirty-five-year-old CEO of the company he'd built from the ground up, generous and philanthropic, beloved in the community, charming, boyishly handsome—not the sort of man someone like me dated. I'd read all about his reputation as a playboy. The women he went out with were models and socialites, women whose sophistication and allure far outweighed my own. Maybe that was why his interest took me so by surprise.

I was relaxed, enjoying the soothing view of the Sound and the salty smell of the sea air, when he handed me a glass of something pink.

"A Bellini. It will make you feel like it's summer." An explosion of fruit filled my mouth, and the combination of tart and sweet was delectable.

"It's delicious." I looked out at the sun setting over the water, the sky painted gorgeous shades of pink and purple. "So beautiful. You must never tire of this view."

He sat back, his thigh next to mine making me more lightheaded than the drink.

"Never. I grew up in the mountains and didn't realize what an enchantress the sea is until I moved east."

"You're from Colorado, right?"

He smiled. "Doing some research on me?"

I took another sip, emboldened by the alcohol. "You're not exactly a private figure." It seemed like I couldn't open a newspaper without reading about wonder boy Jackson Parrish.

"Actually I'm a very private person. When you reach the level of success that I have, it's hard to know who your real friends are. I have to be careful who I let get close to me." He took my glass and refilled it. "But enough about me. I want to know more about you."

"I'm not very interesting, I'm afraid. Just a girl from a small town. Nothing special."

He gave me a wry smile. "If you call getting published at fourteen nothing special. I loved the piece you did for *is* magazine about your sister and her brave fight."

"Wow. You did your research too. How did you even find that?"

He winked at me. "I have my ways. It was very touching. So, you and Julie had both planned on going to Brown?"

"Yes, from the time we were little. After she died, I felt like I had to go. For both of us."

"That's rough. How old were you when you lost her?"

"Eighteen."

He put his hand on mine. "I'm sure she's very proud of you. Especially what you're doing, your dedication. The foundation is going to help so many people."

"I'm so grateful to you. Without your help it would have taken me years to get a space and a staff."

"I'm happy to do it. You were lucky to have her. I've always wondered what it would have been like to grow up with brothers and sisters."

"It must have been lonely being an only child," I said.

He had a faraway look. "My father worked all the time, and my mother had her charity duties. I always wished I had a brother to go outside and throw a football with, to go shoot some hoops." He shrugged. "Oh, well, plenty of people had it much worse."

"What does your father do?"

"He was the CEO of Boulder Insurance. Pretty big job. He's retired now. My mother was a stay-at-home mom."

I didn't want to pry, but he seemed like he wanted to talk. "Was?"

He suddenly stood up. "She died in a car crash. It's a bit chilly. Why don't we go inside?"

I stood, feeling woozy, and put a hand on the chair to steady myself. He turned toward me then, his eyes intense, caressed my cheek, and whispered, "When you're with me, I don't feel lonely at all." I said nothing as he scooped me into his arms and carried me into the house and up to his bed.

Parts of that first night we spent together are still a blur. I hadn't planned on making love to him—I had felt it was too soon. But before I knew it, we were naked and tangled up in the sheets. He held my eyes the entire time. It was unnerving, like he was staring into my very soul, but I couldn't look away. When it was over, he was tender and sweet, and he fell asleep wrapped in my arms. I watched his face in the moonlight and traced the outline of his jaw. I wanted to erase all his sad memories and make him feel the love and nurturing he'd missed as a child. This gorgeous, strong, and successful man that everyone looked up to had shared his vulnerabilities with me. He needed me. There is nothing more enticing to me than being needed.

When morning came, I had a pounding headache. I wondered if I'd been simply another conquest, if now that he'd had me, we'd go back to being business associates. Would I join the ranks of his ex-lovers, or was this the start of a new relationship? I worried that he was comparing me to the glamour girls he was used to sleeping with, and that I came up short. He seemed to read my mind. Propping himself up on one elbow, he traced my breast with his right hand.

"I like having you here."

I didn't know what to say, so I simply smiled. "I bet you say that to all the girls."

His face darkened, and he pulled his hand back. "No, I don't."

"I'm sorry." I took a deep breath. "I'm a little nervous."

He kissed me then, his tongue insistent, his mouth pressed to mine. Then he pulled away and caressed my cheek with the back of his hand. "You don't have to be nervous with me. I'll take good care of you."

A mixture of feelings washed over me. I untangled myself from his arms and gave him a sincere smile. "I need to go. I'll be late."

He pulled me back to him. "You're the boss, remember? You don't answer to anyone but the board." He was on top of me then, his eyes holding mine again in that hypnotizing stare. "And the board doesn't mind if you're late. Please stay. I just want to hold you a little longer."

Everything had begun with such promise. And then, like a windshield chipped by a tiny pebble, the chip turned into deep cracks that spread until there was nothing left to repair.

THIRTY-SEVEN

Dating as a means to getting to know someone is highly over-rated. When your hormones are raging and the attraction is magnetic, your brain takes a vacation. He was everything I never knew I needed.

At work, I was back in my comfort zone, though I kept flashing back to our night together with a smile. Hours later, a commotion outside my small office made me look up. A young man was pushing a cart with vase after vase of red roses. Fiona, my secretary, was behind him, her face flushed and hands waving.

"Someone sent you flowers. Lots of flowers."

I stood up and signed for them. I counted a dozen vases. I put one bunch on my desk and looked around, wondering what to do with the rest. We placed them along the floor of my small office, since we had nowhere else to set them.

Fiona shut the door when the deliveryman left and plopped down in the chair across from me. "Okay, spill."

I hadn't wanted to discuss Jackson with anyone yet. I didn't even know what we were. I reached over and pulled out the card.

Your skin is softer than these petals. Missing you already.

J

They were everywhere. It was too much. The cloying smell of the flowers overwhelmed me and made my stomach roil.

Fiona was staring at me with an exasperated expression. "Well?"

"Jackson Parrish."

"I knew it!" She gave me a triumphant look. "The way he was looking at you when he stopped by to see the offices the other day, I knew it was just a matter of time." She leaned forward, her chin in her hands. "Is it serious?"

"I don't know." I shook my head. "I like him—but I don't know." I gestured toward the flowers. "He comes on awfully strong."

"Yeah, what a jerk, sending you all these beautiful roses." She got up and opened door.

"Fiona?"

"Yes?"

"Take a couple for your desk. I don't know what to do with the rest."

She shook her head. "Sure thing, Boss. But I gotta tell you, he's not going to be so easy to cast off."

I needed to get back to work. I'd figure out Jackson later. I was about to make a phone call when Fiona opened the door again. Her face was ashen.

"It's your mother."

I grabbed the phone and held it to my ear. "Mom?"

"Daphne, you need to come home. Your father's had a heart attack."

"How bad is it?" I choked out.

"Just come. As soon as you can."

THIRTY-EIGHT

The next phone call I made was to Jackson. As soon as I managed to get the words out, he took over.

"Daphne, it's going to be okay. Deep breaths. Stay where you are. I'm on my way."

"But I have to get to the airport. I need to find a flight. I—"

"I'll take you. Don't worry."

I'd forgotten he owned a plane. "Can you do that?"

"Listen to me. Stay there. I'm leaving now to get you. We'll go by your place and get some clothes and be in the air in about an hour. Just breathe."

The rest was a blur. I did what he told me, threw things in a suitcase, followed directions until I was seated on his plane, grasping his hand tightly while I looked out the window and prayed. My father was only fifty-nine—surely he couldn't die.

When we landed in New Hampshire at a private airport, Marvin, a waiter at the inn, was waiting for us. I guess I made the introductions, or maybe Jackson just took over. I don't remember. All I remember is the feeling in the pit of my stomach that I might never get to talk to my father again.

As soon as we arrived at the hospital, Jackson took charge. He found out who Dad's doctor was, assessed the facility, and immediately had him moved to St. Gregory's, the large hospital an hour from our small town. There is no doubt in my mind that he would have died had Jackson not seen the ineptitude of his treating doctor at County General and the lack of sophisticated equipment.

Jackson arranged for a top cardio doctor from New York to meet us at the hospital. The doctor arrived shortly after we did, and upon examining my dad, declared that he hadn't had a heart attack after all, but an aortic dissection. He explained that the lining of his heart had torn, and if he didn't operate immediately, my father would die. Apparently his high blood pressure had been the cause. He warned us that the delay in the diagnosis had diminished his chance of survival to fifty percent.

Jackson canceled all his meetings and never left my side. After a week, I was prepared for him to go back to Connecticut, but he had something else in mind.

"You girls go on ahead," he told me and my mom. "I've talked to your dad about it already. I'm going back to the B&B to make sure everything runs smoothly."

"What about your company? Don't you need to get back?"

"I can handle things from here for now. I've rearranged things a bit. A few weeks away isn't going to kill me."

"Are you sure? There's staff that can fill in for now."

He shook his head. "I can conduct my business from anywhere, but the B&B is a hands-on operation, and when the boss isn't around, things slide. I intend to protect your dad's interests until he's moved back to the inn and your mother can keep an eye on things."

My mother gave me one of those looks then that said, *Don't let go of this one.* She put her hand on Jackson's shoulder. "Thank you, dear. I know Ezra will breathe easier knowing that you're there."

With typical Jackson efficiency and flair, he threw himself into making sure everything ran smoothly—even better than when my father was at the helm. The kitchen was stocked, he oversaw the staff, he even made sure the bird feeders were never empty. One evening when we were short-staffed, I came back to the inn to see him waiting tables. I think that's when I really fell for him. It was a huge load off my mother, and when she saw how easily he stepped in, she was free to spend all her time at the hospital without worrying what was going on back at the B&B.

By the end of the month, my mother was as bewitched as I was.

"I think you've found the one, sweetheart," my mother whispered one night after Jackson had left the room.

How had he managed to do that? I wondered. It was as though he'd been around forever, already a part of the family. All my earlier reservations about him evaporated. He wasn't some self-indulgent playboy. He was a man of substance and character. In the space of a few short weeks, he had become indispensable to all of us.

THIRTY-NINE

Dad was home from the hospital, still weak, but doing better, and Jackson and I were flying to New Hampshire to spend Christmas with my family. My cousin, Barry, and his wife, Erin, were coming with their daughter, and we were all excited about spending Christmas together.

We arrived Christmas Eve to falling snow and the perfect New England setting. The inn was decked out in holiday cheer. Standing in the small church where I'd gone every Sunday from the time I was a little girl, I felt at peace, my heart overflowing. My father had survived, and I was in love. It was like a fairy tale—I'd won the prince I never even knew existed in real life. He caught me looking at him and smiled that dazzling smile at me, his cobalt-blue eyes shining with adoration, and I could hardly believe that he was mine.

When we got back to the inn, my father opened a bottle of champagne and poured a glass for each of us. He put his arm around my mother. "I want you all to know how much it means to have you here. A few months ago, I wasn't so sure I'd live to see another Christmas." He brushed a tear from his cheek and lifted his glass. "To family. Those of us here, and to our darling Julie, in heaven. Merry Christmas."

I took a sip, closed my eyes, and said my own silent Merry Christmas to my sister. I still missed her so much.

We sat down on the sofas by the tree to exchange gifts. My parents had started a family tradition of giving us three gifts, symbolic of the ones the wise men gave to Jesus. Jackson had a pile of three to open as well, and I was grateful that my mother had thought to include him. The gifts were modest but special—a sweater she'd knitted him, a Beethoven CD, and a hand-painted sailboat ornament for his Christmas tree. Jackson held the fisherman's sweater up to his chest.

"I love it. This will keep me nice and warm." He stood up and walked over to the tree. "My turn." He took great delight in handing out the gifts he had selected for everyone. I had no idea what he had bought; he wanted to keep it all a surprise. I had mentioned to him that the gifts would be modest, and asked him not to go overboard. He started with my little niece, who was eight at the time. He had gotten her a lovely silver charm bracelet with Disney characters, and she was thrilled. For Barry and Erin, a Bose Bluetooth speaker, top-of-the-line. I was starting to get a little nervous thinking of the book on classic cars they had given to him and how they must feel. He took no apparent notice, but I could see from the expression on Barry's face that he was uncomfortable.

Jackson took something from his pocket and, kneeling in front of me, handed me a small foil-wrapped box.

My heart began to pound. Was this really happening? My hands shook as I tore the paper. I removed the black velvet box and popped the top open.

It *was* a ring. I didn't realize how much I'd hoped it would be until just then. "Oh, Jackson. It's beautiful."

"Daphne, would you do me the honor of becoming my wife?"

My mother gasped and clapped her hands together.

I threw my arms around him. "Yes! Yes!"

He slipped the ring on my finger.

"It's gorgeous, Jackson. And so big."

"Nothing but the best for you. It's a six-carat round cut. Flaw-less. Like you."

It fit perfectly. I held my hand out and turned it this way and that. My mother and Erin rushed to my side, oohing and aahing.

My father stood apart, strangely quiet, an inscrutable expres-sion on his face. "It's a little fast, isn't it?"

The room went silent. An angry look passed quickly over Jack-son's face. Then he smiled and walked over to my father.

"Sir, I understand your reservations. But I have loved your daughter from the moment I set eyes on her. I promise you, I will treat her like a queen. I hope you'll give us your blessing." He held his hand out to my father.

Everyone was watching them. My father reached out and clasped Jackson's hand in his.

"Welcome to the family, son," he said, and smiled, but I think I was the only one who noticed that the smile didn't quite reach his eyes.

Jackson pumped his hand and looked him straight in the eye. "Thank you." Then, with a cat-that-swallowed-the-canary look, he pulled something from his pant pocket. "I wanted to save this until last." He handed an envelope to my father.

My father opened it, a frown pulling at his mouth. There was a look of confusion in his eyes as he gave it back to Jackson. He shook his head. "This is too extravagant."

My mother walked over. "What is it, Ezra?"

Jackson answered. "A new roof. I know you've been having problems with leaks with this old one. They'll do it in the spring."

"Well, that's so thoughtful, but Ezra's right, Jackson, it's way too much."

He put his arm around me and smiled at them both. "Nonsense. I'm a part of the family now. And family takes care of each other. I absolutely won't take no for an answer."

I didn't know why they were being so stubborn. I thought it was a wonderful gesture and knew it wouldn't put a dent in Jackson's finances.

"Mom, Dad, let go of that Yankee pride of yours," I tried to tease. "It's a wonderful gift."

My father looked directly at Jackson. "I appreciate it, son, but it's not the way I do things. It's my business, and I'll put a new roof on when I'm good and ready. Now I don't want to hear any more about it."

Jackson's jaw clenched, and he dropped the hand from my shoulder. He deflated before my eyes, put the envelope back in his pocket, and spoke again, this time barely a whisper.

"Now I've offended you when I just wanted to do something nice. Please forgive me." His head was bent, and he raised his eyes to look at my mother, like a boy in trouble looking for reprieve. "I wanted to be a part of your family. It's been so hard since my mother died."

My mother swooped over and put her arms around him. "Jackson, of course you're part of the family." She gave my father a disapproving look. "Family does help family. We'll be happy to accept your gift."

That was the first time I saw it—that little smile that played at his lips, and the look in his eyes that read *Victory*.

FORTY

Though he'd recovered from the surgery, Dad wasn't doing well, and I didn't know how long he really had. Part of the reason we rushed to get married was so that I could be sure he would be around to walk me down the aisle. The wedding was a small affair. My father insisted on paying for it, and despite entreaties, would not be persuaded to allow Jackson to contribute. Jackson had wanted to have a huge wedding back in Bishops Harbor and invite all his business associates. I promised Jackson that when we returned from our honeymoon, we could have a party to celebrate, and that appeased him.

We got married in February at my family's Presbyterian church and held the reception at the B&B. Jackson's father flew in for the wedding, and I was a nervous wreck before meeting him. His father was bringing a date, and Jackson wasn't happy about it. Jackson had sent his private plane for them and had a driver waiting at the airport to bring them to the inn.

"I can't believe he's bringing that simpering idiot. He shouldn't even be dating yet."

"Jackson, that's a bit harsh, isn't it?"

"She's a nothing. It's an insult to my mother. She's a *waitress*."

I thought of the lovely women who worked at the restaurant at the inn and felt my defenses go up. "What's wrong with being a waitress?"

He sighed. "Nothing, if you're in college. She's in her sixties.

And my father has a lot of money. She's probably latching on to him as her next meal ticket."

I felt a nagging feeling in the pit of my stomach. "How well do you know her?

He shrugged. "I've only met her once. A couple of months ago when I flew to Chicago on business, we had dinner together. She was loud and not particularly bright. But she hung on his every word. My mother had a mind of her own."

"Are you sure you're not just having a hard time seeing him with someone other than your mother? You've told me how close you were to her. I'm sure it's not easy seeing her replaced."

His face turned red. "My mother is irreplaceable. That woman will never be able to hold a candle to her."

"I'm sorry. I didn't mean it that way." He hadn't shared much about his parents, beyond that his father was a workaholic who never had time for him when he was growing up. I suppose, being an only child, he had an even closer relationship with his mother. Her death the year before had hit him hard, and from what I could see, his grief was still raw. I didn't want to dwell on the un-welcome thought racing through my head—that he was a snob. I chalked it up to angst over his mother and pushed it to the back of my mind.

When I met Flora, I thought she was nice enough, and his father seemed happy. They were cordial to my parents, and everyone got along fine. The next day, when my father walked me down the aisle, all I could think about was how lucky I was to have found the love of my life and to be starting a new life with Jackson.

"Don't you think it's time you let me in on the big secret?" I asked as we boarded his plane for our honeymoon. "I don't even know if I packed the right clothes."

He leaned in and kissed me. "Silly girl. There are suitcases upon suitcases full of clothes I've bought for you already on board. Just leave everything to me."

He'd bought new clothes for me? "When did you have time to do that?"

"Don't you worry about it, my darling. You'll find that I'm very good at planning ahead."

Once we got settled in our seats and I took a sip of my champagne, I tried again. "So when do I find out?"

He pulled the shade to my window down. "When we land. Now lie back and relax. Maybe even get some sleep. And when you wake up, we'll have a little fun in the clouds." His hand moved up and down my inner thigh as he spoke, and desire spread through me like hot liquid.

"Why don't we have that fun right now?" I whispered as I pressed my lips against his ear.

Jackson smiled, and when I looked into his eyes, I saw the same craving I felt. He rose and took me into his muscular arms, carrying me to the bedroom where we fell to the bed, bodies entwined. We slept afterward—I'm not sure how long, but soon after we awakened and made love again, the captain phoned Jackson to let him know we would be making our descent in a few minutes. He was careful not to name a destination, but when I peered out the window, I saw miles and miles of blue water beneath us. Wherever we were, it looked like paradise. Jackson threw off the bedcovers and came to my side by the window, putting his arm around my naked waist. "See that?" He pointed to a glorious mountain that seemed to emerge like a noble monolith out of the sea. "That's Mount Otemanu, one of the most beautiful sights in the world. And soon I'll show you the magnificence of Bora Bora."

Polynesia, I thought. I turned to look at him. "You've been here before?"

He kissed my cheek. "I have, my darling girl. But never with you."

I was somehow disappointed but didn't quite know how to put it into words. I made a clumsy attempt. "I just assumed we would go someplace neither of us had ever been, so that, you know, we could experience everything together. For the first time."

Jackson pulled me down onto the bed and tousled my hair. "I've traveled a lot. Any place worth going to is a place I've been. Would you have preferred Davenport, Iowa? That's a place I haven't seen. You know, I did have a life before we met."

"Of course," I said. "I just wanted this time to be new for both of us, something only the two of us shared." I wanted to ask him if he'd been here alone or with another woman, but I was afraid to ruin the mood even more. "Bora Bora," I said. "It's a place I never thought I'd go to."

"I've booked an over-water bungalow. You're going to love it, my sweet." And he pulled me into his arms once again.

We were back in our seats as the wheels went down, and we landed at the airport on the tiny islet of Motu Mute. The door opened, and we walked down the jet stairs to be greeted by smiling islanders who draped leis around our necks. I reached out to touch his.

"I like your lei better. Blue's my favorite color."

He took it from his neck and put it around mine. "Looks better on you anyway. By the way, in Bora Bora, they're called *heis*."

The warm, fragrant air was intoxicating. I was already in love with the place. We were whisked by boat to our bungalow, which looked more like a lavish floating villa, with glass floors that offered a vision of the lagoon life below.

Our luggage arrived, and I changed into a casual sundress, Jackson into navy pants and a white linen shirt. His tanned skin against the white shirt made him look even more handsome, if that was possible. We had just settled on our private deck when an outrigger canoe pulled up to our bungalow to serve us champagne and caviar. I looked at Jackson in surprise. "Did you order this?" I asked.

He looked at me as if I were a naive little country girl. "This is part of the service, my dear. They'll bring us anything we want. If we choose to stay in for dinner, they'll bring it to us; in for lunch, we get lunch—whatever our whims dictate." He spooned a dollop of caviar onto a round cracker and held it to my mouth. "Only the best for my girl. Get used to it."

To tell the truth, caviar and champagne were two of my least favorite things, but I supposed I needed to develop a taste for them.

He took a long sip of champagne, and we sat there feeling the fresh air waft across our faces, mesmerized by the turquoise water before us. I leaned back and closed my eyes, listening to the sound of the water lapping against the pilings.

"We have a dinner reservation at eight at La Villa Mahana," he said.

I opened my eyes and looked at him. "Oh?"

"It's a little gem with just a few tables. You'll love it."

Once again I had that initial feeling of disappointment. Obviously he'd been to the restaurant before. "I suppose you can tell me precisely what to order and what the best things on the menu are," I said, somewhat flippantly.

He gave me a cold look. "If you'd rather not go, I'll cancel the reservation. I'm sure there are throngs of couples on the waiting list who would love to dine there."

I felt like an ungrateful fool. "I'm sorry. I don't know what got into me. Of course we'll go."

Jackson had already unpacked and carefully hung everything he'd bought for me. The clothing was lined up not only by type of outfit but also by color. Shoes sat on a top shelf over the rod and were separated into flat sandals and heels, every color, every type. He held up a long, white dress with slender straps and fitted bodice. There were more clothes than days we would be there: evening shoes, sandals, bathing suits, cover-ups, jewelry, casual daytime outfits, and floaty slip dresses for evening. "Here," he said. "This will be perfect for tonight, my beautiful girl."

It felt so odd, someone choosing my clothes for me, but I had to admit the dress was lovely. It fit perfectly, and the turquoise drop earrings he'd picked were set off beautifully by the pure white material.

We stayed in the second night and had dinner brought to us. We sat on our deck and savored the food as well as the setting sun that made pink and blue ribbons across the sky. It was magical.

This was our pattern—alone in our bungalow one night, the next night at a restaurant like Bloody Mary's or Mai Kai or St. James. They each had their own delightful ambience, and I especially loved the casual island feel of Bloody Mary's, with its sand floor and delicious rum cake. Even the bathrooms had sand floors. When we had dinner out, we'd walk along the beach holding hands and make love after getting home. On the nights we ate in, our lovemaking began earlier and lasted longer. My skin was turning a warm brown, and it felt clean and taut, after days in the sun and water. I'd never been so aware of my body, the touch of someone's hand on me, the thrill of coming together and feeling as one.

Every moment had been planned by him, from swimming and snorkeling to private tours and romantic dinners. We made love on the sands of a private beach, in a boat on the lagoon, and, of course, in the private haven that was the bungalow. He had thought of everything, down to the smallest detail. And even though there were times I had a small, nagging feeling in my stomach, I never consciously understood how much his need for order and control would overpower my life.

FORTY-ONE

I was packed and ready when he came home, excited at the prospect of four uninterrupted days at the Greenbrier with my new husband. We had been married a little over three months. My suitcase was sitting on the bed, and after kissing me hello, he went over to it and opened it.

"What are you doing? Your suitcase is right there." I pointed to the matching one by his dresser.

He gave me an amused smile. "I'm aware." He pulled out what I had packed, a frown appearing on his face as he looked through all my clothes.

I stood there, wanting to tell him to take his hands off my things, but the words wouldn't come. I watched, frozen, as he rifled through everything and looked at me.

"You do realize this is not some hick bed-and-breakfast like your parents run?"

I recoiled as though I'd been struck.

He noticed my expression and laughed. "Oh, come on. I didn't mean it that way. It's just that this is the Greenbrier. They have a dress code. You need a few cocktail dresses."

My face was hot with embarrassment and anger. "I know what the Greenbrier is. I've actually been there before." I hadn't, but I had looked at it online.

He raised his eyebrows and studied me for a long moment. "Really? When was that?"

"That's not the point. What I'm getting at is that you don't have to go through my things as though I'm a child. What I've packed is fine."

He threw his hands up in surrender. "Fine. Have it your way. But don't come crying to me when you realize you're wildly underdressed compared to the other women."

I strode past him, zipped my case, and flung it to the floor. "See you downstairs." I went to pick it up when he stopped me.

"Daphne."

I turned around. "What?"

"Leave it. We have help for that." Then he shook his head and muttered something under his breath.

I picked it up. I still hadn't gotten used to all these people underfoot, waiting to do for me what I could easily do for myself. "I'm perfectly capable of carrying my own suitcase." I stormed into the study and poured myself a glass of whiskey. Throwing it back in one swig, I closed my eyes and breathed deeply. It burned going down, but then I felt a calmness pervade me and thought, *So this is how people become alcoholics.* Walking to the window, I drank in the water view, and it settled what was left of my jangling nerves.

I was learning that emotional intimidation could be just as unsettling as physical. Little things had begun to grate on his nerves, and despite my best efforts to please him, nothing was ever good enough. I'd chosen the wrong wineglass or left a damp towel on the wood table. Maybe it would be that I'd forgotten my hair dryer on the counter. What made it even more difficult to live with was the uncertainty. Which Jackson was I talking to now? The one with the easy laugh and charming smile that put everyone at ease? Or the one with the scowl and critical tone who let me know with just one look that I had done something else to disappoint him? He was a chameleon, his transitions so quick and seamless they left me breathless at times. And now he didn't even think I had the ability to pack my own suitcase.

A hand on my shoulder startled me.

"I'm sorry."

I didn't turn around or answer him.

He began to massage my shoulders, moving closer until his mouth was on my neck, and his lips sent quivers down my spine. I didn't want to respond, but my body had other ideas.

"You can't talk to me like that. I'm not one of your minions." I pulled away.

"I know. You're right. I'm sorry. This is all a little new for me."

"Me as well. Still . . ." I shook my head.

He stroked my cheek. "You know that I adore you. I'm used to being in charge. Give me some time to adjust. Let's not have this fight spoil our trip." He kissed me again, and I felt myself respond. "I'm really more interested in what you're *not* wearing this weekend."

So I let it go, and off we went.

We were both in good moods by the time we arrived, and when we entered the sumptuous suite, with deep-red carpets and walls, thick gray draperies, and ornate mirrors and paintings, I felt like I'd stepped back in time. It was enormous and formal and a bit intimidating. There was a dining room table that could seat ten, a formal living room, and three bedrooms. Suddenly I wondered if I *had* packed the right clothes.

"It's beautiful, but why do we need such a large suite? It's just us."

"Only the best for you. I wasn't going to have us cramped in a little room. Is that what you did when you came here?"

I tried to picture the rooms I'd seen on the website and waved my hand dismissively. "I stayed in a regular room."

"Really? And when was that again?"

He was looking at me with an amused expression, but his eyes—his eyes were angry.

"What difference does it make?"

"You know, I had a best friend. We used to do everything together from the time we were kids. When we were in college, we were supposed to go on a camping trip with his family. He called me the night before and canceled—said he was sick. I found out on Monday that he'd been at a local bar with his girlfriend." He was pacing now. "Do you know what I did?"

"What?"

"I seduced his girlfriend, had her break up with him for me, then I dumped them both."

My blood ran cold. "That's horrible. What did the poor girl ever do to you?"

He smiled. "I'm joking about the girl. But I did end the friendship."

I didn't know what to believe. "Why are you telling me this?"

"Because I think you're lying. And if there's one thing I cannot abide, it's a liar. Don't take me for a fool. You've never been here before. Admit it now, before it's too late."

"Too late for what?" I asked in a voice braver than I felt.

"Too late for me to trust you."

I burst into tears, and he walked over and put his arms around me.

"I didn't want you to think I'd never been anywhere nice or been exposed to things you take for granted."

He lifted my chin and kissed my tears away. "My darling, you don't ever have to pretend with me. I love being the one to show you new things. You don't have to try and impress me. I love that everything is new to you."

"I'm sorry for lying."

"Promise me it will be the last time."

"I promise."

"All right, then. It's all good. Let's unpack, and then I'll show you around."

As I hung my meager ensembles next to his custom suits and ties, I turned to him with a sinking feeling. "How would you like to do a little shopping after that tour?" I asked.

"Already in the plans," he answered.

The next two days were wonderful. We went horseback riding, spent hours in the spa, and couldn't get enough of each other in bed. It was our last day, and just as we were on our way to breakfast, my phone rang. It was my mother.

"Mom?" I could hear in her voice that something was wrong.

"Daphne. I have some bad news. Your fa—" The sound of her crying came over the line.

"Mom! What is it? You're scaring me."

"He died, Daphne. Your dad. He's gone."

I started to cry. "No, no, no."

Jackson rushed over and took the phone from me, pulling me to him with the other arm. I couldn't believe it. How could he be dead? I'd just talked to him last week. I remembered his cardiologist's warning that his full recovery was far from complete. Jackson held me as I sobbed, and gently led me to the sofa while he packed us up.

We flew straight to the inn and stayed there for the next week. As I watched my father's casket being lowered into the ground, all I could think about was the day we'd done the same thing for Julie. Despite Jackson's strong arm around my shoulder and my mother standing next to me, I felt utterly and completely alone.

FORTY-TWO

Jackson wanted kids right away. We'd only been married for six months when he talked me into putting away my diaphragm. I was twenty-seven, he reminded me; it could take a while. I got pregnant the first month. He was delighted, but it took me longer to warm up to the idea. Of course, we had already been tested to make sure he didn't carry the CF gene. I had the recessive gene, and if he had it as well, we wouldn't have been able to have a child without the risk of passing on the disease. Even after the doctor's assurances that we had the all-clear, I still found it hard to get rid of my anxiety. There were plenty of other diseases or birth defects that might await our child, and if I'd learned anything growing up, it was that the worst can and often does happen. I shared my concerns with Jackson over dinner one night.

"What if something's wrong?"

"We'll know. They'll do the testing, and if it isn't healthy, we'll terminate."

He spoke with such detachment that my blood ran cold. "You say it like it's no big deal."

He shrugged. "It isn't. That's why they do the tests, right? So we have a plan. Nothing to worry about."

I wasn't finished discussing it. "What if I don't want to have an abortion? Or what if they say the baby's fine and it isn't, or they say it isn't and it is?"

"What are you talking about? They know what they're doing," he said, an impatient edge in his voice.

"When my cousin's wife, Erin, was pregnant, they told her that her baby was going to have major birth defects, but she didn't end the pregnancy. That was Simone. She was perfect."

An exasperated sigh. "That was years ago. Things are more precise now."

"Still . . ."

"Damn it, Daphne, what do you want me to say? Whatever I tell you, you come up with an illogical retort. Are you trying to be miserable?"

"Of course not."

"Then stop it. We're going to have a baby. I certainly hope this nervous Nellie act goes away before the birth. I can't abide those anxious mothers who worry about every little thing." He took a swig from his tumbler of Hennessy.

"I don't believe in abortion," I blurted out.

"Do you believe in allowing children to suffer? Are you telling me that if you found out that our baby was going to have some horrible disease, you'd have it anyway?"

"It's not so black-and-white. Who are we to say who deserves life and who doesn't? I don't want to make decisions that only God can make."

He raised his eyebrows. "God? You believe in a God who would allow your sister to live a life of suffering and then die when she was still a child? I think we've seen where God's position on these things takes us. I'll make my own choices, thank you very much."

"It's not the same thing at all, Jackson. I can't explain why bad things happen. I'm just saying that I'm carrying a life inside me, and I don't know if I could terminate, no matter what. I don't think I'm capable of that."

He got very quiet, pursed his lips, then spoke deliberately. "Let me help you out then. I cannot raise a disabled child. I know that that is something that I am not capable of."

"The baby is probably fine, but how can you say you can't raise a child with a disability or an illness? It's your child. You don't throw a life away because it's not what you consider perfect. How can you not see that?"

He looked at me a long time before answering. "What I see is that you have no idea what it's like to grow up normally. We shouldn't even be having this conversation yet. If—and that's a big if—it turns out we have something to worry about, we'll discuss it then."

"But—"

He put a hand up to stop me. "The baby will be perfect. You need help, Daphne. It's obvious that you're incapable of letting go of the past. I want you to see a therapist."

"What? You're not serious?"

"I've never been more serious. I won't have you raising our son with all your phobias and paranoia."

"What are you talking about?"

"Everything is colored by your sister's illness. You can't separate that and what it did to you from your present life. You've got to move past it. Put it to bed, for God's sake. Therapy will close the issue once and for all."

I didn't want to dredge up my childhood and live through it again. "Jackson, please, I *have* let go of the past. Haven't we been happy? I'll be fine, I promise you. I was just thrown a little. That's all. I'll be fine. Really."

He arched a perfect brow. "I want to believe you, but I have to be sure."

I gave him a wooden smile. "We're going to have a perfect baby and all live happily ever after."

His lips curled upward. "That's my girl."

Then something he'd said a moment ago registered. "How do you know it's going to be a boy?"

"I don't. But I'm hoping it will. I've always wanted a son—someone I could do all the things with that my father never had time to do with me."

I felt a nervous stirring in my gut. "What if it's a girl?"

He shrugged. "Then we'll try again."

FORTY-THREE

Of course, we had a girl—Tallulah, and she was perfect. She was an easy baby, and I reveled in being a mother. I loved nursing her at night when the house was quiet, staring into her eyes and feeling a connection that I'd never felt before. I followed my mother's advice and slept when she slept, but I was still more exhausted than I'd anticipated. At four months, she still wasn't sleeping through the night, and because I was nursing, I'd refused Jackson's offer of a night nurse. I didn't want to pump and have her fed from a bottle. I wanted to do it all. But that meant I had less time for Jackson.

That's when things began to unravel. By the time he fully revealed himself to me, it was too late. He had used my vulnerability to his advantage, like a general armed for battle. His weapons were kindness, attention, and compassion—and when victory was assured, he discarded them like spent casings, and his true nature emerged.

Jackson faded to the background, and all my time and energy was focused on Tallulah. That morning, I'd pulled the scale out from under the vanity, thrown my robe off, and stepped on—139. I stared at the number in shock. I heard the door open, and he was standing there, looking at me with a strange expression on his face. I went to step off, but he put a hand up, walked toward me, and peered over my shoulder. A look of disgust crossed his face so quickly that I almost missed it. He reached out and patted my stomach, raising his eyebrows.

"Shouldn't this be flat by now?"

I felt the color rush to my face as shame filled me. Stepping off the scale, I grabbed my robe from the floor and threw it on. "Why don't you try having a baby and see how your stomach looks?"

He shook his head. "It's been four months, Daph. Can't use that excuse anymore. I see lots of your friends at the club in their tight jeans. They've all had kids too."

"They probably all had tummy tucks after their C-sections too," I shot back.

He took my face in his hands. "Don't get defensive. You don't need a tummy tuck. You just need some discipline. I married a size four, and I expect you to get back into all those expensive clothes I've bought you. Come on." He took my hand and led me to the love seat in the corner of our bedroom suite. "Sit down and listen."

He put an arm around my shoulder and took a place next to me on the love seat.

"I'm going to help you. You need accountability." Then he pulled out a journal.

"What's that?" I asked.

"I picked it up for you a few weeks ago." Flashing a smile, he continued. "I want you to weigh yourself every day and write it here. Then write down what you've eaten in the food journal part here." He pointed to the page. "I'll check it every night when I get home."

I couldn't believe it. He'd been holding on to this for weeks now? I wanted to curl up and die. Yes, I still wasn't back to my pre-baby weight, but I wasn't fat.

I looked at him, afraid to ask but needing to know. "Do you find me unattractive?"

"Can you blame me? You haven't worked out in months."

I held back the tears and bit my lip. "I'm tired, Jackson. I'm up with the baby in the middle of the night, I'm tired in the morning."

He covered my hand with his. "That's why I keep telling you to let me hire a full-time baby nurse."

"I cherish that time with her. I don't want a stranger here at night."

He stood up, anger in his eyes. "You've done it for months, and look where it's gotten you. At this rate, you'll be as big as a house. I want my wife back. I'm calling the service today and getting a nurse here. You will sleep through the nights again and have your mornings back. I insist."

"But I'm nursing."

He sighed. "Yeah, that's another thing. It's disgusting. Your breasts are like two overblown balloons. I don't want your tits hanging to the floor. Enough is enough."

I stood on shaky legs, nausea overtaking me, and ran to the bathroom. How could he be so cruel? I took my robe off again and examined myself in the full-length mirror. Why hadn't I noticed all that cellulite before? I took a hand and swiped at it on one of my thighs. Like jelly. Pushing both hands on my stomach was like kneading dough. He was right. I turned around and looked over my shoulder, my eyes drawn to the dimpling in my buttocks. I had to fix this. It *was* time to return to the gym. My eyes rested on the breasts my husband found disgusting. I swallowed the lump in my throat, got dressed, and went downstairs. Picking up the grocery list sitting on the counter, I added another item: formula.

Margarita had prepared a breakfast buffet that morning to rival the Ritz. When Jackson came in, he filled his plate to overflowing with pancakes, bacon, strawberries, and a homemade muffin. I thought about the journal he'd just given me and felt the heat spread to my face. He was crazy if he thought I'd have him dictating what I ate. I'd start my diet tomorrow and on my own terms. I grabbed a plate and picked up the fork on the pancake platter, ready to take one, when he cleared his throat. I looked over at him. He inclined his head ever so slightly toward the fruit platter. I took a deep breath, stabbed three pancakes with my fork, and dropped them onto my plate. Ignoring him, I grabbed the syrup and poured until they were swimming in it. As I lifted the fork, I held his gaze as I stuffed a fluffy slice of pancake slathered in syrup into my mouth.

FORTY-FOUR

paid for my little act of rebellion. Not right away, because that wasn't his style. By the time he executed his plan three weeks later, I had nearly forgotten about it. But he hadn't. My mother was coming for a visit. After my father died, she came often—every few months—and I encouraged her visits. The night before she was due to arrive, he exacted his revenge. He waited until Tallulah had been put down and came into the kitchen, where I was talking to Margarita about the menu for dinner the next night. He was standing in the archway, leaning against the doorframe, arms crossed, with an amused expression on his face. When she left, he walked over to me, pushed a lock of hair from my forehead, then leaned down to whisper in my ear.

"She's not coming."

"What?" My stomach turned to jelly.

He nodded. "I just got off the phone with her, let her know you're not feeling well."

I pushed him away from me. "What are you talking about? I feel fine."

"Oh, but you don't. You have a terrible stomachache from stuffing yourself with pancakes."

Was he really still holding a grudge from weeks ago? "You're joking, right?" I said, hoping he was.

His eyes were cold. "I've never been more serious."

"I'm calling her right now." He grabbed my arm before I could move.

"And tell her what? That your husband lied? What would she think of that? Besides, I told her that you had food poisoning and asked me to call her. I assured her you would be better in a few days." Then he laughed. "I also mentioned that you'd been a bit stressed and that having her visit so often was putting a strain on you, that maybe she should let a little more time elapse between visits."

"You can't do this. I won't let you make my mother think I don't want her here."

He squeezed my arm harder. "It's done. You should have heard how sad she sounded. Poor, dumb hick." He laughed.

I wrenched my arm away and slapped him. He laughed again.

"Too bad she didn't die when your father did. I really hate having in-laws."

I exploded. I raked my nails down his face, wanting to tear it to shreds. I felt wetness on my hands and realized I'd drawn blood. Horrified, I backed away, my hand to my mouth.

He shook his head slowly. "Now look what you've done." Pulling his phone from his pocket, he held it in front of his face. It took me a minute to realize what he was doing. "Thanks, Daph. Now I have proof that you have an explosive temper."

"You intentionally provoked me?"

A cold smile. "Here's a little tip: I will always be ten steps ahead of you. Keep that in mind when you decide you know better than I do what's good for you." He moved toward me, and I stood rooted to the floor, too shocked to move. He touched my cheek, and the look in his eyes grew tender. "I love you. Why can't you see that? I don't want to punish you—but what am I to do when you insist on doing things that are bad for you?"

He's crazy. How did it take me this long to see that he's crazy? I swallowed hard and flinched when his fingers traced the tears running down my cheeks. I ran from the room, grabbed a few things from the bedroom, and went into one of the guest rooms. I caught a glimpse of myself in the mirror—white as a ghost, whole body shaking. Moving into the guest bathroom, I washed my hands, cleaning his blood from under my nails, and tried to come to grips with how I had let myself lose control. I'd never done something like that before. His cavalier comment about my mother dying made me realize there was no going back after tonight. I had to leave. Tomorrow I would pack up the baby and go to my mother's.

After a few minutes, I went in to check on Tallulah and found him standing over her crib. I hesitated at the doorway, something about the picture not striking me as quite right. His stance was menacing; his face in shadow, ominous. My heart beat faster as I approached.

He didn't turn toward me or acknowledge my presence. In his hands he held the enormous teddy bear he had bought for her when she was born.

"What are you doing?" I whispered.

As he spoke, he continued to stare at her. "Did you know that over two thousand babies die of SIDS each year?"

I tried to answer, but no words would come.

"That's why you put nothing in the crib." Then he turned to face me. "I keep telling you not to put her stuffed animals in with her. But you are so forgetful."

I found my voice. "You wouldn't dare. She's your child, how could you—"

He threw the bear onto the rocking chair, and his expression was neutral once again. "I was just joking around. You take everything so seriously." He grabbed both of my hands in his.

"Nothing will ever happen to her as long as she has two parents looking out for her."

I turned from him to watch my baby breathing in and out, and was crushed by her vulnerability.

"I'm going to sit here for a while," I whispered.

"Good idea. Do some thinking while you're at it. I'll be waiting for you in bed. Make sure you don't take too long."

I glared at him. "You can't be serious. I'm not getting near you."

A thin smile played on his lips. "You might want to rethink that. Tire me out, or I may sleepwalk and find myself back in the nursery." He stretched his hand out to me. "On second thought, I want you now."

Silent and dying inside, I took his hand, and he led me to our room and to the bed. "Take your clothes off," he commanded.

I sat on the bed and began to pull off my slacks.

"No. Stand up. Do a strip-tease for me."

"Jackson, please."

I gasped as he yanked me by my hair toward him. He pinched my breast hard. "Don't piss me off. Do it. Now."

My legs were so jellylike, I don't know how I remained standing. I made my mind go blank, shut my eyes, and pretended I was anywhere but there. I unbuttoned my blouse one button at a time, opening my eyes and looking at him to see if I was doing it right. He nodded, and as I stripped, he began to stroke himself. I didn't know who this man was, sitting on my bed, looking like my husband. All I could think to ask myself was how he had done it. How had he played the part for over a year? What kind of a person can keep up a charade for that long? And why was he showing me the truth now? Did he think that I'd stay with him just because we had a child together? Tomorrow, I would go, but tonight, I'd do what he said, do whatever it took to make him think he'd won.

I continued the performance until I was naked. He reached out for me and threw me onto the bed. Then he was on top of me, his touch maddeningly tender and attentive. I would have preferred for him to take me roughly, and for the sake of my daughter, I forced my body to betray me and respond—for he was nothing if not perceptive, and I knew he would never abide my holding back.

FORTY-FIVE

The next morning after he'd left for work, I raced through the house, packed up as much as I could, put the baby in the car, and began the long drive to New Hampshire. I knew my mother was going to be shocked when she found out the truth, but I would be able to count on her support. It would take us around five hours to reach the inn. My thoughts raced as I tried to sort out how this would all shake out. I knew he'd be furious, of course, but there was nothing he could do once we were gone. I would tell the police about his threats to the baby. Surely they could protect us.

He called my cell phone when we reached Massachusetts. I let it go to voice mail. My text tones kept sounding: **ping, ping, ping**—rapid-fire like a machine gun. I didn't look at the texts until I stopped at a rest stop for gas.

What are you doing in Massachusetts? Daphne, where is the baby?
You haven't hurt her, have you? Please answer me.
I didn't think you were serious last night. Don't listen to the voices.
Daphne, please answer! I'm worried about you.
Call me. Please. I'll get you help. Just don't hurt Tallulah.

What was he doing? And how did he know where I was? I hadn't given him any indication that I was leaving. I had made sure that none of the staff had seen me. Did he have a tracker on my car somehow?

I picked up the phone and dialed him. He answered on the first ring.

"You bitch! What the hell do you think you're doing?" I could feel his fury over the phone.

"I'm going to see my mother."

"Without telling me? You turn that car around and get back here now. Do you hear me?"

"Or what? You can't tell me what to do. I've had enough, Jackson." My voice shook, and I glanced at the backseat to make sure Tallulah was still asleep. "You threatened to hurt our baby. Did you really think I'd let you do that? You're not getting near her again."

He started to laugh. "You're such a little fool."

"Go ahead and insult me. I don't care. I'm going to tell my mother everything."

"This is your last chance to come back, or you'll regret it."

"Good-bye, Jackson." I pressed end and put the car back in gear. My text tone started pinging again. I turned the phone off.

With every passing mile, my resolve strengthened, and my hope blossomed. I knew I was doing the right thing, and no amount of threatening on his part would sway me. I was still in Massachusetts when a flash of lights in my rearview mirror gave me pause. As the police car closed the gap between us, I realized he wanted *me* to pull over. I was only going a few miles over the speed limit. I pulled the car to the side of the road, and the state trooper approached.

"License and registration, please."

I retrieved them from the glove box and handed them over.

The officer returned to his car with them, and after a few minutes he came back. "Please step out of the car."

"Why?" I asked.

"Please, ma'am. Out of the car."

"Have I done something wrong?"

"An emergency confinement order is in effect. It claims you're a danger to your child. The baby will have to stay with us until your husband arrives."

"She's *my* child!" That bastard had actually called the police on me.

"Please don't make me cuff you. I need you to come with me."

I got out of the car, and the officer took hold of my arm.

Tallulah had woken up and started crying. Her little face was beet red, her cries turning to screams. "Please, she's frightened. I can't leave my baby!"

"We'll take care of her, ma'am."

I pulled my arm away and tried to get to the car, to take her from her seat and comfort her. "Tallulah!"

"Please stop. I really don't want to have to restrain you." He pulled me away and into the waiting cruiser, and I had to leave her there with the police while they drove me to a local hospital.

I didn't find out until the next day that Jackson had put a contingency plan into effect weeks before. He'd convinced a judge that I was suffering from depression and had threatened to harm the baby. He even had two signed statements from physicians— doctors I'd never even met. I could only imagine that his money had bought them. My claims that I'd been set up fell on deaf ears. Crazy people have no credibility, and I was now considered crazy. During my hold at the hospital, I was evaluated by a number of doctors who agreed that I needed treatment. No one believed me when I told them what he had done, how he'd manipulated the situation. They looked at me like I was a lunatic. The only thing they would tell me was that Jackson had picked Tallulah up right away from the police station and taken her home. I'd been informed that I was being transferred to Meadow Lakes Hospital, which was in Fair Haven, the town neighboring Bishops Harbor. After seventy-two hours of screaming, begging, and crying, I was no closer to being released than when I'd first arrived, and by then I was doped up with who knew what. My only hope rested in convincing Jackson to get me out.

Once they moved me to Meadow Lakes, he left me there for seven days before he finally came to see me. I had no idea what he'd told my mother or the staff about why I was gone. When he showed up in the common room, I wanted to kill him.

"How could you do this to me?" I hissed under my breath, not wanting to make a scene.

He sat next to me and took my hand in his, smiling at a woman across from me who didn't bother to hide her curious stare as she observed us.

"Daphne, I'm only looking out for you and our child." He made sure to speak loudly enough for everyone to hear.

"What do you want from me?"

He squeezed my hand hard. "I want you to come home, where you belong. But only when you're ready."

I bit my tongue to keep myself from screaming. Taking deep breaths until I could speak without my voice shaking, I said, "I'm ready."

"Well, that's for your therapist to decide."

I stood. "Why don't we take a walk on the grounds?"

Once we were outside and no one could hear us, I let my anger show. "Cut the crap, Jackson. You know I don't belong here. I want my baby. What did you tell everyone?"

He looked straight ahead as we walked. "That you're sick and will be home as soon as you're better."

"What about my mother?"

He stopped and turned to look at me. "I told her that you had been increasingly depressed about Julie and your dad, and had tried to kill yourself."

"What?" I shouted.

"She wants you to stay as long as necessary—make sure you get better."

"You're hateful. Why are you doing this?"

"Why do you think?"

I started to cry. "I loved you. We were so happy. I don't understand what happened. Why did you change? How can you expect me to stay with you when you threaten our child and are so horrible to me?"

He started to walk again, maddeningly calm. "I don't know what you're talking about. I didn't threaten anyone. And I treat you like a queen. You're the envy of everyone you meet. If I have to keep you in line occasionally, well, that's part of being married. I'm not whipped like your father was. This is how a strong man handles his wife. Get used to it."

"Get used to what? Being abused? I'll never get used to that." My face was burning.

"Abused? I've never laid a hand on you."

"There are other kinds of abuse," I said. I searched his face for any sign of the man I had first believed him to be. Deciding to try a different tactic, I softened my voice. "Jackson?"

"Hmm?"

I took a deep breath. "I'm not happy, and I don't think you are either."

"Of course I'm not happy. My wife tried to steal my child out from under me with no warning."

"Why do you want me to come home? You don't love me."

He stopped walking and looked at me, his mouth agape. "What?

Are you serious? Daphne, I've spent the past two years teaching, coaching, grooming you to be a wife I can be proud of. We have a beautiful family. Everyone looks up to us. How can you ask me why I'd fight to keep my family?"

"You've mistreated me since Tallulah was born, and it gets worse every day."

"Accuse me again, and you'll stay here forever and never see her again." He started walking again, fast this time.

I struggled to catch up, dropping the conciliatory tone. "You can't do that!"

"Just watch me. The law's on my side. And did I mention that I just donated ten million dollars for a new wing at this hospital? I'm sure they'll be happy to have you stay for as long as I like."

"You're insane."

He swung around, grabbed me, and pulled me close. With his mouth inches from mine, he spoke. "This is the last time we're having this conversation. You are mine. You'll always be mine, and you'll listen to what I say from now on. If you are a good little wife and obey, everything will be fine." He leaned closer, put his lips on mine, then bit down hard. I yelled and sprang back, but his hand on my head prevented my pulling away. "If you don't, then trust me: you'll spend the rest of your life wishing you did, and your child will have a new mother."

I knew he had me. It didn't matter that he was the one who was crazy. He had the money and the influence, and he'd played his hand brilliantly.

How had this happened? I struggled to get a deep breath, to come up with something, anything, that would help me to believe there was a way out. Looking at my husband, this stranger who held my future in his hands, I could come up with nothing. Filled with despair, I whispered, "I'll do whatever you say. Just get me out of here."

He smiled. "That's my girl. You'll have to stay for a month or so. It wouldn't look right if you came right out. Your therapist and I go back a long way. We've been friends since college. He had a little trouble a few years back." He shrugged. "Anyhow, I helped him out, and he owes me. I'll tell him to release you in thirty days. He'll claim it was a hormonal imbalance or something easily fixed."

Thirty-five days later, I was released. We had to go to family court to prove I was a fit mother. We met with his attorney, and I played along. He made me corroborate his lie that I was hearing voices telling me to hurt my baby. I had to agree to keep seeing Dr. Finn, Jackson's friend, which was a total joke. He was always solicitous, asking how I was adapting to being home again, but we both knew the sessions were a charade. Now Jackson had something else to hold over my head, to make sure I never left again, and I knew Dr. Finn's notes would say whatever Jackson wanted them to. When I was finally allowed to go home, the only thing I cared about was being back with Tallulah. I told myself that eventually I'd find a way to escape him. In the meantime, I did what any good mother would do: I sacrificed my happiness to protect my child.

FORTY-SIX

'd only been at Meadow Lakes for a little over a month, but it felt like years. Jackson came to fetch me himself, and I sat in the passenger seat of his Mercedes roadster, looking out the window, afraid to say the wrong thing. He was in a good mood, humming as if this were any ordinary day and we were simply out for a drive. When he pulled up to the house, I felt strangely outside myself, like I was watching someone else's life. Someone who lived in a beautiful estate on the water who had lots of money and everything she could want. Suddenly I longed for the haven of my room at the hospital, far from the prying eyes of my husband.

The first thing I did when I got inside was race up the stairs to Tallulah's nursery. I flung open the door, eager to gather her in my arms. Sitting in the chair rocking Tallulah was a beautiful dark-haired young woman I'd never seen before.

"Who are you?"

"Sabine. Who are you?" She had a thick French accent.

"I'm Mrs. Parrish." I held out my arms. "Please give my daughter to me."

She stood, turned her back on me, and moved away. "I'm sorry, madame. I need to hear from Mr. Parrish that it is okay."

I saw red. "Give her to me," I screamed.

"What's going on?" Jackson strode into the room.

"This woman won't give me my child!"

Jackson sighed and took the baby from Sabine and handed her to me. "Please excuse us, Sabine."

She threw a look at me and left.

"Where's Sally? Did you hire that, that . . . creature? She completely disrespected me."

"Sally's gone. Don't blame Sabine, she didn't know who you were. She was looking out for Tallulah. Sabine will teach her to speak French. You have to think of our child's well-being. Things are running smoothly now. Don't try and come back here and upset the apple cart."

"'Upset the apple cart?' She's *my* child."

He sat down on the bed. "Daphne, I know you grew up poor, but there are certain things that will be expected of our children."

"What do you mean, I grew up poor? I'm from a middle-class family. We had everything we needed. We weren't poor."

He sighed and threw his hands up in the air. "Excuse me. Okay, you weren't poor. But you certainly weren't rich."

I felt my stomach tighten. "Our definitions of rich and poor are vastly different."

His voice rose. "You know damn well what I'm trying to say. You're not used to how people with money do things. Doesn't matter. The point is, leave it to me. Sabine will be a big asset to our family. Now that's enough. I have a special dinner planned. Don't spoil it."

All I wanted was to be with the baby, but I knew better than to complain. I couldn't risk being sent back to Meadow Lake. Another month there, and I would have truly lost my mind.

All during dinner, he was in an unusually good mood. We shared a bottle of wine, and he'd had Margarita prepare my favorite seafood dish—crab imperial. There was even cherries jubilee for dessert—all very festive, as though my exile hadn't been by his design and had instead been a relaxing vacation. My mind was racing the entire evening as I tried to keep up with his uncharacteristic nonstop chatter and be engaging. By the time we went upstairs to bed, I was exhausted.

"I bought you something special for tonight." He handed me a black box.

I opened it with trepidation. "What is this?" I pulled the black leather straps out, studied it, not sure exactly what it was supposed to be. There was a thick collar too, with a round metal ring attached to it.

He walked around behind me and slid a hand down to my hip. "It's just a little role-playing fun." He took the collar from my hand and put it up to my neck.

I shoved his hand away. "Forget it! I'm not wearing that . . . thing." I threw it on the bed along with the corset of straps. "I'm bushed. I'm going to sleep." I left him standing there and went into the bathroom to brush my teeth. When I came out, he was in bed, his light out, eyes closed.

I should have known it was too easy.

I tossed and turned until I heard the soft sound of his snoring and relaxed enough to drift off. I don't know what time it was when I was awakened by the feeling of something hard and cold on my lips. My eyes flew open, and I was trying to swat it away when I felt his hand grip my wrist.

"Open your mouth." His voice was low, guttural.

"What are you doing? Get off of me."

His grip tightened, and with the other hand, he yanked my hair until my chin was pointing to the ceiling. "I'm not asking again."

I opened my mouth and tensed as he shoved a cylinder into it until I started to gag. He laughed. Then he was straddling me, reaching for the lamp by my side of the bed. When the light came on, I realized what was in my mouth—the barrel of a gun.

He's going to kill me. Panic swallowed me, and I laid perfectly still, terrified to move. I watched in horror as his index finger moved to the trigger.

"What will I tell Tallulah when she grows up?" he sneered. "How will I explain that her mother didn't even love her enough to live?"

I wanted to yell out but was afraid to move. I felt tears rolling down the side of my face into my ears.

"I guess I could lie and say suicide runs in your family. She'd never know. Maybe one day I'll even tell her that Aunt Julie killed herself." He laughed. Leaning forward, he kissed my forehead, and then his eyes grew cold. "Or you could start doing what you're told."

He pulled the gun from my mouth, traced my neck, my breasts, and my stomach with it, like a lover's caress. I squeezed my eyes shut, and all I could hear was the blood pounding in my ears. *I'm never going to see my child grow up.* My body tensed in anticipation.

"Open your eyes."

He moved away, the gun still pointed at me.

I exhaled, and a sigh of relief escaped.

"Put on the outfit."

"Whatever you want, just, please, put the gun away," I managed in a whisper.

"Don't make me say it again."

I slid from the bed and retrieved the bag from the chair where I'd thrown it. My hands were shaking so hard that I kept dropping the bustier. Finally, I figured out how to get it on.

"Don't forget the collar."

I fastened the leather collar around my neck.

"Make it tighter," he commanded.

I reached back and moved the collar one more notch. My heart was pounding, and I struggled to steady my breathing. Maybe if I just did what he said, he'd put the gun away.

A lazy smile appeared, and he walked toward me, grabbed the metal ring on the collar, and pulled hard. I jerked forward. He pulled harder until I fell to the floor.

"Get on your knees."

I did as I was told.

"That's a good little slave." Walking over to his closet, he snatched a necktie and brought it over. "Put your hands behind your back." He wrapped the tie around my wrists and knotted it tight, then stood back and held his hands as if pretending to frame a picture. "Not quite right." He walked back to the closet and came out carrying a ball.

"Open wide." He stuffed the soft plastic gag in my mouth.

"That's nice." He put the gun on his nightstand and, grabbing his cell phone, started snapping pictures. "This will make a delightful scrapbook." He undressed and walked toward me. "Let me replace that ball with something else." He pushed himself inside my mouth and snapped more pictures. He pulled away and looked at me with derision. "You don't deserve me. Do you know how many women would love to put their lips on me, and you act like it's a chore?"

"I'm sorry."

"You should be. You stay there and think about what it means to be a good wife, how to prove to me that you find me desirable. Maybe I'll let you pleasure me in the morning." He got in bed. "And don't even think of moving until I give you permission—or the next time, I'll pull the trigger." He slid the gun under his pillow.

The room went black as he turned out the light, and suddenly, I almost wished he had.

FORTY-SEVEN

lived in constant fear of losing Tallulah. The social worker, the attorneys, the bureaucrats, they all looked at me the same way—with a mixture of suspicion and disgust. I knew they were thinking, *How could she threaten to hurt her child?* In town, I heard the whispers—it's impossible to keep something like this quiet. I confided in no one, couldn't tell any of my friends the truth, not even Meredith. I had to live the hateful lie that he had thrust upon me, and after a while, even I almost believed it.

From then on, I did whatever he said. I smiled at him, laughed at his jokes, bit my tongue when I was tempted to argue or talk back. It was a tightrope walk, because if I acted too compliant, he'd get angry and accuse me of being a robot. He wanted some spunk, but I never knew how much. I was always off balance, one leg dangling over the abyss. I watched him with Tallulah, terrified he'd hurt her, but as time went on I realized his twisted games were focused only on me. Anyone looking at us from the outside would have believed we were the perfect family. He took great pains to ensure that I was the only one who saw the mask drop. When we were around anyone else, I had to act like the adoring wife to a wonderful husband.

The days turned to weeks and months, and I learned how to be exactly what he wanted. I became an expert at reading his face, hearing the strain in his voice, doing everything I could to avoid some imagined slight or insult. Months would go by when nothing horrible would happen. He'd even be nice, and we'd go through the days acting as though we were a normal couple. Until I got too complacent and forgot to complete an errand he'd asked me to do, or ordered the wrong caviar from the caterer. Then the gun would make an appearance again, and I always wondered if that would be the night he'd kill me. The next day a gift would arrive. A piece of jewelry, a designer purse, some expensive perfume. And every time I had to wear any of it, I'd be reminded of what I'd endured to receive it.

When Tallulah turned two, he decided it was time for another baby. One night, I was in the bathroom looking in the drawer for my diaphragm—I put it in nightly, never knowing when he'd want to have sex. I wished I could take the pill, but I'd had an adverse reaction to it and my doctor insisted I use something else. When Jackson came into the room, I turned to him.

"Have you seen my diaphragm?"

"I threw it out."

"Why?"

He walked over and pushed himself against me. "We should make another baby. A boy this time."

I felt my stomach turn and tried to swallow. "So soon? Tallulah's only two."

He led me over to the bed and untied the belt holding my robe shut. "It's perfect timing."

I stalled. "What if it's another girl?"

His eyes narrowed. "Then we'll keep going until you give me what I want. What's the big deal?"

The telltale vein in his temple started pulsating, and I rushed to smooth things over before he lost his temper. "You're right, darling. It's just that I've enjoyed being able to focus my attention on you. I wasn't thinking about another baby. But if that's what you want, then I want it too."

He tilted his head and leveled a long stare at me. "Are you patronizing me?"

I inhaled. "No, Jackson. Of course not."

Without another word he pulled my robe off and fell on top of me. When he finished, he grabbed two pillows and put them under my hips.

"Stay that way for half an hour. I've been tracking your cycles. You should be ovulating."

I started to protest, but stopped myself. I could feel the frustration and anger welling up until it was a physical force that wanted to erupt, but I breathed deeply and smiled at him instead. "Here's hoping."

It took nearly nine months this time, and when it finally happened, he was so happy that he forgot to be cruel. And then we went for the twenty-week visit—the one that would reveal the sex of the baby. He'd cleared his schedule so he could go with me that day. I was on eggshells all morning, dreading his reaction if it didn't go his way, but he was confident, even whistling in the car on the way over.

"I've got a good feeling about this, Daphne. Jackson Junior. That's what we'll call him."

I looked at him from the corner of my eye. "Jackson, what if—"

He cut me off. "No negativity. Why do you always have to be such a downer?"

As the ultrasound wand moved around my belly and we looked at the heartbeat and the torso, I was making such a tight fist that I realized my nails were digging into my palm.

"Are you ready to know what you're having?" the doctor asked in her cheery, singsong voice.

I looked at Jackson's face.

"It's a girl!" she said.

His eyes went cold, and he turned and left the room without a word. The doctor looked at me, surprised, and I came up with something on the fly.

"He just lost his mother. She always wanted a girl. He was embarrassed for you to see him cry."

She gave me a strained smile and spoke stiffly. "Well, let's get you cleaned up, and you can go home."

He didn't speak to me the entire ride home. I knew better than to try and say anything to make it better. I had screwed up again, and even though I knew that of course it wasn't my fault, I felt my anger turn inward. Why couldn't I just have given him a son?

He stayed in the New York apartment for the next three nights, and I was grateful for the reprieve. When he came home the next night, he almost seemed back to normal—or whatever normal was for him. He'd texted me to let me know he'd be home at seven, and I'd made sure to have stuffed pheasant ready for dinner, one of his favorites. When we sat down to eat, he poured himself a glass of wine, took a sip, then cleared his throat.

"I've come up with a solution."

"What?"

He sighed loudly. "A solution to your ineptitude. It's too late to do anything about this one." He gestured at my stomach. "Everyone already knows you're pregnant. But the next time, we're getting an earlier test. CVS. I looked it up. It can tell us the sex, and we can do it well before your third month."

"What will that accomplish?" I asked, even as I knew what the answer would be.

He raised his eyebrows. "If the next one's a girl, you can abort it, and we'll keep trying until you get it right."

He picked up his fork and took a bite. "By the way, can I trust you to remember to send in Tallulah's application to St. Patrick's preschool? I want to make sure she gets into the threes program next year."

I nodded mutely as the asparagus in my mouth turned to mush. I discreetly spit it into my napkin and took a swallow from the glass of water in front of me. *Abortion?* I had to do something. Could I get my tubes tied without him finding out? I'd have to figure something out after this baby was born. Some way to make sure it was the last pregnancy I ever had.

FORTY-EIGHT

The children were what helped me to keep my sanity. As the saying goes, the days were long but the years were short. I learned to put up with his demands and his moods, only occasionally messing up and daring to talk back or refuse him something. On those occasions, he made sure to remind me of what was at stake if I screwed up. He showed me an updated letter from two doctors certifying my mental illness, which he kept locked in a safe-deposit box. I didn't bother asking what he had on them to get them to go along with his lies. If I tried to leave again, he said, this time he'd lock me up in the loony bin forever. I wasn't about to test him.

I became his pet project. By the time Bella was in first grade, both girls were in school all day, and he decided my education should continue as well. I had a master's degree, but that wasn't enough. He came home one night and handed me a catalog.

"I've signed you up for French lessons three days a week. The class starts at 2:45. That way you can still get to the foundation on your two days there and the gym beforehand."

The girls were doing their homework at the kitchen island, and Tallulah looked up, pencil poised in the air, waiting for me to answer.

"Jackson, what are you talking about?"

He looked at Tallulah. "Mommy's going back to school. Isn't that great?"

Bella clapped her hands. "Yay. Will she come to my school?"

"No, darling. She'll go to the local university."

Tallulah pursed her lips. "Didn't Mommy already go to college?"

Jackson walked over to her. "Yes, my sweet, but she doesn't know how to speak French like you two do. You don't want a stupid mommy, do you?"

Tallulah's eyebrows furrowed. "Mommy's not stupid."

He laughed. "You're right, sweetie. She's not stupid. But she's not polished. She came from a poor family where they don't know how to behave in polite society. We need to help her learn. Right, Mommy?"

"Right," I answered through clenched teeth.

The class was right in the middle of the day, and I hated it. The professor was a snobby Frenchwoman who wore fake eyelashes and too-red lipstick and talked about how crass Americans were. She took special delight in pointing out the flaws in my accent. I'd only been to one class and was already sick of it.

I was nonetheless getting ready to go back the next week when I got an emergency call from Fiona at the foundation. One of our clients needed to get his son to the hospital, and his car wouldn't start. I offered to take him, even though it meant missing a class. Of course, I never mentioned a thing to Jackson.

The following Monday, I received a frantic call from the girls' school just as I got back to the house after a long massage and facial.

"Mrs. Parrish?"

"Yes."

"We've been trying to reach you for three hours."

"Is everything okay? Are the children all right?"

"Yes. But they are quite upset. You were supposed to pick them up at noon."

Noon? What was she talking about? "They don't get dismissed until three."

An exasperated sigh on the other end. "It's a teacher planning afternoon. It's been on the calendar for a month, and we sent a note home. You should also have received an e-mail and a text."

"I'm so sorry. I'll be right there. I didn't receive any calls on my cell," I said apologetically.

"Well, we've been dialing it for hours. We couldn't reach your husband either. He's apparently out of town."

Jackson wasn't on a business trip, and I had no idea why his assistant hadn't put her through.

I hung up and ran to the car. What could have happened? I pulled out my phone and looked at it. No missed calls. I checked my texts. Nothing.

At the red light, I searched through my e-mails and didn't see any from the school. A sick feeling wound its way from my belly up to my chest. Jackson had to be responsible, but how? Had he deleted the e-mails and texts from my phone? Could he have blocked the school phone number? And why would he do this to the girls?

I skulked up to the main office, dying of embarrassment, and took my little girls from the office of the disapproving headmistress.

"Mrs. Parrish, this isn't the first time. This behavior cannot continue. It's not fair to your daughters, and frankly, it's not fair to us either."

I felt my cheeks go warm, and I wished the floor would swallow me up right then and there. Only a couple of weeks before, I'd been over an hour late for pickup, and Jackson had been called to retrieve the children. Earlier that day, he'd come home for lunch, and after he'd left, I was suddenly exhausted and lay down for a quick nap. I didn't wake up until the three of them came in the door at four o'clock. I had slept right through the phone alarm.

"I'm sorry, Mrs. Sinclair. I don't know what happened. I don't have any of the e-mails or texts, and for some reason my phone never rang."

Her expression made it clear she didn't believe a word I was saying. "Yes, well. Please see to it that it doesn't happen again."

I went to take their hands, and Bella pulled hers away, stomping ahead of me toward the car. She didn't speak to me the entire ride home. When we got to the house, Sabine was waiting, fixing a snack for them.

"Sabine, were you here this afternoon? The school was trying to reach me."

"No, madam. I was at the grocer's."

I picked up the house phone and dialed my cell. It rang in my ear, but the cell phone in my hand didn't buzz. What was going on? With a sinking feeling, I unlocked my phone and went to Settings, tapped Phone, and looked at My Number. My mouth dropped open as it revealed a number I didn't recognize. I took a closer look. It was a new phone. My old one had a tiny crack in the plastic by the home key. Jackson must have replaced it. Now I wondered about the other time I'd been late for pickup. Had he drugged me?

"Daddy's home!" Bella squealed.

As she ran into his arms, he leveled a look at me over her head. "How's my girl?"

She stuck her lip out. "Mommy forgot us at school again. We had to sit in the office all day. It was terrible."

A look passed between Jackson and Sabine.

He hugged her tighter and kissed the top of her head. "My poor darling. Mommy has been very forgetful lately. She missed her French class too."

Tallulah looked over at me. "What happened, Mom?"

Jackson answered for me. "Mommy has a drinking problem, sweetie. Sometimes she just gets too drunk to do what she needs. But we'll help her, won't we?"

"Jackson! That's not—"

I heard Sabine gasp.

"Don't lie anymore, Daphne. I know you missed your French class last week," he interrupted. He took my hand in his, squeezing hard. "If you just admit you have a problem, I can help you. Otherwise, you may need to go back to the hospital."

Tallulah jumped up, tears springing to her eyes. "No, Mommy! Don't leave us." She threw her arms around my waist.

I struggled to find my voice. "Of course not, sweetheart. I'm not going anywhere."

"Sabine will pick you up from now on. That way, the school won't get the wrong idea if Mommy forgets again. Right, Mommy?"

I took a deep breath, trying to slow the pounding in my chest. "Right."

He reached out and touched the sleeve of my shirt. "And that's a really ugly outfit you have on. Why don't you go change? Bella, go help Mommy find a nice dress for dinner."

"Come on, Mommy. I know what would look pretty on you."

FORTY-NINE

All of a sudden, everywhere I looked, there were turtles. They hid behind photographs, peered out from bookshelves, perched menacingly on dresser tops.

In the early days, before I learned not to share my soul, I'd told Jackson why I hated them. When Julie and I were young, my father bought a turtle for us. We'd always wanted a dog or a cat, but unrelated to her CF, Julie was allergic to both. My mom had asked him to get a box turtle, but he brought home a snapping turtle instead. It had been returned to the store after a year because its previous owner couldn't care for it anymore. That very first day, I was feeding him a carrot, and he snapped and bit my finger. His jaw was so strong I couldn't free it, and I screamed while Julie ran to find my mother. I can still remember the pain and my panicked feeling that he would bite it off. My mother's quick thinking of offering him another carrot worked, and his mouth opened again. I pulled my bleeding finger out of its mouth, and we went to the emergency room. Of course, we returned the turtle, and I was left with a permanent fear of anything with a hard shell.

Jackson had listened, murmuring comfort, and it had felt good to unburden myself of another childhood trauma. When Bella was a baby, I put her down for her nap one day, and as I was leaving her nursery, something leaning over the shelf caught my eye. It was positioned among her stuffed animals. I called Jackson at work.

"Where did the turtle in Bella's room come from?"

"What?"

"The turtle. It was in with her stuffed animals."

"Are you serious? I'm in the middle of a killer day, and you're asking me about a stuffed animal. I have no idea. Is there anything else?"

I suddenly felt foolish. "No. Sorry to bother you."

I took the damn thing and threw it in the trash.

The next day, Meredith stopped by for a visit, and I invited her to have coffee in the conservatory. She walked over to the floor-to-ceiling bookcases and picked something up.

"This is lovely, Daphne. I've never noticed it before." She was holding a white-and-gold porcelain turtle.

I dropped my cup, spilling hot coffee all over myself.

"Oh my gosh, what a klutz," I sputtered and rang for Margarita to clean up. "Jackson must have picked that up. I hadn't noticed." I clasped my hands together to stop them shaking.

"Well, it's quite beautiful. Limoges."

"Take it."

She shook her head. "Don't be silly. I was only admiring it." She gave me a strange look. "It's time I was going. I'm meeting Rand at the club for lunch." Then she put her hand on my arm. "Are you okay?"

"Yes, just tired. I'm still adjusting to the baby's schedule."

She smiled. "Of course. Try and get some rest. I'll call you later."

After she left, I searched online to find the turtle. Over $900!

That night, I placed it on the table in front of his plate. When he sat down to dinner, he glanced at it, then back at me.

"What's this doing here?"

"That's exactly what I'd like to know."

He shrugged. "It belongs in the conservatory."

"Jackson, why are you doing this? You know how I feel about turtles."

"Do you hear how crazy you sound? It's just a little figure. Can't hurt you." He was looking at me with that smug expression, challenging me with his eyes.

"I don't like them. Please stop."

"Stop what? You're being awfully paranoid. Maybe that postpartum depression has returned. Should we talk to the doctor?"

I threw my napkin on my plate and stood up. "I'm not crazy. First the stuffed animal, and now this."

He shook his head and made a circular motion with his finger by his ear—like kids do in school to indicate someone is cuckoo.

I flew up the stairs and slammed the bedroom door. Flinging myself on the bed, I screamed into my pillow. When I lifted my head, two marble eyes were staring at me from my nightstand. I picked up the glass turtle and threw it as hard as I could against the bedroom wall. It didn't shatter, but merely landed on the floor with a soft thud. It sat there, appraising me with its reptilian eyes, perched as though it was preparing to crawl toward me and punish me for what I had done.

FIFTY

When you discover you are married to a sociopath, you have to become resourceful. There's no point in trying to change him—once the pot is in the kiln, it's too late. The best I could do was study him—the real him, the one hiding behind his well-polished veneer of humanity and normalcy. Now that I knew the truth, it was easy to spot. Things like the small smile playing at his lips when he was pretending to be sad. He was a brilliant mimic and knew just what to say and do to ingratiate himself into the affections of others. Now that he'd dropped the facade with me, I had to figure out how to beat him at his own game.

I took him up on his suggestion to take more courses at the university. But I didn't study art. I bought the textbooks for the art class and figured I would read up on my own in case he quizzed me. Instead, I signed up for psychology courses, paying cash for them and registering under a different name with a post office box. The campus was large enough that there was little chance of my French professor seeing me while I was pretending to be someone else, but just in case, I wore a baseball cap and sweats to those classes. It's worth noting that by this point in my marriage, these measures didn't seem extreme to me. I had adjusted to a life where subterfuge and deceit were as natural as breathing.

In my abnormal psychology class, I began to put the pieces together. My professor was a fascinating woman who had a private practice. Hearing her describe some of her patients was like listening to a description of Jackson. I took another abnormal psych course with her as well as her class on personality. Then I spent hours at the university library reading everything I could get my hands on about the antisocial personality.

Interviews with sociopaths have revealed that they're able to identify a potential victim merely by the way the person walks. Our bodies apparently telegraph our vulnerabilities and sensitivities. Spouses of sociopaths are said to have an overabundance of empathy. I found that bit of information hard to understand. Is there really such a thing as too much empathy? It had a certain poetic irony, though. If sociopaths are said to lack empathy and their victims to have too much, they would seem to make a perfect match. But of course, empathy can't be divvied up. *Here, you take some of mine; I have extra.* And sociopaths can't acquire it anyway—the lack of it is what defines them in the first place. I think they're wrong, though. It's not too much empathy. It's misplaced empathy, a misguided attempt to save someone that can't be saved. All these years later, I know what he saw in me. The question I still wrestle with is, what did I see in him?

When Bella turned two, he'd begun badgering me to get pregnant again—he was dying for a son. There was no way I would willingly bring another child of his into this world. Unbeknownst to him, I went to a free clinic in another town, used a fake name, and got fitted for an IUD. Every month he charted my cycles, knew exactly when I was ovulating, and made sure that we had even more sex during that window. We had a big blowout one day when I got my period.

"What the hell is wrong with you? It's been three years."

"We could see a fertility doctor. Maybe your sperm count is low."

He scowled. "There's nothing wrong with me. You're the dried-up old prune."

But I had sown a doubt; I could see it in his eyes. I was counting on the fact that his ego could never handle any threat to his virility.

"I'm sorry, Jackson. I want it as much as you do."

"Well, you're not getting any younger. If you don't get pregnant soon, it's never going to happen. Maybe you should get on some fertility drugs."

I shook my head. "The doctor will never do that. They have to do a complete workup on both of us. I'll call Monday and make an appointment."

A look of indecision crossed his face. "This week's bad for me. I'll let you know when I have some time."

It was the last time he brought it up.

FIFTY-ONE

needed Jackson to be in a good mood. I'd been looking forward to having my mother here for Tallulah's birthday party, and I had to work even harder to please him the entire month leading up to it so he wouldn't cancel her visit at the last minute. That meant initiating sex at least three times a week, instead of waiting for him to, wearing all his favorite outfits, praising him to my friends in front of him, and keeping up with the growing piles of books on my nightstand that arrived weekly from his online orders. My books by contemporary authors such as Stephen King, Rosamund Lupton, and Barbara Kingsolver were replaced with books by Steinbeck, Proust, Nabokov, Melville—books he believed would make me a more interesting dinner companion. These were in addition to the classics that we were reading together.

It had been six months since Mom's last visit, and I was desperate to see her. Over the years, she'd come to accept that we were no longer close, believing that I'd changed, that the money had gone to my head, that I had little time for her. It's all what he made her believe.

It had taken everything I had not to tell her the truth, but if I had, there was no knowing what he would have done to us, or even just to her. So I went along and only invited her twice a year, for the girls' birthdays. The inn kept her occupied for the holidays, which eliminated my having to tell her she wasn't welcome. Jackson refused to allow us to travel to see her, claiming it was important for children to be in their own home during the holidays.

This year, Tallulah was turning eleven. We were having a big celebration. All of her friends from school were coming. I'd arranged for a clown, bouncy house, ponies—the works. None of our adult friends were invited, except Amber. We'd been friends for a few months by then, and I was starting to feel like she was family. I'd arranged for plenty of help to keep watch over the children. We'd have both nannies there. Sabine only worked during the week, so Jackson had hired a young college student, Surrey, to spend the weekend with us and help with whatever needed doing. However, Sabine wanted to be there for the party. I was telling Amber about the planning. She'd stopped by to return a movie she'd borrowed.

"I'd really love to meet your mother, Daphne," she gushed.

"You will. I'll have you over while she's here, but are you sure you really want to come to the party? It's going to be twenty screaming children. I'm not sure I even want to go." I was joking, of course.

"I can help you. I mean, I know you have hired help and all, but it's nice to have a friend too."

Jackson hadn't been happy when I'd told him she was coming.

"What the hell, Daphne? This is a family affair. She's not your sister, you know. She's always around."

"She has no one here. And she's my best friend." I realized my mistake as soon as the words left my lips. Was she? I hadn't had one for years. It's impossible to be close to someone when you're living a lie. All my relationships, except for the ones with my children, were superficial by necessity. But with Amber, I felt a bond that no one else could understand. As much as I loved Meredith, she couldn't relate to how I felt losing my sister.

"Your best friend? You may as well say Margarita's your best friend. She's a nothing."

I corrected myself. "Of course, you're right. That's not what I meant. I meant she's the one person who understands what I've been through. I feel like I owe her something. Besides, she always says how welcome you make her feel and how much she admires you."

That mollified him. For a man so smart, you'd think he would have seen through it. But that was the thing with Jackson: he always wanted to believe that everyone adored him.

So she'd come, and it *was* nice to have a friend. To watch Jackson interact with her, you would never know how he truly felt. When she arrived, he gave her a big smile and embrace.

"Welcome. So glad you could come."

She smiled shyly and murmured a thank-you.

"Let me get you a drink. What'll you have?"

"Oh, I'm fine."

"Come on, Amber. You're going to need it to get through the day." He gave her a dazzling smile. "You like Cabs, right?"

She nodded.

"Be right back."

"Where can I put my gift?" she asked me.

"You shouldn't have."

"It's just a little something I thought she would like."

Later, when Tallulah was opening her gifts, I watched with interest as she came to Amber's present. It was a book on the life of Edgar Allan Poe.

Tallulah looked over and gave her a subdued thank-you.

"I remembered you were reading his stories that day in New York," Amber called over to her.

"Isn't she a bit young for Poe?" my mother asked within Amber's earshot, never one to hold back.

"Tallulah's very advanced for her age. She's reading at an eighth-grade level," I said.

"There's a difference between intellectual development and emotional development," my mother pointed out.

Amber said nothing, merely looked at the ground, and I felt torn between defending her and validating my mother's concerns.

"I'll look it over, and if you're right, I'll put it aside until she's older." I smiled at my mother.

I looked up to see Surrey running to retrieve some presents that were scattered on the floor.

"Good heavens, what is going on?" my mother asked.

"Bella threw them from the pile," Amber said.

"What?" I ran over to see what had happened.

Bella was standing in front of the table, hands on her hips, her bottom lip stuck out as far as it would go.

"Bella, what's wrong?"

"It's not fair. She gets all these presents, and no one brought me anything."

"It's not your birthday. You had your birthday six months ago."

She stomped her foot. "I don't care. I didn't get this many presents. And I didn't have ponies." She raised her little fist and smashed it down on the corner of the cake.

I didn't need this today. "Surrey, would you please take Bella inside until she calms down?" I pointed at the cake. "See if you can fix that."

Surrey tried to get Bella to go with her, but Bella refused, running in the other direction. I was glad that none of the other children's mothers were around to witness it. I didn't have the energy to go after her. At least she wasn't bothering anyone now.

When I walked back to Amber and my mother, I was fixed with a disapproving look from the latter.

"That child is spoiled rotten."

The blood pounded in my ears. "Mother, she just has a hard time managing her emotions."

"She's overindulged. Maybe if you didn't leave the parenting to the nannies, she'd be better behaved."

Amber gave me a sympathetic look, and I took a deep breath, afraid of saying something I'd regret.

"I would appreciate it if you kept your parenting opinions to yourself. Bella is my daughter, not yours."

"No kidding. If she were mine, she wouldn't act like that."

I jumped up and ran into the house. Who was she to judge me? She had no idea what my life was like. *And whose fault is that?* a little voice asked. I wished she was a bigger part of my life, that she understood my reasons for the way I parented. But right now her disapproval and critical comments were just one more voice in a sea of accusations that I lived with daily.

I grabbed a Valium from my purse and downed it dry. Amber walked into the kitchen, came over, and put a hand on my shoulder.

"Mothers," she said.

I blinked back the tears and said nothing.

"Don't let her get to you. She means well. You're a terrific mother."

"I try to be. I know Bella's a handful, but she has a good heart. Do you think I'm too easy on her?"

She shook her head. "Of course not. She's a darling. Just impet-
uous, but she'll grow out of it. What she needs is understanding
and nurturing."

"I don't know."

I couldn't blame my mother. It *did* look like I turned a blind
eye to Bella's misbehavior. What my mother didn't know was
that Bella cried herself to sleep more nights than not. Jackson
may have been the doting father in public, but in private, he
knew just the right things to say to pit the girls against each
other and to make Bella feel inferior to her older sister. Bella
struggled with her reading and was behind her schoolmates.
First grade was almost over, and she was not even close to reading. When Tallulah finished first grade, she was reading at a
fifth-grade level. Jackson was quick to remind Bella of that.
Poor Bella was lucky if she could get through the primers. Her
teacher strongly recommended testing, but Jackson refused.
We'd had an argument about it in the car on the way home
from the conference.

"She may have a learning disability. It's not so uncommon."

He kept his eyes straight ahead and answered me through
clenched teeth. "She's just lazy. That child does what she wants to
when she wants to."

I felt frustration well up. "That's not true. She tries so hard.
She's in tears every night trying to get through a page or two. I
really think she needs help."

He slammed his hand on the steering wheel. "Damn it, we're
not having her labeled as dyslexic or whatever. That will follow
her forever, and she'll never get into Charterhouse. We'll hire a
private tutor, and I don't care if she has to work five hours a day,
she *will* learn to read."

I'd closed my eyes in resignation. There was no use in arguing with him. When the girls reached high school, he planned to send them away to Charterhouse, an exclusive boarding school in England. But I knew in my heart that before that day ever came, I would find a way for us to escape. In the meantime, I pretended to go along.

I'd hired a tutor with a background in special education. Without Jackson or Bella realizing it, she had evaluated her and suspected dyslexia. How was Bella going to get through school without any accommodations, without anyone knowing the way she learned? I knew she was in the wrong place. St. Luke's didn't have the resources to provide her with what she needed, but Jackson refused to discuss moving her anywhere else.

The poor child went to school all day and then came home to more lessons with the tutor just to keep up. They worked together for hours, Bella's progress torturously slow and further impeded by her resistance to more desk time. She wanted to go play, and she should have been able to. But every night at dinner, Jackson would insist she read to us. When she stumbled over a word or took too long to sound something out, he'd drum his fingers on the table until she began to stutter even more. The ironic thing was, he didn't understand how his impatience was having the opposite of its intended effect. He actually thought he was doing the right thing, being on top of her schooling—or at least that's what he claimed. We all began to dread family dinners. And Bella, poor thing, was exhausted all the time, overwrought and beset with self-doubt.

One particular night haunts me. Bella had had a horrible day at school and a meltdown with the tutor. By the time we sat down to dinner, she was like a volcano ready to erupt. After we'd finished eating, Margarita brought out the dessert.

"None for Bella until she reads," Jackson commanded.

"I don't want to read. I'm too tired." She reached for the plate with the brownies.

"Margarita." His voice had been so sharp that we'd all turned to look at him. "I said no."

"Mister, I will bring them back for everyone after."

"No, Tallulah can have hers. *She's* a smart girl."

"That's okay, Daddy. I can wait." Tallulah had looked down at her plate.

Margarita had reluctantly put the plate on the table and made a hasty retreat.

Jackson had gotten up from his seat and handed Bella the book he had brought home. She'd thrown it on the floor, and his face had turned bright red.

"You've been getting help for six months now. You're in first grade. It should be easy for you. Read the first page." He'd bent to retrieve it from the floor.

I'd looked at the book. *Charlotte's Web*. There was no way she could do it.

"Jackson, this isn't accomplishing anything."

Ignoring me, he'd slammed the book down on the table, making Bella jump.

My eyes were drawn to the throbbing vein in his forehead. "Either she reads this damn book, or I'm firing her worthless tutor. Let's see what you've learned. Now!"

Bella picked up the book with shaking hands, opened it, and in a trembling voice, began to read. "Wwwww hhheerrr s Pap a ggggoinn g wiith thaat ax?"

"Oh, for crying out loud. You sound like a moron! Spit it out."

"Jackson!"

He'd given me a dark look and then turned to Bella. "You look ugly when you read like that."

Bella had burst into tears and ran from the table. I'd hesitated only a moment, then rushed after her.

After I calmed her down and tucked her in, she'd looked at me with those big blue eyes and asked, "Am I stupid, Mommy?"

I'd been pierced to the core.

"Of course not, sweetie. You're very smart. Lots of people have trouble learning to read."

"Tallulah doesn't. She was born with a book in her hand. I'm the one that's thick as a brick."

"Who told you that?"

"Daddy."

I wanted to kill him. "You listen to me. Do you know who Einstein is?"

She looked up at the ceiling. "The funny-looking man with the crazy hair?"

I forced a laugh. "Yes. He was one of the smartest men ever, and he didn't learn to read until he was nine. You are very smart."

"Daddy doesn't think so."

How could I make this better? "Daddy doesn't mean those things. He just doesn't understand the way different brains work. He thinks if he says those things, you'll work harder." It sounded lame even to my ears, but it was all I could offer.

She yawned and her eyes fluttered shut. "I'm tired, Mommy."

I'd kissed her on the forehead. "Good night, angel."

So she misbehaved sometimes—who wouldn't with that kind of pressure? But how do you explain to people around you that you're cutting your child some slack because her father has reduced her to rubble?

FIFTY-TWO

When Jackson was bored, he liked to hide my things, putting things in places where I'd never find them. My brush often turned up in the guest bathroom, my contact lens solution in the kitchen. Today I was running late for an important meeting with a potential donor at Julie's Smile, and my keys were nowhere to be found. Our driver, Tommy, was off for a family emergency, and Sabine had taken the girls to the Bronx Zoo, as school was closed for another teacher planning day.

Jackson was aware that I had been preparing for the meeting all week, and I knew it was no coincidence that my keys had gone missing. I needed to be there in fifteen minutes. I called a cab and got to my meeting with one minute to spare. I was so frazzled that I was off my game. When the meeting was over, I picked up the phone and dialed Jackson.

"You might have cost the foundation hundreds of thousands." I didn't bother with any preamble.

"Excuse me?"

"My keys are missing."

"I have no idea what you're talking about. Don't blame me because you're disorganized." His tone was maddeningly patronizing.

"I always put them in the drawer in the hall table. Both sets were gone, and Tommy is conveniently off today. I had to call a cab."

"I'm sure there's someone who would find the quotidian details of your day interesting, but it doesn't happen to be me." He ended the call.

I slammed the phone down.

He worked late and didn't get home until after nine. When he arrived, I was in the kitchen, icing cupcakes for Bella's class bake sale. He opened the refrigerator and started cursing.

"What's the matter?"

"Come here."

I braced myself for whatever this latest tirade was going to be and came up behind him. He pointed.

"Can you tell me what's wrong?"

I followed the line of his finger. "What?" Everything had to be perfect; he had started using a measuring tape to ensure the glasses were exactly an eighth of an inch apart. He would have surprise inspections of drawers and cabinets to make sure everything was in its place.

He shook his head and looked at me with loathing. "Do you not see that the Naked juices are not lined up alphabetically? You've got the cranberry behind the strawberry."

The absurdity of my life struck me, and I began to giggle uncontrollably. He was looking at me with increasing animosity, and all I could do was laugh. I tried to stop, felt the terror rise from my stomach. *Stop laughing!* I didn't know what was wrong with me, even when I saw his eyes get dark with anger, I couldn't stop—in fact, it made me laugh even harder. I was becoming hysterical.

He grabbed the bottle, twisted the top off, and poured it on my head.

"What are you doing?" I jumped back.

"Still think it's funny? You stupid cow!" In a rage, he started pulling everything out and throwing things to the floor. I stood, transfixed, as I watched. When he got to the eggs, he began throwing them at me. I tried to shield my face but felt the sting on my cheeks as he whipped them at me as hard as he could. Within minutes, I was covered in fluids and food. He shut the refrigerator door and stared at me for a long moment.

"Why aren't you laughing now, slob?"

I stood rooted to the spot, too afraid to speak. My lip trembled as I muttered an apology.

He nodded. "You should be sorry. Clean this shit up, and don't even think of asking any of the staff for help. It's your mess." He walked over to the plate of cupcakes I'd been frosting and threw it on the floor. He unzipped his pants and urinated all over them. I started to cry out, but caught myself in time.

"You'll have to tell Bella you were too lazy to make her cupcakes." He wagged his finger at me. "Bad Mommy."

Then he turned around and opened the drawer where I kept my keys and jangled them in his hands before throwing them at me. "And your keys were here the whole time, dummy. Next time, look harder. I'm so tired of having such a lazy, stupid wife." He stormed from the kitchen and left me there, huddled in the corner, shaking.

It took me over an hour to clean everything up. In a numb haze, I threw away all the ruined food, mopped, wiped, and cleaned until all the surfaces shone again. I couldn't let the staff see a mess when they arrived early tomorrow morning. I would have to stop at the bakery tomorrow and pick up cupcakes to replace the ones he'd ruined. I dreaded going upstairs, hoping he'd be asleep by the time I showered and got in bed—but I knew that it excited him to humiliate me. The lights were out when I finished drying my hair and walked over to my side of the bed. His breathing was even, and I heaved a sigh of relief that he was asleep. I pulled the covers up to my chin and was just about to drift off when I felt his hand on my thigh. I froze. *Not tonight.*

"Say it," he commanded.

"Jackson—"

He squeezed harder. "Say it."

I closed my eyes and forced the words out. "I want you. Make love to me."

"Beg me."

"I want you now. Please." I knew he wanted me to say more, but that was all I could force out.

"You don't sound very convincing. Show me."

I pushed the covers back and lifted my nightgown off. Straddling him the way he liked, I positioned myself so that my breasts were in his face.

"You're such a whore." He thrust into me with no regard to my readiness. I gripped the sheets and made my mind blank until he finished.

FIFTY-THREE

The next day, as usual, there was a gift. This time it was a watch—a Vacheron Constantin worth upward of fifty grand. I didn't need it, but of course I'd wear it, especially around his business associates and at the club, so everyone could see how generous my husband was. I knew how it would go. He would be charming for the next few weeks: compliment me, take me out to dinner, act solicitous. In truth, it was almost worse than his derision. At least when he was debasing me, I could feel justified in my hatred. But when he went for days on end masquerading as the compassionate man I fell in love with, it was confusing, even when I knew it was all an act.

He checked in with me every morning to go over what I had planned for the day. That morning I had decided to skip my Pilates class and get a massage and facial instead. He called me at ten, like he did every day.

"Good morning, Daphne. I've e-mailed you an article on the new exhibit at the Guggenheim. Make sure you take a look. I'd like to discuss it tonight."

"Okay."

"On your way to the gym?"

"Yes, see you later," I lied. I wasn't in a mood for a lecture on the importance of exercise.

Later that night, I was having a glass of wine in the sunroom and reading the damn Guggenheim article while the girls were being bathed. As soon as I saw his face, I knew something was wrong.

"Hello." I made my voice bright.

He was holding a drink. "What are you doing?"

I lifted my iPad. "Reading the article you sent."

"How was Pilates?"

"Fine. How was your day?"

He sat down across from me on the sofa and shook his head. "Not great. One of my managers lied to me."

I looked up from the screen. "Oh?"

"Yeah. And about something really stupid. I asked him if he'd made a phone call, and he said yes." He took a long swallow from his glass of bourbon. "Thing is, he hadn't. All he had to do was tell me, say he'd planned to later." He shrugged. "It would have been no big deal. But he lied."

My heart fluttered, and I picked up my wineglass, taking a sip. "Maybe he was afraid you'd be angry."

"Well, that's the thing. Now I am. Really pissed, actually. Insulted too. He must think I'm an idiot. I *hate* being lied to. I'll put up with a lot of things, but lying, I can't abide it."

Unless he was the one doing the lying, of course. I gave him a neutral look. "I get it. You don't like liars." Now who was treating someone like an idiot? I knew there was no manager, that it was his passive-aggressive way of confronting me. But I wouldn't give him the satisfaction. I did wonder how he knew I'd skipped my class. "So what did you do?"

He walked over to me, sat down, put his hand on my knee. "What do you think I should do?"

I slid away from him. He inched closer.

"I don't know, Jackson. Do whatever you think is right."

He pursed his lips, started to say something else, then sprang up from the sofa.

"Enough of this bullshit. Why did you lie to me today?"

"About what?"

"Going to the gym. You were at the spa from eleven to two."

I frowned at him. "How do you know that? Are you having me followed?"

"No."

"Then how?"

He gave me a vicious smile. "Maybe people are following you. Maybe cameras are watching you. You just never know."

My throat started to close up. I couldn't catch my breath, and I gripped the side of the sofa as I tried to stop the room from spinning. He said nothing, merely watched with an amused expression. When I finally found my voice, the only word that came out was "Why?"

"Isn't it obvious?"

When I didn't answer, he went on.

"Because I can't trust you. And I was justified. You lied to me. I won't be made a fool of."

"I should have told you, I was just tired today. I'm sorry. You can trust me."

"I'll bestow trust on you when you deserve it. When you stop lying."

"Someone must have really hurt you in the past, made a fool out of you," I said in a sympathetic tone, knowing it would get under his skin.

Anger flashed in his eyes. "No one made a fool out of me, and no one ever will." He grabbed my glass of wine, walked over to the wet bar, and poured the remains in the sink. "I think you've consumed enough calories—especially considering you were too lazy to exercise today. Why don't you go and change for dinner? I'll see you then."

After he left, I poured myself a new glass and thought about this latest revelation. I bet he was spying on me in other ways too. I couldn't let my guard down at all. Maybe he'd bugged the phone or put cameras in the house. It was time for action on my part, and I needed a plan. He controlled all of the money. I was given a cash allowance for incidentals but had to give him receipts for everything I spent. All the rest of the bills went to his office. He gave me no discretionary spending—just one more way he tried to keep me under his thumb. He didn't know that I'd accumulated my own secret stash.

I'd set up an e-mail account and cloud credentials under a fake name on one of the laptops in the office and hid the computer in a closet underneath brochures and flyers—somewhere he'd never think to look. I sold some of my designer purses and clothing on eBay and had the money wired into an account he knew nothing about. I had everything go to a post office box I'd set up in Milton, New York, a thirty-minute ride from the house. It was slow going, but over the past five years, I'd put together a decent enough emergency fund. To date, I'd saved close to $30,000. I also bought a pack of burner cells that I kept at the office. I didn't know yet what I was going to do with all of it, only that I'd need it one day. Jackson thought he had every angle covered, but, unlike him, I was unfettered by delusions of grandeur. I had to believe that somehow they would be his undoing.

FIFTY-FOUR

Christmas used to be my favorite holiday. I sang in our church choir every Christmas Eve, and Julie was always front and center, cheering me on. Then we'd go back to the inn and have dinner, happy to be the ones waited on for a change. We could give one gift early and save the rest for Christmas Day. The last Christmas that I spent with Julie, she'd been fidgety all through dinner, as though she was bursting with some secret she couldn't wait to share. I gave her my gift—a pair of gold ball earrings that I'd scrimped and saved for with my tips at the inn. When it was her turn, she handed me a small box, her eyes bright with excitement.

I tore open the paper and lifted the lid. I gasped. "No, Julie. This is your favorite."

She smiled and took the heart pendant from the box, holding it toward me to put on. "I want you to have it."

She'd been so much weaker lately. I think she knew, or at least accepted, before we did that her time was running out.

I held back tears and grasped the thin chain in my hand. "I'll never take it off." And I didn't. Until after I married him, and I knew that if I didn't hide it away, he'd take it from me too. It was safely nestled under the cardboard bottom of one of the many velvet jewelry boxes that contained his gifts to me.

For the past ten years, Christmas had been nothing more than an obscene display of consumption. We didn't go to church. Jackson was an atheist and refused to expose our children to what he called "a fairy tale." But he had no problem perpetuating the Santa myth. I had stopped trying to reason with him.

I did take pleasure in the girls' enjoyment. They loved the decorating, baking, and sights and sounds of the season. This year, I had another reason to be excited. I had Amber. I had to hold myself back from showering her with too many presents. I didn't want to embarrass her. There was something about her that made me want to take care of her, to give her all the things she never had. It was almost like I was giving Julie all the things she'd never lived to enjoy.

We got up before the girls and went down to have our coffee. It wasn't long before they swept in, little tornados attacking the mountains of gifts with glee, and yet again I worried at the message we were sending them.

"Mommy, aren't you going to open any presents?" Tallulah asked.

"Yeah, Mommy. Open a present," Bella chimed in. Mine were stacked in a tall pile—beautifully decorated in gold foil and elaborate red velvet ribbons. I knew what the boxes would contain—more designer outfits that he'd chosen, jewelry to show off how good he was to me, expensive perfume that he liked, none of the things I would have picked for myself. Nothing at all that I wanted.

We had both agreed that the children's presents to us would be handmade, though, and I was looking forward to that.

"Open mine first, Mommy," Bella said. She dropped the half-unwrapped package she had been opening and ran over to me.

"Which is yours, sweetie?" I asked.

She pointed to the only package covered in Santa paper. "We wrapped it special so it'd be easy to spot," she said proudly.

I tousled her curls as she handed it to me, smiling as she perched on tiptoes, watching me wide-eyed. "Can I open it for you?"

I laughed. "Of course."

She ripped the paper and threw it on the floor, then pulled the lid off the box and gave it back to me.

It was a painting—a family portrait. It was quite good. I hadn't realized what a sharp eye she had.

"Bella! It's amazing. When did you do this?"

"In school. My teacher said I have talent. Mine was the best one. You couldn't even tell what most of the others were. She's going to talk to you about art classes for me."

The picture was twelve by twelve, and it was painted in watercolors. We were all standing on the beach, the ocean behind us, Jackson in the middle with me on one side and Tallulah on the other. Bella stood across from the three of us, noticeably larger than we were. Jackson, Tallulah, and I were dressed in drab grays and whites, Bella in bright oranges, pinks, and reds. Jackson and Tallulah were both turned, looking at me, Tallulah looking glum, Jackson smug, and I was staring at Bella with a wide smile. The picture unsettled me. It didn't take a psychologist to figure out that the family dynamics were off-kilter. I shook off the troubling thoughts and pulled her to me for a hug.

"It's beautiful, and I love it. I'm going to hang it in my office so I can look at it all day."

Tallulah looked over. "Why are you so much bigger than the rest of us?"

Bella stuck her tongue out at her sister. "It's called pesperective," she said, stumbling on the word.

Jackson laughed. "I think you mean perspective, my dear."

Tallulah rolled her eyes and brought me her present. "Open mine now."

It was a clay sculpture that she'd made of two hearts united with a ribbon, on which she'd painted the word *love*.

"It's you and Aunt Julie," she said.

My eyes filled with tears. "I love this, darling. It's perfect."

She smiled and embraced me. "I know sometimes you get sad. But your hearts will always be together."

I was so grateful for this thoughtful child.

"Open one of mine," Jackson said as he handed me a small box wrapped in red foil.

"Thank you." I took the package from him and began tearing the paper to reveal a plain white box, then lifted the lid to find a gold chain with a gold circle charm attached. I pulled it from the box and gasped.

Tallulah took the necklace from my hand and looked at it and then at me. "Who's YMB, Mommy?"

Before I could find my voice, Jackson spoke, the lie coming smoothly off his lips. "They're the initials of your mom's grandmother, who she loved very much. Let me put it on for you." He fastened it around my neck. "I hope you'll wear it all the time."

I gave him a big smile that he would know was fake. "Just another reminder of how you feel about me."

He pressed his lips to mine.

"Eeew!" Tallulah said, and both girls giggled.

Bella had gone back to her pile of presents and was tearing through the rest of the packages when the doorbell rang.

Jackson had agreed to let Amber come over and have dinner with us, since she was going to be alone for Christmas. It hadn't been easy, but I staged the conversation in front of some of our friends, and he wanted to look like the Good Samaritan by including her.

He greeted her like she was family, got her a drink, and we all sat around very agreeably for the next few hours, while the children played with their things and we made small talk.

Amber gave us all lovely gifts—a book for Jackson that he actually seemed to appreciate; books for the girls plus some shiny jewelry for Bella, which she loved. When she handed me my gift, I was a little nervous, hoping she hadn't spent too much. Nothing could have prepared me for the thin silver bangle, with two round charms engraved with the names Julie and Charlene.

"Amber, this is so thoughtful and beautiful."

She held her arm up, and I saw that she wore the same bracelet. "I have one too. Now our sisters will be with us all the time."

Jackson was watching the exchange, and I could see the anger in his eyes. He was always telling me I thought about Julie too much as it was. But even Jackson couldn't take my joy away. Two gifts that honored my sister and the love I felt for her. I felt heard and understood for the first time in so long.

"Oh, and one other little thing." She handed me a small gift bag.

"Another present? The bracelet was enough."

I pushed aside the tissue paper and felt something hard. My breath caught in my throat as I lifted it from the bag. A glass turtle.

"I know how much you love them," she said.

Jackson's lips curled into a smile, and delight shone in his eyes.

And just like that, my feeling of being known and understood evaporated.

FIFTY-FIVE

Meredith was throwing her husband a surprise fiftieth birthday party at Benjamin Steakhouse. Truthfully, it was the last thing I was in the mood for. I was still tired from all the Christmas preparations and we were leaving for St. Bart's in two days, but I didn't want to let Meredith down. She was insistent that the party be on the twenty-seventh, Rand's actual birthday, since over the years it had always been underplayed due to its proximity to Christmas.

I'd just arrived in the city; Jackson had asked me to meet him at the Oyster Bar at Grand Central. That way, we'd be right down the street from the restaurant, and it would only take us a few minutes to walk there.

Even as I put on the Dior dress, I knew I was making a mistake. It was a favorite of mine, but Jackson didn't like the color. It was a pale gold silk, and he claimed it made my skin sallow. But it was a party for *my* friend, and I wanted to make a decision for a change. The moment I saw his face, the barely perceptible furrow of the brow, the small wrinkle worrying between his eyes, I knew he was angry. He stood to kiss me, and I took a seat on the stool next to him. He picked up the crystal tumbler and, with one flick of his wrist, downed the remaining amber liquid and flagged the bartender over.

"I'll have another Bowmore, and a Campari and soda for my wife."

I was about to protest—I'd never even tasted Campari—but I

choked back the words before they escaped. It would be best to let whatever plan he had concocted play itself out.

"Meredith asked that we get to the restaurant by seven so we don't run into Rand. She wants him to be surprised."

Jackson arched a brow. "I'm sure the bill will be surprise enough."

I laughed dutifully, then looked at my watch. "We've got about half an hour, and then we'd better get going."

The bartender placed the drink in front of me.

Jackson lifted his glass. "Cheers, darling." He toasted me with such force that my drink ended up all over the front of my champagne-colored dress, now splashed with red.

"Oh dear, look what you've done." He didn't even try to hide his smirk.

Heat spread to my cheeks, and I took a deep breath, willing myself not to cry. Meredith was going to be so disappointed. I looked at him with no change in expression. "What now?"

He threw his hands up. "Well, obviously you can't turn up to the restaurant like that." He shook his head. "If only your dress were darker, or if you weren't such a klutz."

If only you were dead, I wanted to answer.

He called for the check. "We'll have to go to the apartment and get you changed. Of course, by the time we do that, it'll be too late to make it in time for the surprise."

I forced my mind to go blank and followed him numbly from the bar. We got into the limo, and he ignored me while reading e-mails on his phone. I pulled my phone out and texted my apologies to Meredith.

Because of traffic, it took over forty-five minutes for us to get there. I smiled at the doorman, and we rode the elevator in silence. I went to the bedroom, threw the dress on the floor, and stood looking at the closet. I felt him before I heard him—his breath on my neck, then his lips on my back.

I suppressed the urge to scream. "Sweetheart, we don't have time."

His mouth traveled down my back, to the top of my panties. He slid them off and cupped my buttocks with his hands. He moved closer, and I realized he'd taken off his pants. I could feel him hard against me.

"There's always time for this."

His hands moved to cup my breasts, then he grabbed my hands and placed them flat against the wall, his pressed on top of them. I braced myself as he took me, hard and rough, moving into a frenzied crescendo. It was over within minutes.

I went into the bathroom to clean myself up, and when I emerged, my black Versace was hanging on the bedroom door. I grabbed it and laid it on the bed.

"Hold on," he said, walking toward me. "Wear this underneath."

It was a black Jean Yu thong with a matching strapless bra. He'd had it made to order for me, and it felt amazing—like a silk caress—but the sight of it only reminded me of what he'd done before he gave it to me. I took it from him though, and gave him my best imitation of a smile.

"Thank you."

He insisted upon dressing me, pulling the stockings up my legs, stopping every few moments to brush his lips against my skin as he did so.

"Are you sure you wouldn't rather stay home and let me ravish you again?" He gave me a rakish smile.

Did he really believe I had any desire for him? I licked my lips. "As tempting as that sounds, we did promise. And Randolph is an old friend."

He sighed. "Yes, of course, you're right." He zipped my dress and tapped me on the behind. "Let's go, then."

When I turned around, he looked me up and down. "It's lucky you spilled your drink—that one's much better on you anyway."

By the time we arrived, an hour and a half later, everyone was just nibbling on the passed appetizers. I gave Meredith an apologetic look as we rushed over to greet her.

"I'm so sorry we're late—"

"Yes," Jackson cut in, "I tried to tell her we were running behind, but she insisted on squeezing in a massage. It put us behind about an hour." He shrugged.

Meredith's face registered shock, and she turned to me, hurt obvious in her eyes. "Why did you text me that you spilled something on your dress and had to go home and change?"

I stood there, paralyzed by indecision. If I told her the truth, I'd have to contradict Jackson. Public humiliation would bring a heavy price. But now my good friend thought I'd lied to her just so I could indulge in some pampering.

"I'm sorry, Mer. It was both. I had a pulled muscle, I spilled . . ." I stumbled on my words. Jackson watched me, an amused smile on his face. "What I mean, is that, yes, I did get a massage—my back was really bothering me—but we still would have made it in time if I hadn't spilled my drink all over myself like an idiot. I'm really sorry."

Jackson shook his head and smiled at Meredith. "You know how clumsy our little Daphne can be. I'm always telling her to be more careful."

FIFTY-SIX

When I first met Amber, I could never have imagined that she would become someone I depended on. I'll admit, my first impression was of a somewhat homely and meek young woman with little to interest me except for the fact that she'd experienced a similar heartache. Her grief seemed so raw and fresh that it helped me put my own pain on the back burner to help her. I wanted to make it all better, to give her a reason to wake up in the morning.

Looking back, I suppose I should have seen the signs. But I was eager for a friend, a true friend. No, that's not quite right. I was desperate for a sister—for *my* sister, which was of course, impossible. The next best thing was a friend who'd suffered the same loss I had. It's bad enough to lose a sibling, but to watch one die a little each day—there's no explaining that to someone who hasn't experienced it. So when Amber appeared so unexpectedly in my life, she felt like a gift. I had no one in my life that I could trust. Jackson had done his job well, isolating me from everyone in my past and erecting impenetrable walls around my life. None of my friends knew the reality of my marriage or my life. But with Amber, I could share genuine emotion. Even Jackson couldn't do anything about that.

The flowering friendship made him nervous—he didn't like for me to see any of my friends more than once every few weeks unless, of course, he was there. When I'd asked him to find a job for her at Parrish, he'd been indignant at first.

"Come on, Daphne. Isn't this little charity act wearing thin yet? What could you possibly have in common with that frumpy mouse?"

"You know what we have in common."

He rolled his eyes. "Give it a rest, will you? It's been twenty years. Haven't you mourned enough? So her sister died too. That doesn't mean I want her working in my company. She's around our family too much as it is."

"Jackson, please. I care about her. I do everything you want, don't I?" I forced myself to walk over to him and put my arms around his neck. "She isn't a threat to you. She really needs a job. Her family back home depends on her. I can brag to everyone about how you rescued her." I knew he'd like playing the hero.

"Hilda does need an assistant. I suppose we could give her a chance. I'll call Human Resources and have her set up for an interview."

I didn't want to take any chances. "Couldn't you try her out without an interview on my word? She's smart as a whip; she's done a better job as my cochair than anyone before her. And working at Rollins, she knows a lot about your business. She worked on the commercial side."

"Rollins! That's not saying much. If she's so good, why'd they let her go?"

I had hoped to avoid telling him, but I saw no out. "Her boss was sexually harassing her."

He started laughing. "Is he blind?"

"Jackson! That's cruel."

"Seriously, that dirty-dishwater hair, the ugly glasses, and don't get me started on her lack of fashion sense," he said, shaking his head.

I was glad that he didn't find her attractive. Not because I cared if he strayed, but because I didn't want anything to cause me to lose her as a friend. And working for Hilda Battley, she'd be cocooned from any funny business from the men there. I felt good about helping her and knowing that no one would traumatize her again.

"Please, Jackson. It would make me very happy, and you'd be doing a good thing."

"I'll arrange it. She can start Monday. But you have to do something for me."

"What?"

"Cancel your mother's visit for next month."

My heart sank. "She's been looking forward to it. I've already bought tickets to *The Lion King*. The girls are really excited."

"It's up to you. If you want me to hire your friend, then I'll need some peace and quiet. When your mother's here, I can't relax. Besides, she was just here for Tallulah's birthday."

"All right. I'll call her."

He gave me a cold smile. "Oh, and tell her that you're canceling because the girls want to take Sabine instead of her to the show."

"There's no need to be cruel."

"Okay. No job."

I picked up the phone and dialed. When I hung up, heartsick at the hurt in my mother's voice, he gave me an approving nod.

"Well done. See? You don't need anyone but me, anyhow. I'm your family."

FIFTY-SEVEN

loved having a best friend again. I hadn't realized how lonely I was until Amber came along. Her manipulation was so subtle and gradual that I never had a twinge of suspicion.

It wasn't long until we were always in touch with each other: texting when something funny happened, phone calls, lunches. I wanted her at the house all the time. I was ready to leave to meet her when I heard his car in the driveway. Stomach lurching, I contemplated sneaking out the back, but when I looked out the window, he was out of the car and talking to Tommy, our driver. *Shit.*

He slammed the front door and stalked over to me. "Why do you need Tommy tonight? He said he's picking up Amber too. Are you planning on drinking yourselves into oblivion like some sluts?"

I shook my head. "Of course not. Just a glass or two, but I don't want to drive. She's been so busy with work, we wanted an evening to catch up. I thought you were taking clients out tonight—"

"The dinner was canceled." He studied me for a long moment. "You know, she's the help now. It's actually rather unseemly for you to be friends with her. What if someone sees you together?"

The heat spread from my neck to my face. "She's become like a sister to me. Please don't ask me to stop being friends with her."

"Upstairs," he commanded.

The girls were getting their baths; I had already said my good nights. "I don't want the girls to hear me. I'll have to go through the routine all over again."

He grabbed my hand and pulled me into his office, slammed me against the wall, and locked the door. He unzipped his pants and pushed me down to my knees.

"The quicker you get to it, the faster you can leave."

Hot tears of humiliation ran down my face, ruining my makeup. I wanted to refuse him, to tell him how much he repulsed me, but I was terrified. The slightest resistance to anything he wanted could result in the gun coming out again.

"Stop crying! You make me sick."

"I'm sorry."

"Shut up and get to it."

After I finished, he tucked his shirt back in and zipped up his pants.

"Was it as good for you as it was for me?" He laughed. "By the way, you look like shit. Your makeup's all smeared."

He unlocked the door and left without another word.

I stumbled to the bathroom and ran some water under my eyes. I texted Tommy and told him to get Amber and come back for me. I couldn't let anyone see me this way.

When I finally got to the bar and saw Amber waiting, I wanted nothing more than to pour out my heart, tell her what he was really like. Her friendship had lulled me into such a strong sense of security that I almost told her the truth about why I was late. But the words wouldn't come. And what could she do anyway?

As she looked at me with stars in her eyes, asking about my perfect marriage, I wanted to lay it all bare. But she couldn't help me, and there was nothing to be gained by being truthful. So I did what I had learned to do best: I pushed the reality to the back of my mind and pretended that my charmed life was all that it seemed.

FIFTY-EIGHT

The night that Meredith came to tell me that she'd discovered that Amber wasn't her real name, at first I believed Amber's explanation, that she'd been abused and had to run from her crazy father. After all, I understood what it was like to be a captive. If I thought I could survive and Jackson wouldn't find us, I'd have gladly assumed a false identity. But something in her story was familiar. Then it hit me: she'd used the same phrase—*I'm so ashamed to tell you this*—when she told me about her boss making a pass at her. The more I thought about it, the more her story sounded suspicious. I decided to listen to my gut and investigate, but I pretended to believe her. I had my own reasons, but Meredith thought I was crazy. She'd come over the day after the confrontation.

"I don't care what she says, Daphne. You can't trust her. She's an impostor. I wonder if she even has a sister."

That was impossible, though. Even if she'd lied about everything else, she had to have a sister. I couldn't bear to believe that someone could be so cruel as to pretend she had suffered as I had, to make up stories about a sister struggling with this dreadful disease. That would make her a monster. And my best friend couldn't be a monster.

"I believe her. Not everyone has the resources that we do. Sometimes lying is the only option."

She shook her head. "There's something very off with her."

"Look, Mer. I know you're only trying to protect me. But I know

Amber. Her grief over her sister is genuine. She's had a rough life, and I understand that. Please, have a little faith in my judgment."

"I think you're making a mistake, but it's your call. For your sake, I hope she's telling the truth."

After she'd gone, I ran up to my bedroom, opened my nightstand drawer, and pulled out the glass turtle Amber had given me. Holding it by the edges, I placed it in a plastic bag. I threw my hair into a ponytail, pulled a baseball cap low on my face, and changed into jeans and a T-shirt. I left the house with only my wallet and the burner phone I'd bought a few months earlier and walked the two miles into town. The cab I'd called was waiting in front of the bank on Main Street, and I jumped in the back.

"I need to go to Oxford. This address please."

I handed him the slip of paper and slid back in the seat, looking around to make sure no one I knew had seen me. My thoughts were racing as I considered the implications of Meredith's findings, and I felt sick. Was it possible that our entire relationship was built on pretense? Was she using me for my money, or was she after my husband? Slow down, I thought. Wait and see.

Forty minutes later, the cab came to a stop in front of the brick building.

"Can you wait for me?" I gave him a hundred-dollar bill. "I won't be long."

"Sure, ma'am."

I went up to the fourth floor and found the door marked "Hanson Investigations." I'd found the agency online, using a computer at the library. I went inside to a small, empty reception area. No one sat behind the desk, but a door behind it opened, and a man walked out. He was younger than I'd expected, clean-cut and kind of cute. He smiled and walked toward me, his hand outstretched.

"Jerry Hanson."

I shook his hand. "Daphne Bennett," I said. The chances that he knew Jackson or anyone in our world were slim, but I wasn't taking any chances.

I followed him into a pleasant room with bright colors. Instead of sitting behind his desk, he took one of the armchairs and indicated I should take the one across from him.

"How can I help you? You sounded pretty shaken up on the phone."

"I need to find out if someone who's gotten close to me is who she says she is. I have her fingerprints." I handed him the bag. "Can you find who they belong to?"

"I can try. I'll start with a criminal check. If her prints aren't there, I'll see if I can reach out to some folks who might be able to tap into private databases where she might have been printed for a job."

I handed him the newspaper article with her picture. I had circled her face. "I don't know if this will help. She claims to be from Nebraska, but I don't know if she made that up. How long will it take before you find anything out?"

He shrugged. "Shouldn't take more than a few days. If we find a hit, I can put together a full report for you. To be safe, let's say next Wednesday."

I stood. "Thanks so much. Text me if there's any delay; otherwise, I'll see you on Wednesday. Is noon good?"

He nodded. "Yeah, that works. Listen, Mrs. Bennett, be careful, you hear?"

"Don't worry. I will."

I took the stairs, feeling as though I would jump out of my skin if I didn't keep moving. I thought about all the intimate conversations, the parts of me I had shared with her. Julie. My darling Julie. If she did anything to make a mockery of my sister's memory, I didn't know what I would do. Maybe it would just be a misunderstanding.

I got back into the cab to head home. Now all I had to do was wait.

FIFTY-NINE

t's not good, Mrs. Bennett," Jerry Hanson said as he slid the manila folder across the desk toward me. "There's quite a bit to look through. I'm gonna take a walk, get some coffee. I'll be back to discuss everything with you in about half an hour."

I nodded, already immersed in the file. The first thing I saw was a newspaper article with Amber's photo. Her eyes were heavily lined with black, and her hair was bleached platinum blond. She looked sexy, but hard. Only her name wasn't Amber. It was Lana. Lana Crump. I read the article, then looked through the rest of the document. My hands shook as I put down the last piece of paper. I broke out in a sweat, reeling from the betrayal. It was far worse than I'd imagined. She had made everything up. There had been no sick sister, no abusive father. I had let her into my life, my children's lives, let her get close to me and told her things I'd never shared with another human being. She had played me, and brilliantly. What a fool I'd been. I'd been so blinded by my grief over Julie that I'd actually invited that jackal into my life.

My heart actually ached. She was a criminal, a fugitive. And what she had done—it showed such a clear lack of conscience, no remorse. How could I not have seen it?

Her entire life was here in these pages. A new picture began to form. A poor girl from a small town consumed by jealousy and want: covetous, predatory. She'd mapped out a plan, and when it had failed, she'd exacted her revenge. She had fooled everyone there too, had turned another family's life upside down, irrevocably damaged them, then run away. Then she'd taken on a different identity. A chill passed through me as I thought of the real Amber Patterson's disappearance. Had Lana had a hand in it? Now I understood why she always hid from cameras. She was afraid of someone she'd known in her other life seeing her photo.

The door opened, and the detective returned. "How did someone like you get mixed up with someone like her?"

I exhaled. "Doesn't matter. Tell me, according to this, there's an open warrant out for her. What would happen if I called the police?"

He leaned back in his chair and tented his hands. "They'd pick her up, call the Missouri police, and have her taken back there to stand trial."

"What kind of sentence does perjury and jury tampering carry?"

"Varies by state, but it's a felony and usually carries a prison sentence of at least a year. The fact that she skipped out on bail is going to add some time as well."

"What about what happened to that poor boy? Will that factor in?"

He shrugged. "There's not a punitive component to the criminal charges, so not technically. But I'm sure the despicable intent will sway a sentencing judge, even if he or she doesn't admit it."

"This is all confidential, right?"

He raised his eyebrows. "Are you asking me if I'm obligated to turn her in?"

I nodded.

"I'm not an officer of the court. This is your report; you do what you want with it."

"Thank you. Um, this has nothing to do with Amber, but I

need you to look into one more thing for me." I filled him in, handed him a folder, and left.

I hailed a cab and had it take me to the bank—the one twenty miles from home, where Jackson didn't know I had an account or a safe-deposit box. I looked through the file one more time before putting it away. A picture caught my eye: a woman who must have been Amber's mother. That's when I realized the other thing she had done—and that is what convinced me beyond a shadow of a doubt that Amber, aka Lana, was as devoid of a conscience as Jackson. That revelation was liberating. It meant that I could proceed with the plan that I had begun to formulate in my mind.

I wasn't going to turn her in. No, she wasn't going back to Missouri to serve a measly couple of years in prison. She was going to get a life sentence right here in Connecticut.

SIXTY

If there's one thing living with an abusive psychopath has taught me, it's how to make the best of a bad situation. Once I recovered from the betrayal, I realized Amber could be the answer to everything. It was now obvious that she'd only used me to get close to Jackson. She had manipulated me into getting her a job so she'd be right there every day. But the problem was, Jackson wouldn't be as easily fooled as I was. And as cunning as Amber was, she had only half the picture, no real idea what made him tick, what turned him on. That's where I'd come in. I would feed her the information she needed to succeed in turning his obsessive focus from me to her. Little by little, I would play her, just as she'd played me.

I had to make him want her more than he wanted me. His money, power, and meticulous planning ensured that my only way out was for him to let me go. Up until then, he'd had no reason to do so. That was all about to change. I decided that I needed to pretend that he had once cheated on me. I wanted her to believe there was a crack in my marriage, that Jackson was capable of being tempted.

We met at Barnes & Noble that Saturday, and when she approached, I almost didn't recognize her.

"Wow. You look fantastic." Her hair was no longer dishwater brown, but a beautiful ash blond, her brows shaped into perfect arches over thick, luscious lashes and perfectly applied eyeliner. Contoured cheekbones, just the right amount of blush, and glossed lips completed the picture. She looked like a different woman. She hadn't wasted any time transforming herself.

"Thanks. I went to one of those makeup places at Saks and they helped me. I couldn't go to work in a fancy New York office looking like a country mouse."

Please, that was a Red Door makeover if I ever saw one. I wondered where she'd gotten the money. "Well, you look wonderful."

After browsing a bit, we went across the street to a café for lunch.

"So how are things going? Still loving the job?" I asked.

"Yes. I'm learning so much. And I really appreciate Jackson giving me the chance to fill Battley's shoes. I know it wasn't easy for him, after working with her for so many years."

I had to hand it to her, she gave nothing away. I don't know how she did it, but when Jackson came home a few short months after Amber had started and told me that Battley had resigned, I'd suspected she'd had a hand in it. "She was a gem. So loyal. Jackson didn't really tell me why she decided to retire early. Do you have any idea?"

She raised her eyebrows. "Well, she was up there in age, Daph. I think she was really more tired and taxed than she let on. I had to cover for her more than once." She leaned in toward me conspiratorially. "I probably saved her getting fired on a few occasions when she deleted an important meeting from Jackson's calendar. Luckily I caught it in time and fixed it."

"How lucky for her."

"Well, I guess she realized it was time. I think she was ready to have more time for her grandkids too."

"I'm sure—but enough about work. What's going on with your personal life? Any cute guys at the office?"

She shook her head. "Not really. I'm starting to wonder if I'll ever meet someone."

"Have you considered a dating service?"

"No. I'm not really one for those kinds of things. I'm a big believer in fate."

Sure she was. "I get it. You want the old-fashioned boy-meets-girl story."

She smiled. "Yes. Like you and Jackson. The perfect couple."

I gave a small laugh. "Nothing's perfect."

"The two of you sure make marriage seem easy. He looks at you like you're still on your honeymoon."

I had my opening to make her think there was trouble in paradise. "Not lately. We haven't had sex in two weeks." I cast my eyes downward. "Sorry—I hope you don't mind my talking about this."

"Of course not, that's what friends are for." She twirled the straw in her iced tea. "I'm sure he's just tired, Daph. It's been crazy at work."

I sighed. "If I tell you something, do you promise not to tell a soul?"

She leaned in closer. "Of course."

"He cheated on me before."

I saw the delight in her eyes before she was able to disguise it. "You're kidding? When?"

"Right after Bella was born. I still had some extra weight, and I was tired all the time. There was this client—she was young and pretty and hung on his every word. I had met her at a social function, and from the way she looked at him, I knew she was trouble."

She licked her lips. "How did you find out?"

Now I was just making it up as I went along. "I found her pant-ies in the apartment."

"Are you kidding? He took her to your place in New York?"

"Yes. I think she left them deliberately. When I confronted him, he fell apart. Begged my forgiveness. Told me that he'd just felt so ignored with all the time I spent with the new baby, and she'd flattered him so much. He admitted that her adoration was just too hard to resist."

"Wow. That must have been so hard for you. But at least you bounced back. The two of you seem very happy. And you have to give it to him for not lying."

I could see the wheels turning in her mind. "I think he did feel bad. He swore it would never happen again. But now I'm seeing some of the same signs I did back then. He's working late all the time, not initiating sex, seems distracted. I think there must be someone else."

"I haven't seen anything suspicious at the office."

"There's no one there that seems to be hanging around him more than usual?"

She shook her head. "Not that I can think of. I'll keep an eye on him for you, though, and let you know if I think there's anything you have to worry about."

I knew she'd keep an eye on him—and maybe more than that. "Thanks, Amber. I feel so much better knowing you're there look-ing out for me."

She put her hand on mine and gave me a steady look. "I would do anything for you. We have to stick together. Soul sisters, right?"

I squeezed her hand back and smiled. "Right."

SIXTY-ONE

t was easy to arrange. He had been looking forward to seeing *Hamlet*, and I knew he wouldn't want to waste the valuable second ticket. Bella wasn't really sick, but I purposely bowed out of the show, hoping he'd invite Amber. He was furious that I'd missed it. My phone rang that night at midnight.

"Don't you ever do that again; you hear me?"

"Jackson, what's wrong?"

"I wanted you with me tonight. I had plans for you after the play."

"Bella needed me."

"*I* needed you. The next time you break plans with me, there'll be serious consequences. You got it?"

Apparently Amber had no idea about his bad mood. She called me the next morning with just the right things to say.

"Hello?"

"Hi, Daph, it's me."

"Hey. How was the play?"

Rustling papers on her end. "Amazing. My first Broadway play. I was in awe the whole time."

Her Pollyanna act was getting old.

"I'm glad. So what's up?"

"Oh, well, I just wanted to let you know that by the time we got out, it was late, and so we stayed at the apartment."

"Oh?" I made my voice sound appropriately on guard.

"Jackson insisted that it was silly for me to go all the way home when I had to be back so early in the morning. I took the sheets off the guest room bed and put them in the laundry room so the housekeeper would know they needed to be changed."

Clever of her. She couldn't come out and state that she'd stayed in the guest room, or she'd be implying that there was a chance she'd slept with my husband, but she was letting me know that nothing had happened.

"That was thoughtful. Thanks."

"And I borrowed your red Armani suit, the one with the gold buttons. I hope you don't mind. I obviously hadn't brought a change of clothes."

I tried to figure out how I would feel if I still thought she was my friend. Would I have minded?

"Of course not. I bet it looks great on you. You should keep it." Let her see that it meant nothing to me, that Jackson's wife had so much, I could afford to give her my castoffs as if they were no more significant than a pair of gloves. A sharp intake of breath came over the line.

"I couldn't. It's a two-thousand-dollar suit."

Did I detect just the slightest bit of reproach in her voice? I forced a laugh. "Did you google it?"

A long moment of silence. "Um, no. Daphne, are you angry? I think I've upset you. I knew I shouldn't have gone. I just—"

"Come on, I'm just teasing. I'm glad you went. Got me off the hook. Don't tell Jackson, but I find Shakespeare a bore." That wasn't true, but I knew she'd use that bit of misinformation to her advantage. "I mean it about the suit. Please, I want you to have it. I have more than I can wear. What are friends for?"

"I guess, if you're sure. Listen, I've got to run. Jackson needs me."

"Sure. Before you go, are you free this Saturday? We're having a few friends over for a dinner party, and I would love it if you'd come. There's someone I'd like you to meet."

"Oh, who?"

"A guy from the club who happens to be newly single and perfect, I think, for you." I had invited Gregg Higgins, a trust-fund baby. He was in his late twenties and extremely good-looking, which was fortunate for him, since he didn't have much going on upstairs. His father had given up hoping that Gregg would take over in the family business, but had given him a big office and title and let him spend his days having long lunches entertaining clients. He would be putty in Amber's hands and falling all over her, which is just what I wanted Jackson to witness. He wasn't in the same league as Jackson by any stretch, so I didn't worry about him actually distracting her, but he would be irresistible to her for the time being—her ticket to the club, glamorous events, and someone to pamper her until she achieved her ultimate goal. I figured she was also smart enough to realize a little competition would be good for arousing Jackson's interest.

Her voice was warm now. "That sounds interesting. What time should I be there?"

"Starts at six, but you're welcome to come a little early. Why don't you come at noon, and we can hang at the pool for a while and then get ready around two? Bring your clothes, and you can shower and dress here. In fact, why don't you plan to spend the night?"

"Fantastic, thanks."

I wanted Jackson to see Amber in her bikini, and given how she'd stepped up her game lately, I knew she'd come over looking like something from the pages of the Victoria's Secret catalog.

I ended the call, grabbed my tennis racket, and left. I was meeting Meredith for a doubles game. Things were still a little

strained between us since her confrontation with Amber. I knew
Meredith was angry that I had bought Amber's story about being
on the run from an abusive father, but once she saw I was immov-
able, she'd finally let it go. I hated for our friendship to become
a casualty of my plan, but for the first time in ten years, I felt a
flicker of hope. I wasn't going to let anything get in my way.

I ate a ton of carbs all the next week. Cookies, crackers, chips.
Jackson had just left on a business trip, so he wasn't there to stop
me. The girls were thrilled to have some junk food in the house.
Normally, he inspected the refrigerator and cabinets daily and
threw out anything remotely resembling snack food. I had to
swear the girls to secrecy and even hide it from Sabine, who'd
already gone running to Jackson when I kept Tallulah up late
one night watching a movie. But yesterday I'd insisted she take a
couple of days off, and her delight outweighed her sense of duty.

I wanted to make sure to pack on a few pounds before Saturday, so Jackson would notice how much better Amber looked in
her bathing suit than I did in mine. It's amazing how quickly the
weight comes back when you're used to eating fewer than twelve
hundred calories a day. I was on my fourteenth food journal—
Jackson inspected it every day when he got home and kept all the
completed ones lined up in his closet, his little keepsakes proving
his control over me. Occasionally I would write down a food that
wasn't on the approved list—he was too smart to believe I never
cheated on my diet. On those days, he'd sit and watch while he
made me run five miles on the treadmill in our home gym to
make up for it. I hadn't decided yet whether or not I would include some extras on the journal this week or just pretend that

perimenopause was to blame for the extra weight. The idea that my fertility was declining would make Amber that much more appealing in comparison.

I'd forgotten how good sugar tasted. By Friday my stomach had a nice little pooch to it, and my whole body was a bit puffy. I put all the wrappers and cartons in a trash bag and drove them to the dump. When he returned Friday night, the kitchen was in tip-top shape again. It was just past nine when I heard his car in the garage. I grabbed the remote and clicked off the television. I pulled roast duck out of the oven and set a place for him at the island.

He walked in the kitchen as I was pouring myself a glass of pinot noir.

"Hello, Daphne." He nodded toward the plate. "I ate on the plane. You can put that away."

"How was your flight?"

He picked up the glass of wine and took a swallow. "Fine, uneventful." His brow creased. "Before I forget, I looked through the Netflix queue. I see that you watched some low-rate drama. I thought we talked about this."

I'd forgotten to wipe the queue clean. Damn it. "I think it came on automatically after the biography of Lincoln I'd been watching with the girls. I must have left the Netflix on."

He leveled a look at me and cleared his throat. "Be more responsible next time. Don't make me cancel the subscription."

"Of course."

He scrutinized my face, put a hand on my cheek, and pressed. "Are your allergies acting up?"

I shook my head. "I don't think so, why?"

"You look puffy. You haven't been eating sugar, have you?" He opened the cabinet containing the trash and looked through it.

"No, of course not."

"Get me your diary."

I ran upstairs and retrieved it. When I came back to the kitchen, he was looking through all the cabinets.

"Here."

He snatched it from my hands, sat down, and went through it, tracing each item with his finger. "Aha! What's this?" He pointed to an entry from yesterday.

"A baked potato."

"That turns right into sugar. You know that. If you have to be a pig and eat a potato, make sure it's a sweet potato. At least that has some nutritional value." He looked me up and down. "You make me sick. Fat pig."

"Daddy?"

Tallulah was standing in the doorway. She looked at me, worry in her eyes.

"Come give Daddy a hug. I was just telling your mommy she has to stop stuffing her face. You don't want a fat mommy, do you?"

"Mommy's not fat," she said, her voice cracking.

He looked at me and scowled. "You stupid sow. Tell your daughter that you need to watch what you eat."

"Daddy, stop!" Tallulah was crying now.

He threw his hands up in the air. "The two of you! I'm going to my study. Put the crybaby to bed, and then I want to see you in my office." Then he leaned in and whispered in my ear. "If you're so hungry all the time, I'll give you something to suck on."

SIXTY-TWO

Amber reached for the bottle of tanning lotion and squirted some in her hand. After she applied it to her arms and face, she handed it to me. "Would you do my back?"

I took it from her and caught a whiff of coconut as I rubbed my hands together.

"Want to go sit on the bench in the pool?" It was sweltering, and I wanted to cool off.

"Sure."

Amber's bikini was practically pornographic—all she had to do was sit the wrong way and all the goods would be on display. I was glad Tallulah and Bella were out for the day with Surrey. It was obvious that she hadn't missed any time at the gym, although with the hours she was putting in working for Jackson, I didn't know how she fit it in. I had purposely worn a one-piece that hugged my body and revealed the little pooch my belly was sporting. Jackson would notice it as soon as he looked at me.

We sat side by side on the built-in seat in the shallow end. The water was a perfect eighty-five degrees and felt wonderful. I looked out at the vast stretch of blue and the beach beyond, relaxing as I took a deep breath of salt air.

Jackson came outside for his daily swim.

"Hi, girls, I hope you put some sunscreen on. Hottest time of the day."

I smiled. "I have, but Amber here is covered in tanning oil."

She sat up straighter, sticking out her chest for full effect. "I like to tan."

"That's because you're too young to know the sun gives you wrinkles," I said.

Jackson walked to the diving board and surprised me by turning around and executing a perfect back dive into the pool. Was he showing off? When he broke the water's surface, Amber clapped.

"Bravo! Well done."

He swam to the side of the pool, pushed himself up and out and gave a little bow.

"It was nothing."

"Come join us for a minute," I said.

He grabbed a towel from the outdoor armoire behind the bar and sat on one of the cushioned seats across from us.

"I've got a little work to do before the party."

"Anything I can help with?" Amber asked.

Jackson smiled. "No, no. It's your day off. Don't be silly. Besides, Daphne would kill me if I put you to work."

"That's right. You're a guest today."

"I'm really hot, just going to get all the way wet." She pushed off the bench and slipped underwater. My eyes were on Jackson, who was watching Amber as she swam to the steps and climbed out, giving him a front-row seat to her wet body and see-through suit.

"That felt great," she said, looking straight at him. She was getting quite brazen.

"Well, I've got to get to it," Jackson said as he walked back to the house.

Amber came back to where I was and took a seat once again. "Thanks again for inviting me over today. This is such a treat."

Did she think I was an idiot? "What time is everyone coming again?"

"Around six. We can relax for a couple of hours and then go shower and change. I've asked Angela to come by at three to do our hair." I had more planned for the afternoon, intending to let her see every little benefit Jackson's money provided.

"How wonderful. Does she always do your hair?"

"Only when we entertain or I'm going somewhere special. We have her on retainer, so she pretty much drops whatever else she has if I need her." What I now recognized as a look of resentment flashed in her eyes, but she quickly recovered.

"Wow."

"Of course, I try to give her notice. Don't want to intentionally mess up someone else's plans."

"Is it fancy tonight?"

I stretched my legs out in front of me. "Not really. Three other couples from the club and Gregg, the guy I want you to meet."

"Tell me more about him."

"He's in his late twenties, reddish-blond hair, blue eyes. Your typical good-looking preppy." I laughed.

"What does he do?"

"His father owns Carvington Accounting. He works in the family business. They have gobs of money."

Now I had her attention. "I'm not sure he'll be interested in me. He's probably used to debutantes and girls from important families."

This pitiful act was beginning to tire me. I looked up to see the two masseuses walk out to the tile patio. "I have a surprise for you."

"What?"

"We're each getting a nice, long massage."

"Don't tell me they're on retainer too?" Amber asked.

"No. They're part-time. Jackson and I couldn't survive without at least two massages a week." It wasn't true, but I wanted her green with envy.

The afternoon passed in a pleasant haze. After the hour-long massage, I soaked in the tub while Amber's hair was done; then she sat and talked to me while Angela did mine. By three thirty, we had drinks in hand and sat in the sunroom overlooking the Sound. In a few hours, phase two of my plan would begin.

By six o'clock, we were having drinks on the veranda, and Gregg, as I had anticipated, was falling all over Amber. I couldn't help but compare the girl who had come to that first committee meeting with the poised and self-assured young woman standing there. No one meeting her for the first time would have a clue that she was out of place. Everything about her telegraphed money and refinement. Even her dress, a Marc Jacobs shift, was worlds away from the L.L.Bean separates she used to wear.

I walked over to her and Gregg. "I see you've met our Amber."

He gave me a broad smile. "Where've you been hiding her? I haven't seen her at the club." He gave her a knowing look. "I would have remembered."

"I don't belong," she said.

"Then you'll just have to come as my guest." He looked at her empty glass. "Can I get you a refill?"

She put a hand on his arm. "Thank you, Gregg. You're such a gentleman. I'll walk over with you."

Gregg's hand rested on the small of her back as they made their way to the bar, and I looked up to see that Jackson was watching them. There was a proprietary look in his eyes, one that said, *You're pissing on my lawn.* It was working.

I walked over to him.

"Looks like Amber and Gregg are clicking." I could see that she was playing him, but all Jackson could see were the pheromones jumping off Gregg.

"She can do better than that idiot."

"He's not an idiot. He's a nice young man. He hasn't taken his eyes off her all night."

Jackson drank the rest of his bourbon in one swallow. "He's as dull as a stone."

By the time we were seated for dinner, Gregg was thoroughly infatuated. Amber already had him wrapped around her finger. All she had to do was look thirsty, and he was waving the server over to get her another drink. The other women didn't miss it either.

Jenka, a brunette beauty married to one of Jackson's golf buddies, leaned over to me and whispered, "Doesn't it make you nervous? A girl like that right outside his office every day? I know he loves you, but he is a man, after all."

I laughed. "I trust Jackson implicitly, and Amber's a good friend."

She looked dubious. "If you say so. There's no way I'd let Warren hire somebody who looked like that to be his assistant."

"You're too suspicious, darling. I've nothing to worry about."

Gregg was the last to leave. He gave Amber a chaste kiss on her cheek. "See you Sunday. Pick you up at noon."

When he'd gone, I turned to her. "Sunday?"

"He's invited me to have lunch with him at the club and then see *Cat on a Hot Tin Roof* at the Playhouse."

"How lovely. Well, I'm exhausted. Shall we go to bed?"

She nodded.

I gave her the guest room across the hall from us. I wanted Jackson to know she was close by.

He was in bed when I came into the bedroom.

"Nice evening, right?" I said.

"Except for that moron, Gregg. I don't know why you invited him in the first place," Jackson grumbled.

"It would have been awkward for Amber not to have a companion. He's nice enough. Just drinks a little too much."

"A little too much? The guy's a drunk. I detest people who can't control themselves."

I slid under the covers. "Amber has a date with him on Sunday."

"She's too smart for him."

"Well, she seems to like him." Good. He was jealous.

"If he didn't have a rich father, he'd be living in a studio apartment over someone's garage."

"Jackson, I need to ask you something."

He sat up and turned the light back on. "What?"

"You know how much I miss Julie. Amber's the closest thing to a sister I'll ever have. Your interest in her seems more than just professional."

His voice rose. "Now just a minute. Since when have I ever given you a reason to be jealous?"

I put a gentle hand on his arm. "Don't be mad. I'm not accusing you of anything. But I see how she looks at you. She adores you. And who can blame her?" Did I sound convincing? "I just don't want anything to happen between you. Anyone can slip. Amber is my only true friend. If you should find yourself attracted to her, please don't give in to it. That's all I'm saying."

"Don't be ridiculous. I'm not interested in other women."

But I knew that look. The determination in his eyes. No one told Jackson Parrish what he could and couldn't have.

SIXTY-THREE

Duplicity suited me. All the years of living with Jackson had taught me a thing or two. It was hard at times, knowing that Amber believed herself so clever and me so stupid, but it would be worth it in the end. It had been tortuous that weekend she was at the lake house with the girls and me. I hated going to that house, period. My mother was really only an hour away, and he wouldn't let me invite her. He chose it specifically for that purpose—to make my mother believe that I was so self-absorbed that I didn't think to include her. She had too much pride to ever ask to come. But inviting Amber to the lake had been necessary for moving my plan along. That was the weekend I gave her the vital tidbit that I hoped she would pounce upon—the fact that Jackson desperately wanted a son, and I couldn't give him one. I also gave her a key to the New York apartment, knowing it wouldn't be long before she found an excuse to use it.

When I got her text Friday morning asking if it was okay to use the New York apartment for the weekend, I came up with a plan. Jackson had been working from the lake house all week, making life miserable for the girls and me. He didn't believe in letting schedules slide, even on vacation. When he wasn't there, we'd lounge by the lake all day, eat when we wanted, stay up late and watch movies. But when he was around, it was lunch at noon, dinner at seven, girls in bed by eight. No junk food, only organic and healthy. I'd have to hide the books on my nightstand and replace them with his selection of the week.

That week, though, I did little things to irritate him. I came in from swimming with smeared makeup under my eyes, left my hair a mess, left crumbs on the counter. By Friday, I could tell he was reaching the breaking point. We'd just finished lunch, and I'd made sure that a piece of spinach was lodged between my front teeth.

He looked at me with disgust. "You're a pig. You have a big green thing in your teeth."

I pulled my lips back and leaned close to him. "Where?"

"Ugh. Go look in a mirror." He shook his head.

As I got up, I purposely bumped my hip into the table, and my plate went clanging to the floor.

"Look where you're going!" His eyes traveled up and down my body. "Have you put on weight?"

I had actually—ten pounds. I shrugged. "I don't know. There's no scale here."

"I'll bring one next week. For the love of . . . What the hell do you do when I'm not here? Stuff yourself with junk?"

I picked up the plate and walked to the sink, deliberately leaving a piece of cucumber on the floor.

"Daphne!" He pointed.

"Oops, sorry."

I ran the dish under the water and put it in the dishwasher—facing the wrong way.

"Oh, Jackson. The Lanes are coming over for dinner tonight." I knew that would be the final straw. Our neighbors at the lake lived in Woodstock the rest of the year, and their politics were to the left of Marx. Jackson couldn't bear to be in the same room as them.

"Are you serious?" He came up behind me, grabbed my shoulders, and turned me around. His face was inches from mine. "I've been very patient with you this week, put up with your slovenly appearance, your ineptitude around the house. This is too much."

I looked at the floor. "Stupid me! I thought this was a week you'd be away. I got the dates confused. I'm so sorry."

He sighed loudly. "In that case, it will be. I'm heading home today."

"I've arranged to have all the carpets cleaned over the weekend. You really shouldn't be there, with all the chemicals."

"Shit. I'll go to the apartment then. I should go into the office anyhow. Thanks for screwing everything up once again."

He stormed off to the bedroom to pack.

I would text Amber in the morning with the text I'd "meant" to send today—informing her that Jackson was coming to the apartment, and she couldn't use it after all. I'd tell her that I'd forgotten to hit send, and hoped that she hadn't been startled when Jackson showed up.

Walking into the bedroom, I tossed *Ulysses* to the floor and replaced it with the latest Jack Reacher. I stretched out on the bed and took a deep breath. We'd have pizza for dinner. The Lanes were enjoying the concert they were attending; they'd told me about it when they were over for dinner the week before.

Hours later, my phone rang.

"What the hell are you up to?" Jackson said.

"What do you mean?"

"Amber's here. What kind of game are you playing, Daphne?"

I feigned surprise. "I texted her and told her you were using the apartment. Wait. Let me look at my phone." I waited a few seconds. "I'm such an idiot. I never hit send. I'm so sorry."

He cursed. "You are intent on ruining my weekend. I just want some peace and quiet. I don't feel like making small talk with the help."

"Tell her to leave, then. Do you want me to call her?"

He sighed. "No, I'll handle it. Thanks for nothing!"

I hit send and typed another message to Amber. **Sorry. Meant to let you know Jackson was headed to the apartment. May want to stay out of his way. He's not in the best mood, thanks to me.**

That should be enough to have her lending him a sympathetic ear. After that, it would just be a hop, skip, and a jump before they were in bed together.

SIXTY-FOUR

He's got it bad. Amber must be really good. Most nights he claimed to be working too late to come all the way home, so he decided to stay at the apartment. Just to test my theory after the third night in a row, I offered to come in and keep him company, but he demurred, saying he would be at the office until all hours. It was also apparent in Amber's demeanor. She thought she was so clever and that I couldn't tell, but I noticed the looks that passed between the two of them when she was at the house, and the way she was beginning to finish his sentences.

During our trip to London, her perfume lingered on his clothes and in his hair every time he came back from a meeting. Apparently the infidelity turned him on, because he wanted sex even more than usual. I never knew when he would grab me. The sex was different too—faster and rougher, like a dog staking his claim. I pretended to Amber that he hadn't touched me in weeks. I needed her to believe he had eyes only for her—except for the one time I let my pride get the better of me and told her that we'd just slept together. The look of shock and anger on her face was delicious. I was worried, though, that it might be only a matter of time before he would tire of her and return to me, more obsessed than ever. My only hope was for Amber to elicit in him the same feelings I had evoked when we first met. He had to become focused on possessing her. She was already doing her part—trying to make herself into a younger version of me. I'd noticed her copying my perfume, wearing her hair the same as mine; she'd even copied my lipstick color. And I continued to feed her the ammunition. But would it be enough? What was taking her so long to get pregnant? Of course, unless it was a boy, it would do no good. We'd been down that road before. He had no use for another daughter.

I made myself look even more pitiful to him. I wanted him to see Amber as my perfect replacement. I wore long underwear under my clothes so I would sweat and blamed it on hot flashes. I started dropping hints that I was going through early menopause, so he would know that if he stayed with me, his dream of a son would go unfulfilled. I was placing all my hope on her getting pregnant with a boy. But if that didn't work, I was hoping she was clever enough to find another way to hook him.

The night he came back from Paris, he was in a good mood. She had told me she was taking a few days off to go visit a friend so I wouldn't be suspicious. But I'd known she was with him, had seen the lingerie he tucked into his suitcase at the last minute.

I was almost asleep when he walked into the bedroom and turned on a bedside lamp.

"You weren't sleeping, were you?" He came around to my side of the bed and stood looking down at me.

"I was."

"I'm hurt. I thought you'd be waiting up for me. You know how I miss you when I'm gone."

My eye started twitching. I gave him a tight smile. "Of course I missed you. But I thought you'd be tired anyway."

A slow smile spread across his face. "Never too tired for you. I brought you a present."

I sat up and waited.

It was the red and black corset I'd seen in his suitcase. I took it from him, and the smell of Incomparable wafted over me. The sick bastard wanted me to wear this after she had.

"Here are the stockings that go with it. Get up and put them on."

"Why don't you let me pick something out and surprise you?" I didn't want them touching my skin after they'd been on her body.

He threw the corset at me. "Now!" He grabbed my hand and pulled me from the bed. "Arms."

I lifted my arms, and he pulled off my nightgown so that I was standing there in only my panties.

"You're getting fat." He pinched the flesh on my waist and made a face. "I'm going to have to buy you a girdle soon. Don't make any plans for the rest of the week. You'll be spending it with the trainer every day. We have dinner at the club on Thursday, and I've bought you a new dress. It had better fit." He shook his head. "Lazy bitch. Now put on the outfit your nice husband went to all the trouble of buying for you."

I pulled the stiff fabric up over my hips and stomach. It was tight, but I managed to make it fit. My face was hot with shame, and I had to look up at the ceiling to keep from crying. When I had fastened the stockings, he made me do a pirouette for him.

He shook his head. "Looks like shit on you." He pushed me down. "All fours."

I fell to the floor, the hard wood sending waves of pain through my knees. Before I could brace myself, I heard his pants unzip and felt him behind me. He was rough, and I felt like I was being torn in two. When he finally finished, he stood up and looked down at me. "Still the best around, Daph."

I felt my body go weak as I slumped to the floor in anguish. Had all of this been for nothing? Was he already tired of Amber? Now that I had allowed myself to envision a life away from him, there was no way I was giving up. One way or another, I would be free.

SIXTY-FIVE

She must have given him an ultimatum. I heard him whispering on the phone in the bathroom last night, telling her he needed more time. She'd better play her cards right, I thought, or it could all blow up. Jackson was not a man to be threatened. I'd seen her the day before when I stopped by the office, and I could tell. She was definitely pregnant, at least three months along. I wondered if it was a boy or girl. I don't think I've ever prayed so hard for anything in my life since Julie died.

All of us walked on eggshells all through dinner. I could hear his phone pinging with texts from the dining room. At one point he got up, threw his napkin on the chair, and stormed from the room. Minutes later he was back, and I didn't hear any more texts coming in.

After I put the girls to bed, we watched a documentary on penguins. Finally, around ten, he looked at me.

"Let's turn in."

To my relief, he washed up, got into bed, and fell asleep. I lay there in the dark, wondering what was going on between them. I had started my period last night and had just gotten up to take something for my dull headache, then got back into bed and fell asleep.

I thought I was dreaming. Something bright was hurting my eyes, and I tried to turn but found myself immobilized. My eyes flew open. He was straddling me, shining a flashlight at them.

"Jackson, what are you doing?"

"Are you sad, Daphne?"

I shielded my eyes from the light and turned my head to the side. "What?"

He pushed my cheek so that I was looking into the light again. "Are you sad that you got your period? Another month and no baby."

What was he talking about? Could he have somehow found out about the IUD? "Jackson, please, that hurts."

He turned the light off, and I felt the cold steel of the gun against my neck.

He clicked the flashlight on again. Then off. On and off while the hand holding the gun pressed against my neck. "Are you laughing behind my back every month? Knowing how much I want a son?"

"Of course not. I would never laugh at you." The words came out in a whisper.

He slid the gun from my neck up to my face and positioned it over one eye. "It would be hard to cry without an eye."

He's going to kill me this time.

Then he moved it to my mouth and ran it around my lips. "It would be hard to talk about me without a mouth."

"Jackson, please. Think of the children."

"I am thinking of the children. The ones I don't have. The son I don't have because you're a withered-up old prune. But don't worry. I have a solution."

He moved the gun to my stomach and drew a figure eight. "It's okay, Daphne, if you're too used up to carry a baby in here. I've decided we can adopt."

"What are you talking about?" I was too afraid to move, worried the gun would go off.

"I know someone who's going to have a baby, and she doesn't want it. We could take it."

My whole body tensed. "Why would we want to adopt someone else's baby?"

I heard him cock the gun. He leaned over and turned the lamp on so that I could see.

He smiled at me. "There's only one bullet. Let's see what happens. If I pull the trigger and you live, we'll adopt. If you die, we won't. Sound fair?"

"Please . . ."

I watched in terror as his finger moved back and held my breath until I heard the click. The breath whooshed out of me, and a cry escaped my lips.

"Good news. We're going to have a son."

[P A R T   I I I]

SIXTY-SIX

A mber left the apartment on East Sixty-Second Street carrying a small suitcase, her credit card, and a wad of money. Jackson had called earlier to let her know he'd be there by nine in the evening, and she was going to make sure he walked into an empty apartment. She was tired of this waiting game. One day he was going to tell Daphne, and the next day he had an excuse for why he couldn't. She wasn't going to take it any longer. This was showdown time.

She'd booked a room at a small hotel under a different name. The note she left said simply:

> *I'm afraid you don't love me or our son. I don't think you have any intention of leaving Daphne to marry me. If you don't want this child, I will see that he doesn't come into this world.*
> *With great sorrow,*
> *Amber*

At ten past nine her cell phone began ringing. She ignored it. In a few minutes it rang again, and once more she refused to answer. This continued for twenty minutes, and then he left a message. *Amber, please. Don't do anything foolish. I love you. Please call me.*

Amber heard the pleading and panic in his voice, smiled, and turned off her ringer. Let him call all night and wonder where she was and what she'd done. She turned on the TV and laid down on the bed. This would be a long, boring night, but the time had come for a drastic move on her part. I'm not going to be the patsy again, she thought, and fell into a fitful sleep.

She'd gotten up several times through the night to go to the bathroom, and each time she checked her phone. Call after call from Jackson, and messages and texts that alternated between begging and fury. The last time she got up was four in the morning, and finally she slept uninterrupted until eight o'clock. She got up and called room service. Decaffeinated tea and yogurt were delivered twenty minutes later, along with the morning paper. She scanned the pages with little interest, and then she waited. And waited. And waited.

At two in the afternoon she punched in Jackson's number. He answered before the first ring was complete. "Amber! Where are you? I've been trying to reach you since last night."

She whispered into the phone with a quivery voice. "I'm sorry, Jackson. I love you, but you forced me." She let out a quiet sob to emphasize her pitifulness.

"What are you talking about? What have you done?"

"I have an appointment in an hour, Jackson. I'm sorry. I love you." And she hung up.

Let him stew with that for a while, she thought. Her phone rang again, and this time she picked it up on the fifth ring.

"What?" she said.

"Amber, listen to me. Don't do this. I love you. I love our son. I want to marry you. I will marry you. I'll tell Daphne tonight. Please. Believe me."

"I don't know what to believe anymore, Jackson." She made her voice sound weak and tired.

"Amber, you can't go through with this. You're carrying my son. I won't lose my son." He sounded furious.

"You've forced me to do it, Jackson. It's your fault." She heard him sigh, and then his tone changed.

"No, no. I know I've been dragging my feet, but it's all for us. I was waiting for the right time."

"That's just it. It seems like the right time is never going to come. I can't wait forever, Jackson. And neither can this appointment."

"You would actually kill our child? I can't believe that. Our beautiful little boy?"

"I can't have this baby by myself and unmarried. Maybe you think it's all right, but I wasn't raised that way."

"I promise you we'll be married before he's born. I promise. But come back to me, Amber. Where are you? I'll come get you now."

"I don't know—"

Jackson cut her off. "We'll go back to my apartment. You can stay there. Forever. Please."

Her lips curled into a catlike smile.

Jackson was there within the hour. She got into the back of the limo and gave him what she hoped was a pitiful look. His lips were white, and his face was set in a scowl.

"Don't you ever do that to me again."

"Jackson, I—"

He grabbed her hand and squeezed it tight. "How could you threaten to kill our child? To hold him hostage."

"You're hurting me."

He dropped her hand. "I don't know what I would do if something happened to my son. Or to you."

There was something in his manner and voice that unnerved

her, but she shrugged it off. Of course he was angry. Worried. He wasn't acting like himself.

"I won't, Jackson. I promise."

"Good."

They went back to the apartment, and she coaxed him into bed. They stayed there until dark, Amber begging him for forgiveness while trying to ensure that their plans were still on track.

"Are you hungry?" she asked him.

"Starving. How about an omelet?" Jackson said, throwing the covers back and bouncing out of bed. Amber followed him to the kitchen, and he began to crack eggs into a bowl. Now is the time to get down to it, she thought. Before he changes his mind.

"I've been thinking, Jackson. You're not going to move out of the house, are you? It was yours before you married her."

Amber had wanted that house from the first day she saw it. She wanted to be the mistress of the house, have Bella and Tallulah have to listen to *her*. They would be guests in *her* house now, and Bella would feel the sting of her hand if she continued with her shenanigans. The first thing she was going to do would be to have a portrait of herself done—one of those full nudes while she was pregnant. She'd hang it in a place where they'd have to see it every time they came to visit. She'd make it so miserable for them that they wouldn't want to come for weekends, and she'd make sure that Jackson didn't care either. In time, she would make him see that they were little bloodsuckers, just like their mother.

"I can't very well kick her out when I'm the one leaving the marriage," he said, flipping the eggs over.

"I suppose you're right. But . . . she hates that house. She's told me how pretentious she thinks it is. I really don't think she deserves it. She'll probably move her mother in with them. Do you really want that beautiful house to belong to her? Will she even keep it up?"

She could see his wheels turning.

"Well, I did have it long before I met her. Let me see what I can do. Maybe I can persuade her to let me have it."

"Oh, Jackson! That would be wonderful. I love that house. We're going to be so happy there."

The only thing that would make her happier than moving in and staking her claim would be if Daphne had to move in to Amber's one-room hovel. She knew she was being a bitch, but she didn't care. Daphne had been spoiled for far too long. It would do her good to see how it felt to have the designer shoe on the other foot. She might have pretended to be Amber's friend, but Amber knew that, deep down, Daphne still considered her the help. Reaching down like Lady Bountiful to help poor, pathetic Amber. It infuriated her to realize that Daphne had never considered her a threat. Daphne thought she was so much more beautiful than Amber, was so secure in Jackson's love for her. *Well, guess what, Daphne. He loves me now. He belongs to me now. And I'm giving him a brand-new family. You and your brats are obsolete.*

SIXTY-SEVEN

I t was finally happening! Jackson had called her that morning and asked her to come to the New York apartment to discuss something "serious." Daphne didn't need to wonder what it was about because, thanks to a lesson with private eye Jerry Hanson, she'd learned how to clone a cell phone. She'd been privy to texts between Amber and Jackson for the past month. She had to give it to Amber, that disappearing stunt of hers was a stroke of genius. Jackson would do just about anything to ensure he didn't lose the son he'd been waiting to have for so long.

She arrived at five o'clock, and when she walked into the apartment, she could smell Amber's perfume. The two of them were sitting on the sofa.

She pretended to be shocked. "What's going on?"

"Sit down, Daphne," Jackson answered. Amber said nothing, merely sat there with a tight smile and a malicious look in her eyes. "We need to talk to you."

Daphne continued to stand and looked at Amber. "We?"

Amber looked down at her hands, but her lips were still curled in a smile.

"Whatever is going on, just tell me."

Jackson leaned back and stared at her a long moment. "I think it's pretty clear that we've been unhappy lately."

Unhappy lately? Daphne wanted to say. *When have we ever been happy?* "What are you talking about?"

He stood up and started pacing and then turned to look at her. "I'm divorcing you, Daphne. Amber is pregnant with my son."

For their benefit, Daphne feigned shock and sank into the chair. "Pregnant? You're sleeping with her?"

"What did you expect?" His eyes traveled up and down her body. "You've let yourself go. Fat, slovenly, and lazy. No wonder you couldn't produce a son for me. You treat your body like shit."

It took everything she had not to tell them how stupid they both were. Instead, she pasted on a sad expression and looked at Amber. "How long have you been sleeping with my husband?"

"I didn't mean for it to happen. We fell in love." At this, she looked at Jackson, and he took her hand in his.

"Really?" Daphne's voice rose. "Then how long have you been in love?"

"I'm sorry, Daphne. I never meant to hurt you." Her eyes told a different story. It was obvious that she was relishing every moment.

"I trusted you, treated you like a sister, and this is how you repay me?"

She sighed. "We couldn't help ourselves. We're soul mates."

Daphne almost started laughing, and a sound escaped that she hoped they mistook for a sob.

"I'm really sorry, Daphne," she repeated. "Sometimes these things just happen." She put a hand on her belly and rubbed. "Our children will be related, so I hope in time you'll come to forgive me."

Daphne's mouth dropped open. "Seriously? Are you cra—"

"Enough," Jackson interrupted. "We want to get married, and I want to do it before my son is born. I'll make it worth your while to give me a quick divorce."

Daphne stood. "I have a lot to think about. When I'm ready to discuss it, I'll let you know. And I don't want *her* there."

As soon as she walked out of the apartment and out of their line of sight, she broke into a smile of her own. It was already worth her while, but she wouldn't tell him that. How can you put a price on your freedom? But she'd take the money for her children's sake. Why should Amber have it all? No, she'd make sure that the settlement was generous, and then she'd grant him his quick divorce.

SIXTY-EIGHT

Amber closed her eyes as the manicurist massaged her hands with creamy lotion. She'd told the girl that she was getting married, and immediately she'd gushingly suggested a French manicure. How completely tacky. She opened her eyes and looked at her left hand. It was the first time she'd taken the Graff diamond—one carat larger than Daphne's—off her finger. She smiled and watched as the polish went on and then suddenly pulled her hand away.

"I don't like that color. Take it off and let me see what else you have," she demanded.

The young woman obediently gathered more bottles and set them before Amber. She took her time looking them over and finally chose a champagne nude. "This one." She pointed to the bottle and sat back in the leather chair. She'd had the works today—massage, facial, pedicure. Tomorrow she would look beautiful, and all her dreams would become a reality as she stood before a clerk of the court and became Mrs. Jackson Parrish. Jackson's divorce had become final just in time. The baby was due any day, and she wanted to be Jackson's wife when he was born. Jackson had been in a state of ecstasy about the coming birth of his son, and he wanted a huge wedding to introduce his pregnant new wife to all of his friends.

"We'll have it at the house and invite everyone. It'll be huge, at least three hundred people. I want them all to meet my gorgeous wife. We'll announce the impending arrival of our amazing son," he'd said.

"Jackson, really. Everyone knows about the baby. The divorce, the pregnancy, our engagement—it's all been the choicest gossip for the last six months. Besides, I want something small and intimate. Just the two of us." There was no way she was going to have all the snobs in Bishops Harbor looking at her fat and pregnant, talking behind her back at her wedding and reporting back to Daphne. "We can have a big party later, after the baby's born." She laughed and gave him a peck on the cheek. "Besides, then I won't have this enormous belly and can wear something beautiful. Please?" She wanted to make sure that the first time she appeared in print as Jackson's wife, she looked the part. She wasn't worried any longer about being recognized. No one from her Podunk town would make the connection. They would never in a million years imagine that Lana Crump had become the fabulous Amber Parrish. And besides, if anyone came nosing around, she'd have plenty of money to make any pesky problem disappear.

He had pursed his lips and nodded. "Okay. We'll do it later. But what about Tallulah and Bella? They should be there."

She wasn't about to let an angry and morose Tallulah and a spoiled Bella take center stage at her wedding. They would ruin everything. Better that they hear about it after the fact, when it was too late for any tears and tantrums that might discourage their father.

"Yes, you're right. I wonder, though, do you think it will upset them to see me pregnant? I don't want them to be sad that it's not their mother who's having the baby. I would hate for them to be hurt or feel they're being replaced. Maybe it'll be easier once he's born. He'll be their brother, and it won't really matter who the mother is. Let them wait for the big celebration afterward. I think that will be much easier for them."

"I don't know. It might not look right if they're not there," he'd said.

"They'll have much more fun at the party we throw later."

"I guess you're right."

"I just want them to like me. Accept me as their stepmother. I've even discussed it with the pediatrician. She thought it might be too much for them, but said to run it by you." Amber had made up the pediatrician part, but her eyes were wide with a look of innocence.

"You have a point. I suppose it's not really necessary. After all, none of our other family will be there."

Amber had smiled at him and taken his hand. "We'll be one big, happy family. You'll see. I'm sure they'll love their little brother."

"I can't wait to meet this little guy."

"Soon," she'd said. "But in the meantime, how would my handsome husband-to-be like a little gratification?" Amber reached over and unbuckled his belt.

"You turn me on like no one else," he said and slumped back in his chair. As she got on her knees, she reminded herself that once she was Mrs. Parrish, she wouldn't have to pretend to enjoy this anymore.

Amber rose early the next morning. She had told Jackson that it was bad luck for the bride and groom to see each other the night before they got married, so he'd taken a hotel room at the Plaza while she stayed at the apartment. She didn't give a crap about those silly superstitions, but she wanted the morning to herself.

There were calls she wanted to make, and she didn't want Jackson around to hear them. She had a light breakfast of yogurt and fruit and checked her e-mails. There were three from Jackson's new administrative assistant. Amber had taken her time and chosen very carefully from a slew of applicants. She thought her selection perfect—young, attractive, smart, technologically up-to-date, outside-the-box thinker, and, best of all, male. Of course the checkbook would be coming home, too. Only Amber would see what was spent in their household. She would never make the stupid mistakes that Daphne had.

After a luxurious bath, she dried herself off, spread some exorbitantly expensive body cream all over, and turned sideways to see her belly in the mirror. The huge ball disgusted her. She couldn't wait for this kid to be born and to get her figure back. She shook her head and, looking away, grabbed one of the terrycloth robes. She'd gotten one for each of them, monogrammed and plush and expensive. She laughed to herself. Whenever she bought something, she went to the Internet and typed in "most expensive" whatever it was. She was a quick learner.

Amber and Jackson were meeting at city hall at one o'clock, so she still had plenty of time to get dressed and call for the limo. She reclined on the velvet chaise longue in the bedroom and punched in the telephone number on her mobile.

"Hello?" It was Daphne.

"I want to speak to the girls."

"I'm not sure they wish to speak with you." Daphne's words were clipped and chilly.

"Listen, you can stand in my way all you want, but it behooves you to cooperate with me, or your little brats will be out of the picture faster than you can say 'divorce agreement.'"

Amber heard nothing for a moment, and then the sound of Tallulah's voice came on. "Hullo?"

"Tallulah, sweetheart, where's your sister? Can you put her on the extension?"

"Hold on, Amber."

Tallulah yelled for Bella to pick up the phone and waited a few minutes. "Bella, are you on the phone?"

"Yes."

"Tallulah, are you still there?" Amber asked.

"Yes, Amber."

"I want to tell you both that I'm very sad you won't be at the wedding today. I told your father I wanted it to be only family and not a big party. I just wanted the two of you and no one else, but your father thought you were too young to be there." Amber made a sniffling sound, as if she were crying. "You have to understand that your father is very excited to be having a baby boy, so sometimes he forgets about you two. I want us to be very good friends, and I will make sure that you're part of our new family. Do you understand?"

"Yes," Tallulah said flatly.

"Bella, what about you?" Amber pressed.

"My daddy loves me. He won't forget me."

Amber could picture Bella stamping her imperious little foot.

"Of course you're right, Bella. I wouldn't worry if I were you. By the way, did I tell you that the new baby will have your father's name? Jackson Marc Parrish Junior?"

"I hate you," Bella said and clicked off.

"I'm sorry, Amber. You know how Bella gets," Tallulah said.

"I know, Tallulah. But I'm sure you'll be able to talk some sense into her, right?"

"I'll try," she said. "Talk to you later."

"Bye, sweetheart. The next time we talk, I'll be your stepmother."

Amber hung up, satisfied that she had gotten her message across. Tallulah was a peacekeeper and would present no problems. Some sparkly jewelry and new toys would be enough to eventually bring Bella around. Not that Amber intended for them to be at the house often enough for it to matter.

She pulled her computer next to her and answered the e-mails that needed attention, then rose to dress. There wasn't much she could do to look sexy and desirable for Jackson, but apparently the baby belly was enough to induce his euphoria anyway. She squeezed herself into a cream-colored dress and put on the new Ella Gafter pearls Jackson had bought her as a wedding present. She wore no other jewelry except her emerald-cut diamond ring.

When she arrived, Jackson and Douglas, his new assistant, stood waiting for her in front of the building. "You look absolutely beautiful," Jackson said, taking her hand.

"I look like a beached whale."

"You are an image of loveliness. I don't want to hear another word."

Amber shook her head and turned to Douglas. "Thank you for agreeing to be our witness today."

"My pleasure."

Jackson put his arm around her, and the three of them climbed the stairs to the entrance.

They waited their turn, and when it was time, they stood in front of an officiant. Before they knew it, he was telling Jackson he could kiss his bride. *His bride.* Amber tasted the word in her mouth. She savored how delicious it was.

"Well, I guess I'll get back to the office. Congratulations," Douglas said, reaching out and shaking Jackson's hand.

As Douglas walked away, Amber leaned against her new husband and felt a thrill of electricity go through her body. A thin platinum band now complemented the diamond on her ring finger. They were finally married. *Anytime now* was the silent message she sent their unborn son. As they got in the limousine and she sat back against the fine leather, she envisioned the life ahead of her—expensive homes around the world, fantasy trips, nannies and maids at her command, designer clothes and jewelry.

The stuck-up women in Bishops Harbor would soon enough be bowing before her—that much she was sure of. It only took lots and lots of money and a powerful husband. They'd be falling over themselves to be her friend. Ha. She loved it. Everyone in the club would be clamoring to sit at her table at the annual regatta dinner. She'd had to do a little damage control to make sure that Gregg's family didn't do anything to mess that up for her. Once she and Jackson had broken the news to Daphne, Amber had invited Gregg out to meet her for a drink. She figured he'd have an easier time keeping a stiff upper lip if they were out in public. They'd met at the White Whale in Bishops Harbor, a little tavern on the water. She was already seated at a table when he arrived. He walked over and leaned down to kiss her. She turned her face so that he got her cheek. Off balance, he took the seat across from her.

"Is everything okay?"

She'd blinked back tears and pointed at the glass of whiskey in front of him. "Take a sip. I ordered it for you."

A look of confusion had passed over his face, and he'd taken a long swallow. "You're scaring me."

"There's no easy way to say it, so I'm going to just come out with it. I've fallen in love with someone else."

His mouth had dropped open. "What? Who?"

She'd put a hand over his. "I didn't mean for it to happen. It's just—" She'd stopped and brushed a tear from her cheek. "It's just that we were together every day. Working together day in and day out, and we discovered we're soul mates."

He'd frowned and looked even more puzzled.

Is he that stupid? She'd suppressed a sigh. "It's Jackson."

"Jackson? Jackson Parrish? But he's married. And so much older than you. I thought you were in love with me." His lower lip trembled.

"I know he's married. But he wasn't happy. Sometimes these things happen. You know how it is to work closely with someone and how feelings can develop. I've seen the way your assistant looks at you at the office."

He'd narrowed his eyes then. "Becky?"

She'd nodded. "Yes. And she's quite lovely too. You must have noticed how enamored she is of you."

She'd had to stay for another two drinks before she could leave, and he'd told her he understood. She'd begged him not to take his friendship from her, made him believe that she needed him to be there for her in this time of uncertainty and public judgment. And the idiot fell for it. There would be no trouble from him at the club. And Becky should thank Amber. She was about to be promoted from assistant to fiancée.

Jackson and Amber Parrish would be the new golden couple of Bishops Harbor. And as soon as this baby was born, she'd be sure it would be the last. She was going to have her body back. The glow of happiness and satisfaction surrounding her at that moment could have lit up Manhattan.

SIXTY-NINE

Daphne knew it would only take one visit to the house that used to be theirs to make the girls never want to go back. Up to now, the visits had taken place in neutral territory. But Amber and Jackson wanted to have them over for the weekend, and she'd finally relented.

Amber had moved into his social circles seamlessly, and if Daphne had cared more about the women she'd spent the last ten years with, she might have been hurt that they embraced her husband's new wife so easily. But then again, no one in this town would dare to snub the new Mrs. Jackson Parrish. The one friend who didn't desert Daphne was Meredith. She had remained a true friend. Daphne wished she could tell Meredith the full truth, but she couldn't risk it. So she let her think that she was foolish and naive.

They pulled up to the house and got out of the car.

"Let me ring the bell," Bella shouted as the two of them ran up to the front door.

"Whatever," Tallulah answered.

A uniformed man appeared. *So they have a butler.* She didn't know why she was surprised.

He opened the door. "You must be Bella and Tallulah. Mrs. Parrish is expecting you."

Hearing Amber called Mrs. Parrish was jarring, but Daphne walked in behind them, nodding at him.

"Please wait here, and I'll get madam."

Moments later, Amber breezed in, holding her new son.

Bella looked up at her and asked, "Where's my daddy?"

"Bella, don't you want to meet your little brother, Jackson Junior?" Amber asked as she brought the baby closer.

Bella stared at the child, a pout on her face. "He's ugly. He's all wrinkled."

A look of hatred flashed across Amber's face, and she turned to Daphne. "Why don't you teach your children some manners?"

For once, Daphne was grateful for Bella's bluntness. She gave Amber a cool look and put a hand on Bella's shoulder. "Darling, don't be rude."

"Maybe your father forgot you were coming," Amber said. "He's buying toys for baby Jackson. He loves him so much. Do you want me to call and remind him?"

Tallulah looked up at Daphne in horror. Daphne wanted to kill Amber right then and there.

"Maybe we should reschedule the visit—" Daphne started, but Bella stomped her foot and interrupted her.

"No! We haven't seen Daddy in weeks."

"Of course you should stay," Amber said. She turned to her butler. "Edgar, would you take Bella and Tallulah to the drawing room where they can wait for Mr. Parrish? I have things to do."

"Please stay until Daddy comes," Tallulah whispered to her mother.

Daphne squeezed Tallulah's hand and whispered, "Of course I will."

"Amber."

"Yes?"

"I'll wait with the girls. How long do you think he'll be?"

She rolled her eyes. "You're so overprotective. Suit yourself. I'm sure he'll be home soon."

Daphne took both of the girls' hands in hers, and they followed Edgar to the "drawing room," where an enormous portrait of Amber, pregnant and naked, was perched on the wall above the marble fireplace. One hand covered her breasts, and the other rested on her pregnant belly. The entire room showcased photos from their wedding, and Daphne realized that Amber wanted them to see it. She'd orchestrated Jackson's being gone, knowing that Daphne wouldn't leave the girls until he returned.

"I hate her," Tallulah announced.

"Come here." She pulled Tallulah into her arms and whispered, "I know she's horrible. Try to ignore her and just enjoy your father."

"Girls!" They looked up to see Jackson come in, and they both ran into his arms.

"I guess that's my cue." Daphne stood. "I'll be back on Sunday to pick them up."

Jackson wouldn't even look in her direction, and she watched as the three of them left the room.

She went back to the foyer, and as her hand reached for the doorknob, Amber's voice rang out.

"Bye, Daph. Don't worry. I'll take good care of your little brats."

Daphne swung around, glaring at her. "You harm one hair on their heads, and I'll kill you."

She laughed. "You're so dramatic. They'll be fine. Just don't be late picking them up. I have naughty plans for *my* husband. He can't get enough of me."

"Enjoy it while you can."

Her face darkened. "What's that supposed to mean?"

Daphne smiled. "You'll find out soon enough."

SEVENTY

Daphne was about to play her trump card. They had been divorced for two months now, and Daphne had already put the millions she walked away with to good use. She had gotten custody of the girls, and Jackson had weekend visitation rights. She was here to change that.

She walked up to Jackson's assistant's desk.

"Good morning, Douglas. Is he alone?"

"Yes, but is he expecting you?"

"No, but I'll only take a moment. Promise."

"Okay."

She walked into Jackson's office.

He looked up, surprised. "What are you doing here?"

"Good morning to you too. I have a bit of news that you'll find most interesting," she told him as she shut the door and handed him a file.

"What the hell is this?" His face turned white as he scanned the contents. "This can't be right. I've seen her passport."

"Amber is a missing person. Your wife, Lana, is using her identity. How does it feel to be the one on the other side? She's nothing but a common con artist." She laughed. "Makes you wonder if she really wants you or just your money."

The vein in his temple was pulsating so hard she thought it might break through the skin.

"I don't understand," he sputtered, continuing to look the article over.

"It's quite simple. Amber—I mean Lana—targeted you. She insinuated herself into my life with the express purpose of landing a rich husband. Of course, once I was onto her, she became my golden ticket out."

"What are you talking about? You knew she and I were together?"

"I orchestrated it. I practically gift-wrapped her for you. The weekend at the lake, I drove you right into her arms. And the reason I couldn't get pregnant? Well, let's just say it's hard to get pregnant when you're using an IUD."

His eyes opened wide in surprise. "You played me?"

"I learned from the best."

"You fuc—"

"Now, now, Jackson. It won't do to lose your cool."

His breath was coming faster. "Are you planning on exposing her?"

"That depends on you."

"What do you want?"

"For you to terminate your parental rights."

"Are you crazy? I'm not signing away my rights to my children."

"If you don't, I'll go to the police and tell them who she is. They'll arrest her. Is that the legacy you want for your son? A convict for a mother? He'll never get into Charterhouse with that kind of background."

He slammed his fist on the desk. "You bitch!"

Daphne arched an eyebrow, feeling calm in his presence for the first time in years. "If you're going to start name-calling, I'll just go ahead and phone the police. Maybe the newspapers too, so they can see your new wife leave the house in handcuffs."

He took several loud, deep breaths, clenching and unclenching his fists. "How do I know once I sign away my rights you won't turn her in anyway?"

"You don't. But you know I'm not like you. I just want to get away from you once and for all. As long as you're with Amber, I know you'll leave me alone. That's all I want. So you'll sign?"

"What will people think? I can't have them thinking I've abandoned my children," he said.

She shook her head. "You tell them I wouldn't grant you the divorce unless you agreed to let me go to California; that I've been cheating on you, whatever you want. You're good at making things up. Paint me as the horrible parent and pretend you come out to see them every chance you get. No one will know."

"You don't care how you look?"

"No. That's your game." All she cared about was getting her children and herself as far away from him as possible. "You'll have everything you want. And before you even think of doing anything to stop me, please know that if anything happens to me, all the evidence will be forwarded to Meredith. And I've made other contingency plans as well."

He had no idea what private detective she had used or how many fail-safes she had set up. The detective had all the information, for one, and if anything were to happen to Daphne, he'd go to the police. She'd also told her mother everything and given her copies of Amber's file.

"Do you have the papers with you?"

She opened her purse and took out the envelope. "Have your attorney review them. There's a place for his signature. They need to be notarized. There's also a statement from you that you made up all the charges against me with the Department of Children and Families."

"Why would I sign that?"

"Because if you don't, I'll call the police. I'm not letting you have any more leverage over my life. Sign it, and no one will ever see it unless you try and come after the kids."

He sighed. "Fine. You can have your life back, Daphne. I was tired of you anyway. You're old and used up." His eyes traveled up and down her body. "At least I got your youth."

She shook her head, unaffected by his words. "I almost feel sorry for you. I don't know if you were born this way or if your parents screwed you up, but you're a miserable son of a bitch. You're never going to be happy. But the truth is, I can't even regret being with you. Because if I hadn't, I wouldn't have the two most amazing gifts in my life. So I'll trade those horrible years with you for my children. And I have plenty of love and life left in me."

He yawned. "Are you finished?"

"I was finished years ago." She stood. "And by the way, you're a terrible lover."

He exploded with fury and flew from his chair toward her.

She opened the door and retreated.

"I'll expect those papers tomorrow," she said as she left.

SEVENTY-ONE

A mber's happiness was short-lived. After the baby was born, Amber and Jackson had gone on a belated honeymoon to Bora Bora. He'd been everything she could have hoped for in a husband. All she had to do was ask for whatever she wanted, and it was hers. Round-the-clock nurse care for their son, unlimited shopping allowance, and all the pampering she desired. She loved the way everyone in the stores and the spas kowtowed to her, and she enjoyed being able to be as rude as she wanted with no repercussions. No one would dare insult Mrs. Jackson Parrish, especially with the kind of money she threw around.

Amber didn't have to worry about having those little monsters around since Daphne had moved with them to California. Jackson told her he would visit them there.

So when she woke that morning to Jackson standing over the bed, staring at her, she had no idea what was to come. She rubbed her eyes and sat up.

"What are you doing?"

He was scowling. "Wondering if you're ever going to get your lazy ass out of bed."

She thought at first he was joking.

Laughing, she answered. "You love this ass."

"It's getting a little fat for my taste. When's the last time you went to the gym?"

She was pissed now. Throwing off the covers, she jumped up. "You may have been able to talk to Daphne that way. But not me."

He pushed her, and she fell back on the bed.

"What the hell—"

"Shut up. I know all about your past."

Her eyes widened. "What are you talking about?"

He threw a file folder on the bed. "That's what I'm talking about."

The first thing she saw was a copy of a newspaper article with an old picture of her. She picked it up and quickly scanned it. "Where did you get this?"

"Doesn't matter."

"Jackson, I can explain. Please, you don't understand."

"Save it. No one makes a fool of me. I should turn you in, let you go to jail."

"I'm the mother of your child. And I love you."

"Do you, now? Like you loved him?"

"I . . . it wasn't like that . . ."

"Don't worry. I'm not going to tell anyone. It wouldn't be good for my son to have a mother in jail." He leaned closer to her, his face inches away. "But I own you now. So I will talk to you however I want. And you'll take it, do you understand?"

She'd nodded, frantically calculating her next move. She thought he was just angry—that once she could come up with a believable story, he'd calm down and things would go back to the way they were.

But instead, things began to escalate. He put her on a strict allowance, making her account for every dime she spent. She was still trying to figure out how to fix that. Then he wanted to choose her clothes, her books, and her leisure activities. She had to go to the gym every day. He expected her to volunteer for that stuck-up garden club Daphne had been so involved in. She could tell that the women didn't want her there, and she couldn't give a crap about it. Why did she need to learn about gardening? Isn't that what gardeners were for? And the journal—the damn food journal that he insisted she keep, along with her daily weight. It was humiliating. That was what put her over the edge and made her call his bluff. It was just last week.

"Are you crazy? I'm not reporting to you on what I eat every day. You can take that journal and stick it up your ass." She'd thrown it on the floor.

His face had turned red, and he stood looking at her like he wanted to kill her. "Pick it up," he'd said through clenched teeth.

"I will not."

"I'm warning you, Amber."

"Or what? You already said you weren't going to turn me in. Stop threatening me. I'm not weak and malleable, like your first wife."

At this he'd exploded. "You can't hold a candle to Daphne, you low-class whore. You can read all you want, study all you want, and you'll never be anything but poor white trash."

Before she had time to think, her hand was around the crystal clock on the table next to her, and she'd thrown it at him. It crashed to the floor, missing him completely. She watched as he advanced toward her, a murderous look in his eyes.

"You crazy bitch. Don't you ever try and hurt me." He'd grabbed her wrists and squeezed until she yelled out in pain.

"Don't threaten me, Jackson. I'll take you down." Inside she was trembling, but she knew she had to put on a brave face if she had any hope of keeping the upper hand.

He'd abruptly let go, turned, and left, and she thought she'd won.

※

When he came home that night, neither of them said a word about the fight. Amber had asked Margarita to prepare something French for dinner—coq au vin. She'd googled it, along with the right wine and dessert to serve. She'd show him who had class. He arrived home at seven and went straight to his study, where he stayed until she called him for dinner at eight.

"How do you like it?" she asked after he took a bite.

He gave her a droll look. "Why do you ask? It's not as though you made it."

She threw her napkin on the table. "I chose it. Look, Jackson, I'm trying to make peace here. I don't want to fight. Don't you want things to go back to the way they were between us?"

He took a sip of his wine and looked at her. "You tricked me into leaving Daphne. You made me think you were something you're not. So, no, Amber. I don't think things can go back to the way they were before. If it weren't for our son, you'd be in prison."

She was sick of hearing about the sainted Daphne. "Daphne couldn't stand you. She used to complain all the time that you made her skin crawl." Daphne had never said any such thing to Amber, but it shut him up.

"What makes you think I believe a word that comes out of your mouth?"

She was making things worse. "It's true. But I love you. I *will* win your trust back."

They finished their dinner in silence. Afterward, Jackson went to his office, and Amber stopped by the nursery to look in on Jackson Junior. Mrs. Wright, the nanny, was sitting in the rocking chair, reading a book. Amber had talked Jackson into hiring a live-in nanny to help with the baby. Sabine was gone. Amber didn't need that stuck-up French slut around. Surrey still helped out on the weekends. Bunny had referred Mrs. Wright, and she'd come with excellent credentials. She was also a respectable age, and no one that Jackson would ever look at twice.

"Any problem putting him down?" Amber asked.

"No, ma'am. Drank his bottle and went right to sleep. He's a sweet one, that one."

Amber leaned over and planted a soft kiss on his head. He was a beautiful child, and she looked forward to the day when he'd become interesting. When he could carry on a conversation and play games instead of just lying around like a lump.

Amber got in bed and pulled out the detective novel she'd hidden in her nightstand. Close to an hour later, Jackson finally came up, and she put it away before he could see it. It had been two weeks since they'd had sex, and she was getting worried. When he slipped under the covers, she reached over and began to stroke him. He pushed her hand away.

"Not in the mood."

She tossed and turned and finally fell asleep, still wondering how she was going to restore harmony between them.

Suddenly she couldn't breathe. She woke up in a panic and realized he was straddling her, his hand over her nose. She pried his fingers from her face, and gasping, cried out.

"What are you doing?"

"Ah, good. You're awake."

He flipped the lamp on. Her eyes flew open when she saw that he was holding a gun; the same gun she'd found in Daphne's closet all those months ago.

"Jackson! What are you doing?"

He pointed the gun at her head. "If you ever throw anything at me again, you won't wake up the next time."

She went to push his hand away, certain he was just playing around. "Ha, ha."

He grabbed her wrist with his other hand. "I'm serious."

Her mouth fell open. "What do you want?"

"Bye, Amber."

She screamed as his finger depressed the trigger. *Click.* Nothing happened.

She felt something wet and realized her bladder had emptied. A look of disgust filled his face.

"You're weak. Pissing the bed like a child."

He jumped off, still pointing the gun at her.

"This time you get a pass. Next time you might not be so lucky."

"I'll call the cops."

He laughed. "No, you won't. They'd end up arresting you. You're a fugitive, remember?" He pointed to the bed. "Get up and change the sheets."

"Can I take a shower first?"

"No."

She got up and began to strip the bed, sobbing as she did so. He stood, watching the entire time, not saying a word. After she'd finished, he spoke again.

"Go take a shower, and then we'll have a little talk." She began to walk away, and he called her back.

"One more thing." He threw the gun at her, and it fell to the floor before she could catch it. "Don't worry, it's not loaded. Take a look at the initials."

She picked it up and saw the letters she'd first read months before: YMB. "What does it stand for?"

He smiled. "You're mine, bitch."

⁂

So now she listened to everything he said, like an obedient child. When he told her to lose five pounds, she didn't argue, even though she was back to her pre-baby weight already. When he called her "stupid" and "white trash," she didn't argue with him, but apologized for whatever perceived infraction she'd committed. He showered her with expensive clothes and jewelry, but now she understood that it was all for show. And in public they were the golden couple, she the adored and adoring wife, he the handsome indulgent husband.

The sex became more demeaning and debasing—he'd demand oral pleasure from her when she was on her way out the door, or after she'd just gotten dressed, so he could make sure to leave his mark and humiliate her further. What had she ever done to deserve this? Life was so unfair. She'd worked so hard to escape her life in that wretched town where everyone looked at her like she was trash. Now she was Mrs. Jackson Parrish, one of the richest women in town, surrounded by the best of everything. And yet she was still being looked down on, still being treated like garbage. All she'd wanted was the life she deserved. It didn't occur to her that she had gotten it.

SEVENTY-TWO

Eight Months Later

Daphne gripped the phone tightly in her hand while looking out the window of the New York cab. She'd been too nervous to eat anything on the plane, and her stomach was growling insistently now. Rooting through her bag, she found a mint and put it in her mouth. She took a deep breath and braced herself when they pulled up to the front of Jackson's office building. After today, she could leave Connecticut behind her for good and get on with the new life she was forging.

Once the divorce was final, Daphne had taken the girls and gone to see her mother at the inn. She hadn't called ahead—she didn't really know how to begin. After they'd settled in and the girls had gone to sleep, she and Ruth sat together and she told her everything from beginning to end.

Her mother had been heartbroken. "My poor girl. Why didn't you ever tell me? You should have come to me."

Daphne had sighed. "I tried. When Tallulah was a baby, I left. But that's when he had me committed and put together all that evidence against me. There was nothing I could do." Daphne reached out and grabbed her mother's hand. "And there was nothing you could do."

Ruth was crying. "I should have known. You're my daughter. I should have seen through him. Realized you hadn't really changed into the person he made you out to be."

"No, Mom. You couldn't have known. Please don't blame your-self. What matters is that I'm free now. We can be together now."

"Your father never liked him," Ruth had said quietly.

"What?"

"I thought he was being overprotective. You know, just a dad not wanting his little girl to grow up. He thought he was too slick, too practiced. I wish I'd listened."

"I wouldn't have listened. It would have only pushed us further apart than we already were." She put her head on her mother's shoulder. "I miss him so much. He was a wonderful father."

They'd stayed up all night, catching up and reconnecting. Her mother surprised her the next day with her decision.

"How would you feel if I sold the inn to Barry and moved with you to California?"

"I'd be thrilled! Are you serious?"

She'd nodded. "I've missed enough. I don't want to miss any more."

The girls had been ecstatic to learn that their grandmother would be living with them.

Southern California had been good for all of them. The con-stant sunshine and happy dispositions of everyone around them had done wonders. The girls still missed their father, of course, but every day it got a little easier. They blamed Amber for the estrangement, and Daphne was happy to let them. When they were old enough, she would tell them the truth. In the meantime, the girls were healing, with the help of a gifted therapist, a neigh-borhood full of kids, and a yellow lab they called Mr. Bandit— renamed for his tendency to steal their toys.

They'd found a lovely four-bedroom home in Santa Cruz a mile and a half from the beach. At first she was worried that the girls would find it hard to go from living in their estate on the water to this charming but cozy two-thousand-square-foot house. She had more than enough money from the settlement to buy something bigger, but she was finished living that kind of life. Her mother had sold the B&B to Barry and insisted on contributing to the purchase of the house. Daphne had put the money from the settlement in a trust for the girls, which provided enough interest for them to live on. Douglas would be taking the reins at Julie's Smile, and Daphne would be on his board. She'd go back to working, of course, but not yet. Now was a time for healing.

When she brought the girls to look at the house, she had held her breath, waiting for their reaction. They had immediately run up the stairs to see where their rooms would be.

"Oh, can this be mine, Mommy? I love the pink walls!" Bella had asked after checking them all out.

Daphne had looked at Tallulah. "Fine with me. I like the one with the built-in bookcases," Tallulah said.

"It's settled, then." She'd smiled. "You like it?" They'd both nodded.

"Mommy, will this be your room?" Bella had taken her hand and pulled her to the master bedroom.

"Yes, this will be mine, and Grandmom will have the third floor to herself."

"Yay! You'll be so close to me."

"That makes you happy?" she'd asked.

Bella had nodded. "I used to get scared in that big house, with you and Daddy so far from me. This is so nice."

Daphne had hugged her. "Yes, it is." And she'd said a silent thanks that she would never have to lock her bedroom door again.

The refrigerator was filled with their favorite foods; there was ice cream in the freezer and candy in the pantry. Daphne had left her scale in Connecticut and felt healthier and more beautiful than she ever had. Sometimes she would still reach for her food journal, and she'd have to remind herself that she didn't have to write things down anymore. She'd brought it with her as a reminder never to let anyone control her again. She was delighted to keep those extra ten pounds she'd put on, which gave her a feminine and shapely form. Walking into the family room and hearing SpongeBob's braying laughter, watching her daughters revel in the silliness, overjoyed her. She relished the freedom to make her own choices without fear of reprisal. It was like letting out a sigh of relief that had been pent up for years.

School would let out in another three weeks, and they were all looking forward to a lazy summer collecting seashells and learning how to surf. She loved the simplicity of their life here. No more packed schedules and regimented days. When she drove them to school on their first day, Bella had looked at her with surprise.

"Aren't we going to have a nanny that will drive us?"

"No, darling. I'm happy to take you."

"But don't you need to get to the gym?"

"Why do I need the gym? I can ride my bike to the beach and take a walk. Lots of things to do. It's too beautiful here to be stuck inside."

"But what if you get fat?"

It had been like a knife to the heart. Clearly Jackson's imprint wasn't going to be as easy to wash away as she'd hoped.

"We're not going to worry about fat or thin anymore—only healthy. God made our bodies very smart, and if we put good things in them and do fun things for exercise, it will all be okay."

Both girls had looked at her a bit dubiously, but she'd work on it over time.

Daphne's mother had arrived last week, and had been as enchanted with the house and the area as Daphne. It felt so good to have her mother back in her life for real.

Now the cab was pulling to a stop, and Daphne paid the driver. When she walked into the office building, the familiar feeling of dread engulfed her. She squared her shoulders, took a long breath, and reminded herself that now she had nothing to fear. She didn't belong to him anymore. She sent a text and waited. Five minutes later, Douglas, Jackson's assistant, came down on the elevator and walked over. He gave Daphne a hug.

"I'm glad you made it. I just got the call. They'll be here any minute."

"Does he have any idea?"

Douglas shook his head.

"How bad is it?"

"Bad. I've been giving them the spreadsheets for months now. I was finally able to get some of the account numbers two weeks ago. Pretty sure that's what clinched it."

"Shall we go up?" Daphne asked.

"Yes, let me sign you in." He turned around and looked behind her. "They're here," he whispered.

There were four men clad in shiny blue raid jackets, the gold letters "FBI" embossed across the left breast, entering the building. They approached the security desk, flashing their credentials.

"Come on, let's get upstairs before they do," Douglas said.

As the elevator ascended, she felt a throbbing pulse in her wrists and a tingling all the way to her fingertips. Her face was hot, and she felt a sudden wave of nausea overwhelm her.

"Are you okay?" Douglas asked.

She swallowed, put her hand on her stomach, and nodded. "I'll be fine. Just felt a little woozy there for a minute." She tried to smile. "Don't worry. I'm all right."

"You sure? You don't have to be here, you know."

"Are you kidding? I wouldn't miss this for the world."

The elevator doors opened, and Daphne followed Douglas into the suite of offices and went with him to his, directly outside Jackson's.

She had a thought and quickly turned to Douglas. "I'll be right back."

"Where are you going?"

"I have something to say to him before they go in."

"You'd better hurry."

She flung open the door without bothering to knock, and after a confused second, Jackson looked at her in surprise. He rose from his chair, looking impeccable in his custom suit, an angry scowl on his face.

"What are *you* doing here?"

"I've come to give you a little going-away present," Daphne answered sweetly, pulling a small package out of her handbag.

"What the hell are you talking about? Get out of my building before I have you thrown out." Jackson picked up the phone on his desk.

"Don't you want to see what I have, Jackson? The gift I've brought for you."

"I don't know what your little game is, Daphne, but I'm not interested. You're boring me. You always bored me. Get the hell out of here."

"Well, guess what. Your life is about to get really interesting. No more boredom." She tossed the package onto his desk. "Here you go. Enjoy your time away."

She opened the door and held her breath when she saw the men from the lobby advance toward the offices. Their faces were unsmiling and ominous.

Jackson and Daphne turned to look as Douglas escorted the suited quartet into Jackson's office.

Daphne stepped aside as one of the men held out his credentials. "Jackson Parrish?"

Jackson nodded. "Yes."

"FBI," the older agent said, as the others fanned out around Jackson.

"What is this all about?" Jackson's voice cracked as he raised it. The office was now deathly quiet. Chairs pivoted toward the commotion, all eyes on Jackson.

"Sir, I have a warrant for your arrest."

"This is bullshit. For what?" Jackson said, his voice having returned.

"For thirty-six counts of wire fraud, money laundering, and tax evasion. And I assure you it is not bullshit."

"Get the hell out of here! I haven't done anything. Do you know who I am?"

"I most definitely do. Now if you would kindly turn around and put your hands behind your back."

"I'll sue your asses. You'll be lucky to be writing parking tickets when I'm through with you."

"Sir, I am going to ask you one more time to turn around and put your hands behind your back," the agent said as he firmly pivoted Jackson, leaning him against the wall.

With his cheek against the wall, he sputtered, "You! This is your doing, isn't it?"

Daphne smiled. "I wanted to see the justice system in action. You know, it's educational. You taught me that I should always be improving my mind."

He lunged for her, but the men stopped him and cuffed him. "You bitch! No matter how long it takes, I'll get even with you."

He struggled against the agent holding him. "You'll be sorry you did this."

A rather large agent standing behind Jackson pushed the chain of the cuffs that were in his hand gently toward the ground. Having no choice, Jackson dropped to his knees, wincing in pain.

Daphne shook her head. "I'm not sorry. And you can't hurt me anymore. You have no one to blame but yourself. If you hadn't gotten greedy and set up those offshore accounts, and if you'd paid taxes on that money like you should have, none of this would be happening. All I did was make sure your new assistant was someone with the integrity to turn you in."

"What are you talking about?"

Douglas came and stood next to Daphne. "My sister has CF. Daphne's foundation saved her life." He looked at one of the men and nodded.

"Excuse me, ma'am . . . sir, I need the two of you to step back, please." The agent sneaked in a wink and a wry smile. "Let's go, Mr. Parrish," he said, lifting him off his knees and in the direction of the elevator.

"Wait," she said. "Don't forget your present, Jackson."

She grabbed the package from the desk and slipped it into his pocket.

"Sorry, ma'am. I need to see that." The tallest of the men put his hand out.

She took the package from him and unwrapped it, holding up a cheap plastic turtle from the dollar store. "Here you are, sweetie," she said as she dangled it in front of him. "Something to remember me by. Like you, it has no power over me anymore."

SEVENTY-THREE

Daphne had one more stop to make. She got out of the cab and told the driver to wait for her. It still felt strange, having to ring the bell to her former home. Margarita opened the door and threw her hands up in surprise. "Missus! It's so good to see you."

She gave her a hug. "You too, Margarita." She lowered her voice. "I hope she's treating you okay."

Margarita's face became a mask, and she looked around nervously. "Did you come to see Mister?"

She shook her head. "No, I'm here to see Amber."

Her eyebrows rose. "I be right back."

"What are *you* doing here?" Amber appeared, looking rail-thin and pale.

"We need to talk."

She looked at Daphne suspiciously. "About what?"

"Let's go inside. I don't think you want your staff overhearing."

"This is *my* house now. I'll do the inviting." She pursed her lips and then looked around nervously. "Fine, follow me."

Daphne followed her into the living room and took a seat in front of the fireplace. An enormous portrait of Amber and Jackson on their wedding day had replaced the family portrait. Even though Amber had been pregnant and showing at the time, she'd had the artist paint her sylphlike, without the bulging belly.

Looking at Daphne warily, she spoke. "What gives?"

"Don't ever bother my children again."

She rolled her eyes. "All I did was send them an invitation to their brother's baptism. Did you fly all the way from California just to complain about that?"

Ignoring Amber's taunting, Daphne leaned toward her. "You listen to me, you little bitch. If you ever send them so much as a postcard, I'll have your head. Is that clear, Lana?"

She leaped out of the chair and came close. "What did you call me?"

"You heard me . . . Lana. Lana Crump." Daphne wrinkled her nose. "Such an unfortunate last name. It's no wonder you don't use it."

Amber's face was red, and her breath came fast. "How did you know?"

"I hired a detective after Meredith confronted you. I found out everything then."

"But you were still my friend. You believed me. I don't understand."

"Did you really think I was that stupid? That I didn't know exactly what you were up to? Please." She shook her head. "*Oh, Amber, I'm so worried about Jackson cheating. I could never give him a son.* You ate it all up, did everything just the way I'd hoped you would, even ordered the perfume I was 'allergic' to." She put air quotes around *allergic*. "And once you were carrying his son, I knew you had him. The reason I never got pregnant was because I had an IUD."

Her mouth dropped open. "You planned all of this?"

Daphne smiled. "You thought you were getting the perfect life, the perfect man. How do you like him now, Lana? Has he shown you his true colors yet?"

Amber glared at Daphne. "I thought it was just me. That it was because of what he found out. He told me I was nothing better than white trash." She looked at Daphne with hatred. "You're the one who gave him the file?"

She nodded. "I read all about how you framed that poor boy Matthew Lockwood for rape when he wouldn't marry you. How you let him sit in prison for two years for a crime he didn't commit."

"That son of a bitch deserved it. He kept me his dirty secret, slept with me all summer while his rich girlfriend was away. And his mother—you'd think she'd have wanted her grandchild. But she said I should have it aborted, that any child of mine would be nothing but trash. I laughed while they put her precious son away. I loved seeing the Lockwood name tainted with scandal and dirt. They thought they were so wonderful, so high-and-mighty."

"You still feel no remorse? Even though because of you, he was beaten in prison and is in a wheelchair for the rest of his life?"

Amber stood up and began to pace. "So what? If he was too much of a weakling to take care of himself in prison, that's not my fault. He's nothing more than a coddled mama's boy." She shrugged. "Besides, he has money; he's well taken care of. And his simpering girlfriend married him."

"And what about your son?"

"What *about* Jackson Junior?"

"No, your *other* son. How could you just abandon him?"

"What should I have done? My mother found my diary and went to the police. They found that juror I convinced to fight for the conviction, and he agreed to testify against me. They arrested me. What kind of mother turns in her own daughter? She said she felt sorry for Matthew—like that spoiled brat deserved any sympathy. Once I got out on bail, I had to run. No way was I going to prison just for giving Matthew what he deserved." She took a deep breath. "But I would like to get my son back, punish Matthew and his fat cow wife. She's raising him like she's his mother. He's my kid, not hers. It's not fair."

"Fair?" Daphne laughed. "He's so much better off without you. Tell me something, who is Amber Patterson? Did you have anything to do with her going missing?"

She rolled her eyes again. "Of course not. I hitched a ride out of town with a trucker from Missouri to Nebraska. I got a job waitressing there, and one of my regulars was a guy who worked in the records department. He got me the credentials."

"How did you get her passport?"

She smiled then. "Oh, well, you know how small towns are. After a while, I finagled a way to meet her poor mom. She worked at the grocery store in town. Took a few months, but I guess I reminded her of her lost daughter. It helped that I wore my hair the way she had and talked to some of her friends and pretended I liked the same things. Her mom would make me dinner once a week—what a shitty cook. I found out Amber was supposed to have gone to France with her senior class—that's the only reason the stupid hick had a passport. So I stole it." She shrugged. "She also had a nice sapphire ring. I took that too. She didn't need it anymore."

Daphne shook her head. "There really is nothing beneath you."

"You could never understand. Growing up dirt-poor, with everyone looking down on me, I learned early on that if you want something, you have to get it for yourself. No one's going to just hand it over."

"And do you have what you want now?"

"I did at first. Until he found out about my past." Her earlier bravado was waning. She straightened and looked at Daphne. "If you hadn't given him that file, I could leave him, get child support and alimony. But if I do, he'll turn me in." Her demeanor changed suddenly, and Daphne could almost see the transformation taking place. "Daphne, you know what he's like. We're both victims now. You have to help me. You figured out a way to escape. There must be something I could use on him. Is there?" She was the old Amber now; the one Daphne had believed was her friend. She was narcissistic enough to believe that she could still manipulate her.

Daphne looked at her. "Tell me something, honestly: did you ever consider me a friend?"

Amber took Daphne's hand in hers. "Of course I was your friend. I loved you, Daph. It was just too tempting. I had nothing, and you had everything. Please forgive me. I know what I did was wrong, and I'm sorry. Our children are related. It's like we *are* sisters now. You're a good person. Please, help me."

"So if I help you, then what? You'll leave him, and we can go back to being friends again?"

"Yes. Friends again. For Julie and Charlene." As soon as the words left her mouth, Amber realized her mistake.

"Yeah. For Charlene. Who never existed." Daphne stood up. "Enjoy your bed, Amber. You'll be spending lots of time in it. Jackson's a man of strong appetites."

Amber scowled at Daphne. "You want to know the truth? I was never your friend. You had all the money, all the power, and you gave me your crumbs. You didn't even appreciate what you had. All that money he spent on you and your bratty kids. It was obscene. All the while, I was working in his office like a dog." Her eyes were cold. "I did what I had to do. It was so boring, listening to all your depressing stories. *She's dead!* I wanted to scream. *No one cares about Julie. She's been rotting in the ground for twenty years. Let it go.*"

Daphne grabbed her wrist and held it tight. "Don't you ever

speak my sister's name again—do you hear me? You deserve everything you're getting." She let go of her. "Take a look around. Try and commit to memory what it was like living the good life, because it's over now."

"What are you talking about?"

"I've come from Jackson's office. The FBI just took him out of his office in handcuffs. Seems they got access to his offshore accounts. Pity. He never paid taxes on that money. I'm pretty sure when all is said and done, you'll be lucky if the two of you can afford to live in your old apartment. That is, if they don't give him jail time, but knowing Jackson, he'll figure a way out of that. He'll have to deplete all his resources, of course. Maybe you can help him start a new business."

"You're lying." Her voice was shrill.

Daphne shook her head. "You know that male assistant you made sure he hired so there'd be no funny business at the office? Douglas? Well, he's an old friend of mine. See, his sister *does* have CF. Julie's Smile has been a tremendous help to his family. He's been spying on Jackson, and he finally got the account numbers he needed to go to the feds. Take a good look around. You may not have all this for long." She started to walk away, then stopped and turned back. "But at least you still have Jackson."

Daphne walked out of the house for the last time. As the driver pulled away, she watched as the house receded from sight. How different it looked to her now from when she'd first seen it. Settling back against the seat, she took in, for the last time, the magnificence of each house they passed, and wondered what secrets each of them held. She grew lighter with each passing mile, and when they drove out of the pristine borders of Bishops Harbor, she left the pain and shame she'd lived with while she was still its prisoner behind her. A new life awaited—one where no one terrorized her in the middle of the night or made her pretend to be something she was not. A life where her children would grow up secure and loved, free to be whomever and whatever they desired to be.

She looked up at the sky and imagined her beloved Julie watching from above. She pulled out a pen and the small notepad she kept in her purse and began to write.

My darling Julie,

I often wonder if I'd have made different choices if you were still here. A sister can keep you from making those big mistakes. You wouldn't have allowed my need to save everyone blur my vision. If only I could have saved you, maybe I would have tried harder to save myself.

How I miss confiding in you, in having that one person that I always knew was in my corner no matter what, sharing my life. And how foolish I was to think that I could ever find that same solace from anyone else.

I suppose I have been looking for you everywhere since I lost you. But I know now, I didn't lose you. You're still here. In the twinkle in Bella's eyes and the kindness in Tallulah's heart. You live on in them and in me, and I'll hold tight to the precious memories of the time we had together until, one day, we are reunited. I feel you watching over me: you are the warmth of the sun as I romp with your nieces on the beach, the cool breeze that caresses my cheek in the evenings, the feeling of peace that now resides in the place of turmoil. And despite my desperate wish to have you back, I must believe that you, too, are finally at peace, forever free from the disease that bound you.

Remember when we saw our first Shakespeare play? You

were just fourteen and I was sixteen, and we both thought Helena was a fool for wanting a man who didn't want her. It occurs to me that I've become Helena in reverse.

And so, my dear Julie, a chapter has closed and a new one begun.

I love you

Daphne put the notebook in her purse and leaned back. Smiling and looking up, she whispered the Bard's famous words from that play she and Julie had seen so long ago:

"The king's a beggar, now the play is done:

All is well ended . . ."

ACKNOWLEDGMENTS

Long before a book is born, there is a group comprised of friends, family, and professionals that make its eventual existence possible. We are deeply grateful to them for their indispensable roles in that process.

To our wonderful agent, Bernadette Baker-Baughman of Victoria Sanders & Associates, thank you for being our biggest champion and advocate and for making the journey so enjoyable with your graciousness, wit, and dedication. You are an answer to a prayer, and it is a joy to work with you.

To our fabulous editor, Emily Griffin, your infectious excitement and dedication to excellence took the story to the next level and made it so much better than we ever could have done without you.

To the stellar team at Harper, thank you for your excitement about the book and all you did to make it happen. Jonathan Burnham, thank you for your electrifying enthusiasm and most inspiring note, making us certain we'd found the right publishing home. Jimmy Iacobelli, who designed our brilliant cover, and the creative team who designed the interior pages — we fell in love with your vision the minute we laid eyes on it. Thanks to Nikki Baldauf for her expert steering through copyediting and production. Heather Drucker and the PR team, thank you for your incredible passion and talent. Katie O'Callaghan and the marketing team, we know we are in the very best of hands. Huge thanks to Virginia Stanley and the amazing Library Sales team for a fantastic job getting the early word out. Deepest appreciation to Carolyn Bodkin, who worked so diligently in managing the foreign rights. To Amber Oliver (aka the Other Amber), and to all the incredibly hard working people at HarperCollins, our deepest gratitude for all you do.

Appreciation and love to our sisters-in-law and sisters in heart, Honey Constantine and Lynn Constantine for reading, rereading, reading again, and cheering and encouraging us every step of the way.

To Christopher Ackers, wonderful son and nephew, for listening in and offering advice on our numerous plot conversations and always infusing them with your customary humor.

Thank you to our beta readers: Amy Bike, Dee Campbell, Carmen Marcano-Davis, Tricia Farnworth, Lia Gordon, and Teresa Loverde, your enthusiasm was a great motivator.

To the wonderful authors and friends who make up the Thrillerfest community, an incredible well of camaraderie, understanding, and mutual support, many thanks.

To David Morrell for your thoughtful advice. Thank you for always being available to talk.

To Jaime Levine for your continual support and encouragement and being there from the beginning.

To Gretchen Stelter, our first editor. You brought clarity and insights that ratcheted up the tension and made the manuscript more compelling.

Thanks to Carmen Marcano-Davis for your psychological expertise that helped us to shape Jackson, and to Chris Munger for authenticating the FBI scenes in the book.

To Patrick McCord and Tish Fried of Write Yourself Free for sharing your talent and skill. Your workshops made us better writers.

Lynne thanks her husband, Rick, and her children, Nick and Theo, for their unwavering support and forbearance while she spent hours locked in her office skyping with Valerie on plot lines or working late into the night to meet deadlines. And to Tucker, for always being by her side while she works. All my love to all of you always.

Valerie thanks her husband, Colin, for his constant encouragement and support, and her children, her greatest cheerleaders. I love you all.

ABOUT THE AUTHOR

LIV CONSTANTINE is the pen name of sisters Lynne Constantine and Valerie Constantine. Separated by three states, they spend hours plotting via FaceTime and burning up each other's e-mails. They attribute their ability to concoct dark story lines to the hours they spent listening to tales handed down by their Greek grandmother. You can find more about them at: livconstantine.com.